# MICHELLE KIDD

## Guilt

*Enjoy!*

# ?

Question Mark Press

First published by Question Mark Press 2021

First edition

This book was professionally typeset on Reedsy.
Find out more at reedsy.com

# Chapter One

*Tuesday 30<sup>th</sup> October 2018*

1.05am

He slipped the empty dog lead into his pocket and pulled the thick woollen balaclava down over his face. He didn't have a dog - just a lead. But if any of the late night dog-walking fraternity of this part of town questioned his lack of a four-legged friend, they did so silently.

But tonight was not a night for dog walking.

There was nobody around to see him; he was sure of that. He'd done his homework, just like he always did. But he still gave the fog-shrouded street one last look before making his way across to number seventeen.

The house was cloaked in darkness; no security lights flashed to announce his presence, and the street lights had long since been extinguished. If anyone *was* watching, all they would see was his shadow.

He slipped soundlessly around the side of the house, the aroma of spent fireworks clogging the freezing night air. Stretching a gloved hand towards the back gate, he gave it a push. It clicked open - just as he knew it would. Carefully side-stepping around the patio furniture, he headed for the back door.

Again, he knew it would be unlocked. People were strange creatures and old habits died hard. But he knew the Jacksons' habits would change after tonight - albeit too late to change the course of events set in motion.

The family would be asleep, oblivious to his presence – and the thought gave him an unexpected thrill.

With a smile flickering across his hidden lips, he pushed down the handle and stepped inside.

* * *

*Tuesday 30<sup>th</sup> October 2018*

*5.15pm*

Detective Inspector Nicki Hardcastle nudged open her office door with a booted foot, a bundle of files under each arm. Spending the entire day at Ipswich Crown Court hadn't been top of her wish list for her first day back. And the nightmare return journey along the A14 hadn't improved her mood. She let the files slide onto the desk and sighed.

Back at work just one day and already her desk was buried. Suddenly, the memories of her week-long stay at the Bedford Lodge Hotel and Spa was a dim and distant memory.

"Evening, boss." DC Darcie Butler popped her head around the door frame, grinning out from underneath her dark fringe of glossy black hair. "Nippy out, isn't it?" She stepped into Nicki's office armed with two takeaway coffee cups. "I picked these up on my way back in."

Nicki smiled, gratefully, and accepted the cup of what smelt like her favourite mocha. "You could say that," she replied, wriggling out of her woollen coat. "What kind of a day have you had?"

"I went out to an address in Moreton Hall – another reported burglary overnight." Darcie nodded towards Nicki's cluttered desk. "I printed out the report for you – such as it is."

Nicki glanced down at the court files she'd slid onto her desk, noting the A4 sheets of paper buried beneath. "Thanks, Darcie. I'll get to it in a moment." Pulling out her chair, Nicki sank down and wrapped her fingers around the cup, grateful to feel the heat spreading through her frozen fingers. Even the short walk from the car park had been enough for the chill to seep into her bones. "Is it similar to the others?"

Darcie nodded, perching on the corner of Nicki's desk and sipping her own coffee. "Seems to be. Scene of crime investigators were there when we left, so I guess you'll get something from them soon."

Nicki flashed another grateful smile and glanced at her watch. "You heading off home?"

Darcie nodded, an impish grin crossing her face. "Yep. I might have a date tonight!"

Nicki rolled her eyes skywards. "Not another poor soul from that dating app of yours?" The dimples on the young detective's cheeks, together with the sparkle in her smoky grey eyes, told Nicki all she needed to know. "Well, you just be careful. I know I sound like your mother, but there are some funny people out there!"

"Yeah, maybe - but not in this sleepy town." Darcie pushed herself off the desk and headed for the door. "But I'll be careful – you don't need to worry." Before slipping out into the corridor she turned and flashed a smile at Nicki. "Oh, and by the way, you'll love the new guy!"

Nicki watched as the young DC skipped out of the door, wondering what it felt like to be so young and carefree. At thirty-two years of age, she wasn't exactly over the hill herself, but the thought of going out on the dating circuit again filled her with nothing but dread. Her relationship history was best described as patchy, with a smattering of dissatisfaction mixed with disillusionment.

With her fingers starting to defrost, she settled back in her chair and closed her eyes, letting the warmth of the hot coffee perform its magic. Wiggling her toes inside her sheepskin boots, she contemplated an evening run. Followed by a hot bath. *That* was her idea of a perfect evening.

Darcie's parting shot then caused her eyes to snap open. The new guy?

Before she could gather her thoughts any further, she heard the desk phone trilling. Pulling it free from beneath the files she'd unceremoniously dumped just moments earlier, Nicki immediately recognised the deep West Country tone of DCI Malcolm Turner.

"Nicki – glad I caught you. Welcome back. How's he settling in?"

Nicki paused, the coffee cup hovering in front of her lips. How was *who* settling in? She'd called into the station briefly early this morning to pick up the court files before heading over to Ipswich. She'd had a brief catch up with Darcie, filling her in on her week away at the spa, but had then headed straight out. Placing her coffee down and reaching for her diary, she flicked the page over to today's date.

And there it was.

Royston Carter – her new DS.

"Sorry, I've been out at court all day, but I'm sure he's been made to feel welcome. I was just going to track him down when you rang." Nicki hoped her tone didn't betray her. How could she have forgotten they had a new member of the team starting today? Maybe the week spent at the Spa had turned her brain to mush.

"Good, good. I'm sure he'll have been tied up with all that HR nonsense for most of the day. He won't start properly until tomorrow. We'll catch up in the morning." The DCI paused and Nicki thought she could hear the rustling of paperwork in the background – or maybe it was a food wrapper. It was well known that DCI Turner had a penchant for a certain Cornish delicacy from the pasty shop not far from the station.

"That works for me," replied Nicki, reaching for her cup again. "It'll be good to have another pair of hands on the team."

After the exchange of a few more pleasantries, and the skilful side-stepping of any mention of her family, Nicki hung up and surveyed her desk. She'd managed to clear most of the backlog of paperwork before going on leave, but now noted her in-tray was groaning once again. She took another gratifying mouthful of coffee before pulling the burglary report towards her.

Five minutes.

Five minutes and then she'd go and hunt down this new DS Royston Carter.

\* \* \*

*Tuesday 30<sup>th</sup> October 2018*
  5.25pm

"Time to get your shoes on or you'll miss it!"

Lucas Jackson sat cross-legged in front of the 64-inch television, oblivious to the repeated calls from his mother. It was his favourite TV show and he wasn't moving until it was finished.

"Lucas!"

Sophia Jackson pushed open the door to the living room, a harassed look on her face. Her strawberry blonde hair was swept back into a messy pony tail, and tell-tale smudges of icing sugar dusted her cheeks. "Turn that TV off now! We're leaving in five minutes!"

With no response from her son, Sophia hurried into the room, her pale grey eyes scouring the sofa and chairs for the remote control. It was nowhere to be seen. With a sigh, she strode across the carpet and snapped the TV off at the button.

"Aw, I was watching that!" Lucas Jackson's six-year-old eyes peered mournfully up at his mother. "It's the best bit!"

Sophia Jackson regarded her son for a moment, before reaching down to sweep him up onto his feet. She hugged him close, breathing in the soft, sweet scent of coconut shampoo from his hair. She could never resist those eyes – the wide, staring cornflower blue eyes he'd inherited from his father. Releasing her grip, she pecked him on the cheek. "Well, come on birthday boy! If you want to go to the fair, you need to get ready now!"

"I am ready!" Lucas looked down at his Batman costume. "Can I have a cake first?"

Sophia brushed away the icing sugar that still decorated her cheeks "When we come back – the icing still needs to set." She guided Lucas towards the door that led out into the hall. "Go and find your boots, and you'll need your big coat on. It's cold out tonight."

Lucas skipped away and scrambled upstairs.

"And don't forget your gloves!" Making her way back towards the kitchen, Sophia eyed the two wire racks sat on the worktop filled with delicately iced cupcakes. Each had Lucas's favourite Batman logo on top – a yellow background and a silhouetted black bat. She afforded herself a small smile, pleased with how they'd turned out. She'd pop some candles on top when

5

they got back home later.

Lucas had been obsessed with funfairs ever since their trip to Hunstanton last summer. And when the flyer landed on their doormat advertising the Winter Fayre was coming to town on his birthday, he'd jumped up and down with delight.

"Mum, do we have to go?" Amelia Jackson appeared in the doorway. At twelve years old, funfairs weren't on her list of acceptable activities. Especially with her brother.

"Yes we do," chided Sophia, turning to lock the back door. "It's your brother's birthday and he wants to go."

"I could always stay here?" Amelia's mobile phone pinged in the palm of her hand. "I won't open the door to anyone, I promise. And I'll keep everything locked."

Sophia shivered. The crime scene investigators had only been with them for an hour or so that morning, dusting the back door and other areas in search of fingerprints, but their presence lingered in her mind far longer. "Nice try," she replied, checking the back door was locked one more time. "But you're too young to be left home alone, especially after last night. Come on, it'll be fun!"

Sophia turned back towards her daughter, noting the scowl that decorated her brow. "Do it for your brother. Go and get your coat and gloves."

"But Esme and Katie are doing this video thing online tonight. I'll miss it." Amelia saw the resolute look on her mother's face and sloped back into the hallway, giving a dramatic huff as she went. "It's not fair," she muttered, stomping her way towards the stairs.

Sophia followed her disgruntled daughter out into the hall and unhooked her long coat from the coat stand, pursing her lips. She rued the day that she'd given in and agreed to get Amelia a mobile phone. Now it was permanently glued to her hand every second of the day. She never went anywhere without it. The constant 'ping' drove Sophia to the edge of madness.

But what could she do when all Amelia's friends had one? And Sophia knew Liam would've bought it for her in a heartbeat. Amelia was a daddy's girl, through and through. Anything she wanted, Liam always succumbed – something that Amelia had been well aware of and milked to the brim. So, now, when Sophia tried to put her foot down, Amelia would go into a mini-rage and blame her for ruining all their lives. She'd then go through the well-rehearsed process of slamming as many doors in the house as she could possibly find.

It's the grieving process, she'd been told by a family therapist not long after Liam's accident. It'll pass in time.

Well, I wish it would pass a bit quicker, thought Sophia as she heard Amelia's heavy-footed stomps across the bedroom floor upstairs.

It was times like these that Sophia found the hardest to cope with. The loss of Liam had hit her hard, but she'd bounced back. She'd had to for the sake of the children. She couldn't afford to wallow in grief and lock herself away. She had to be strong for her family.

With a heavy heart, Sophia pulled on her coat and sought out her trainers from the pile of shoes by the door. She was exhausted. The stress of discovering the burglary when they'd got up that morning had kept her on edge all day. Someone had been in the house while they slept. The thought made her shiver once again.

If she was honest, there was nothing she'd like better than staying home, locking all the doors, and relaxing in a nice hot bath with a glass of wine. But she couldn't let Lucas down; not on his birthday. Pulling his red wellington boots out from beneath the pile of shoes, Sophia turned to call up the stairs.

"Come on you two! I'm leaving in one minute! And I'll eat all the toffee apples myself!"

Five seconds later, Lucas bundled down the stairs two at a time, landing in a heap at the bottom. His sandy, fair hair was ruffled and standing up in unruly tufts, but Sophia just smiled. He had Liam's hair, too. She bent down and helped Lucas into his boots while Amelia slunk down the final few steps, her face thunderous and her phone still clamped to her hand. She'd pulled on a purple puffa jacket and wound a scarf around her neck.

Sophia looked up. "That's better. Your trainers are down here somewhere. Pop them on and we'll get going. You don't want to miss all the best rides!"

Amelia continued her slow journey to the bottom of the stairs, avoiding her mother's gaze. She did her best to deepen her frown as she huffed and puffed, seeking out her trainers from the haphazard pile of random shoes by the door.

But Sophia could see a sparkle in her daughter's pale blue eyes and tried to suppress the giggle that threatened to spill from her mouth. "There'll be candyfloss..."

That did it.

Warmth flooded Amelia's face and her eyes lit up like sparklers. Candyfloss was her favourite. She quickly pulled on her trainers, shoving her mobile phone into the pocket of her puffa jacket. "Come on, then," she squealed, wrenching open the front door. "What are we waiting for?"

* * *

*Tuesday 30th October 2018*

5.30pm

He placed the chair in the centre of the room and smiled. The sight of it always gave him a fluttering sensation in the pit of his stomach – the sense of anticipation, the intoxicating sense of what was yet to come.

The room was slightly bigger than the one back home. He'd boarded up the single window, telling his brother he needed the room to be dark for his photography. He didn't quite know where that lie had come from, springing from his mouth before it had fully formed in his brain. But his brother had merely shrugged and kept out of his way.

He'd then turned off the radiator to give the room its customary damp chill. It was better like that. It was what he remembered. He'd been pleased to see that the room had largely been abandoned by his brother, leaving it to develop patches of mould on some of the walls. Thick, sticky cobwebs hung down like curtains from the peeling ceiling.

It was perfect.

He'd already cut the precise lengths of thin rope, which now sat curled up at the foot of the chair. Waiting.

Everything else in the room had been stripped bare – just the wire-framed bed pushed up against the wall beneath the window and a bucket in the corner for waste. He felt another ripple of excitement. Sometimes this was the best part – the waiting. Not fully knowing what might happen. It was a thrill he never tired of – not now he'd tasted it for himself.

It'd been some time since he'd taken the last one. But the memory of him was still fresh in his mind. He'd been a good boy – obedient and quiet. Just how he liked them. It had been difficult forcing himself to wait this long for another; at times the urge had felt almost impossible to resist.

But now he was ready.

He checked his watch and smiled. He had a feeling that this one would be easy.

Stepping out onto the upstairs landing, he pulled the padlock from his pocket and slotted it into place. He knew his brother wouldn't pry, but he locked it just the same. The padlock gave a satisfying click, and another smile spread to his lips.

It was time.

* * *

# Chapter Two

*Tuesday 30^th October 2018*
  6.00pm

The Winter Fayre had taken over every inch of the Abbey Gardens. Stretching over fourteen acres, the Gardens sat on the site of a former Benedictine Abbey, with the ruins still contained within its grounds. As they walked in through the main entrance under the Abbey Gate, Sophia's senses were immediately assaulted with the most wondrous mix of aromas. Rich, sweet toffee apples were joined by hot, roasted chestnuts – all joined together with warming vegetable soups and hot dogs. As they moved steadily through the growing crowds, the smells only intensified.

The rides may not be as big as those you might find at the seaside, or even a travelling fair, but to Sophia it was just perfect.

"So, what's it to be? Hot dogs or rides first?" Sophia turned towards Lucas and Amelia, who had both already skipped ahead, hand in hand. Her heart ached when she saw the two of them together like this. Liam had never got the chance to see his children growing up, but he would've loved to have seen the children like this. Amelia pretended her baby brother was a pain in the neck, huffing and puffing if she was ever asked to keep an eye on him or, god forbid, *play* with him. But Sophia knew that she secretly adored him.

Amelia turned and waved towards the hot dog stand, her eyes shining in the glare of the Victorian-style lamps erected overhead.

"Hot dogs it is, then," smiled Sophia, following her excitable children towards the intoxicating smell of frying onions.

There wasn't too much of a queue at the hot dog stand and Sophia stood in line while Lucas and Amelia chatted away, nineteen to the dozen. Glancing around while she waited, she noticed several groups of police officers drifting through the crowd. She'd noticed them at the entrance under the Abbey Gate, too.

"Why are the police here, Mummy?" Lucas jumped up and down by Sophia's side, his red wellington boots stamping on the frozen grass beneath. "Do they like coming to the fair, too?"

Sophia smiled and ruffled the top of his head before pulling his bobble hat down firmly. "They do! But I think they like the hot dogs better! What are you going to have on top of yours?"

Sophia nudged both her children ahead of her in the queue, taking another look over her shoulder at the departing police officers. As she did so, the headlines from the previous summer months filled her head. It had been awful – two children abducted and murdered less than forty miles away. The local news had been full of nothing else for weeks.

A chill rippled through her as she recalled the pictures that had been splashed over the front pages. The haunted look in their parents' eyes was something that remained with her to this very day. Even without a mirror, Sophia knew that she'd had the very same look on her own face after losing Liam.

She felt a tugging on her arm and saw Lucas pulling her towards the front of the hot dog stand – it was their turn. She smiled and ordered three hot dogs, doing her best to push her thoughts of Liam, and the grief that always followed, to the back of her mind.

It didn't take them long to devour the food – they'd barely eaten that day, what with the early morning visit from the police and then the crime scene investigators. She'd shut Lucas and Amelia in the living room with a giant sized packet of popcorn and some biscuits, but that had pretty much been it.

Sophia wiped her chin with a paper serviette. The hot dogs had gone down very well – her own cooked just the way she liked it, smothered in onions and tomato ketchup. Lucas was a much pickier eater, insisting on just a plain sausage and leaving most the bread roll, while Amelia opted for just a dash of mustard. There was a contented silence as all three munched their way through their food, sitting high up on a stone wall, watching the world go by.

The Fayre was getting much busier now, and Lucas was fidgeting by her side – losing interest in his sausage and wanting to go and sample some of the rides.

"Let's go, then, Batman," smiled Sophia, helping Lucas down off the wall. "Put your rubbish in the bin first, though."

Lucas and Amelia obediently ran across to the wheelie bin opposite, depositing their serviettes and any leftover food inside, before scampering off in the direction of the rides.

"And keep together!" Sophia picked her way through the throng that was now descending into the Gardens, keeping them in sight yet secretly delighting in their independence at the same time. Amelia was at that awkward age – verging on adolescence, but still very firmly seated in childhood. Children grew up so quickly these days, she knew that. She wouldn't have much time left with Amelia before she started to pull away and become a stranger to her; the mother-daughter relationship she'd been used to, transforming into something altogether very different.

Pushing such thoughts from her mind, Sophia headed towards the waltzer, tucked away in one of the far corners of the Gardens next to the children's playground. She'd already spotted both Lucas and Amelia waiting in the queue.

After three goes on the waltzer, Sophia's feet were beginning to freeze. Wishing she'd put on an extra pair of socks, she suggested that they walk around the stalls for a bit to warm up and maybe get a hot chocolate. They strolled through the rest of the Fayre, stopping now and again at the more traditional fairground stalls, such as the Hook-a-Duck and the coconut shy. Amelia's face lit up when she won an enormous four-foot-high teddy bear on the Hoopla stall, immediately thrusting it towards her brother.

"Happy birthday, squirt!" she grinned, laughing at how the teddy bear was taller than he was.

Lucas squealed and hugged the bear, twirling around on the spot.

"Careful, you'll make yourself sick!" Sophia spied a hot chocolate stall that also sold treats. "Anyone have room for a toffee apple?"

Sophia took hold of the four-foot teddy bear, plus Lucas's coat, as both children ran off in the direction of the stall. Lucas had insisted on removing his coat, despite the cold, saying he was getting too hot in his Batman costume beneath.   Joining them at the confectionary stall and reaching for her purse, Sophia smiled.

"So, what'll it be? Toffee apples or candyfloss?"

* * *

*Tuesday 30<sup>th</sup> October 2018*

Time 6.30pm

They'd been easy to spot. The boy had his Batman costume on, just as he knew he would. The sister, had just won some great big teddy bear on one of the stalls and the mother was now faced with carrying both that and the boy's discarded jacket.

He began to grin. He could sense that the perfect time would be coming soon – all he needed to do was be patient. And wait. He moved through the swelling crowd, nobody paying him even the slightest degree of attention. It was as though he were invisible.

Occasionally, he would catch the eye of an excited child, or a weary parent, but they paid him no heed. His grin broadened.

He'd followed them at a discreet distance, staying close but just far enough away not to be seen. Not once did he lose sight of them. That was the great thing about crowds – the more people there were, the easier it was to hide.

The boy was excited, barely sitting still long enough to eat his hot dog. The aroma from the fried onions had made his own stomach rumble, but there was no time for food. Not for him. Not tonight.

Not when he was hunting.

Eventually, the two children ran towards the Waltzer and he'd followed in their wake. He'd already dismissed the idea of taking the boy from there

– once inside that swirling car they were untouchable. Instead he merely watched, hanging back in the shadows, biding his time. While he waited, he thought back to the room that was waiting for them. The chair had been almost identical to the one he remembered; he'd been excited to find it lurking at the back of the garage. His brother had paid him no heed as he'd dragged it up the stairs.

As the Waltzer made yet another stomach-churning circuit, he noticed two police officers sauntering past. He'd seen the police presence as soon as he'd arrived, but took satisfaction in the fact that none of them had paid him the slightest attention.

As they walked away, his smile broadened.

They weren't looking for him.

Not yet.

* * *

# Chapter Three

6.45pm

Nicki brought the drinks to the only table in the pub. At just fifteen feet by seven feet, and the smallest pub in Britain, one table was all there was room for in The Nutshell. DS Royston Carter cast a wary look at the pint glass set before him.

Nicki grinned. "Try it. You'll like it!" Sitting down at the cramped table, she took a sip of her wine and eyed her most newly acquired detective with a narrow gaze across the rim of her glass. "So, Mr Royston Carter – how did your good self end up on my patch? I don't detect a Suffolk accent there."

The young detective let a broad grin graze his lips just as he took his first tentative sip of the pint of dusky brown liquid in front of him. A surprised look crossed his face.

"Not bad, eh?" Nicki raised her own glass again and took another sip.

"Not bad at all, ma'am." DS Carter glanced around the compact pub. "This place is great. We don't have anything like this back home."

"And back home being?" Nicki leant back against the wood panelled wall and momentarily considered kicking off her boots. Her bones ached from the day spent cooped up in the prosecution room at the Crown Court, where time had dragged by, millisecond by millisecond. And then there was the tedious car journey back. An evening run was still not out of the question if she limited herself to just the one glass.

"Originally Newcastle. But we moved about a bit with my Dad's job – ended up in Peckham before I joined the force. But I suppose you could call me a Geordie at heart."

Nicki smiled. "I thought I could detect a hint of a north-eastern twang in there." She nodded out towards the window. "So, what do you think of our little town?"

Another broad smile broke out on DS Carter's face. "It's great. Feels really small and friendly. I'm used to London, and that's neither small *nor* friendly."

"Whereabouts are you staying?"

"I've got a room in a shared flat above a phone shop at the moment. It's fine for now."

A few moments of comfortable silence passed while they both sipped their drinks and another customer entered the cramped space. With three people in the bar, it almost felt packed. Nicki always made a point of bringing any new recruits on her team to The Nutshell – a chance to get to know them, and them to know her, outside of the confines of the station. It was her favourite pub in the town, so full of character and history – it gave her a warm, snug feeling every time she set foot in it.

"So, Royston." Nicki broke the silence. "There are one or two rules when working on my team. It's best you get to know them early on."

A faint look of trepidation crossed the detective sergeant's face, which made Nicki fight to restrain the giggle building up within her.

"Firstly, I don't function without coffee. If you want to have a serious conversation with me before midday, come armed." Nicki paused and took another sip of her wine. A smile twitched behind her glass. "Secondly – there's no ma'am or guv, here. Call me boss if you *really* have to – but I usually answer to Nicki. But don't *ever* call me Nicola – that's reserved for my parents and my parents alone. And thirdly." Nicki paused once more, her eyes taking on a soft tone. "If you think you have something to say, say it. There's no pecking order in my team. We're all doing the same job for the same reasons, so we all get the same right to voice our opinions. That all good with you?"

Another wide grin covered DS Carter's face. "It's more than good. Cheers." Holding up his pint, he chinked Nicki's wine glass and let his grin widen. "There is just one thing though…"

"Oh?"

"Can you call me Roy? My mother's side of the family is originally from Nigeria and my Grandma persuaded my parents to call me after my grandfather. So I got lumbered with Royston." He made a face behind his pint glass. "But I prefer Roy. Or even Carter."

"Roy it is, then!" Nicki raised her glass once more and took a large sip. "So, Roy, what made you want to join up? Family tradition?"

Roy Carter placed his pint glass back down on the table and reached for a handful of the peanuts that had appeared alongside their drinks. He threw a few into his mouth before replying.

"I'm the first in the family to join the police, so I guess you could say it came as a bit of a surprise. My Dad's a chef, my Mum's a teacher. I think they both thought I'd follow one or other of them – but my cooking skills aren't great and I'd had enough of school by the time I left at eighteen."

Nicki continued to eye her new detective across the tiny table, noticing a darkness drift into his gaze, snuffing out the sparkle that'd been evident earlier. She caught his eye. "OK, but what's the real reason? I know most of the coppers back at the station probably can't cook either, but…something else made you join up, didn't it? I can tell."

DS Carter gave Nicki a lop-sided smile, accompanied by a faint shrug. He took another mouthful of his beer. "I guess I felt I wanted to help. Give something back." He paused, the cloudiness in his eyes deepening. "I lost someone close to me – a good friend – while I was at college. He died of an overdose, right in front of me. There was nothing I could do. I just watched him die." DS Carter replaced the pint glass back on the table. "It felt like the right thing to do – joining up, I mean. Maybe I could make a difference somehow."

"I'm sorry, Roy. That must've been very hard to deal with." Again, Nicki looked across the table into the young detective's eyes and this time she saw something else; something familiar.

Guilt.

"Losing someone close to you can have that effect." Nicki smiled and nudged the china bowl of peanuts across the table. "Whatever the motivation, we're glad to have you here with us."

They both sat and chatted for a while longer, Nicki skilfully avoiding any questions as to her own motivations for joining the force. *That* was definitely a conversation for another day. Taking a last mouthful of wine, she rose from her seat.

"As much as I'd love to stay and chat some more, Roy, I've a hungry cat at home waiting for me to feed her. Plus, I need to get out of these boots."

\* \* \*

*Tuesday 30<sup>th</sup> October 2018*

7.30pm

Wrapping her frozen fingers around the warming cup of caramel hot chocolate, Sophia let the sweet-scented vapour waft towards her nostrils. Amelia had predictably opted for a bag of candyfloss and Lucas a toffee apple – but by the size of the apple, Sophia reckoned they would be taking most of it home with them.

As they turned away from the stall, Lucas's eyes lit up and he began to jump up and down on the spot, his Batman cape flapping around his shoulders. "Mummy! Mummy! Can I, please?" With a hand sticky with toffee, he grabbed hold of Sophia and dragged her towards an inflatable slide in a quieter section of the Gardens by the river.

The slide was busy, swarming with children climbing up the rope ladder at the side, and more slipping and sliding their way down into the ball pit at the bottom. All Sophia could see were bobbing heads in a variety of woollen hats, the air full of the sound of children's delighted screams. A selection of mums and dads, brothers and sisters, gathered in groups around the base, stamping their frozen feet into the ground. An array of shoes and boots littered the ground.

"It looks very busy, Lucas," replied Sophia, warily. "Maybe later."

"Aw, no Mummy. Now. Please Mummy, now!" Lucas looked up at her with those wide, cornflower-blue eyes and Sophia knew she would relent. She could almost see Liam's smiling face, waiting to catch his son as he came flying down into the ball pit.

"OK, but take your wellies off first." Sophia watched as Lucas promptly sat down on the frozen ground and obediently pulled off his boots, still gripping his toffee apple in one hand. "And it looks like there's a bit of a queue," she added. "You'll have to wait your turn, Batman."

"I will, Mummy." Lucas scrambled to his feet, his eyes shining. "Can I pay the man, Mummy? I'm six now!" He held out a gloved hand and began dancing from foot to foot.

Sophia smiled and dug into her pocket for some change. "All right. But make sure you don't move from that queue. I'm only going to be over here." Sophia nodded towards a seating area behind them. "You come straight over here when you're finished and I'll be watching you the whole time."

"I will, Mummy." Lucas closed his fist around three pound coins.

"Amelia, go and stand with him. Make sure he's OK."

Amelia opened her mouth to object, but was immediately silenced by the stern look on her mother's face. "OK," she huffed, passing her bag of candyfloss to Sophia and thrusting her hands into the pockets of her puffa jacket.

Sophia turned and made her way to an arrangement of wooden chairs behind them, sitting down to finish the last of her hot chocolate. She balanced the four-foot teddy bear on its own seat and sat back to see Lucas skipping happily towards the inflatable slide, and Amelia trudging on behind. Smiling, she sipped her drink and savoured the sugar hit. Tiredness began to wash over her; she hadn't stopped all day, what with preparing for Lucas's birthday, and now found herself feeling a little lightheaded.

The burglary last night hadn't really sunk in yet, not properly. Waking up that morning, she'd immediately sensed that something was different. Not wrong as such, just different.

And she hadn't seen it - not straight away. She'd got up as usual, making her way downstairs to make a cup of tea and switch on the radio. It wasn't until she felt the chill draught on the back of her neck as she waited for the kettle to boil, that she saw the back door was open. She was certain she'd shut the door before they went to bed last night, but had she locked it?

The thought that someone had been inside the house while they slept made Sophia shiver once again, and she took another mouthful of hot chocolate. It was a horrible feeling – it made you feel violated and dirty. Exposed. As far as she could tell, nothing of much value had been taken. Not that they really had that much to take anyway. Her handbag was still on the kitchen worktop; her purse and car keys still inside. All she could see was that two ten pound notes had gone – but the other cash, a five pound note and a twenty, remained untouched. The detectives that had arrived later that morning advised her to cancel her cards anyway, just in case, and make sure she locked her back door in future.

All in all, she considered she'd got off lightly.

Shuddering again, she forced the thoughts from her head and gazed towards the slide. Lucas had joined the queue and was munching on his apple as he waited. Amelia stood behind him, her face glued to the screen of her mobile phone.

As she leant back in the uncomfortable wooden chair, Sophia let her eyes wander around the rest of the Fayre. They'd strolled around most of it now, but there were still a few stalls to look at before they called it a night. The crowd was thickening, everyone wrapped up in coats and scarves to do battle against the cold, frosty air. Despite the freezing temperatures, many of the children, just like Lucas, appeared to be in some form of fancy dress or dressing up costume, with coats and jackets discarded. With tomorrow being Hallowe'en, there were a fair few ghosts, ghouls and zombies scampering past, plus a smattering of Marvel superheroes.

There must be a face painting stall somewhere, she mused, as she watched two young boys run past – one with a full Spiderman face, the other with some form of green monster. A lone vampire with a deathly-white face and bloodied lips brought up the rear.

Suddenly, Amelia came striding into view, a familiar frown decorating her brow. "Lucas is on the slide now - he's got six goes. I'm not hanging around there for him. The place is full of kids."

Sophia smiled and patted the seat next to her. "Have a sit down for a couple of minutes, then. We can watch the slide from here."

Amelia slumped down next to her mother and pulled out her phone from her pocket. Sophia saw the familiar glare from the screen light up her daughter's face and heard the usual 'ping' of an incoming message.

"You know, you could go and take a picture of your brother on the slide." Sophia leant across and nudged Amelia's arm. "Go on, get a birthday photo of him."

Amelia let out another huff before pushing herself out of her chair and storming back across to the inflatable slide, returning a minute or so later to thrust her phone towards her mother. "There."

Sophia took the phone and saw a series of four pictures – two of Lucas at the top of the slide, one of him halfway down the slide, and another when he landed in a heap in the ball pit at the bottom. In all four he was still clutching his half-eaten toffee apple.

"I'm sure he shouldn't still have that apple with him," remarked Sophie, handing the phone back.

"He wouldn't give it up," replied Amelia, turning her face back towards the phone screen. "I think the man just let him on with it to keep him quiet."

After another few minutes of people watching, Sophie glanced at her watch. She pushed herself up from the wooden chair, feeling the cold starting to seep back into her bones, the warming effects of the hot chocolate having worn off. She picked up the oversized teddy bear and Lucas's jacket.

"Let's go and find Lucas. He must've finished sliding by now."

The first inkling Sophia had that something was wrong came when she saw the discarded toffee apple lying on the frozen grass at the exit from the ball pit. It took a while for the realisation to hit, but when it did, a spreading sickness swamped her. Whipping her head round from side to side, Sophie scoured the masses of children running to and from the entrance to the slide.

"Where is he?" Sophia's voice barely carried above the sound of excited, sugar-filled children. "Where's Lucas?"

With fear rising, Sophia stumbled as quickly as she could towards the heap of discarded boots and shoes. It didn't take her long to spy Lucas's bright red wellington boots. She pushed her way through the gaps between the waiting parents, ignoring the grunts that followed, and scoured the slide once again, searching for the tell-tale Batman cape.

There were so many children it was hard to focus. Each and every one blurred into the next, a mass of multi-coloured shapes swimming before her eyes. There were ghosts and ghouls, even a few zombies and green-eyed monsters, but there was no Batman.

There was no Lucas.

\* \* \*

# Chapter Four

*Tuesday 30<sup>th</sup> October 2018*
  7.45pm

After saying their goodbyes outside The Nutshell, Nicki crossed over towards Whiting Street and the short walk home. The air was cold and damp, with an ever thickening fog on the horizon. The unmistakable smell of the Fayre, which would now be in full swing at the Abbey Gardens, reached her nostrils. A mixture of burgers and hot dogs, the sickly sweet smell of candyfloss and chocolate – all wrapped up with a covering of the rich, nutty aroma of roasted chestnuts.

With bonfire night less than a week away it was the beginning of a magical time of the year for the town. The annual Christmas Market at the end of the month would signal the unofficial start of the festive season, and for the first time in a very long while, Nicki actually felt like she was looking forward to it.

The week at the Bedford Lodge Hotel and Spa had done her good. The tightness in her shoulders, the twinges in her lower back, had all melted away beneath the full-body massages and hot-stone treatments. It had been an indulgence, but Nicki didn't regret a single penny.

Stress.

That had been the cause of her ailments, according to her massage therapist. He could literally feel the knots in her muscles beneath his hands as he worked; tight clusters of stress that slowly began to yield under his touch.

But stress was a peril of the job; something that had to be lived with. Sometimes it just couldn't be helped. A previous case, an investigation into people trafficking and child prostitution, had almost thrown her over the edge, prompting DCI Turner to suggest she take some time off. 'Suggest' was probably the wrong word. It had been more like an order. A command. But meant in the best possible spirit.

Quickening her stride, she soon reached her home on College Lane and felt the cold night air prickling at her cheeks. With an early meeting with DCI Turner in the morning, and that towering in-tray to deal with, the thought of an evening run was becoming less and less enticing.

Instead, she reached into her pocket for her house keys, looking forward to a hot bath and an early night.

Unbeknown to Nicki, she would achieve neither.

\* \* \*

*Tuesday 30ᵗʰ October 2018*
   7.45pm

Six-year-old Lucas Jackson could still taste the sickly sweetness of the toffee apple on his tongue beneath the sticky tape that stretched across his mouth. The hot dog from earlier was churning in his stomach.

Trying to move, he found his hands were bound tightly behind his back, and his ankles tied together with some sort of rope. All he could do was lie still and stare up to the ceiling. He was in a van – he knew that much. It was the same type of van the man from next door drove. He would often see it parked on the man's driveway and Lucas wondered what was inside. Mummy had said he was a plumber – but Lucas didn't really know what that was.

The bindings around his wrists were hurting, cutting into his flesh. Each time he tried to wriggle free, they bit into his skin, deeper and deeper with every turn. It felt like when Darren Porter from the year above at school would grab him in the playground and give him a Chinese Burn, digging his fingernails into his arm just for fun.

But this wasn't fun.

Lucas felt himself shiver, and not just from the coldness inside the van. He wanted his Mummy, and he wanted Amelia. Where were they? Why did they let that man take him?

The thought of the man sent another shudder coursing through Lucas's tiny body and he felt the unmistakable sensation of warm urine seeping into his underwear.

Tears prickled at the corners of his eyes. "Mummy, where are you?"

$$* * *$$

*Tuesday 30th October 2018*

7.45pm

Sophia ran from one side of the inflatable slide to the other, screaming Lucas's name. Hot tears flooded her cheeks, stinging as they met the chilled air. Flinging the four-foot teddy bear to the ground, she yelled again.

"Lucas!" she screamed, pushing through a group of parents waiting by the pile of abandoned shoes. "Lucas!" Her words sounded dull and empty; no sooner had they escaped her mouth than they were swallowed up in the damp air, snuffed out like a spent candle.

"Amelia!" Sophia ran back towards her daughter who was standing, rooted to the spot, by Lucas's discarded toffee apple.

Amelia's face was as white as a sheet. "Mum? What's happened to Lucas, Mum?" The strain in her voice was palpable, her bottom lip beginning to tremble.

Sophia grabbed hold of Amelia and pulled her close. "I don't know, sweetheart. I don't know." Roughly wiping away her tears with the back of her hand, Sophia turned back towards the slide. "Let's check again. He has to be here. Check the slide again."

Both Sophia and Amelia scoured the slide once more for any sign of Lucas;

for any sign of the excitable six-year-old in the Batman costume.

But there was none.

"Has anyone seen my son?" Sophia began to run, forcing herself between the waiting parents, randomly grabbing hold of arms and elbows. "My son? Lucas. He's six? He's six today." She choked back fresh sobs as people parted to let her through the crowd, most eyeing her warily and stepping out of her way. "My son," she yelled. "Can anybody help me?!"

Nobody seemed to hear.

The sounds of the Fayre were dim and distant, as if she were encased in her own bubble of cotton wool. Words were muffled and incoherent. She could no longer hear the screams of the children as they tumbled down the slide; the music from the nearby merry-go-round was faint and subdued. All she could hear was her own rapid breathing and the hammering of her own heart.

Sophia's eyes roamed the faces staring at her, each one swimming in and out of focus. "He's got a Batman costume on. He's six!" she screamed, making a lunge for a man, who wrenched his arm away from her and shrank back into the crowd. "He's got blue eyes and fair hair. He's called Lucas!" More wary faces eyed her suspiciously and turned away, dragging their children with them. "Why won't anyone help me?" she sobbed. "Why won't anyone help me?!"

Sophia felt her legs give way as she sank down onto the frost covered muddy grass below. "Please help me, please...."

The next thing Sophia felt was a pair of sturdy hands guiding her to her feet. She turned and collapsed into the arms of a police constable.

\* \* \*

Tuesday 30<sup>th</sup> October 2018
9.15pm

The free-standing bath was Nicki's pride and joy; the first thing she installed in the house when she'd bought it some seven years ago. Perching herself on the edge, she watched the water slowly begin to rise – the small bathroom soon filling with the intense aroma of bergamot and patchouli. Her week away at the Spa had taught her the importance of looking after her mind, body and spirit – all of which had been neglected at some point over the last few years - and one way to achieve all three was a deeply-filled bath full of luxurious essential oils. Lighting some candles while she waited, Nicki breathed in the relaxing scent.

It had been a rotten first day back – but the first day back usually was. Spending most of the day in court had not been part of her initial plan. Still, tomorrow was another day, she mused, and she began to unbutton her blouse and step out of her trousers. As she did so, her Russian Blue cat nosed its way into the bathroom.

"Come here, Luna," coaxed Nicki, stretching out a hand. "I've missed you so much." The cat obliged and sniffed Nicki's fingers, rewarded in turn with a rub behind the ears and underneath the chin. A gentle, soft purr could just about be heard above the cascading water from the bath taps. "There's a good girl."

Luna sniffed the air, her wet nose twitching. She eyed the bath somewhat apprehensively, and took a few steps backwards.

"It's not for you," laughed Nicki, reaching for the glass of wine she'd poured herself on getting back to the house. Despite the reassurance, Luna backed out of the bathroom and disappeared.

The house was a compact, one-bedroomed home set on three levels – if you counted the rooftop; which Nicki did. Straight in off a narrow lane, two steps took you down into the living room, complete with an open fireplace that now housed a wood-burning stove. A small galley-kitchen to the rear led out into an enclosed courtyard, hardly big enough to swing the proverbial cat – although Nicki had never tried, much to Luna's relief.

From the living room, a narrow set of open wooden stairs led up to the first floor, which housed one decent-sized bedroom and the small bathroom.

But Nicki's favourite space, and the decider when it came to putting in an offer for the house, was up on the roof. Originally just a flat, concrete roof space, Nicki had instantly seen it as a rooftop garden. And that was exactly what she had created.

Accessed from the first floor landing, it was her 'go-to' space. Her thinking space. Her space to escape from the world below. Just being up there transported her to another world. It was quiet and tranquil – any sounds from the streets below melted into the ether by the time they reached her. She could lie back on her rattan lounger furniture and stare up at the sky above, losing herself in the huge expanse of nothing.

With the house being only a stone's throw away from the Greene King brewery, the air often bore a tinge of brewing hops – a sweet, malty aroma that warmed her from within.

Too cold to venture up onto the roof tonight, Nicki stepped into the hot water of her aromatherapy bath and sank beneath the surface. Her skin tingled as the heat hit, making her shudder. Resting her head back, she reached for the glass of wine and closed her eyes.

It was then that the phone rang.

\* \* \*

# Chapter Five

The station at night was a completely different beast than during the day -
something about it being out of hours altered its aura. Nicki snapped on the
lights to the main incident room, squinting against the sudden glare. Her
hair was still damp from her thirty seconds or so in the bath and it clung,
coolly, to the back of her neck. She'd pulled on a pair of lycra sports tights
and an old sweatshirt before dashing out of the house in her running shoes,
grabbing a waterproof jacket on the way. Luna had barely lifted a whisker at
her sudden departure, used to Nicki's impulsive comings and goings by now.

Following her into the room were both DC Butler and the newly appointed
DS Carter.

"Darcie? What happened to your date?"

Darcie gave a grimace. "He cancelled on me just as I got home. Something
'came up', apparently."

"You didn't need to tip out as well, Roy," Nicki added. "You don't start
properly until the morning."

DS Royston Carter held up his hands. "Happy to help. It'll be morning
soon enough."

Nicki smiled, gratefully, at her newest member of the Major Incident Team.
"The details we have so far are somewhat sketchy. But the report is of a
missing child." She strode over to one of the whiteboards that hugged the

walls of the incident room. Picking up a marker pen, she began to write.

"Lucas Jackson. Aged six. Disappeared from the Abbey Gardens approximately two and a half hours ago. Last seen around seven-thirty pm. An initial search of the Gardens hasn't thrown up any sightings. An outer cordon has been set up preventing anyone entering or leaving the Gardens, and patrol cars have been despatched to the surrounding streets."

"Could he just have wandered off?" ventured Darcie. Her tone suggested her words were borne more out of hope than anything else. "Gone home?"

"I pray to God that's what's happened, Darcie." Nicki paused and chewed her lip. "But at six years old? The family live on the Moreton Hall estate, so it's not an easy walk, especially in the dark."

"Let's just hope he's got lost and he's hiding somewhere, scared out of his wits." Darcie tried to inject some optimism into her voice.

"We'll work on that assumption, but not rule anything else out. The Gardens are being cleared of the public, and an initial team on site are taking details from anyone who was close to where he was last seen. All exits from the Gardens have been closed where possible; others have a uniformed officer preventing anyone else entering or leaving. Whilst not a crime scene at the present time, the DCI made it quite clear we're to do everything by the book." The words 'just in case' hovered on her tongue. Swallowing them back, Nicki placed the marker pen down and stared at the almost empty whiteboard. Except for the name 'Lucas Jackson' it remained blank. Nicki shuddered, hoping it stayed that way, and the young boy was quickly returned to his family. She turned to her team. "Let's head out there and see what we're dealing with."

"You think this is more than just a wandering child?" Roy asked the question that was on each of their lips.

Nicki hesitated and then slowly began to nod. "I'll keep an open mind, but...a child doesn't just disappear from a crowded place like that, not in my experience."

"The parents must be in bits," added Darcie, her slim shoulders shuddering.

Nicki recalled the scant details she'd been given when DCI Turner's call had ended her luxurious bath. "From what the DCI has told me, it looks like a single parent household – just Sophia Jackson listed as mother. There's one other child - a daughter. We'll get a family liaison officer out to be with them as soon as we can."

"You all right, boss?" Roy had noticed the pale tone gracing Nicki's cheeks as she spoke, and the deep concern in her eyes.

With one last glance towards the name 'Lucas Jackson' on the whiteboard, Nicki turned back to her team, clasping her hands together to hide their trembling. The sickness she'd felt earlier when she'd received the call was intensifying, creeping through to every crevice of her body. She'd stood there, dripping wet from the bath and shivering in the hallway, gripping the phone receiver with a shaking hand as DCI Turner relayed the details to her.

Details that sounded so familiar. Details that transported her back to *that time.*

She tried a wan smile. "Let's just get out there and see what we can do."

From bitter experience, she knew they didn't have much time to lose.

* * *

*Tuesday 30th October 2018*
10.15pm

He'd taken his time transferring the boy to the house, making sure there were no busybody neighbours twitching at their net curtains. Even in the dark you could never be quite sure who was watching. The house was set back from the road, secluded behind tall hedges that masked it from prying eyes. At this time of night, he should be safe – everyone should be tucked up in bed, their curtains drawn, lights turned out until morning.

But he'd waited anyway. You couldn't be too careful.

After enough time had passed, and the darkness outside had deepened, he'd opened the back of the van and inhaled the damp, fetid smell of urine. It reminded him of the toilet block in his old school. Wrinkling his nose, he'd reached in and pulled the boy towards him by his feet. He'd wriggled and kicked to begin with, but by the time they'd reached the house he'd quietened down.

He'd had the foresight to open the doors to the double garage before backing the van up close. All it now took was one last effort to haul the boy onto his feet and then tip him over his shoulder. The only detectable sound was a muffled cry from behind the masking tape.

Safely inside the double garage, he'd lowered Lucas Jackson to the floor and activated the button to shut the doors. Once the doors were fully closed, he'd snapped on the interior light and cast his eyes down at the boy by his feet.

He'd come surprisingly willingly – which was either a testament to his own powers of persuasion, or the abhorrent parenting skills of the mother. Maybe it was a bit of both. He was sure he'd seen a vague flicker of doubt in the boy's blue eyes when he'd first approached him, as if he was aware he was doing something that maybe he shouldn't. But it didn't last long.

He hadn't been sure it would work. There was so much that could've gone wrong, no matter how much preparation and planning he'd done. But he'd noticed the slide almost immediately, and instantly knew it would be the place. He didn't know why, but he could just feel it. The boy wouldn't be able to resist.

Allowing him to queue up alone was genius. The mother had inadvertently dropped the child right into his lap. The sister was so distracted with her phone that she never saw him waiting, hovering by the side of the slide. He blended in well; he knew that. And his confidence soared every time he locked eyes with the little boy in the Batman costume.

And it couldn't have been easier in the end.

The sister had lost interest quite quickly, more interested in the messages on her phone, and the mother was distracted by the sights and sounds of the fair. Seated not that far away, she wasn't watching the slide; not really. She never once looked across to see the man watching her son.

And just like that – they were gone.

Gazing down at the boy's body cowering at his feet, he could almost hear the words that must now be circulating around Lucas Jackson's head, as if he were saying them out loud.

But he looked friendly, Mummy.

He said nice things, Mummy.

He said it would be all right, Mummy.

He said he would bring me back.

A smile grazed his lips. Not that the boy would be able to see.

With the garage door now firmly shut, he bent down and picked the boy up. He didn't weigh much, and whatever fight had been in him at the beginning of the journey had now dissipated. He felt the boy's body shudder beneath his touch, the thin fabric of the Batman costume clinging to his bones. Just a faint whimper could be heard behind the tape stretched across his mouth.

As he dragged the boy to his feet, the faint aroma of fried onions and hot dogs reached his nostrils, even through the fabric of his mask. It made his stomach growl.

With the hunting over, now he could feast.

\* \* \*

Tuesday 30<sup>th</sup> October 2018

10.30pm

The smell of sizzling sausages still hung in the dampened air, making everyone's stomachs churn with a sickening nausea. An internal cordon had been erected around the slide where Lucas had last been seen, roped off with blue and white police tape. As Nicki and her team arrived, the last huddles of fairgoers were being ushered away, details taken and the scene cleared.

The Abbey Gardens Winter Fayre had come to an abrupt end.

Sophia Jackson was still sitting in the back of a St John Ambulance, refusing to leave. Nicki could already hear her heart-rending wails from where she was standing by the inner cordon, adjacent to the inflatable slide. All the shoes, boots and trainers had been collected – all that now remained on the cold, frosty grass was one pair of bright red wellington boots belonging to

Lucas Jackson.

Seeing the boots all alone, and without a six-year-olds legs wriggling inside, made the situation very real. Nicki's heart ached.

Officers were already scouring the rest of the Gardens once again, spreading out towards the Cathedral grounds. There were several ways in and out of the Abbey Gardens – each one potentially a route that Lucas Jackson took. Each one had been closed and a uniformed officer placed on guard.

Behind the inflatable slide, the River Lark slid silently by. Nicki's eyes wandered towards the dark waters and considered whether Lucas could have merely slipped and fallen into the river, unseen and unheard. Skirting the police tape, she stepped across to the banks of the river and peered over the railings into the chilled, murky waters below. The river was dark and quiet, silently continuing its journey, oblivious to the commotion going on all around. Nicki knew it wasn't going to be giving up any of its secrets that easily. The thought of having to deploy police divers made her stomach clench.

Turning away, she made her way back around the edge of the cordon, coming face to face with DCI Turner as she did so. His tall, powerful frame towered above her, reminding her in so many ways of her father. An enormous man at six feet five inches, Detective Superintendent Hugh Webster had been a gentle giant. And for a split second, standing there in the freezing fog of the Abbey Gardens, memories of being enveloped in those thickset arms and held close to his beating heart flooded her brain. She was five years old again and the apple of her Daddy's eye.

How quickly times can change.

Nicki pushed the unbidden thoughts from her mind and caught DCI Turner's eye. Despite the darkness surrounding them, he could see the pale and haunting expression on her face.

"Nicki?" The DCI's thick West Country accent cut through the damp foggy air. Thick droplets of moisture were clinging to everything around them, and visibility was decreasing sharply with every passing second. Freezing rain looked to be on the horizon. "Are you OK?"

Nicki nodded a little too quickly, swallowing past the lump in her throat.

She buried her chin into the collar of her jacket, but didn't open her mouth to speak. She had a feeling no coherent words would escape.

DCI Turner's eyebrows raised a notch. "Are you sure? I don't think you should be here."

Nicki eventually found her voice. She shook her head. "I'm fine. I want to do this."

The DCI's face softened, but didn't lose the concerned tint in his steely-grey eyes. "If you're sure. But anytime you want to hand this one over, do so. Without hesitation. I can bring someone else in if you'd prefer."

Nicki shook her head more fiercely this time and forced a weak smile onto her frozen lips.

DCI Turner nodded, but his concerned look remained. "Well, so far we've got the stall holders gathered by the main entrance at Abbey Gate. Officers are taking names, addresses and seeing if anyone recalls seeing the young lad this evening. All exits are closed and guarded."

Nicki's eyes flickered towards the abandoned stalls. The Gardens now had an eerie, deserted feel to them.

DCI Turner continued. "All officers now have a photograph of Lucas and there'll be continued searches of nearby streets overnight, just in case he's wandered off. The CCTV operators have been alerted and also sent images of Lucas."

Nicki caught the DCI's eye. "You don't believe that's the case, though, do you? That he's just wandered off?" It was a statement more than a question. Both the DCI's and Nicki's gaze were drawn towards the abandoned pair of red wellington boots lying on the frosted grass just inside the inner cordon. If Lucas Jackson had decided to go wandering, then he'd done so in his socks.

DCI Turner cleared his throat and pulled his gaze away from the abandoned boots. "I'd like to think it was, but.... I'm scaling this up to a potential crime scene."

"Because of the Norfolk cases?"

"I want to play down the similarities with the Norfolk abduction and murder cases. Keep a lid on it until we're certain. The last thing we want to do is cause a mass panic. We keep a level head at all times and investigate it by the book."

Nicki nodded. It made sense. Linking the cases right here, right now, wouldn't help their search for Lucas tonight.

"And I mean it, Nicki." The DCI touched Nicki lightly on the arm as they both turned away from the police tape circling the inflatable slide. "The minute all this gets too much, you let me know. You're my best DI, you know that, and I can't think of anyone I'd rather have as my deputy – but if you need to take a step back...?"

Nicki gave what she hoped was a reassuring smile and excused herself, heading over to where DC Butler and DS Carter were gathered next to the St John Ambulance that housed Sophia Jackson and her daughter. She noticed DS Carter already had his notebook in hand.

"What have you got for me so far, Roy?"

"Sophia Jackson and her daughter, Amelia, last saw Lucas on the inflatable slide at around seven-thirty. Amelia waited in line with Lucas until he bought his ticket and went through the entrance onto the slide itself. After a minute or so, she left him there and went to join her mother in the seating area over there." Roy pointed a gloved finger towards a muddy section of grass behind them where a selection of wooden chairs was arranged.

"Approximately how long was he on the slide? How long was he out of their sight for?"

"That's hard to tell. They're both extremely distraught, as you can imagine. I'm not sure they can put times to anything right now. But I wouldn't say it could've been for very long. I mean..." Roy paused and looked back towards the slide. "It wouldn't take that long to climb up and slide down, would it? If he paid for six goes, then...." Roy gave a shrug. "Five minutes maybe? Ten?"

Nicki nodded. "And he's never done anything like this before? Wandered off? Got himself lost?"

Roy shook his head. "Not according to Mum. He never goes anywhere on his own, and isn't the type to run off. Always has his sister there watching out for him."

Nicki felt a sudden chill envelop her which had nothing to do with the plunging temperatures, and an all too familiar pull wrenched her stomach.

She cleared her throat and refocused her mind. "OK. I'll have a quick word with her, but then I think we need to get them back home. They can't do anything constructive out here."

Roy and Darcie stepped to the side as Nicki made her way towards the St John Ambulance. With one of the rear doors already open, she popped her head inside and felt her heart immediately clench when she saw the ragged expression on Sophia Jackson's face. It went beyond pain; as deep as it was humanly possible to go.

Nicki pulled herself up into the ambulance and tugged the door closed behind her, shutting out the blue flashing lights and raised voices that filled the air outside. It was quiet inside the ambulance and, for the briefest of seconds, it felt possible that by staying cocooned within it, they could shut out the world. And by doing so, what had happened to Lucas could be pushed so far back into the distance that it had never happened at all. Just so long as they could stay in here.

But Nicki knew that wasn't an option. Soon the doors to the ambulance would have to be opened again, and Sophia Jackson would need to face the grim reality of life as it now was.

Soon. But not yet.

She sat down on the edge of an examination trolley and instinctively reached across to where Sophia was sitting, grabbing hold of the terrified woman's hands and giving them a squeeze. Her skin was as cold as ice and her hands trembled beneath Nicki's touch.

"Mrs Jackson? Sophia? I'm Detective Inspector Nicki Hardcastle. I'm so sorry for everything that you're going through right now – all I can say is that we are doing everything we can to find your son."

Nicki looked deeply into Sophia Jackson's eyes, but all she saw was a hollowness in return. It was a look she'd seen all too often, and knew that nothing she could say would bring any form of reassurance or comfort. She didn't intend to prolong the poor woman's agony.

"Officers are searching every inch of the Gardens and beyond. We have patrols out on the streets covering each of the exit routes." Nicki paused again and gave Sophia Jackson's chilled hands another squeeze. "We'll do all we can to bring him back to you."

Turning towards the rear door, ready to break the walls of the cocoon and let the harsh realities of the outside world in once again, Nicki gave a grateful smile to the St John Ambulance volunteer who hadn't left Sophia Jackson's side for one minute. "We'll send a car to get them both home as soon as we can."

Just as Nicki pushed open the rear door, Amelia's quivering voice stopped her in her tracks.

"It's all my fault, isn't it?"

Nicki spun around to find Lucas's twelve-year-old sister staring mournfully up at her, clinging to her mother's arm.

"It's my fault he's gone."

Nicki pulled the door closed once again and stepped back towards the shaking girl. She crouched down and held Amelia's tear filled gaze in her own.

"That's not true, Amelia." Nicki felt her own eyes begin to prick with tears as she reached out and placed a hand on the trembling girl's forearm. "None of this is your fault."

"But I should've been watching him." Amelia's face was deathly white, tears tunnelling their way down her frozen cheeks and dripping from her chin onto the fabric of her puffa jacket. Nicki felt a wayward tear splash onto the back of her hand. "Mum told me to watch him."

"Please don't think like that," continued Nicki, softly. "Sometimes..." The words caught in the back of her throat. "Sometimes bad things happen and it's outside of our control...any of us. You mustn't think that this is your fault."

Nicki watched as Amelia's face crumpled yet again. She knew her words sounded hollow and meaningless. Of course she was going to blame herself. There was nothing anyone could do or say that would change that. She would blame herself forever.

Nicki straightened up and backed out of the ambulance, closing the door behind her. Let the Jackson's have a few more momento inside their cocoon before they had to face the harsh reality of the night's events and the world as they knew it came crashing down around them.

"You OK, boss?" Darcie stepped forwards to take hold of Nicki's arm, noticing how the detective inspector was swaying slightly on her feet and looked deathly pale even in the muted light of the Gardens. "You look dreadful."

Nicki met Darcie's gaze and forced a wan smile. "I'm fine." She patted the detective constable's hand and started towards the main exit out onto Mustow Street. "I think we've seen enough for now. Let's get back to the station and plan the next move."

Both Darcie and Roy began to follow. "Maybe, with any luck, by the time we get there he'll have been found." Darcie tried her best at sounding optimistic.

"Maybe." Nicki's own voice was flat.

'It's my fault he's gone.'

'I should've been watching him.'

Amelia's words echoed inside Nicki's head as they headed back towards the car.

'It's all my fault.'

Before opening the driver's door, she hurriedly wiped a hand across her cheek, brushing away the tears that had started to trickle. She knew just how Amelia would be feeling right now – right now and forever afterwards.

Amelia thought it was all her fault.

"Just as it was mine." Nicki breathed out into the fog. "Just as it was mine."

* * *

# Chapter Six

*Wednesday 31ˢᵗ October 2018*

1.00am

Closing the door behind her, Nicki sank back against the cool wood and closed her eyes.

What a night.

They'd spent an hour or so back at the station, compiling what information they'd managed to glean, which at this stage wasn't much. The patrols would continue throughout the night, as would the monitoring of CCTV, but it wasn't until daylight that they would be able to begin the search properly. If Lucas had merely wandered off, then there was a faint hope he was just sheltering from the cold somewhere. But if not... Nicki found herself shuddering at the thought.

Already, she'd actioned enquiries into the family arrangements of the Jacksons. Unfortunately, in the area of child abductions – if this *was*, indeed, an abduction – then in the vast majority of cases the perpetrator was known to the family, as sickening as that sounded. Initial enquiries showed the Jacksons to be a small family unit – with just the mother, Sophia, and her two children. But every family had its secrets. It was just a question of uncovering them.

After an hour, Nicki had sent her team home. They looked wrecked. There was little that they could physically do tonight that wasn't already being done, and dawn would be upon them before they knew it. Tomorrow would be the moment they faced the question of whether this was just a simple case of a child wandering off and getting lost, or whether they were, in fact, facing something far more sinister.

Pushing herself away from the door, she kicked off her running shoes and slipped out of her jacket. Heading out to the small galley-style kitchen at the rear of the house, she hesitated for a second by the kettle. Shaking her head, she pulled open the fridge and selected a chilled bottle of Chablis and a large glass from the shelf above.

Padding back through to the living room she lit the wood burner, adding a couple of extra logs, and then settled down into the sagging sofa, pouring herself a glass of wine as she did so. Within seconds, Luna jumped up onto the sofa and started to knead Nicki's legs. She ruffled the back of the cat's ears and stroked her bobbing head.

The case of Lucas Jackson had rocked her. At the first mention of a child going missing from a fairground, her heart had squeezed inside her so painfully she thought it might break. Memory after memory flooded her brain.

Deano.

She thought about Deano most days – at some point or other his cheeky, impish face would flash into her mind, causing her to smile at the fun he'd brought into their lives. But not tonight. Tonight she felt raw; as if she'd been transported back to her ten-year-old self and was forced to relive the horror of that night all over again. Second by agonising second.

And even here, in the safety of her living room, she thought she could still smell the jarringly sweet aroma of the candyfloss. She'd never once eaten it again – not after that night.

* * *

*Thursday 7th November 1996*
    6.45pm

The smell of sweet candyfloss grazed her nose, making her teeth tingle. And there was popcorn! It was just like being at the cinema, but better.

Ten-year-old Nicola Webster hopped and skipped her way towards the candyfloss stall, her hand closed tightly around the coins in her pocket. She'd had to beg her mother to give her next week's pocket money early, promising that she'd tidy her room and clean out the rabbit hutch at the weekend. Her mother had given her one of 'those looks' but parted with the money anyway. Dad had taken her to one side and slipped two extra fifty pence pieces into the palm of her hand, bringing a finger to his lips.

"It's our secret, Nix. Don't tell your mother."

Nicki couldn't wait for the fair to arrive. She'd seen the posters in the town for weeks; and her friends at school couldn't talk about anything else. It was the biggest and best fair to come anywhere near them – and *everyone* was going. She'd even marked the days off on her Take That calendar but time was dragging past so slowly. It was always the same. Everything you ever looked forward to – birthdays, Christmas, the summer holidays – the days would drag on for weeks; hours would tick by so slowly it was as if time was going actually backwards. But things you didn't look forward to – trips to the dentist, the first day back at school – they sped closer and closer at breakneck speed.

But the day had finally arrived - it was time to go to the fair!

Nicki had begged and begged to be allowed to go with her friends, but her parents had insisted that it was to be a family outing – otherwise she wasn't going to be allowed to go at all. Reluctantly, she waited by the front door, tapping her foot impatiently on the mat. It was taking ages to get Deano ready – she could hear them upstairs trying to get him to put his socks on. Stomping up and down the hallway in her snow boots, she grimaced at how late he was making them.

There were to be fireworks as well tonight. If he made her miss them....

Eventually, her parents jogged down the stairs followed by her five-year-old brother, Dean.

"Come on, we'll be late!" she urged, already tugging open the front door and letting in a rush of chill November air.

"The fair's not going anywhere, sweetie," replied her mother, stopping to pull a woollen bobble hat onto Dean's head. "We've got plenty of time."

They traipsed out of the cul-de-sac and headed out onto the main street. The fair was in a field close to the seafront, and Nicki could tell just by the amount of people streaming along the pavement that it was going to be packed. A tiny thrill swirled inside her stomach. It wasn't often anything exciting happened in the village. Tonight was going to be a night she would never forget.

"Stay where I can see you, Nicola," her mother called out. "And you need to wait for your brother."

Nicki just frowned and quickened her step.

It didn't take them long to reach the fair, even with Deano's small legs. "Take Dean on that ride over there, and stay with him." Nicki's mother pointed to a small caterpillar ride, where each carriage was painted a bright green, and the one at the front depicted the caterpillar's smiley face. It looks bug ugly, thought Nicki, her top lip curling in distaste. And so babyish. She glanced around to see if there was anyone from school nearby; she didn't want to be seen queuing for a baby ride. Thankfully, she didn't see anyone that she recognised.

Nicki took hold of Dean's hand and headed over towards the queue.

"We're going to find some coffee," her mother called out. "Wait for us here when it's finished. And don't go wasting your pocket money on that candyfloss. It rots your teeth. We'll get some burgers later on."

Raising a hand in acknowledgment, Nicki felt her frown deepen. She really wanted candyfloss. The smell was everywhere around her; that sickly, sweet sugary smell that made your mouth water. She didn't want a burger; she could have one of those any day of the week.

They reached the queue for the caterpillar ride which, thankfully, wasn't very long. While she waited, Nicki's gaze fell onto the popcorn and candyfloss stall opposite. She could see the huge metal bowl churning away, whipping up the frothy pink strings inside. Her stomach grumbled and her mouth began to tingle.

She *really* wanted some candyfloss...

Reaching the front of the queue, Nicki paid for Dean's ticket and hurriedly stepped out of the way. There was no way she would be seen dead on a ride like that. What if her school friends walked past and saw her? She watched as Dean clambered aboard his carriage and whooped with delight as the ride began its journey. She found herself smiling as she saw the delight painted across his frost-chapped cheeks. He wasn't bad, as far as baby brothers go. Annoying at times, but they sometimes had fun together - when no one else was looking. She watched the caterpillar make its first turn, listening to Dean's cries of joy as it went round the bend.

Nicki's eyes were then drawn once again across to the stall opposite.

It would only take a minute. Two at most. She could be there and back before the ride stopped.

She had plenty of time.

But the candyfloss had taken longer than expected. When she'd arrived at the stall, the metal bowl was virtually empty and the stall holder was making a fresh batch. She waited in line, casting the occasional glance over her shoulder to see that the caterpillar was still looping around the track, hearing the children's cries as it climbed the gentle slopes.

The sky had darkened overhead, the moon snuffed out behind a bank of cloud that carefully inched its way across the sky. The chill in the air was threatening snow, she could feel it. She loved the snow, but living by the coast they rarely saw much more than a light dusting if they were lucky. She could only remember one winter when they had a proper snowfall – Dad was in the back garden rolling huge balls to make into a snowman. And every so often he would stop to throw snowballs at her, sending her running into the kitchen shrieking with laughter.

Nicki grinned at the thought and willed the snow to fall again. She turned her attention back to the stall. It was almost ready. A quick look over her shoulder told her that the caterpillar ride was coming to a stop, and the children were starting to clamber out. She craned her neck to see if she could spy Deano's bobble hat, but there were too many parents blocking her view.

He'll be OK. I'll only be a minute. She pulled out a fistful of coins from her pocket and watched, wide eyed, as the candyfloss stick was thrust into the spinning metal bowl and the pink fluffy sweetness span round and round in front of her eyes. She felt her lips start to tingle in anticipation.

Throwing another glance over her shoulder, she tried to see if Dean was waiting by the ride, but there were still too many people milling around for her to see clearly. Just a few more seconds; just a few more seconds. Eventually, the candyfloss had grown as big as it could, and Nicki happily exchanged it for her shiny fifty pence coin. She immediately clenched her teeth around the sticky mass and tugged a portion away from the stick. It melted on her tongue.

Grinning to herself, she turned and skipped back over to the caterpillar ride where another group of excitable children were already climbing aboard the green insect. She scanned the line waiting by the entrance. Where was Deano?

Turning her attention back to the ride, all she could see was the fresh wave of children scrambling for seats – there was no Deano. Again, she looked back at the waiting queue, wondering if he'd enjoyed it so much he wanted another turn.

But he wasn't there either.

No Deano.

Suddenly, the smell of the sickly-sweet pink floss started to churn her stomach, while her blood turned to ice to match the plunging temperature. Frantically, she ran from one end of the ride to the other, and then around the back. Perhaps he'd enjoyed it so much he wanted to watch the next circuit. She completed a full circle and there was still no Deano. Returning to the front of the ride, she searched the nearby stalls, looking for the familiar bobble hat. Nothing at the hot dog stall. Nothing at the tin-can alley. Nothing at the dodgems. She tried to remember what he was wearing, besides the woollen hat. She was sure it was his bright yellow anorak, and yellow boots to match.

She searched the crowd yet again

Dumping the candyfloss in a nearby bin, its smell making hot bile rise up into her throat, she stumbled away from the caterpillar ride and pushed her way through the crowd. But try as she might, there was no yellow anorak or yellow boots to be seen.

Deano had vanished.

\* \* \*

*Wednesday 31ˢᵗ October 2018*

  1.30am

Deano.

Glancing up, Nicki found her gaze resting on the photograph that took pride of place at the centre of the mantelpiece above the fireplace. Dean had been five-years-old when he went missing, and the picture had been taken just days before. It was impossible not to be drawn to that cheeky smile and the mop of dark brown, unruly hair that would sit up in messy tufts no matter what you tried to do with it.

Her parents had never forgiven her – she knew that. Oh, they'd made all the right noises at the time; said all the right things, cuddled and comforted her, and told her that everything would be all right. That *nobody blamed her.*

But she knew, deep down, that they did.

*Nicki* blamed herself, so of course they would too. She hadn't been watching him, plain and simple. If she had, he would still be here today.

Deano would be twenty-seven now – a man. Nicki often wondered what he would be doing, if things had been different. What kind of job would he have? Would he have married? Had children of his own? All those possibilities had been snuffed out the moment she'd taken her eye off the ball. The moment she'd put her own wants and needs first. The moment she'd been selfish.

Losing Deano had been hard, but losing her parents had made it ten times harder. There was a gaping hole in their family – a Deano-sized hole that *she* had caused, no one else. Her dad had tried his best – he'd still given her the same bear-hugs as before, wrapping his arms around her and squeezing her so tightly she could barely catch her breath. But they felt different. They felt colder, more distant - not as warm or comforting as they used to be. And they weren't as frequent, either. Until such time as they stopped altogether.

As the years passed by, Nicki felt both her parents pulling away from her.

Never knowing what had happened to Deano was a pain that never went away. Instead, it gnawed like an open wound that refused to heal. There was no end to the grief and heartache that his disappearance had caused. There was no body they could mourn; no grave they could visit. Just an empty hole where life had once been, but death had yet to fill.

After leaving school and her home at the age of eighteen, Nicki had changed her name – adopting her mother's maiden name instead. It wasn't that she wanted to distance herself from her family, or from Deano; it was more of a professional decision. She was joining the police force, something she'd yearned to do throughout her adolescent years; to follow in her Daddy's giant-sized footsteps. Maybe it was Deano's disappearance that had pointed her in that direction, who knows. But joining the police with her old surname of Webster would've been like having a millstone around her neck, and one that she didn't need. The press coverage at the time had honed in on how she had been with Deano at the time, and how her inattention had led to his disappearance.

How she had lost him.

It was something she would never forget, but she didn't need it clouding her career before it'd even started. So, she'd changed her name and tried to leave what had happened, and all the accusations and blame, behind her. And, up to now, it seemed to have worked. Nobody knew her true identity. Nobody knew who she really was, except for DCI Turner. Her secret was safe.

Nicki took another glug of wine and wiped her glassy eyes on her sleeve. Where did you go, Deano? What happened to you? She knew they were questions she could never answer, but she asked them all the same. She always did.

*I'll never make that mistake again.*

It was a statement she often repeated to herself. She would never put herself first – *ever*. She would never again let selfishness take over. Being selfish had torn her world apart and it had never been rebuilt.

Luna had finished her kneading and settled down in the dip of Nicki's lap, curling herself up into a contented ball. Nicki stroked her head and could feel the soft purrs vibrating through her skin.

As she sunk another mouthful of wine, she rested her head back against the sofa and closed her eyes.

Lucas and Deano.

Where are you?

\* \* \*

# Chapter Seven

*Wednesday 31<sup>st</sup> October 2018*

8.00am

Nicki pulled the blind across the solitary window of the incident room, sweeping her eyes around the room. Her team had reassembled after just a few hours' sleep – if anyone had, indeed, slept. Nicki knew she hadn't and, judging by the pallid-looking faces entering the room, she wasn't alone.

"Firstly, before we crack on, I'd like to formally introduce Royston Carter to the team as our new DS. Some of you will have met Roy briefly last night, but today is his first full day with us. And we couldn't be more grateful to see him."

Various murmured greetings rippled around the room, but the sound was subdued. Darcie beamed over the rim of her coffee cup. Two experienced DCs, Matt Holland and Duncan Jenkins, had answered Nicki's early morning call to join the team and raised their hands in greeting.

"Lucas Jackson has now been missing for approximately twelve hours. A search of the Abbey Gardens overnight and surrounding streets hasn't thrown up any sightings. Today we need to prioritise any CCTV in the Gardens themselves."

"He hasn't just wandered off, has he?" Darcie pulled her jacket close around her, nursing the hot cup of coffee in her hands.

Nicki shook her head. "It's looking that way. Children of that age, as a rule, don't disappear of their own free will." She hesitated, feeling her throat

49

constrict as an image of Deano flashed into her mind. She masked the pause with a gulp of coffee, which was too hot and burnt her tongue. "I feel we're looking at an abduction by a person or persons as yet unknown."

"Tina's heading over to the Jackson's home this morning," added Darcie. "She called in earlier."

Nicki nodded, and took another mouthful of the scalding coffee, oblivious this time to the burn. "Good. We'll check in on the family later today." Nicki knew DC Tina Gallagher well; she would be the perfect Family Liaison Officer. Turning to the almost empty whiteboard behind her, Nicki saw it still sported just the bare bones of the investigation so far – in fact, just the name Lucas Jackson. "I'm contacting the Public Protection Unit for information on any local child sex offenders in the area." The words stuck in her throat as she spoke. "It's a box we have to tick."

Turning back to face her team, Nicki continued. "Everyone here is well aware of the two cases in Norfolk earlier this year. Ivy McFadden and Oliver Chambers were both abducted from public places – Ivy from a fairground on 1st April, Oliver from an open-air cinema on 30th May. Their bodies were found several weeks later and the perpetrator was never caught." Nicki felt another lump form in her throat. "The similarity to Lucas Jackson's disappearance is not lost on us, but we need to keep an open mind. I'll need to speak to the SIO in charge of the Ivy and Oliver cases – Roy, could you make that your first task of the day?"

DS Carter nodded and pulled out his notebook. "Boss."

"Arrange a time for us to talk – and we'll need access to all the case files for both." Nicki watched as Roy scribbled in his notebook. "Darcie, you're coming with me to see Sophia Jackson. Duncan and Matt – can you focus on the CCTV from the Abbey Gardens?"

Everyone in the room nodded.

Darcie got to her feet. "What about the burglaries, boss?"

"I'll get them assigned elsewhere. Lucas Jackson's our priority right now." Nicki turned towards the door. "Be ready to leave in five. I just need to have a quick word with the DCI."

# CHAPTER SEVEN

* * *

*Wednesday 31st October 2018*

8.30am

Sophia Jackson sat on the edge of the sofa, her body tense and rigid. She'd not moved since they'd arrived home sometime after midnight, and had continued to stare out into the darkness throughout the night. She'd persuaded Amelia to go to bed, to get some rest, but she knew her daughter would be lying awake upstairs. In the soft, muted light of the emerging morning she could still hear her muffled sobs from upstairs.

Sophia hadn't wanted to get out of the ambulance at the Abbey Gardens. She hadn't wanted to leave the safety and seclusion it had given her. But staying wasn't an option, she knew that. The police had been kind. Their faces were all a blur to her now, but she remembered a woman coming to sit with her, telling her how hard they were working to find Lucas.

Lucas.

Sophia's heart felt as though it were ripped it two. It was a physical pain like no other. The officer who'd driven them home had made her a cup of sweet tea – it still sat untouched on the coffee table by her side. Someone would be with her in the morning, the officer had said – unless she felt as though she needed someone right away, which could be arranged. Sophia had merely shaken her head and closed the door. She hoped she hadn't come across as rude, but she needed to be alone.

With her shoulders heaving as she suppressed yet another sob, Sophia's gaze came to rest on the pile of unopened post sitting on the arm of the sofa. The letters had rattled through the letterbox yesterday morning whilst she was busy making Lucas's cupcakes and she hadn't got around to opening any of them. The sound of the letterbox always made her tense these days – it never brought her any good news.

One letter she could clearly see was from HMRC – she recognised the brown envelope and postmark. Her tax credits had been frozen and an investigation was underway – she even had a case number now. She was a 'case' – with a number. When the first letter had landed on the doormat several weeks ago, she had no idea it would have snowballed into this. Accusations of falsifying her claim; providing incorrect information; the threat of prosecution. The words danced in front of her eyes, all merging into one. Where they were getting their information from, lord only knew.

The other letter she recognised the post mark on was from her boss. He wanted a face to face meeting to discuss the allegations that had landed, anonymously, on his desk. She understood where he was coming from; he had to investigate, she knew that. What employer wouldn't? But she couldn't afford to lose this job; she just couldn't.

It may only be part-time, and not much more than minimum wage, but it was money she relied on. Money that she needed. Since Liam's accident, she'd done her best to turn the tide and support her children on her own – and, just when she thought she was getting back on her feet and things were getting better, this happened.

Suddenly, everything in her life was turning upside down.

And now Lucas.

A lone tear trickled down her cheek, following the well-worn tracks made by so many others over the last twelve hours.

None of it felt real.

The sky outside had lightened, with last night's fog finally lifting, but Sophia kept the curtains drawn. She didn't want to see the dawn. She didn't want to embrace a new day without Lucas. Just as another round of sobs threatened to wrack her slight frame, the doorbell rang. It would be the family liaison officer they'd promised.

With a heavy heart, Sophia got to her feet.

\* \* \*

*Wednesday 31st October 2018*
  8.45am

Standing in the queue to pay for the loaf of bread and pint of milk he'd selected, his eyes were drawn to the stack of newspapers on the counter. There was no missing the headline.

**'Police hunt for missing boy'.**

As he stood in line, he felt a familiar thrill start to flicker. Adding a copy of the newspaper to his shopping, he paid and left the shop, glaring at an old woman hovering behind the magazine rack. Hurriedly, he stepped out onto the pavement and half walked, half ran back towards the house.

A mixture of emotions swirled inside him as he unlocked the front door and slipped inside. Heading for the kitchen, he placed the milk and bread on the counter and took another glance at the newspaper's front page.

There was a picture of Lucas, as expected, in the centre. It was a very good likeness to the boy he had upstairs, except that the beaming smile was no longer present – replaced, instead, with tear-stained cheeks and a sickeningly white complexion. As he let his eyes take in the rest of the article, his smile widened. Apparently the police were 'following several lines of enquiry' - a stock phrase he'd read many times before. They didn't know who he was; he was sure of that. If they did, they would be here knocking at his front door.

A police spokesperson denied they were linking the six-year-old's disappearance with the murders of Ivy McFadden and Oliver Chambers at this stage, and 'all enquiries were continuing'.

He let his grin widen even more. They might not be making the link, but the media most certainly was. Two further photographs appeared at the bottom of the page – smiling images of Ivy and Oliver that the public had come to know so well over the summer.

They hadn't officially made the link yet, but they would; they had to. The evidence was staring at them, full in the face. If he were a betting man, he'd give them until tomorrow.

With the kettle now boiled, he threw a tea bag into the waiting mug and added a splash of milk before tipping the boiling water on top. There was nothing in the newspaper report that shed any light on his own identity – the police were pissing in the wind. The thought made him chuckle. As he took a sip of tea, his thoughts turned to upstairs where he thought he could hear the beginnings of a faint, muffled cry. The boy must be stirring, although he had been awake most of the night crying behind his gag. Probably hungry and thirsty, and no doubt needing the toilet. Revulsion trickled through him, dampening his mirth.

The boy had continence issues. These young boys and girls – they wet themselves at a moment's notice; and worse. Clearing up after them was unpleasant to say the least and not part of the plan.

His nose wrinkled as he considered the prospect of what might be waiting for him when he climbed the stairs. Maybe he would let the boy sit in his own mess a while longer – teach him some element of self-control.

Yes, the boy could wait. It would be good for him. He reached for the fresh loaf of bread and started to load the toaster.

* * *

*Wednesday 31st October 2018*

   10.30am

Nicki pulled the car to a stop outside number seventeen and sighed. Looking out of the side window, it looked just like any other house along the quiet residential street on the Moreton Hall estate. Two bay windows sat either side of a recently installed UPVC front door; to the front was an immaculately tended garden laid to lawn, with neatly pruned winter-flowering shrubs around the edges. Appearances were sometimes deceptive, however, and nothing on the outside of number seventeen could reveal the grief that would be festering inside.

Darcie followed Nicki along the short garden path, the front door opening as soon as their feet landed on the doorstep. DC Tina Gallagher, Family Liaison Officer appointed for the Jackson family, gave a smile in greeting, and then stepped aside to let them into the hallway.

A pile of mis-matched shoes sat by the side of the doormat; coats, jackets and scarves hung on the coat stand. A stack of unopened letters sat on a small nest of tables.

Normality.

Except nothing would ever be normal for the Jacksons again – not until Lucas was returned to them.

The front room was large and airy, an archway leading through to a dining room beyond. The television was switched on in the corner, playing on mute, tuned to a 24-hour news channel. Sophia Jackson sat, straight-backed, in one of the single armchairs that flanked a two-seater sofa, with a face that confirmed she'd been awake all night.

Despite the warmth from the central heating, the room had that icy-cold chill that only sadness could bring. An untouched cup of tea sat on the coffee table by her side.

"Mrs Jackson? Sophia?" Nicki stepped further into the room, nodding at DC Gallagher that now would be a good time to make a fresh round of tea. Tea was always made in situations such as this – whether it helped or not, nobody knew. But the kettle was always kept busy.

Sophia Jackson raised her head and met Nicki's gaze. Her eyes said it all – she didn't need to voice the question that was on her lips.

Nicki gave a sad shake of the head in response. "No news yet, I'm sorry. But we're doing everything we can." The stock phrase escaped Nicki's mouth before she had time to stop it. She usually hated these expressions – ones that were bandied about so freely - but sometimes there was nothing else that could be said.

They *were* doing everything they could. Nicki's contact with the Public Protection Unit said they'd have an update for her later that day on the location of any known sex offenders in the area. CCTV was being accessed and analysed at this very moment in time. The wheels were definitely moving behind the scenes, although to Sophia Jackson it all meant nothing if they didn't find her son.

The newspapers had relished a fresh story on what would otherwise have been a very quiet news day. Nicki spied a copy of one of the national tabloids folded up on the coffee table next to the cold cup of tea. She couldn't tell if it'd been read, but there was no mistaking the headline emblazoned across the front page.

*'Fairground horror – child abducted'*

Darcie joined Nicki on the two-seater sofa which faced the bay window and looked out across to the quiet street outside. The curtains were drawn, however, and most likely had been all morning. There was no need to open them – there was nothing outside that the Jacksons needed or wanted to see. The world, for them, had stopped turning the moment little Lucas had disappeared.

"We'll try not to take up too much of your time, Mrs Jackson," began Nicki, her tone soft. She knew her words sounded empty. Time. The Jacksons had plenty of that right now. "There's just one or two things we'd like your help with, if that's OK?"

DC Gallagher nudged the door to the front room open and carried in the tea tray, depositing it on the coffee table. Three mugs of tea and a plate of digestive biscuits were passed around. Nicki smiled, gratefully, at Tina. They'd worked together many times before, and Nicki knew that she would be a great support to the family – whether Sophia realised they needed it or not. And a great asset to the investigation as a whole. FLOs were experienced detectives and a crucial link between the family and the investigation. DC Gallagher was adept at getting pertinent information out of even the most tight-lipped of families.

"Of course." Sophia Jackson's first words were so quiet they could barely be heard above the deafening silence that was already suffocating the room.

Nicki discreetly removed her notebook from her pocket. "It's correct that you live here with just Lucas and Amelia, yes?"

Sophia Jackson nodded, her hands clasped tightly around the hot mug of tea. "Yes, it's just us."

"And the children's father, your husband, Liam – he passed away four years ago?"

Another nod from Sophia, this time accompanied with a tentative sip of the scalding tea. If it burnt her lips, she didn't notice. "Yes, Liam died in April 2014."

"I'm sorry to hear that," replied Nicki. And she was. Glancing up at a recessed shelving unit next to the television, she saw a series of silver-framed photographs of a good-looking, sandy-haired man. In one he was standing on a beach, an azure-blue sea stretched out behind him. Another, he was cradling a newborn – whether it was Lucas or Amelia, Nicki couldn't tell. The one that took centre-stage on the mantelpiece, however, was one of Liam and Sophia on their wedding day. Nicki turned her gaze back towards Sophia. "Are your parents still around? Or Liam's?" Nicki had very quickly noticed on arrival that Sophia Jackson was dealing with her grief alone.

Sophia took another sip of tea, wincing as the hot liquid hit her tongue. "My parents are both dead – I don't know where Liam's are."

"No other family at all?"

Sophia stared down into the mug and gave a curt shake of the head. "No," she replied. "We don't have anyone else. I'm an only child."

"What about Liam's side? Any brothers or sisters?"

The question hung in the air for several seconds. Nicki watched closely as Sophia Jackson's demeanour started to change. The muscles in her neck tightened, and a hard look entered her eyes. As she gripped the mug in her lap, the whites of her knuckles showed through her pale skin. Eventually she spoke.

"Liam has two brothers. But after he died, we didn't keep in touch. I think they might live abroad."

"And you don't see his parents? The children's grandparents?"

Sophia's hand tightened further around the mug. "No. As I said, after Liam died we didn't keep in touch."

Nicki made a quick mental note. There was something about Sophia Jackson's reply that suggested all was not well in her relationship with her late husband's family. Slipping her notebook back inside her pocket, she got to her feet.

"Would it be possible to take look at Lucas's bedroom?"

It looked just like any other six-year-old boy's bedroom. The bed was pushed up against the far wall beneath the window, neatly made up with a Batman duvet and pillowcase set. A set of plastic Batman figurines were lined up along the edge of the windowsill. Although not a fan, Nicki could recognise the characters of The Joker, The Penguin, and Batman's side-kick

Robin.

Stepping across the room towards a set of shelving, Nicki noted each level rammed full of books and toys. She cocked her head to one side to read the spines.

Animal Encyclopaedia.

How to count to 100.

Know your shapes and colours.

My first Bedtime Story Collection.

Nicki's heart shuddered and she bit back the tears that threatened to spring from her eyes. Clearing her throat, she crossed over to the single wardrobe next to the bed. The door was slightly open revealing an array of jeans, t-shirts, and jumpers hanging neatly inside. Everything looked so normal.

Darcie had taken Sophia to see Amelia who, according to DC Gallagher, had not spoken a word since the FLO's arrival that morning. Taking advantage of having the room to themselves, Nicki turned towards Tina, indicating that she should nudge the door shut - Amelia's bedroom was only a short way away.

"Tell me more about the family – Liam's family."

DC Gallagher's voice was hushed. "I managed to get Sophia to open up a little, just before you arrived. But she's very hesitant to speak about the family set-up. Any mention of Liam's family and she clams up. But I eventually got her to reveal the names of the two bothers – Marcus and Callum."

"The ones that live abroad?"

DC Gallagher nodded. "But I couldn't get her to elaborate any further. They clearly don't keep in touch."

Nicki agreed. She'd sensed as much from Sophia's reaction earlier. "Anything else of note?"

"Not much at this stage. She's still in a great deal of shock. I get the impression things are frosty with the in-laws as well. Looks like some kind of massive falling out after Liam died."

"Thanks. Keep digging and trying to get her to open up." Nicki made a move towards the door. There was nothing in Lucas's bedroom that was likely to help them. "Keep her talking. Find out all you can about the Jacksons."

* * *

# Chapter Eight

*Wednesday 31<sup>st</sup> October 2018*
   11.00am

Side by side, they sat in silence. The only sound in the modest-sized front room was the faint rustle of the newspaper as Callum Jackson turned the pages. He felt a ripple of excitement start to spread – a feeling he knew would be mirrored by his brother sat next to him.

"I wonder how she's feeling this morning." Marcus Jackson broke the quiet, his voice calm and even. His face was set hard, his steely grey eyes fixed to the newsprint in front of him.

Callum Jackson didn't respond, his own eyes still rapidly devouring the article.

"Nothing more than she deserves," added Marcus, pulling his gaze away and getting to his feet. "Maybe she'll start to realise what she did to us – all of us – and what she put us through." His eyes flickered towards the ceiling. The plan was underway. "I'll be upstairs if you need me."

Just as Marcus reached the threshold to the hallway, the landline phone rang. He hesitated by the doorframe and frowned – there was only one person who used the landline.

Callum remained glued to his seat on the battered two-seater sofa, his gaze still fixed to the newspaper spread out over his knees, seemingly oblivious to the trilling phone.

Marcus crossed the threadbare carpet and snatched up the receiver on its third ring.

"Mother," he greeted. "I take it you've seen the papers this morning?" He paused, listening to their mother's reply, giving a brief nod of the head and glancing across to his brother. "He's reading it now." A cruel smile flickered onto his lips. "Well, didn't I say to you not so long ago that she'd get her comeuppance sooner or later? It was only a matter of time."

Callum lifted his gaze from the headline of the Daily Express – '**Mother's Torment at Missing Son**' – and caught his brother's eye.

"Of course, Mother. I'm being careful." Marcus raised his eyebrows and flashed a grin at Callum. "Just leave it with me." He paused again while their mother gave him her usual lecture, letting his gaze drift up towards the ceiling. He needed to get on; he had work to do. "I need to go, Mother. But rest assured, this is only the start for our lovely Sophia. Her nightmare is only just beginning."

\* \* \*

*Wednesday 31st October 2018*
   11.15am

The room frightened him. It was dark and cold, and it smelt funny.

Lucas Jackson blinked back the tears that streamed from his eyes. His hands were still tied behind his back, so he couldn't brush them away from his cheeks. Instead, they dripped from his chin onto his lap.

The man had been angry at him for wetting himself, and that had earned him the first slap to the face. He'd been forced to sit in the chair, in his wet underpants, all night; his ankles tied to the chair legs with rope. He'd seen the bed by the window, when the man had dragged him inside. But he was secretly quite glad he wasn't made to lie in it – the mattress was dirty and the walls around the window above it were stained with a horrible, creeping mould.

Lucas shuddered. He hated the dark. At home, Mummy let him have his night light on to help him get to sleep. There was no such light in here. The window had thick wooden planks nailed across it, snuffing out any light from outside.

He didn't know whether he'd slept at all in the night. He supposed he must have. His neck felt sore and his bottom was numb.

The man had put a smelly piece of cloth across his mouth when he'd tied him to the chair, muttering about how much noise he was making. Lucas didn't know what else he was meant to do but cry. Why was the man being so nasty? He'd been fun at the fair. He'd made him laugh.

Lucas shuddered again. As his eyes flickered around the darkened room, he saw tangled cobwebs dangling from the ceiling, some of them right overhead. His pale skin shivered with goose bumps. He hated spiders. Almost as much as he hated the dark.

Swallowing back yet more sobs, Lucas turned his head towards the door. He could hear movement on the other side; the opening and closing of doors, floorboards creaking. He wanted to cry out but knew if he did he would only get another slap – or worse. Anyhow, the gag across his mouth meant he could only make a muffled sound at best.

Fresh tears splashed into his lap.

The sounds from outside the door got nearer and Lucas's heart froze when he heard the sound of the padlock snapping open. When the man's face appeared in the doorway, Lucas knew he was angry again.

He couldn't help it; he'd tried to hold it in. He had a nervous tummy and when he needed to go…. He'd spied the bucket in the corner of the room during the night but had no means to get there, shackled to the chair such as he was. And anyway, the thick, matted cobwebs that hung merely feet above the bucket had done nothing to quell the churning in his stomach and the squeezing of his bowels.

The man cleaned him up again – wiping away the mess with a face like thunder. Messing himself again had earned him two slaps this time – one to each side of his head – the force snapping his head back against the wooden chair. He could feel a trickle of blood inching its way down the side of his cheek.

But before Lucas could blink away the fresh tears, the man knelt down in front of the chair and placed his calloused hands around his neck.

And squeezed.

Lucas felt his eyes swim in and out of focus. He couldn't breathe. He tried to kick out with his legs but they were held fast by the thin rope tying him to the chair. He tried to pull his hands out from where they were wrenched behind his back – but that, too, was fruitless.

The more he struggled, the more the man's grip tightened.

He'd begun to gurgle and choke behind the gag, the saliva gathering in his mouth having nowhere to go. Just when he thought he couldn't take it any more, his vision popping with stars and bright stabs of light, the man simply removed his hands and walked away.

Lucas coughed and spluttered, trying to draw in big enough breaths through the gag to fill his lungs. Why was he doing this? Lucas's tiny body shook as he tried to control his breathing. The man had been so nice to him at the fair. He'd waved at him from the side of the ball pit, clapping as he'd made his way down the slide. And with each slide he'd clapped and cheered some more. Lucas could remember giggling and twirling around in his Batman cape.

'*Good slide, Batman,*' had been the man's first words.

Fresh tears coursed down Lucas's cheeks, mixed with the blood from his scalp.

Please Mummy, where are you?

\* \* \*

*Wednesday 31st October 2018*

12.30pm

Nicki stepped back into the incident room to find a hive of activity already underway. Roy had the sleeves of his crisp white shirt rolled up, and was annotating a second whiteboard. He snapped the lid back on his marker pen as Nicki arrived by his side.

"I spoke with the SIO on the Norfolk cases. DI Tony Phillips. He's more than happy to talk to you any time this afternoon. I've started putting the main case details up on here." He nodded towards the whiteboard. "All the relevant statements and reports are on your desk."

Nicki gave an appreciative nod. Ivy and Oliver's names were at the top of the second whiteboard, with a single colour photograph of each pinned next to them. Roy had added the date and location of each of their disappearances, followed by the date and cause of death, and then location of the bodies. It made for grim reading.

"Good work." Nicki pulled off her coat and started to walk towards the back of the incident room where DCs Holland and Jenkins were seated, glued to their computer screens. "Anything yet on the CCTV?"

Matt Holland looked up as Nicki approached. "Not much. The CCTV Manager from the Council has downloaded all footage from the relevant cameras and fast-tracked them through to us. We've located the family entering the Gardens at the Abbey Gate entrance at a little after six pm. But after that, nothing much of significance. A couple of sightings, but nothing too clear. We've still got lots more to sift through."

Nicki thanked both DCs before turning to head back towards the door. Darcie was just getting herself seated at her desk as Nicki passed.

"Darcie? Can you work with Roy on the Ivy and Oliver files? Start going through them from the beginning. See what jumps out."

Darcie nodded. "Boss."

"I'll be in my office if you need me."

\* \* \*

*Wednesday 31ˢᵗ October 2018*
  1.30pm

DC Tina Gallagher brought through the ham and cheese sandwich that she knew would remain untouched – but she placed it at Sophia's side anyway. DI Hardcastle had left some two hours ago and Sophia hadn't moved.

In her other hand she had the morning's post that she'd gathered from the doormat. Placing it next to the sandwich, she noticed yesterday's letters were still unopened. Sophia barely stirred at her presence as Tina sat down on the edge of the sofa.

"Try and eat something," she coaxed, nudging the plate of sandwiches closer. "You need to keep your strength up."

Sophia remained still, staring towards the shrouded window, her mobile phone clutched in her hand. Tina had noted the lack of visitors and well-wishers in the same way that Nicki had. Usually, family members would have descended by now to offer help and support; the phone ringing constantly from those unable to make the trip in person.

So where was Sophia Jackson's family? Where were her friends? Her neighbours even?

Not one person had been in touch since Tina had arrived early that morning. Not one neighbour had called round with a well-meaning offer of comfort.

Sophia had nothing and no one.

Tina's gaze dropped to the mobile phone in Sophia's hand. Maybe she was receiving text messages or emails instead?

"Are you sure I can't call anyone for you, Sophia?" Tina nodded towards the phone. The question elicited no response, so Tina tried again. "A friend maybe? Someone to come and sit with you?"

Again the question remained unanswered. Tina longed to be able to take the poor woman in her arms and give her a hug – somebody needed to – but she feared she might break under her touch. "Maybe you should contact Liam's parents? I'm sure they'd want to know how you are?" And why they hadn't been in touch, Tina wanted to add – but didn't.

The mention of Liam's parents was the first hint of movement Tina had seen all morning – a slight shift in Sophia's position in the armchair. It wasn't much, but detectable all the same. Tina seized the opportunity. She needed to get Sophia talking, for her own sake as much as anything else.

Getting to her feet, Tina crossed the thick-pile carpet towards the shelving unit by the TV, which was still playing on mute. Thankfully, the news of Lucas's disappearance wasn't being shown, the newscaster having moved on to the international row about President Trump's plans to build a wall on the border with Mexico, and how GPs in England and Wales were preparing for finally being able to prescribe cannabis products to patients as from tomorrow.

As she let her eyes wander the shelving, she noted every available surface was littered with silver-framed photographs. Tina picked one up that showed Liam in his Army uniform.

"How long was Liam in the Army?" Tina glanced back towards Sophia, holding up the picture. At the mention of Liam's name, Sophia turned, her face softening. Tina noted fresh tears were brewing.

"He joined when he was eighteen. It was the only job he'd ever had. The only thing he'd ever loved."

Tina replaced the photograph. "You must have been very proud."

Sophia brushed away the freshly-formed tears and nodded. "Always," she breathed.

Tina returned to the sofa, encouraged that Sophia had begun to talk. She again nudged the plate of sandwiches closer. "Try a sandwich, Sophia. It'll do you good. I'm going to take one up to Amelia in a minute. Why don't you come with me?"

Sophia stared at the sandwich for a few seconds, as if contemplating Tina's words, but she then returned her gaze to the curtained window.

Tina saw the phone screen in Sophia's hand light up. Relieved that maybe she was at last getting some contact with the outside world – maybe a message of support from a friend – Tina stood up and made her way back towards the kitchen.

"I'll be upstairs with Amelia if you want to join us." Tina left a few seconds for Sophia to reply, but when no response came she headed out the door. As she disappeared, Sophia lowered her head to the phone screen and let another tear drop from her cheeks.

\* \* \*

*Wednesday 31ˢᵗ October 2018*
  *2.30pm*

Nicki gripped the papers so tightly that her knuckles turned white. Reading the account of both Ivy and Oliver's murders made her heart heave. The similarities to Lucas's disappearance were striking.

DI Tony Phillips had given her a brief overview of both cases – most of it was in the reports she'd already seen, but it was always useful to talk to those on the ground. Sometimes there were additional things, subtle nuances that didn't come across in the computerised files. They'd made the link between Ivy and Oliver's abductions very early on, despite there being no forensic evidence linking them to speak of.

Nicki shivered and swallowed past the lump that had appeared in her throat. For some reason yet to be discovered, the same perpetrator had now shown up on her patch. She was sure of it. A formal link to Lucas Jackson had yet to be made public, but it was only a matter of time – and the media were already speculating. She continued reading, turning to the post mortem reports which were always the hardest part to read. No matter how hard she tried, she couldn't help but imagine herself reading a post mortem report with her brother's name at the top.

The injuries on both children had been horrific. Although in an advanced state of decomposition when found, both bodies had revealed sustained knife wounds to every limb; not enough to cause death, but enough to cause intense pain and suffering. Evidence of sexual assault had not been possible to ascertain from the post mortem, but its absence didn't lessen the shocking nature of the deaths.

Cause of death in both cases had been asphyxiation. Reading how both Ivy and Oliver had been suffocated made Nicki's eyes burn with the threat of hot tears. But they were tears she knew she couldn't shed – not yet, not here. She couldn't show the DCI she wasn't coping. He would take her off the case in a heartbeat. And she needed to see this one through – for her sake, and also for Deano.

*Asphyxiated.*

The word stuck in her throat. Forcing herself up out of her chair, she crossed over to the window and pushed it open.

*Asphyxiated.*

Blurry images of Deano flooded her brain. With three children now abducted in very similar circumstances, she couldn't help but turn the clock back twenty-two years. How could she not? She knew it couldn't be the same offender who took Deano. The gap between the offences made no sense, but the thought chilled her just the same.

Returning to her seat, she flicked to the interviews with both Ivy and Oliver's parents. Grief seeped out of the paperwork before her very eyes, becoming in itself a physical entity. Both Ivy and Oliver had been in the care of their older brothers when they went missing and Nicki didn't have to imagine what state they would've been in after the abductions; she already knew.

Guilt.

It was a funny word. So short – *too* short for the depth of feeling it conjured up. Guilt could do many things to a human being. It could seep into your very soul and devour you from within like a cancer, slowly consuming you until there was nothing left but an empty shell. She'd seen it all too clearly in her own parents. Guilt had taken its toll on the Webster family. She knew they felt guilty about what happened to Deano – guilty for deciding to take them to the fair, guilty for letting them go off on their own, guilty for telling Nicki to watch over her brother. They were his parents and the ultimate responsibility for his welfare lay with them.

Except it didn't; not really.

Responsibility for Deano that night had been down to her, and no one else.

Sighing, she lay the papers down on the desk and glanced up at the clock on the wall above the door. She'd urged Darcie and Roy to take a break – they'd both been in early on the back of a late night, and they'd hardly slept; she could tell that from their faces. Reluctantly, they'd agreed.

She knew she should start taking her own advice, and take a break herself – but she knew that wasn't an option. Not for her. Just as she was contemplating reading the case papers on Ivy and Oliver once again, the door to her office opened and DCI Turner's frame filled the doorway.

"Time for a quick chat?"

68

* * *

*Wednesday 31ˢᵗ October 2018*
   3.00pm

Marcus jogged back downstairs and popped his head around the door frame into the front room. Callum had changed position now, seating himself in the armchair by the window.

"You sure you don't want to come?" Marcus started pulling on his work boots. "It's only a couple hours' work – hanging some new doors. Job's nearly done and it's cash-in-hand."

Callum's eyes remained fixed, staring towards the net curtains that shielded the window. He shook his head without breaking his gaze.

"I could do with another pair of hands?" cajoled Marcus, reaching for the keys to the van. Another shake of the head gave him his answer. "OK, well I won't be gone long. Two hours at most."

Marcus grabbed his toolbox and pulled the front door shut behind him, striding towards the van parked on the driveway. He wrenched open the rear doors and placed his tool box inside. He never left tools in the van overnight anymore. There'd been far too many thefts in recent months – vans like his were easy pickings. And what he did leave in there overnight wouldn't attract even the most desperate of thieves. A few sacks of builders' sand were slung into the far corner, together with several empty buckets caked in dried cement. What tools he did have were rusted and useless. A roll of battered carpet lay wedged up against a side wall.

Slamming the rear doors shut, Marcus hopped into the driver's seat and fired the engine, grateful to hear it splutter into life. The van was old, but it was all they had. It wasn't a great living, but needs must. Everything cash in hand – something he made clear at the very outset – quick and easy jobs, no questions asked. Sometimes he'd take Callum with him, sometimes not. Today was a 'sometimes not' day.

Today's job was at a tiny bungalow a few miles away in the next village. An old lady who looked like she was a hundred, but was probably somewhat younger. Hard of hearing and her eyesight wasn't much better, he'd managed to inflate the price of the job by at least £400. She didn't seem to notice. He could tell that she had money; old women like that always did. Despite the shabby looking exterior of the bungalow, and the overgrown tangled garden, he knew she was a goldmine.

Forcing the ageing van into gear, he reversed off the drive and headed out. He'd get the job done as quickly as possible, cut a few corners here and there, in and out in an hour; the old woman would never notice. Once the cash was in his hand, he'd cut and run.

He needed to get back – he had things to do.

\* \* \*

# Chapter Nine

*Wednesday 31ˢᵗ October 2018*
  3.10pm

Although caffeine was the last thing she really needed, Nicki accepted the mug of strong Costa Rican coffee and wrapped her hands around it. They still hadn't sorted the heating out in the incident room and it could chill you to the bone if you were alone, without bodies inside to warm it up, and the same could be said about her own office. But here, in the DCI's, the radiators were working just fine.

"I know I sound like a stuck record, Nicki, but…" DCI Turner collapsed into his leather swivel chair and sighed. "How are you doing?"

Nicki tried a sip of the coffee, knowing it would be far too hot to drink. Her lips stung as the searing liquid hit. She winced and shuddered at the same time.

"It'll be a tough case to crack. We've got precious few leads, if I'm honest, but it's very early days. We're looking into the CCTV and I've spoken to the SIO for the Norfolk murders. DC Gallagher is working on getting Sophia Jackson to talk."

"That's as maybe, but you know that wasn't what I meant." DCI Turner flashed a fatherly smile. "I meant how are *you* doing?"

Nicki took another sip of coffee, oblivious this time to the scorching heat. Anything to give her time to think. How was she doing? Did she even know the answer to that question herself? She nodded and gave the usual reply.

"I'm fine, Sir. Really, I'm fine."

The fatherly smile slipped a little, replaced with a look of concern. "Well, that's good to hear." His tone suggested he perhaps didn't quite believe her. "You do understand why I have to keep asking, don't you?"

Nicki gave another nod, bringing the mug to her lips and hiding behind the coffee vapour.

"I do still feel this investigation is too close to home for you, but..." DCI Turner held up a hand as soon as he saw the expected bristling from across the desk. "But I know how determined you are. All I will say is that you need to bring your team up to speed – regarding your brother. They won't have a clue how this investigation is affecting you. They deserve to be in the loop."

Nicki knew he was right. It was wrong to keep something so fundamental from her team. She'd come close to telling them about Deano on a few occasions in the past, but something always stopped her.

Guilt.

There was that word again. It managed to crop up when you least expected it. Or maybe she was expecting it this time. It was always with her, after all. It never went away. *Guilt.* Always there, always bearing down from a great height, threatening to crush her when she was at her weakest. Which was why she had to remain strong – and why she couldn't tell anyone, not yet.

"I will, I promise. Just not right now."

DCI Turner nodded, raising his mug to his lips and conceding defeat. He knew this was as far as he could push it. Nicki Hardcastle did things when Nicki Hardcastle was ready. Her resolve and dedication was second to none; which was what made her such an exceptional detective.

"Your father sends his best."

Nicki felt a grimace emerging, forcing her to take another sip of coffee. "Does he?" she managed to reply, keeping the irritated edge from her tone. "That's nice to know."

DCI Turner sighed. "It's hard for him, Nicki. For them both. You must understand that. He's just trying to handle things the way he knows best." The DCI paused, seeking out Nicki's hardened gaze. "He does always ask after you, when we talk. That hasn't changed."

No, but a lot else has, Nicki wanted to reply. But, instead, she nodded. "I know, I know."

And she did, if she were honest. Her father was a close friend of DCI Turner's – they attended lunches, played golf together, even a spot of sea fishing on occasion. And sometimes it made her feel strange – that her boss had a better and closer relationship with her own father than she did. But she tried not to dwell on it too much.

He had his reasons for staying away. They both did; Mum and Dad.

Guilt.

There it was again.

Such a small word, yet so destructive when it snared you.

Instead of bringing them together, guilt had torn them apart.

Nicki gulped down the rest of her coffee, ignoring the painful burn, and rose from her seat. "I should get back, Sir. There's loads to do."

DCI Turner merely nodded and watched Nicki slip away through the door. He hoped he hadn't made the wrong decision in letting her lead this one – but he knew that now she'd started, she wouldn't let it go.

For now, all he could do was look out for her.

And hope for the best.

\* \* \*

*Wednesday 31st October 2018*
  4.30pm

Pulling the door shut, he snapped the padlock back into place. It was the second time today that he'd had to wash the boy down. The initial euphoria of last night's work was already beginning to wane. Jogging back downstairs, he headed for the kitchen.

The morning newspaper was still on the table, and as he rinsed the cloths in the sink he found his eyes drawn back towards it. There it was again; that flicker of excitement. The headline splashed across the front was about *him*. They were talking about *him*.

'*Police hunt for missing boy.*'

A smile worked its way back onto his lips as he stored the wet dishcloth back in the cupboard underneath the sink. He'd bleached the chair and floorboards beneath the boy – again - ridding the room of the cloying smell of stale urine and the faeces that had seeped down his legs. It was a smell that stirred many a memory of his own, no matter how hard he tried to forget.

\* \* \*

Westfield Comprehensive School
*Thursday 14th March 2002*

Running as fast as he could, he reached the boys' toilets and hurtled into one of the vacant cubicles, slamming the door shut behind him.

And only just in time.

The main door crashed open and a barrage of shouting and jeering filled his ears.

"Aw, have you wet yourself, weirdo?!"

"You can't hide in there forever!"

"I can smell you from here, have you shit yourself?!"

Cackles of laughter followed, together with thumps and kicks against the cubicle door. He turned his back against it, pushing as hard as he could to keep it closed. They couldn't break it down, could they?

Each kick came harder than the last; each one jolting him forwards. The lock on the door rattled and strained before he heard the terrifying sound of splintering wood.

Tears pricked the corners of his eyes as he threw himself towards the back of the cubicle. But it was fruitless – there was nowhere to hide. A pair of rough hands grabbed him by the collar of his school blazer and dragged him back out.

The kicks that had rained down on the cubicle door now found their way towards his body – lacking in power to begin with, they soon they grew in ferocity and determination. He cried out in pain as the shoes connected with the bruises still healing from last time.

All around him the sound of laughter, mixed with the thumping sound of boot on flesh, bounced off the cheaply tiled walls.

"Aw, do you need a wash, loser?"

The hands that had grabbed his blazer now dragged him over to the toilet pan; more jeering and whoops of delight following. Yanked onto his knees, his head was forced down into the toilet bowl.

He scrunched his eyes shut; he didn't need to see. He knew what was coming.

Fighting back as hard as he could, he was powerless to stop his head being thrust downwards into the bottom of the toilet bowl - the acrid smell of industrial bleach, mixed with urine and faeces, filling his nostrils and hitting the back of his throat. He resisted the urge to cry out - he knew he didn't want to open his mouth. Not now.

With one last thrust, his face hit the water in the bottom of the toilet bowl and the sound of flushing water filled his ears. More jeering and shouting followed, although now somewhat muffled. Water jetted up his nose, causing him to choke; air squeezed from his lungs, with nothing but water to replace it.

With his eyes smarting from the bleach, he saw nothing but black shapes swimming in and out of focus.

The sound of the school bell flooded his body with relief. One by one his tormentors left, banging the cubicle door shut behind them.

And then there was silence.

The only sound being his own heaving sobs and gasps for air.

\* \* \*

*Wednesday 31st October 2018*
    4.30pm

Placing the bucket underneath the sink, he tried to push the memory from his mind. Whoever said that schooldays were the best days of your life clearly hadn't been to Westfield Comprehensive. Why they'd decided to pick on him, single him out for daily torture, he could never fathom. He'd kept himself to himself after joining the school, avoiding confrontation at all costs. Hell, he'd barely spoken to anyone.

Maybe that was why.

He rubbed his nose, still aware of the lingering smell of the boy's bowels.

The school had been no help. Always turning things around to try and suggest that maybe *he* had a part to play, that *he* was somehow to blame for his own misery and torture, that *he* somehow encouraged or invited it. Why would he ask to have his head rammed down a stinking toilet?

Dad had been the only one to stick up for him.

\* \* \*

Westfield Comprehensive School
*Thursday 14<sup>th</sup> March 2002*

"We wonder if there's a way to make your son's life here a little easier." Mrs Clara Henderson, headmistress at Westfield Comprehensive, peered over the top of her half-moon spectacles. "To help him settle. He's a bright boy."

"Can I ask what action you're taking against the boys that're making his life such a misery? He's only been at this school five minutes." Alan Woods clenched his generous-sized fists in his lap and afforded the headmistress a thunderous look. "Surely there must be some repercussions?"

Daniel Woods stared, forlornly, at his feet; his school shoes scuffed from being dragged the length of the first floor corridor. Again. His school shirt was still damp and clung to his back, his hair lying in tangled strands either side of his tear-streaked face. The smell of bleach and fetid urine still filled his nostrils.

He didn't think kids still did that kind of thing – ramming heads down toilets and pulling the chain. He'd read about it in books, but… He shuddered as the memory of the water choking the back of his throat started to make him gag.

"Mr Woods. I assure you steps will be taken against those responsible."

"Giving them a talking to and a pat on the back? A day's detention? That won't cut it this time. They need to be punished – properly." Alan Woods' jaw clenched. "If you don't, then I will."

"Mr Woods – we don't advocate violence in this school."

"Unless it's against my son?"

Mrs Henderson paused, now wishing she'd taken up the deputy head's offer to sit in on this rather delicate conversation. Mr Woods had been to the school before, several times, and the conversations never ended well. He was a formidable man, with an imposing and overbearing presence, and sometimes she wondered what went on at home. Daniel had only arrived at the school two months ago and she knew the man in front of her was his stepfather. What had happened to the biological father wasn't clear from his previous school records.

"I do understand your frustrations," continued Mrs Henderson. "And your anger. It is entirely reasonable. But we must work within the law at this school – I do not condone any sort of vigilante action. Now, if we could just focus on how we might make Daniel's life here at school a little easier."

* * *

*Wednesday 31ˢᵗ October 2018*

   *4.40pm*

With the boy now clean and hopefully more in control of his bladder and bowels, he made the journey back upstairs. Ivy and Oliver had both been more amenable, more pliable, more obedient. He knew it was the fear that did it. He could see it in their eyes, and the paleness of their skin; the shuddering of their bodies beneath the slightest touch.

All thoughts of urine stained floorboards drained from his head, replaced by the powerful sense of anticipation. When you were on the brink of starting a new adventure, there was nothing quite like it.

He'd always tried to re-create the room exactly how it had been before back home. In the previous house, with Ivy and Oliver, it'd been easier. He'd had the place to himself, no distractions or prying eyes. But the neighbours had become suspicious of his comings and goings. He'd caught one snooping around in his back garden, peering through the kitchen window. Another watched him like a hawk from her house across the street; always up at the window, always watching. He'd had to leave before they saw something they shouldn't.

But here, in his brother's house, things were more difficult. He'd been given the use of the largest bedroom at the back and left to his own devices. It was clearly a room his brother never used; cold and damp with no furniture to speak of, save for a single metal-framed bed.

But that suited him fine.

He'd boarded up the window, just like before, which had earned a frown or two from his brother. His explanation that he needed it for his photography seemed to have done the trick, even though he didn't possess a camera.

With the chair in the middle of the room, it was almost identical to the memories ingrained in his own head. Dad would be impressed at how much he'd remembered.

'*Well done, son,*' he could almost hear his father's low tone. '*That's my boy!*'

Of course, he hadn't appreciated what his father was doing to him at the time, not in the early days. Much like Lucas Jackson didn't appreciate or understand why he was tied to a chair in a stranger's house.

But the boy would soon.

Just like he had.

* * *

5 Arlington Crescent
*Thursday 14th March 2002*

The bolt slid into place, grating against the doorframe. It made him shiver. Not because it was cold, and not because he was scared. Just because. People shivered in this house. He saw Mum shiver all the time, especially when Dad was around.

He knew that Alan Woods wasn't his 'real' Dad, but his memories of his real father were fading fast. And Alan had insisted on being called 'Dad', almost the minute they'd moved in - so he obeyed. You always obeyed Dad if you knew what was good for you. He'd learnt that the hard way.

The window was boarded up from the outside so, despite the late afternoon sunshine, the room was already plunged into a dusky shadow. He sat on the rusty metal-framed bed, the thin mattress beneath him hard and unforgiving.

He was allowed to keep a watch when he was in the back bedroom, so he knew when day turned into night and night into day; the boarded up window otherwise keeping this hidden.

And he was allowed a book – just the one. He always kept a copy of Treasure Island in the back bedroom. It was his favourite. He didn't always understand all the words but it gave him a familiar comfort to read about swashbuckling pirates and buried gold. For that brief moment in time, he was transported away from here, away from school, away from the back bedroom – and instead into a world of his own creation. Dad let him have a candle at night to read by – and in the early days he'd wondered what would happen if he used the flame to burn down the room and escape. But there wasn't much in the back bedroom that would feed the flames – no curtains hung at the window and just the one scratchy blanket covered the stained mattress. No pillows. No sheets. And all he had were the clothes he stood up in.

He knew he'd been bad when Dad led him up the rear staircase after getting home from their meeting with the headmistress. When he was good, he was allowed to sleep in the bedroom at the front of the house – the one with pillows on the bed, and a duvet to curl up in at night. And a window. Although it didn't open – the locks fused tight – it was still a window. And there was a small, tinny radio that he could listen to.

But today was a 'bad' day – today was a 'back bedroom' day.

He rubbed the salted crusts from the corners of his eyes and began to peel off his school clothes. They'd dried now, more or less - his shirt no longer clinging damply to his back. But he could still smell it in his hair –

the bleach, the urine, and worse. It was that unforgettable 'toilet' smell that only schools seemed to possess. How having his head rammed down the toilet had turned out to be his fault, he couldn't quite fathom. But he'd quickly learnt not to ask too many questions.

He wasn't allowed to use the bathroom when he was in the 'back bedroom'. That was out of bounds. He wrinkled his nose as he spied the fresh bucket tucked away in the corner of the room. Although the bucket was fresh, the odour left behind from the last time he'd been in here still lingered.

He pulled off his socks and shoes and stepped out of his charcoal grey school trousers. He'd needed the toilet on the way home, but Dad had made him wait - seeming to enjoy watching his stepson's discomfort, hopping from foot to foot until the inevitable had happened. Which had earned him another slap.

There was a small, cracked sink in the corner, with two rusting taps. Only one of them worked – the cold one. Stepping across the bare floorboards, he began to fill the sink with ice-cold water, submerging his urine stained trousers beneath the surface. There was a small square portion of dried-up soap on the side, which generated no lather. His fingers tingled from the chill water.

Looking at his watch, he saw it was nearly six. Dad only put the heating on in the back bedroom for one hour at six o'clock. The one solitary radiator served as his only source of heat to get his wet clothes dry – although he knew they'd still be damp come morning, but it was better than nothing. It wouldn't be the first time he went to school in damp clothes; something else to add fuel to the fire stoked by the bullies from the year above.

He sniffed the armpit of his school shirt. It didn't smell too bad and would last another day. And then it was the weekend where he would be allowed a change of clothes. And if he was good, he might be taken back to the front bedroom. *If* he was good.

He knew Dad scorned him for letting himself be bullied, always blamed him for failing to stand up for himself - as if it was something he had control over. *'Stand up for yourself boy!' 'Don't let them walk all over you!'*

But he was small. And thin. And weak. His mother told him he'd been born too early. Anyhow, the bullies were much bigger than he was. How could he stand up to them? They were stronger than him, and they knew it. He didn't have many friends in his own class. The other children stayed away from him, no doubt worried that if they were seen to be friends with the 'odd' boy, then the bullies might come for them. And who could blame them? No, staying away was probably best.

He'd arrived mid-term, which hadn't helped either. Everyone else had established friendships, formed little groups, and there was no room for a newcomer.

Especially a newcomer like him – coming from the poor side of town, and living on one of the roughest estates. What a lad from that part of town was doing in *their* school, they couldn't seem to understand. Kids from his estate went to Birchwood Comprehensive - they didn't come here.

So, he'd joined the school as an outcast, and remained so for the rest of term. He'd kept himself to himself as much as he could, hardly daring to speak unless he was spoken to first; intent on getting through each day with the minimal amount of fuss. He'd found some good hiding places and, for a while, it worked.

But he couldn't hide forever.

With his trousers and underpants draped across the stone-cold radiator, waiting for the one-hour window of heat that would make them wearable tomorrow, he wrapped himself up in the scratchy blanket and lay down on the hard mattress. He knew the faint aroma of stale urine would still cling to the fabric of his trousers, and that his classmates would turn their noses up at him if he walked too close. But he did the best he could.

Sighing, he felt his stomach rumble beneath the covers. Dad would be in soon with his supper. While he waited, he reached for his copy of Treasure Island.

* * *

# Chapter Ten

The air was damp with a heavy, suffocating fog – moisture clinging to anything and anyone it touched. Nicki stepped out of the station's front doors, standing behind and a little to the side of DCI Turner. Press releases were a chore at the best of times, but they were a necessary evil in today's fast-paced, digital age. The news-hungry general public would get an update on the Lucas Jackson investigation almost before the words had left the DCI's mouth – long gone were the days when the morning papers carried the latest headlines. Now it was virtually instant.

They'd chosen to do the press release outside the station for two reasons. Firstly, the conference room, if you could stretch to calling it that, was currently being used for storage - as several other parts of the building were being renovated. Currently, it housed a collection of ladders, scaffold boards, paint pots and an array of electrical cables. Secondly, and the reason most favoured by DCI Turner, was that conducting the press release on the steps outside the station, in plunging sub-zero temperatures, would hopefully deter all but the most intrepid reporters from making the journey. And therefore shorten its duration.

As they stepped out into the freezing early evening air, Nicki cast a glance around the gathered media. The ploy looked to have worked. She saw only four reporters huddled together in the dark, mobile recording devices clutched in gloved hands, scarves wrapped tightly around exposed necks. Each had had the foresight to bring a takeaway coffee cup with them, the vapour from which billowed out to join the fog-ridden night air.

DCI Turner flashed a look at Nicki before turning towards the hastily erected microphone. It wasn't really needed for such a small crowd, and he wasn't even sure it was turned on, but it gave him something to hide behind. Clearing his throat, he stood with legs apart, hands clasped firmly behind his back, a steely expression on his face.

"At approximately seven-thirty yesterday evening, Lucas Jackson, a six-year-old boy from the town, disappeared from the Abbey Gardens. An extensive search has, as yet, not led to his discovery. He was last seen at the Winter Fayre playing on an inflatable slide. I appeal to anyone who was in the vicinity of the Abbey Gardens yesterday evening who saw Lucas at any time, and has not already spoken to us, to contact the police as a matter of urgency. A picture of Lucas is on our website along with the relevant numbers to call. He was wearing a very distinctive Batman costume, with cape, plus – for the most part of the evening at least - a pair of red wellington boots." DCI Turner paused and let his eyes rove the congregated reporters.

"I would also like to hear from anyone who was out in the town yesterday evening, who thinks they may have seen Lucas in the company of anyone else. In particular, if you were driving through the town and have dash-cam footage, please contact the police urgently. You may have vital evidence. Please can I also ask residents of Bury St Edmunds to check any sheds, outbuildings, or garages in case Lucas is sheltering somewhere. Investigations continue at the present time, with the hope that we can reunite this young boy with his family. Thank you."

DCI Turner took a step back and lowered his gaze, indicating that the press release was at an end.

Nicki had been relieved when the DCI suggested he be the one to lead the press release. She both loathed and admired the press in equal measure. They did a great job in some respects, publishing details of investigations and appealing for information, helping to jog the public's memory. There were some very high profile cases that would never have been solved without the public's help.

And she had some good friends in the media.

But the press could also be a loose cannon.

It wasn't long before the first question rang out through the chilled air, sounding somewhat muffled in the descending fog. And it was the question they'd all been expecting. The press, as a whole, weren't stupid.

"Are you linking this case with the murders of Ivy McFadden and Oliver Chambers?" The question had come from a small, weasel-like man standing huddled beneath a black umbrella. The collar of his raincoat stood up on end, a dark-coloured scarf wound around his neck. His face had that pinched expression – a combination of the freezing temperatures and his own narrow bone structure. A pair of beady eyes peered out of the gathering gloom.

DCI Turner stepped towards the microphone once again. He knew Richard Cross from one of the local newspapers – their swords having crossed several times before. But he respected the seasoned reporter, acknowledging that the articles he wrote were both informative and accurate in their content. He wasn't usually one to speculate or print inflammatory opinions based solely on conjecture.

"We are aware of the similarities of this case to that of Ivy McFadden and Oliver Chambers." DCI Turner paused and flashed another split-second glance sideways at Nicki. "The investigation team are considering all angles and nothing is being ruled out."

"But you *are* linking them?" persisted Cross, taking a mouthful of the takeaway coffee he'd brought with him. "The killer of Ivy McFadden and Oliver Chambers is here in Bury?"

DCI Turner knew the dogged reporter wasn't going to give up. After a slight inclination of the head from Nicki at his side, he again stepped towards the microphone which he was now convinced was just a prop. "At this point in the investigation – which I stress is still in its very early stages – I can confirm we have been in touch with the team investigating the cases of both Ivy and Oliver, and we are working on the assumption that the cases could be linked."

There. He'd said it. He may as well have – the press would've made the link themselves in any event. They'd already printed as much in the newspapers that morning. It was best to get it out in the open.

Nicki felt a fluttering in the pit of her stomach as she watched the DCI step backwards, away from the microphone. There wasn't much more to be said. Headlines were already being created in the mind of each and every reporter in front of them and would no doubt be appearing online in a matter of minutes.

Part of her hoped that the Jackson's were offline tonight – to spare them the horror that such a revelation would no doubt create. They'd spoken about it earlier that day, so it was unlikely to come as much of a shock, and DC Gallagher had counselled them this afternoon on what to expect. But there was something different about seeing it written in black and white. Something permanent. Something set in stone.

Nicki had seen the expression on Sophia Jackson's face when the realisation hit that Lucas's disappearance was similar to the other two children abducted earlier that year. Children who were found dead some weeks later. If the person responsible for the abduction and murder of Ivy and Oliver now had her little boy...Nicki could only watch as Sophia Jackson's face crumpled before her.

Nicki turned to follow the DCI back into the station. No more questions were voiced by the waiting press; they'd already heard the answer to the one that mattered. With her fingers frozen to the bone, she thrust her hands inside her coat pockets and stepped back inside the building. Just as she did so, another voice carried through the fog.

"And what about the disappearance of Dean Webster? Are you reopening his case in the light of the Norfolk murders and this most recent abduction?"

Nicki's heart froze solid, her whole body jerking to a stop. She remained hovering just inside the entrance, casting a worried look towards DCI Turner.

*Why were they asking about Deano?*

Nicki's already pale face lost even more colour. The faint shrug of the DCI's shoulders told her that he was as much in the dark as she was. Panic threatened to overwhelm her and, despite being frozen to the core, the palms of her hands buried inside her pockets began to feel slick with sweat. With her heart hammering out of control, Nicki again looked towards DCI Turner, her face white.

The DCI took a step back outside, the steeliness in his eyes returning. The reporter who'd posed the question was standing alone a few metres away from the steps. The rest of the media had already started to make the journey back towards their cars. A couple stopped and turned back around, their interest piqued for another story.

The reporter was not one the DCI recognised. He was tall, a good six feet or more, dressed in a smart double breasted suit with regulation beige raincoat. A trilby hat sat perched on top of his head, a cigarette hanging loosely at the side of his mouth. He looked like something that had stepped out of a 1950s detective series.

The DCI cleared his throat once again. "This investigation concerns the disappearance of Lucas Jackson and Lucas Jackson alone. We have already confirmed the suspected link to the cases of Ivy McFadden and Oliver Chambers. That is all."

"But Dean Webster also disappeared, aged five, in very similar circumstances. From a fairground as I recall." The mystery reporter wasn't giving up. "His case was never solved. Don't you agree there are similarities with your current case?"

DCI Turner cast a sideways glance, grateful that Nicki had decided not to return to the front step and was still hovering in the shadows inside the station entrance. "The disappearance of Dean Webster is not a case being investigated by this force. Now, if you would excuse me, this press release is now finished." The DCI turned abruptly and strode back inside the building.

Nicki stepped aside as the DCI brushed past her and disappeared into the corridor, his face full of thunder. Unsure whether she should follow or let the dust settle, Nicki found herself pulled towards the front step.

As she approached, she glanced out into the murky fog and saw everyone had already disappeared from view; they had their headlines and would spend the next few hours putting together their reports.

Everyone bar one.

Taking a long drag on his cigarette, it was the reporter who spoke first.

"You know as well as I do that the circumstances are remarkably similar. You'd be a fool to ignore it." He paused, puffing out a cloud of cigarette smoke. "And Dean Webster? I know he was your brother."

Holding Nicki's panic-stricken gaze in his own, he stepped up onto the threshold of the station and pressed a small piece of card into her right hand.

And then he was gone.

Nicki remained frozen to the spot, her mouth unable to form even the simplest words. Her tongue felt dry, her mouth full of cotton wool – her legs threatening to give way at any second. Grabbing the door frame to support herself, she watched the reporter's figure disappear into the fog.

Why hadn't she asked him who he was?

Glancing down at the card in her hand, her eyes widened further as she took in the printed words.

He wasn't a reporter at all.

Caspar Ambrose

*Private Investigator.*

\* \* \*

# Chapter Eleven

8.00pm

Nicki closed the door behind her and sank to the floor. She was still shaking. The short walk through the town to her home had done nothing to quell the fear that coursed through her like an express train. She still clutched the private investigator's business card in her hand, her knuckles white from the cold.

Caspar Ambrose.

How had he found her? When she'd stumbled back inside the station, DCI Turner had quickly sought her out and whisked her back upstairs to his office, sitting her down with a hot coffee fortified with a little brandy. She'd initially screwed her face up at the taste, not being a brandy fan, but the warmth and then the numbness it brought soon had her welcoming a second mug.

They hadn't spoken immediately, and the DCI merely sat himself behind his desk, quietly sipping his own drink. After enough time had passed, and enough alcohol-infused coffee had seeped into their chilled systems, he spoke - answering the first question at the forefront of Nicki's mind.

"I don't know who he is or where he came from. It was probably just a coincidence." It was difficult to tell from the DCI's tone whether he genuinely believed that or not. His kind eyes peered at Nicki over the rim of his mug. "Are you OK?"

Nicki found herself nodding, although she wasn't really aware of being in conscious control of her reactions. She clutched her mug and allowed the warmth to thaw her hands.

"Good." DCI Turner placed his mug down on the desk and leant forwards, arms resting on piles of papers, his fingers laced together. Nicki gave a weak smile. Her father used to sit like that at his desk at home. She remembered with absolute clarity as if it were only yesterday and not the ten years or so since she'd last seen him. "If anything comes of it, I'll nip it in the bud as quickly as I can."

Nicki found herself nodding again. She took another mouthful of the brandy-laced coffee, this time relishing the burn. Her mind was racing, giving her heart a good run for its money. She couldn't get the man's name out of her head.

Caspar Ambrose.

Private Investigator.

She wasn't quite sure why, but she didn't tell DCI Turner about the card, or the fact that Ambrose clearly knew who she was. Instead, she'd just sat there, sipping her coffee, feeling the business card burning a hole in her pocket, the letters branding and scarring her skin. After a few more minutes exchanging pleasantries and assuring her senior officer she was fine, she'd thanked the DCI for his time, and his brandy, and made her excuses to leave.

And so here she was. Sitting on the cold floor tiles just inside her front door, her hands clutched once again around the small, square card.

Luna slunk silently down the stairs and headed in her direction, the faint mewing sound getting louder as she neared. Nicki reached out and gave the cat a rub behind the ears, welcoming the head bobs that followed. After a few more rubs under the chin, Nicki scrambled to her feet and followed the cat out into the kitchen, where Luna sat patiently by her food bowl.

Nicki reached for the cat food pouches and selected a delicious sounding combination of poultry and lamb. All the while, her mind continued to race. *Caspar Ambrose.*

She'd toyed with the idea of searching for him online. His business card didn't give any website address; indeed, it didn't give any address at all. But her investigative instincts were tapered by fear. She wanted to know who

89

he was, but was afraid of what she might discover when she did. She gave another shudder at the thought.

Luna was happily munching away at her dinner, so Nicki pulled open the fridge and grabbed the nearest bottle. She didn't care what it was, anything would do tonight.

The bottle turned out to be a very decent Chardonnay. She sunk the first glass within a few mouthfuls and, although it was chilled, it warmed her insides as it made its journey into her bloodstream. She still gripped the business card in one hand, unable to let it go. As she poured herself a second glass, she let her mind leave the mystery surrounding Caspar Ambrose and, instead, images of Lucas Jackson filled her head.

She knew she shouldn't get so personally involved – she should distance herself from such a heart-rending investigation, at least for the few hours she had to herself at night. Once you became emotionally involved there was a risk it could impair your judgement; cause you to make rash decisions. But the look on Sophia Jackson's face earlier that day would stay with her forever, burned into every dark recess of her mind. It was a look she knew well. Her mother wore the same expression for months, maybe even years, after Deano went missing.

Nicki wrenched her thoughts back to the present day. She uncurled her hand and studied the business card once again. If you could even call it that. Just a name and a phone number. *Private Investigator*. That was all. No address. No website. No nothing. Something deep inside sparked a warning. The man could be a hoax.

But hoax or not, he'd tracked her down after all these years.

*Found her.*

As far as she knew, even her own parents didn't know exactly where she was living. They knew she'd taken her mother's maiden name and that she was based at Suffolk Police, so it wouldn't take much to find her; not if they really wanted to. Which, judging by their silence for the last decade, they clearly did not. DCI Turner might mention how her father asked after her at one of their golfing sessions, but it wasn't the same.

Nicki sunk the second glass of Chardonnay and began to find herself

CHAPTER ELEVEN

relaxing, that familiar and welcome numbness spreading through her bones. She pulled the velvet throw around her and curled up at the far end of the sofa, closest to the wood burner. She needed to eat something, she knew that. Brandy and wine on an empty stomach, coupled with an early start the next morning, was a ferocious mixture.

But, instead, she reached for the bottle again and poured a generous third glass. It wasn't long before her eyes fluttered shut and she drifted off.

\* \* \*

"Wait for me in front of the ride when you're finished." Nicki nodded towards the queue for the caterpillar ride. "Don't go wandering off."

Dean Webster scampered away, delight spreading across his tiny face.

With Deano safely aboard the caterpillar, she turned her attention back to the candyfloss stall. The aroma was incredible – so sweet, so sticky. Her teeth ached. She could hear her mother's voice echoing inside her head,

*'Don't go wasting your pocket money on that candyfloss. It rots your teeth.'*

Pushing her mother's voice firmly out of her mind, Nicki gripped the coins in her pocket and skipped in the direction of heaven-on-a-stick. It would only take a minute. As she arrived at the stall, the stall holder was in the process of making a fresh batch. He smiled, apologetically as he loaded the metal bowl with fresh ingredients.

Just my luck, mused Nicki, watching the bowl whirr into action as she danced from foot to foot- a mixture of anticipation and cold. Glancing over her shoulder, she noticed the caterpillar ride had just begun its first circuit. She could just about make out the top of Deano's bobble hat in the second carriage.

She hadn't seen anyone from school yet, although everyone had said they would be here. Even Fiona, whom nobody liked that much. Turning her head back towards the candyfloss, she was relieved to see the stall holder reaching for the wooden sticks.

91

Any moment now.

Any moment now and she would be able to taste that sticky, velvety texture on her tongue. Her mother would go mad if she found out; but Nicki didn't care. Right now, all she could think about was candyfloss. As she watched the bright pink floss spin and grow before her eyes, winding itself around the wooden stick, she sensed a shadow behind her; a figure blocking out the light.

Although already a chilly night, with temperatures no better than freezing, she felt the cold creep around her. Whipping her head sideways, she saw a tall man in a light-coloured raincoat, with a trilby hat perched on his head, and a cigarette dangling from the corner of his lips.

Caspar Ambrose.

Nicki woke with a start, her heart hammering. Disorientated, she searched the dark for the mysterious figure. Slowly, her head caught up with the rest of her and she realised she'd been dreaming. The wood burner was now no more than a few glowing embers, and the living room sat in darkness. Her watch told her it was 11.45pm – she'd been asleep for the best part of three hours.

What had woken her? Her cluttered and confused mind raced through the fog, her eyes squinting through the dim light and coming to rest on the front door. Had she locked it when she came in? Uncertainty flooded her bones. With the velvet throw still wound tightly around her, she pushed herself up from the sofa and padded over to the door, her stomach tightening with every step. There was a stale taste of alcohol on her tongue, and the faint beginnings of a headache at her temples.

Trying the handle, she found the door wasn't locked. Reaching for the key, she turned it in the lock and heard its satisfying click - satisfying yet unnerving. The run of burglaries in the town flickered through her mind – the perpetrator had entered properties through unsecured doors and windows. How could she have been so careless?

Standing motionless on the doormat, Nicki looked back through the gloom into the living room, searching for anything that looked out of place. Had there been a noise to wake her up? The thought did nothing to quell her rapidly beating heart. How could she have been so stupid? She remembered nothing about the evening over and above sinking into the sofa with the bottle of Chardonnay.

Images of Deano and Caspar Ambrose then pushed their way back into her head. Admonishing herself for being so silly, she pulled the throw around herself and grabbed the packet of cigarettes and lighter that sat on the small nest of tables by the door. With one last glance around the darkened living room, she knew there was only one place she needed to be right now.

Reaching the roof garden, she found her heartbeat starting to slow. The bitter air hit her face in a strangely welcoming way. Padding across the flagstones with her bare feet, she settled into her favourite recliner. It was damp with moisture from the descending fog, and as cold as ice – but Nicki sank gratefully into its familiarity.

She pulled a cigarette from the packet and lit it, dragging the smoke into her lungs. She wasn't really a smoker – hadn't had one for months. Maybe even longer. And it wasn't a habit that she really enjoyed, but tonight – right now - it was what she needed. She'd already pickled her liver with the best part of a whole bottle of Chardonnay, so may as well add nicotine to the list of self-abuse.

She'd promised herself she'd go for a run tonight. She bit back the bitter laugh that hovered in her throat. *That* hadn't materialised. Again. She silently promised herself she would go tomorrow - tomorrow that was rapidly turning into today - maybe even before she went to the station. But if not then, definitely when she got home.

*Definitely.*

She swallowed another laugh.

The velvet throw did nothing to ward off the biting chill, but Nicki almost welcomed the discomfort. She needed the cold to sharpen her brain. Sophia Jackson needed her to be at her best – not some washed up detective out for the count on the sofa, with only an empty bottle and an unlocked door for company. She needed to be sharp. She needed to be reactive. And most of all she needed to be right. There could be no mistakes, not with this investigation – not if they were to find Lucas Jackson before it was too late.

Time was already against them; the perpetrator already had the upper hand. If they were dealing with the same person who abducted and murdered poor Ivy and Oliver, the outlook was bleak. Lucas may already be dead. But until they knew that for sure, until they found him, Nicki knew she needed to be at her best.

As she drew more cigarette smoke into her lungs, she gazed out over the rooftops. Everywhere was silent. People tucked away inside their houses, sound asleep, shielded from the night. The quiet enveloped her. This was one of her favourite views, high above the rooftops, feeling as though she were on top of the world. But tonight it felt different. *He* was out there; somewhere. And so was Lucas. Maybe she was even looking straight at his house - right here, right now.

And until she found him, Nicki knew she wouldn't rest.

* * *

# Chapter Twelve

*Thursday 1<sup>st</sup> November 2018*

6.45am

Nicki noticed the three missed calls on her phone just as she stepped out of the shower. She'd stood under the warm water for at least fifteen minutes extra this morning, trying to wash away the events of the night before. Once she'd reluctantly left the rooftop garden and tried to sleep, the sense of disquiet had remained. She'd tossed and turned for the rest of the night and eventually risen at a little after 5am. She couldn't help but think back to the unlocked front door and how long she'd been asleep on the sofa. The idea of someone being in the house while she slept made her stomach churn. It was unlikely, she knew that – and a quick glance around her compact one-bedroom house had told her nothing had been disturbed.

But the feeling refused to leave her.

She shivered, despite just stepping out of the hot shower, and picked up her phone. Three calls all from the same number – DCI Turner – and all within the last eight minutes. Her finger hovered over the redial button. Whatever it was, it wasn't going to be good news; not at this time in the morning. She placed the phone back down and reached for another towel, wrapping it around her wet hair. The bathroom had steamed up, the air full of moisture and the scent of lime-fresh shower gel. She wiped a hand across the mirror and pondered her reflection.

Notwithstanding the blurriness of the mirror, and the steamy condensation in the air, there was no mistaking the tiredness plastered across her face. Her eyes looked sunken, with dark circles already starting to form. Her skin, despite the apricot face scrub applied vigorously in the shower, looked wan and slack. Her eyes lacked their usual lustre and sparkle.

And the investigation was only in its very early beginnings – history told her that things would get a whole lot worse before they got any better.

Glancing back down at the phone, she sighed and hit the redial button. Better get it over and done with, she reasoned. Forewarned is forearmed, didn't someone say once?

The DCI answered on the second ring, clearly waiting for her call.

"Nicki," he greeted, a false sense of jollity in his tone. "Hope I didn't wake you?"

Fat chance, she thought, wrapping another towel around her body and stepping through to the bedroom. "No, not at all. Just out of the shower."

"Good, good." The DCI's voice lowered a notch. "Look, there's no easy way of saying this – but have you had a chance to look at the papers this morning?"

\* \* \*

*Thursday 1ˢᵗ November 2018*
7.00am

He'd been awake most of the night, padding silently through the house, his nerves jangling. He'd placed an ear up against the padlocked door several times, but there'd been no sounds from within. The boy must be asleep for once. He'd lain him down on the bed this time, tying his wrists to the bedposts, covering his tiny body with the thin, moth-eaten blanket.

The boy had merely whimpered; no longer crying out from behind his gagged mouth.

Lucas Jackson was learning.

He afforded himself a smile before turning to jog back downstairs. It had taken a while, but after he'd shown him how easy it would be to choke him,

96

the boy had succumbed. He'd initially cried out, his eyes wide open in horror, but he'd soon learnt to swallow his sobs.

By the end, he was submissive and pliable.

Snapping on the kitchen light, he flicked the switch on the kettle. Looking up towards the ceiling, he felt the familiar thrill ripple through him once again. It was at times like these that he thought of his stepfather. Would he be proud? He hoped so; that was all he'd ever wanted. That was why he was doing all this – for him. For the man who had shaped him in the back bedroom of No 5 Arlington Crescent.

* * *

5 Arlington Crescent
*Saturday 16<sup>th</sup> March 2002*

Balancing the plate of bread crusts on top of his mug, he nudged open the kitchen door. Dad unlocked the back bedroom earlier that morning when bringing in his breakfast of bread and water and had left it unlocked. It was a sign that he was, for now, forgiven. He'd spent only two nights in the back bedroom this time, which lightened his heart. The kitchen was flooded with sunlight, the back door wedged open with a heavy, cast iron weight. The day outside had dawned bright and clear.

Mum was at the sink, her hands submerged in a bowl of washing up water, humming quietly to herself as she wiped the soap suds from the dishes. There was a faint aroma of lemon in the air. He crossed the kitchen floor and placed his mug and plate on the draining board and saw his mother glance sideways at him, a faint smile twinkling at her mouth. She looked tired – dark circles hung beneath her eyes, and her skin was pale and lifeless. But she was happy – she had to be happy, she was humming.

A shadow fell across the kitchen. He glanced towards the back door just in time to see his stepfather's hulking frame fill the space, blocking out the sun. He thought he saw his mother flinch, but maybe it was his imagination.

"Ready, son?" Alan Woods held up a muddied football in one hand, a wide grin plastered to his unshaven face.

Hesitating, he warily eyed the football.

"Come on!" urged his stepfather, stepping backwards out into the garden, sunlight suddenly replacing his shadow. "Let's have a kick about. Build up those muscles of yours!"

He found himself edging towards the back door, his legs moving of their own accord. Resistance was futile, he knew that. When Dad wanted to play football, then they played football. Although, really, it was an excuse for his father to run him ragged around the garden, forcing him to jump and squat, all as a pretext of 'building him up'.

*'Let's make you into a man, my boy!'* he would say, before thumping the ball towards him. *'Toughen you up!'*

But it beat being locked up in the back bedroom.

He quickened his step towards the back door, wanting to get it over and done with before he changed his mind, when he heard a faint jangling sound of metal scraping over the kitchen floor. He turned back to see his mother stepping away from the sink and heading towards the fridge. As she moved, the metal chain clasped around her ankle scraped over the ceramic floor tiles.

Mum must've been bad too, he mused, before heading out into the garden.

* * *

*Thursday 1st November 2018*

7.45am

Stirring his freshly brewed mug of tea, he peered more closely at the blurry image on page three of the local newspaper. He'd nipped out to the shop, eager to see what headlines people were waking up to. And he hadn't been expecting what he saw.

It was only a tiny black and white photograph tucked away in the bottom corner, but the recognition was instant. Despite the grainy image, there was no mistaking the face staring back out. Pulling out a chair at the kitchen table, he sat down, heart hammering.

It was the same picture that had been in all the newspapers back in 2004; the same unflattering image that portrayed his stepfather as a monster. He shook his head, brow creasing. They didn't know him like he did. Photographs told only one side of the story.

The mention of his stepfather's name had been an unexpected addition to the morning routine. But so was the picture printed next to it. Dean Webster was the name attached to the photograph. Investigative reporter Adam Sullivan was alleging that 'an unnamed source' had confirmed the investigation into the five-year-old's disappearance in 1996 was to be re-opened.

He let his eyes rest on the boy's grainy black and white photograph. The journalist continued to report that in 2004 the convicted murderer, Alan Woods, was questioned by Sussex police about the disappearance of the five-year-old, but he denied all knowledge from his cell in the Category A prison he now called home. The full-page article concluded with a renewed call to re-investigate the disappearance of Dean Webster and, in particular, his links to 'notorious child killer' Woods.

Notorious.

He'd heard that word spoken many times before when people spoke of his stepfather.

He'd been only eight when they'd moved into No 5 Arlington Crescent, and Alan Woods had become his new Dad. He struggled to remember his real father now, even when he really tried.

He often tried to remember the first time his new father had shown him the boys. But his memory of that time was somewhat hazy these days. Time did funny things to you. Part of him felt there had always been boys in the house, but that couldn't be true, could it?

The back bedroom was where Dad had kept them – when it wasn't being occupied by himself after another 'bad day' at school. The room could be accessed only from the rear of the house; the rear staircase leading to that one room and nowhere else. He didn't often choose to climb those stairs, having no real reason to, but sometimes he felt an inexplicable pull towards it – if for no other reason than morbid curiosity.

Although he couldn't be sure of the exact date, he knew it must've been around fireworks night. He'd just been chased out of the school gates, the bullies threatening to throw bangers at his head and blow him to smithereens. He didn't know if they really had bangers – but he wasn't going to wait to find out. On this occasion, he got away and arrived home unscathed.

Dad had been nowhere to be seen all evening, so it had been just him and Mum at the kitchen table for dinner.

"Where's Dad?" he'd asked, spooning more chicken casserole into his mouth as he spoke. Part of him was glad it was just the two of them – Mum always gave him extra helpings when Dad wasn't around.

His mother hesitated for a second or two, avoiding his enquiring gaze, before pushing back her chair and stepping towards the counter next to the sink. "More bread?" she asked, picking up the bread knife and cutting several more slices from the white bloomer.

Again the metal chain clasped to her ankle scraped across the kitchen tiles as she moved.

"Please," he nodded. "But, where's Dad?"

Returning to the table and placing a thickly cut slice of bread on her son's plate, she resumed her seat, tucking the metal chain underneath her chair. "He's busy tonight, sweetheart. Don't worry."

Busy?

Dad had been busy before and he'd disappeared for days.

After finishing his second helping of casserole, and another slice of bread, he excused himself from the table. His heart pounded as he made his way towards the rear staircase. Some inexplicable unseen force was drawing him towards the back bedroom.

He knew his mother wouldn't be able to follow him. She wouldn't be moving from the kitchen; not until Dad unlocked the chain. And sometimes he didn't do that for a very long time. He was sure that some nights Mum slept on the kitchen floor.

With no lights in this part of the house, the rear staircase was bathed in shadowy darkness. He avoided the stairs that he knew creaked the loudest and arrived at the top, his breath coming in short, sharp rasps. He pressed his own hand to his mouth to silence them.

The landing was small, with just the one door leading from it. That and the hatch leading to the attic above. Gingerly, he stepped forwards, his eyes adjusting to the dark. The door to the back bedroom was still shut tight.

Glancing over his shoulder to check that he was still truly alone, he pressed an ear to the cool wood and listened. Holding his breath, he strained to hear anything from beyond the door. But everything seemed quiet.

With no sounds emanating from the room, he wondered if he'd got it wrong. Maybe Dad wasn't in the house at all. Pausing for a few more seconds, he straightened up onto his tiptoes and placed an eye to the spy-hole.

What he saw almost stilled his heart and snatched the breath from his lungs. Out of everything imaginable, he wasn't expecting to see that.

The boy was sitting on a wooden chair in the middle of the room. His ankles were strapped to the chair legs, his hands tied in front of him. He'd been stripped down to his underclothes, wearing nothing but a pair of underpants and a vest. His face was pale and tear-streaked.

Slowly, he let out the breath he'd been holding in, unable to deprive his lungs of oxygen any longer. His heart hammered painfully inside his chest, so loud he wondered if it could be heard through the thick wooden door.

Who was the boy?

A movement to the side of the room made his eyes shift their focus from the terrified boy to the figure now walking into view. Although the figure's back was towards him, and the room was in a muted darkness, he would recognise those wide, muscular shoulders anywhere.

Questions repeatedly flooded his mind. Who was the boy? What was Dad doing in the back bedroom? Why was the door locked?

Confusion fogged his brain. Dad seemed to be talking now; he could hear hushed tones over the sound of his own breath, but it was muffled and the words sounded distorted. Whatever it was he was saying, the boy still looked petrified.

He saw the gag that had been placed across the boy's mouth, a dirty rag that looked to be stained with something dark. Was that blood?

With his heart racing and beads of sweat popping onto his forehead, he felt an icy cold blast shiver through his bloodstream as his eyes connected with the boy's for the briefest of moments. Visions of the pirates in Treasure Island, and the other adventure books he so loved, swam in and out of his brain. The boy's eyes widened as they locked into his gaze.

Holding his breath once again, he willed his heartbeat to lessen. It was so loud, surely someone would hear? He began to pull away from the door, but felt his gaze still inexplicably drawn to the confusing scene before him. Just as he hesitated, his stepfather's form stepped into view – and for the longest of split-seconds, their eyes met.

And that day was when life, as he knew it, changed. The moment their eyes met through the spy-hole, life would never be the same again; for either of them.

He remembered with remarkable clarity what happened next. He'd been expecting a thrashing for being somewhere he shouldn't; for *seeing* something he shouldn't. But the thrashing never came.

With his feet rooted to the spot, unable to obey the natural instinct to run, the door creaked open and Dad stood in the doorway.

Seconds ticked by; maybe even minutes. Time stood still. And then his stepfather simply turned away, disappearing back inside the back bedroom. He'd hesitated, unsure what to do. The door to the back bedroom – *his* back bedroom – remained open, and any fear he may have felt at being discovered, began to seep away like a receding tide. In its place, curiosity built.

Something inside propelled him forwards. It was as though, something else, *someone* else, had control of his limbs, and he was a mere puppet at their mercy.

He peered around the door frame, eyes wide and unblinking. He could see more clearly now. The boy was still sitting in the wooden chair, unable to move due to the strappings and restraints. A pool of urine sat by his feet. But he didn't seem to be fighting or resisting – if he ever had been. He merely sat, limply, a look of confusion mixed with resignation on his pale face.

Glancing towards the bed, where he himself had spent so many days and nights curled up underneath the scratchy, worn blanket, he saw the boy's clothes discarded on top.

Dad beckoned him forwards. It was an unusually tender gesture, his eyes soft and sparkling, a threat of a smile on his lips. His stepfather's rough, calloused hand enclosed around his own and gently pulled him closer. A touch that usually inflicted pain on him was, instead, warm and comforting. It was an alien feeling and, at first, he was unsure what to do. But no sooner had his stepfather's hand grasped his own, he felt an equally alien swelling sensation in his heart.

As Dad coaxed him closer, his footsteps on the bare floorboards making the smallest of sounds, he heard the boy's soft whimpering, and saw that his bare knees were shaking. Why was the boy so scared? Dad was kind.

It was then, at that very moment, that he realised what his stepfather had been trying to teach him all along. Locking him up in the back bedroom hadn't been a punishment; not really. Neither had the whippings, and worse. It had all been part of his journey – the journey he needed to take to become a man; a man like his stepfather.

He looked up in raw wonderment, seeing his stepfather in an entirely new light. He no longer saw those cold, steely-grey eyes that flashed with anger and irritation – instead he saw love. He found himself breaking into a smile. Dad loves me – he truly loves me.

"Come here, son. Let me show you."

He didn't learn the boy's name until later, when the story of his disappearance hit the newspaper headlines and he'd recognised the boy's face staring out from the newsprint. Jacob Ayers. The name had stuck with him ever since.

There had been a second boy, too – not long after the first – and the name Sean Warren sprang to mind.

Continuing to stir his tea, he looked once more back at page 3 of the newspaper, and at the image of Dean Webster. If the boy had disappeared in 1996, then this was long before he and his mother came to live at 5 Arlington Crescent. But had he been in the back bedroom, too?

He pushed the thought from his mind and flicked back to the front page of the newspaper. He noted a different journalist was confirming that the murders of both Ivy McFadden and Oliver Chambers were now being formally linked to the disappearance of six-year-old Lucas Jackson. Photographs of both Ivy and Oliver's faces smiled out once again from the centre of the one-page article; the same pictures that had adorned every newspaper and TV outlet when the hunt for them was at its most intense.

He traced a finger around Ivy's grinning cheeks. She'd been a beautiful child. Blonde hair. Blue eyes. The archetypal English rose. His heart fluttered. Ivy had been a good girl. He hadn't been sure he was going to convince her to go with him. But in the end it had been easy.

* * *

Sunday 1st April 2018

"I'm gonna win you a teddy!" Christopher McFadden grinned at his younger sister and grabbed hold of the hoopla rings. He eyed the wooden sticks standing up on the far side of the stall. It looked easy, but he knew by the amount of prizes that were still waiting to be won that it probably wasn't. Dad had always told him that the games at the fair were rigged. The coconuts were stuck to the poles so you couldn't knock them off; the darts were weighted so they didn't throw in a straight line. Even so, Christopher McFadden was going to give it a go. If he hooped three posts, then he won the massive Easter Bunny. And he had a good aim; he was on the school cricket team and had a keen eye for a twelve-year-old.

"I need a wee!" Ivy McFadden jumped from foot to foot, a pained expression on her face. Her hands were buried in a pair of woollen mittens, the rest of her encased in a multi-coloured Peppa Pig coat. Their mother had only been prepared to let them out if she agreed to keep her mittens on. Always. Ivy had been quick to agree – she'd agree to anything to go to the fair!

Christopher McFadden ignored his little sister's cries and turned his attention back to the wooden posts on the hoopla stall. Which one should he aim for first? The ones closest to him, or the ones at the back? He had a pretty strong throw, so he decided to concentrate on the ones towards the back of the stall.

"I need a wee!" wailed Ivy, louder this time. "I really do!"

Christopher McFadden put his hoopla rings down and took in the expression on his little sister's face, noting how she did look to be in discomfort. Not wanting an accident on his hands, he quickly glanced across the muddied grass towards the toilet block behind them. A series of port-a-loos sat in a line, three for women, two for men, and at the moment there was only a small queue.

"Look, go over there – join the queue." Christopher McFadden waved towards the toilets. "Then come straight back over here."

Ivy didn't need asking twice, running towards the queue and waiting behind a young mother with a baby in a carry sling. Christopher held up both thumbs and then turned his attention back to the hoopla stall. Picking up the first ring, he narrowed his gaze and took aim.

The first ring missed by a mile.

Maybe his dad was right. Maybe they *were* rigged.

He picked up the next ring and tested the weight in his hands. He'd be more gentle with this one.

Again, he focused his gaze and threw the hoop.

Again, he missed – but not by quite so much this time.

"Unlucky!" laughed the stallholder, picking up the discarded ring. "Keep trying!"

Christopher McFadden shifted his stance. He wasn't going to let this stupid game beat him. He took another quick glance over his shoulder and saw that Ivy was now at the front of the toilet queue, still hopping from one foot to the other. Turning his attention back to the job in hand, he decided to change tack and go for one of the front row posts this time. Focusing intently on the one nearest to him, he flung the hoop into the air and watched as it came down perfectly on target.

"Yes!" he yelled, pumping a fist in the air.

"Good shot!" agreed the stallholder. "You've won a prize!" He pointed to a row of small beanie toys on the bottom shelf of the prize rack. "Three more rings – see if you can win something bigger!"

Christopher McFadden lined up the next hoop. He was going to aim for the same post again – his lucky post. Adjusting his feet, he narrowed his gaze once again and launched the hoop into the air and watched as it bounced off the target and landed on the floor.

He grimaced. He only had two more hoops left and he needed both of them to be perfect if he was going to win Ivy that bunny.

Ivy.

He shot a glance over his shoulder to see that Ivy was no longer in the queue. Thinking she must be inside one of the cubicles, Christopher McFadden turned his attention back to the hoopla stall. It was now or never. He bit his bottom lip in concentration.

Both hoops sailed smoothly to their chosen targets, landing perfectly around each post.

"Yes!" he screeched again, giving the air another punch. "I won!"

The stallholder conceded defeat and plucked the enormous Easter Bunny from the top shelf, passing it across into Christopher's outstretched hand. "Well played, young man!"

Christopher grinned. Now he just needed to tell Ivy!

Turning around, he made his way over to the five port-a-loos and waited at the side. The air was turning really cold now, his breath billowing out in front of him each time he exhaled. He stamped his frozen feet as he waited – he'd get them both a hot chocolate to warm them up before heading for home. And maybe a burger.

The minutes ticked by and Christopher McFadden continued to train his eyes on the port-a-loos. He watched as each door opened and closed, expecting to see her tiny frame bundling out and running across to him once she saw the huge fluffy bunny – but Ivy was nowhere to be seen.

A weird feeling started to trickle through his empty stomach. She'd been standing in the queue; he'd seen her, waiting patiently for her turn. That was all of what, two minutes ago? How long had he been at the hoopla stall? He frowned and peered over the top of the bunny, again watching the toilet doors open and close. She had to be in one of them. She had to be.

Another minute ticked by and there was still no sign of Ivy. He started looking around him, but there were so many people drifting by it was hard to see very far ahead. He knew Ivy was wearing her distinctive multi-coloured Peppa Pig coat so she would stand out in a crowd.

He scoured the streams of people passing him by in both directions. No multi-coloured coat. No Ivy.

Fear now cascaded through him. "Ivy?" Blundering through the crowd, he ran from stall to stall, searching blindly for the multi-coloured coat. "Ivy?"

She had to be here somewhere.

She couldn't just disappear.

\* \* \*

*Thursday 1st November 2018*

7.50am

Tearing his eyes away from the image of Ivy McFadden, he folded up the newspaper and got to his feet. He couldn't sit here all day, thinking about the past. He had things to do.

Placing his empty mug in the sink, he contemplated what to do next. Now Lucas was a little more receptive towards him, he could spend the rest of the day teaching him – just the way his stepfather had taught him. The idea intrigued him.

From reading the newspaper reports, he already knew that Lucas Jackson's father was not around. A smile flickered onto his lips as he made his way towards the stairs.

The boy needed a father's touch.

Grabbing the thick leather belt that hung on the rack by the door, he headed upstairs.

\* \* \*

# Chapter Thirteen

The station was quiet at this time of the morning, with the sun struggling to pierce through the heavy clouds and most people's curtains still drawn. The Lucas Jackson investigation was turning everything on its head – it was the biggest investigation Suffolk Police had had to launch since the Suffolk Strangler some twelve years ago. While not yet a full scale murder enquiry, Nicki knew with sickening realisation that many were quietly thinking things were heading in that direction. It was almost the expected outcome, as hard as that was to stomach.

Operation Goldfish was the random name it had been allocated. Somewhat apt in a strange kind of way. Nicki could recall winning a goldfish at a local fair when she was small. Before Deano. Before life was irrevocably altered.

She pushed open the door to her office and was pleasantly surprised to see a takeaway cup of her favourite coffee sitting amongst the mountain of files and papers decorating her desk. She shrugged out of her coat and hung it on the peg on the back of the door, just in time to see a familiar head poking around the door frame. DS Roy Carter, looking freshly scrubbed and smelling of citrus body wash, smiled in her direction.

"Morning, boss," he greeted. Nicki tried to return the smile, conscious of her own pallid skin and wayward hair. She would say that the display of early morning energy was down to his youth, but in reality she wasn't that much older than he was. Not in years, maybe – but in life experience she felt ancient.

"Morning, Roy. I take it I have you to thank for the coffee?" She raised her eyebrows in the direction of the cup.

Roy grinned. "Well, I remembered what you said, boss." He gave a show of looking at his watch. "As it's way before midday I thought it would be a good idea."

Nicki gave a proper smile this time. "And you thought correctly, sergeant. Thank you."

Roy bowed his head and began to retreat. Before disappearing, he nodded towards the corridor outside. "The DCI wants a quick word once you've settled."

Nicki tried to keep the smile in place while Roy took his leave and disappeared from view. Once out of sight, her face dropped. She grabbed at the coffee cup and took a grateful swig. It was too hot and too sweet, but right now she didn't care or even notice. Her early morning bathroom conversation with the DCI had served to dull whatever senses she had.

The moment she'd heard him say the word 'newspapers' her heart had plummeted. She didn't pass any newsagents on her way to the station and was loath to make a special trip just for that – so DCI Turner had given her the edited highlights. If you could call them that.

It could've been worse, she concluded as she'd put the phone down. At least they didn't mention her name or her connection to Deano. At least the lid was still on *that* can of worms.

But for how long?

'A source close to the investigation' had been quoted several times when mentioning Dean. One tabloid had even gone so far as to suggest that they were considering linking Dean's disappearance to that of Ivy, Oliver and now Lucas. The thought troubled her. Despite the similar nature of the cases, it just couldn't be the same person...could it?

Nicki pushed the thought from her mind as she took another mouthful of sweet coffee. There was, of course, another reason that the thought sickened her. If it were true, and Deano had been taken by the same person they were hunting now...

Bile rose up into Nicki's throat, almost making her gag. With both Ivy and Oliver murdered within a week of their abduction, according to the post mortem reports, there was only one logical conclusion to reach.

She shook her head and forced another swig of coffee into her mouth. No – it wasn't a thought she could ever entertain. No part of Nicki's fragile state of mind allowed her to even consider it.

*No.*

Suddenly the aroma from the fresh coffee was not as enticing as it had been, and Nicki left it on her desk as she made her way towards the DCI's office.

* * *

*Thursday 1st November 2018*

8.30am

The boy was learning, albeit slowly. When he'd unlocked the padlock earlier that morning and stepped inside, Lucas had barely uttered a sound. And when he'd brandished the thick, leather belt he'd only detected the slightest of flinches.

He'd bruised and bled more easily than the others had; the boy's sandy fair hair now clogged with congealed blood.

As he strapped the boy back into the chair, he wrinkled his nose in distaste. Lucas had soiled himself again overnight; this time on the bed. Which had earnt him an extra punishment with the leather belt.

He washed the mattress down as best he could and placed the dirty cloth into the bowl of now discoloured and foul-smelling water, feeling the unpleasant taste of bile rising into the back of his throat as he did so. Thoughts of getting rid of Lucas Jackson were already coursing through his head.

As he straightened up and headed towards the door, he tried to remember how long his stepfather had kept them – Jacob and Sean - but the more he tried to think back the fainter the memories became. Had it been a week? Longer? Less?

He'd wanted to do things just like his stepfather had and even considered writing to him, asking for advice. But he'd rapidly dismissed that idea as ludicrous, almost as soon as it had formed in his mind. Letters were censored in prison, weren't they? Surely they were? So he'd kept his questions to himself.

But that meant he was still no further along in deciding what to do with Lucas. Despite the boy's progress, he was still a nuisance. He'd tried to guess with both Ivy and Oliver, and he was sure he'd got it wrong. He worried he'd not waited long enough before getting rid of the bodies, or hadn't hidden them well enough. They'd both been discovered fairly easily by dog walkers on their early morning walks.

Dog walkers. Why was it always them? Did the animals detect the scent of decay? He hadn't paid much attention in school. Not that they would've taught him anything as useful as that. How long does it take for a body to decompose? How long after death does a body start to smell? And where is the best place to hide one? Those questions had never been answered.

No - school had been a waste of time. Instinctively he let a hand rub the side of his chin

Especially after *the incident.*

* * *

Westfield Comprehensive School
*Monday 8th March 2004*

He hadn't wanted to go back to school - but his mother had insisted. And in the first letter Dad had written to him from inside his prison cell, he'd virtually commanded him to return.

'*You can't let them beat you, son.*'
'*No member of the Woods family has ever been a coward.*'
'*What have I taught you about being strong, about being in control?*'

So, he'd returned to school with his head held high. Walking in the *front* entrance this time, not sneaking in the back way like he used to. He was strong. And who cared what the papers said? He knew his stepfather – and he wasn't a monster. He wasn't anything like what they were saying.

Sometimes he found his mother sitting in the kitchen with her head in her hands, crying; her shoulders heaving with every sob. He'd tried to comfort her the best he could, but how could he? The man she loved had been taken away from her – or at least, he thought that was what she was crying about. Sometimes, when he looked into her eyes, he saw a strange emotion cross her features. In amongst the tears, he caught a fleeting glimpse of relief, almost as though she was smiling inside. As if she were *happy*.

The thought confused him.

The first few days back at school went well, and he slowly began to relax. No one seemed to want to come near him. The fifth year bullies no longer hung around outside his classroom at break time. No longer did they chase him down the corridors and corral him into the boys' toilets for a drowning. No longer did they steal his lunchbox or tip the contents of his school bag out across the playing fields. No longer did they drag him by his blazer outside the school gates and push him into the bushes when they'd finished with him.

This time, people stayed out of his way. Even the teachers. He caught the odd look thrown in his direction, the odd whisper in hushed tones behind his back, but no one actually spoke to him. He sat by himself in all his lessons, the other students moving out of his way as if he were infected, scared to touch him. The thought gave him a tiny thrill. Sometimes, he inched his chair a little closer to someone, or wandered across to their side of the corridor, just to see them flinch and hurriedly move away.

This was the power and control his stepfather had told him about. He was no longer the boy that was bullied – and the thought made him smile.

Maybe he relaxed too much, relishing in the unexpected notoriety of having a father in prison. He now knew that he'd taken his eye off the ball; been lulled into a false sense of security that eventually served to be his downfall and altered the course of his life forever.

It was a Friday – he remembered that as clear as anything. They'd just finished PE and he'd been allowed to shower and change in silence and space. No one so much as looked at him. Maybe they all knew what was coming next.

It was morning break-time and he had a new habit of walking out into the main playground and sitting on one of the picnic benches by the entrance to the kitchens. At this time of day, the smells of the forthcoming lunches wafted through the open windows. He flung his schoolbag down onto the grass and swung a leg over one of the bench seats, inhaling the aroma as he did so. It looked like fish pie was on the menu today.

Reaching down into his bag, he pulled out a chocolate bar. Sweets, including chocolate, weren't allowed in school – but he didn't care. He knew the teachers wouldn't have the heart nor the courage to take it from him – not after what had just happened.

He afforded himself a smile as he ripped off the silver foil wrapping.

He should have seen them coming; if he'd been looking. But they were upon him before he'd had the chance to swallow his first mouthful of chocolate. Six of them, maybe more, surrounded him and dragged him from the bench. He hadn't made a sound, save for a guttural choking as melted chocolate flowed out of his mouth. Sometimes, the back door to the kitchen was left open, allowing the kitchen staff a tea break and breather before resuming the preparation of the lunches.

But not today.

Today the back door remained firmly shut, and nobody saw Daniel Woods being dragged across the grass towards the entrance to the science block.

With it being break-time, the science block was deserted. As the outer door was flung open, the familiar smell of chemicals grazed their nostrils. He tried to twist out of their grip, but it was futile. They were too strong, just like they always were. His legs were kicked out from under him, and several pairs of strong arms pulled him across the linoleum floor.

The first door they came to was the main chemistry lab. As soon as it was kicked open, he smelt the acrid aroma of acid and spent Bunsen burners. Dragging him past the rows of white coats hanging on pegs by the entrance, they flung him across the room towards a wooden worktop housing a series of Butler sinks. Piles of discarded test tubes and glass beakers decorated the worktop, waiting for the lab assistant to work her magic, rinsing and cleaning everything ready for the next class.

He eyed his captors with a narrowed, inquisitive gaze. If they'd wanted to give him a good kicking, they could've done that outside; they usually did. A quick and fast assault, leaving him rolling around on the grass while they made good their escape.

But not this time. This time was different.

He turned his attention to the deserted lab. The door had been slammed shut, a wooden chair placed in front to block entry from outside. He felt his heartbeat quicken a notch and his palms began to moisten with sweat. Turning to face them, he tried to anticipate their next move.

It was then that the cat-calls and whistles began; a cascade of name-calling and taunts filled his ears. "Paedo!" "Child killer!" "Murderer!" The words echoed around his head, bouncing around like a frantic pin-ball machine. He closed his eyes to block them out. They didn't know what they were saying. They didn't know the truth. They just listened to the TV and newspaper journalists, spouting their lies and spreading rumours. He *knew* his stepfather. He wasn't like that. He was a good man.

Closing his eyes had been his mistake.

Because he didn't see it coming.

But the error could also have saved his eyesight.

He couldn't quite remember what he felt first. The sensation of liquid on his face, or the intense burn. One came so quickly after the other. Whichever it was, his eyes flew open and stared, wildly, at his attackers.

The cat calls descended into whoops of joy and exhilaration at exactly the same time that his skin began to dissolve. He crumpled to the ground, his hands instinctively scraping at the intense fire that now raged across the lower half of his face and neck. He heard the door crash open and the retreating footsteps of his tormentors faded into the background.

And then there was nothing; nothing but silence and his own disintegrating skin.

* * *

*Thursday 1ˢᵗ November 2018*
  8.30am

He pulled his roving thoughts back to the present, the cloying smell of faeces still clinging to his nostrils. Satisfied the boy was secure in the chair, although there was no way out once the door was locked, he backed out of the room and jogged downstairs.

Holding the bowl of dirty water as far from him as he could without spilling it, he made his way towards the kitchen. Tipping the soiled water down the sink, he couldn't help but feel that maybe he'd picked the wrong boy this time. Lucas was learning, but not quite quickly enough.

Maybe he needed someone else. Someone new. As he ran fresh water around the sink to flush away the stench of urine and faeces, liberally adding a generous squirt of bleach, the idea stuck in his mind. He'd been thinking about it most of the night. Someone else. A new kid. *Two together.*

The thought intrigued him. And the more he thought about it, the more he believed it could work. Two at once, where was the harm? He had a big enough room, and there was another wooden chair in the garage; he'd seen it. Maybe a new one would teach the boy upstairs how to control his bladder.

Or maybe... Another thrill flickered in the pit of his stomach. Maybe he should get rid of Lucas Jackson completely, and get two fresh ones. Two pliable ones. Two *obedient* ones. The idea made his heart quicken.

Swirling more bleach around the inside of the sink, he felt the acidic vapour irritate his nose and cause the tell-tale pinching at his eyes. Thoughts of Lucas Jackson and his replacement were pushed to the back of his mind. It was always bleach that did it - any kind of bleach instantly took him back to that day.

The day of *the incident.*

He could remember scraping frantically at his face, trying to tear off the burning skin. But all he seemed to do was transfer the corrosive liquid to his fingers.

He didn't know how long he'd lain there, writhing on the floor of the deserted chemistry lab. It had felt like hours, days even. Each passing second stretched like a never-ending mirage of time. All the while, he'd felt his skin melting, and there was nothing he could do to stop it. He'd tried scrambling to his feet, but his legs wouldn't obey him; they merely trembled and collapsed beneath him at every attempt.

After managing to crawl into a kneeling position, he was suddenly met by a wall of cold water, a tidal wave knocking him back to the floor. The first wave was followed quickly by another. And then another. Wave after wave of water thudded against him, finding its way up into his nostrils and making him choke.

"Keep still, Daniel." A muffled voice rose above the sound of the crashing water. "Lie down and keep still. Help is on the way."

The water had kept on coming, as if someone had opened a tap above his head. He'd felt like he was drowning, water choking his throat and soaking into his clothes. But it was better than burning. Prising open one eye, he saw an anxious face staring down at him. He opened his mouth to speak, but found it filled with water as another wave engulfed him.

"Keep still," the voice repeated, the tone calm and reassuring. "We've got you now."

Hydrochloric acid had been what they'd used on him.

Instinctively, he raised a hand to his face. It wasn't until he was in the ambulance on his way to hospital that he'd learned that it was his science teacher, Mr Buchanan, and a passing lab assistant who'd come to his rescue – they'd both seen a group of boys thundering out of the classroom, quickly followed by the sound of screaming.

Quick thinking on their part, drenching him with buckets full of water until the ambulance crew arrived, had saved him from worse disfigurement. All in all, he'd gotten off lightly; the damage could have been far worse. That was what everyone kept telling him – the hospital staff; the surgeons; the psychologists. They all said the same thing, in the same condescending voices.

'It could have been worse.'

Irritation ripped through him as he threw the bucket to the floor. His scars may not be so visible now – some said that you had to be up close to see them – but inside they still ran deep. Those were the scars nobody saw, and nobody cared about. But they were the scars he remembered each and every day.

\* \* \*

# Chapter Fourteen

*Thursday 1ˢᵗ November 2018*
  8.35am

The incident room was starting to fill with bodies; the warmth generated from them and their various mugs of tea and coffee compensating for the lacklustre performance from the antiquated radiators. Despite her own mug of coffee nestled in her hands, her third of the morning, Nicki still felt ice-cold.

Caspar Ambrose.

Just those two simple words served to send a creeping chill down her spine.

She'd spent the last half an hour in the DCI's office reading and then re-reading the newspaper report on Deano's disappearance. Seeing his picture there in black and white had rocked her to the core. And seeing it displayed next to the child killer, Alan Woods, chilled her to the bone.

Alan Woods.

That name had kept her awake at night for many years after Deano's disappearance. The speculation in the press had all but added him to Woods' list of victims. But the child killer had always denied it. So the nightmare had continued – with the name Alan Woods at the very epicentre. Just seeing his picture again made her feel sick to the stomach.

It was something that hadn't gone unnoticed by DCI Turner.

"Step away from the case, Nicki," he'd said, folding up the newspaper and placing it out of sight. "You're too emotionally involved."

The DCI's words still echoed inside her head. She either needed to step away from the case or tell the team about Deano. One or the other. But Nicki had refused to back down. This was her case and Lucas Jackson needed her. She would tell the team when she was good and ready.

And she had also, again, chosen not to tell the DCI about Caspar Ambrose – a decision which she knew she may live to regret. As she turned her focus towards the whiteboard, Nicki pushed all thoughts of the private investigator out of her mind.

For now, Lucas Jackson needed her fullest attention.

"It is now thirty-six hours since Lucas Jackson disappeared. A thorough search of the Abbey Gardens hasn't thrown up much of any significance. Accidentally falling into the river has been discounted as unlikely, due to the height of the railings that surround it. We have divers on stand-by but I don't think we seriously believe poor Lucas to have entered the water." Nicki took a breath, noting that each pair of eyes from her team were fully trained on her.

She cleared her throat and resumed. "Roy, I'd like you to focus on the Jackson family today." She held the young DS's gaze in hers for a moment. "See if there are any other family members out there that we're unaware of. And see if there are any links, no matter how small, to the cases of Ivy and Oliver."

Roy gave a nod.

"Now, for the rest of you – firstly, Darcie – go back over the investigation files for Ivy and Oliver. Just in case we're missing something obvious. Revisit all witness statements, see what jumps out. Liaise with Roy about any links to the Jacksons."

Darcie nodded. "Will do, boss."

Nicki turned towards the row of whiteboards behind her. On the third whiteboard, a large map of Bury St Edmunds had been pinned and Nicki pointed to the section edged in red.

"Here we have a map of the Abbey Gardens and surrounding area. There are a number of entrances and exits, in and out, and we need to focus on which one we feel most likely the perpetrator used. I'm heading back there later this morning, on my way to see Sophia. Matt and Duncan? Anything on the CCTV?"

Duncan Jenkins shook his head. "Nothing useful yet, boss. We're just finishing up with the footage from the Gardens. We'll widen the search to the roads leading away from the exits now."

Nicki nodded her approval. "Take a look in the days before the abduction, too. Our man must have visited the scene beforehand. Lucas's abduction went far too smoothly for it to have been an opportunistic crime. Whoever he is, he planned this. The PPU got back to me about sex offenders living in the area – there are two potential leads being followed up as we speak. But I expect both to be a dead end, as both offenders currently wear electronic tags." Nicki paused and picked up her coffee mug, its contents now stone-cold. As she did so, Darcie raised her hand.

"Boss? There've been two more reports of burglaries overnight – looks like a similar MO to the others. You want me and Roy to follow these up, too?"

Nicki took a sip of the cold coffee and shook her head. "No, you've both got enough to do with the Jackson case, and that has to take priority today." She peered over the rim of her mug, her gaze landing on a familiar figure lurking at the back of the room by the hot water urn. "Graham? Can you please pick up the burglaries? And revisit the ones we already have on file?"

DS Graham Fox looked up, his face instantly darkening. "Really? Domestic burglary? Can't you get someone else to do it?" As if his tone wasn't enough to voice his displeasure, the scowl that accompanied it made it abundantly clear. "It's more suited to a DC, surely?"

Nicki felt a sharp stab of irritation begin to swell, and took another unwanted sip of cool coffee to retain her composure.

"I appreciate you may think domestic burglary is beneath you, DS Fox, but that is what I wish you to focus on." Nicki's tone was even and controlled, but the steely look in her eyes wasn't lost on anyone. "Burglaries are no less distressing for the people involved than other crimes, and are worthy of the same attention from this team."

"But…" DS Fox wasn't giving up without a fight and the scowl remained.

"But nothing." Nicki's cheeks began to colour "You will investigate these burglaries as instructed." She gave the DS a thunderous look before breaking her gaze, the exchange of words clearly at an end. "Any questions from anyone else?"

Nicki saw a range of heads being shaken, and the occasional murmured 'no boss' before the briefing broke up and members of her team began to go about their day. DS Fox thundered towards the door, shouldering DC Holland and DC Jenkins out of the way as he passed, and left the incident room, muttering under his breath.

"He still giving you issues, boss?" Darcie hovered by her chair as the incident room door slammed shut.

Nicki gave a wizened smile. "Nothing I can't handle. Although I could do without him throwing his toys out the pram whenever I ask him to do something." Despite having a list of things to do a mile long, she couldn't get DS Fox's reaction out of her mind. "I wouldn't mind so much, but that idiot is actually a half-decent detective when he puts his mind to it. He did some great work on that people trafficking case I had a while back. I don't know why he has such an issue with me sometimes."

That wasn't quite correct. Nicki had a fairly good idea what was going on with DS Graham Fox, but it wasn't something she felt that she should share with her team. It all stemmed from her first case as the newly promoted DI at the station – which was something DS Fox seemed to have taken umbrage at. Which was a shame – they'd worked together as sergeants and got along, as far as Nicki was aware, really well. At one time she would have classed him as a friend.

But all that changed in a heartbeat and he'd seemed to be baying for her blood ever since. Sullen and uncooperative a lot of the time, Nicki had had reason to pull him up on more than a few occasions for his conduct. Which only seemed to make the situation worse and the huge chasm between them widened even further.

It was a shame. She genuinely liked the guy – when he wasn't acting like a prick. Which was more often than not these days.

"He's an idiot, boss. Don't let him get to you." Darcie held her hand out for Nicki's half-drunk coffee mug. "Fresh one?"

Nicki shook her head. She already had enough caffeine buzzing around her system for one morning. "Not yet, Darcie, I need to head out soon. Thanks anyway."

Ridding herself of thoughts of DS Fox, Nicki gathered up her jacket and made for the door. Just as she was reaching for the handle, the door opened and the head of a passing PC entered.

"Detective Inspector Hardcastle?" The PC edged further into the doorway, brandishing a folded note in his hand.

Nicki nodded and eyed the piece of paper, warily. "Yes?"

"Message for you, from the front desk." The PC handed her the note and retreated back into the corridor and out of sight.

Nicki plastered a smile onto her face for the benefit of the departing PC, but her stomach gave an unwanted churn. She flipped over the folded note but already felt she knew what it would say. Or, at least, who it would be from.

The familiar tightening in her stomach returned as she stepped out into the corridor and dropped her gaze to the message.

'Please return my call. We need to meet 07700 900548'

Caspar Ambrose.

Underneath was a message from the person who had taken the phone call. '*This man has rung five times this morning!*

Nicki's stomach sank further.

He wasn't giving up.

* * *

*Thursday 1st November 2018*

10.00am

Sophia knew that DC Gallagher was only trying to help, but she just wanted to be left alone. She didn't need a newspaper to know what people were saying about her. *She hadn't kept her eye on Lucas. She hadn't watched him closely enough. How could she have been so silly?*

Those were the kinder end of the comments. The rest spiralled into accusations of neglect and even abuse. There were calls from some anonymous social media posts to have her other child taken away from her; she'd demonstrated such a lack of judgment; how could she be trusted with another child's welfare?

The posts continued unabated. As soon as one was reported and removed, another sprang up in its place.

Sophia had got to the point of just switching her phone off.

But her main focus turned to Amelia. What was she reading about her own mother online? Her own family. Her own brother.

Amelia had yet to come out of her room, and Sophia knew she should be up there right now, comforting her and telling her everything would be all right.

But here she was letting DC Gallagher take the strain. She was being more of a mother to Amelia than Sophia was right now, as hurtful as that sounded. And according to the online trolls, maybe that was for the best.

And it wasn't just about Lucas.

Her employers were still being tagged in other posts - much to Sophia's embarrassment. Some of the things being said about her were vile – no wonder her boss wanted a word with her. But he would have to wait.

Right now, Sophia Jackson was in no fit state to talk to anybody.

She knew the police were coming later, DC Gallagher had told her that over a pot of tea earlier this morning. She doubted it would be good news. She could just tell by the look on the family liaison officer's face that it wasn't. They were no nearer finding Lucas than they were yesterday.

With fresh tears starting to spout from the corners of her eyes, Sophia slipped her phone down the side of the armchair, out of sight.

\* \* \*

*Thursday 1st November 2018*
  *10.30am*

Leaving the team to get on with their actions for the day, Nicki had retired to the sanctity of her office. She needed a few minutes' peace before heading over to the Abbey Gardens. Ignoring the mounting paperwork spilling across the desk, she pulled the private investigator's business card out of her pocket and ran a finger along the edge. The sickening feeling in her stomach intensified. She knew she needed to focus on the investigation, but Caspar Ambrose was becoming a distraction.

Taking a deep breath, she reached for her desk phone - this was a call that couldn't wait.

Dialling the number from memory, she found it was answered almost immediately.

"Nicki Hardcastle, as I live and breathe! How the devil are you?"

Nicki couldn't help but allow a small smile to tease her lips. "Jeremy. It's been a while." She pulled the desk phone across several piles of paper and sat down. "How are you?"

"Everything's peachy here." Jeremy Frost, senior reporter with one of the local newspapers, and one of Nicki's closest friends, sounded genuinely pleased to hear from her. "And even more so for hearing your wonderful voice this morning."

"Stop it," chastised Nicki, the smile growing. "I need a favour."

"A favour?" A hint of intrigue entered the reporter's tone. Nicki imagined at least one eyebrow being raised. "Shoot."

Nicki hesitated, taking a deep breath to steady her nerves. She knew DCI Turner would probably disapprove of her reaching out to a member of the press, but right now she felt she had little alternative. There was no one else she could turn to. And Jeremy could be discreet when he wanted to be – for a reporter anyhow. Nicki just hoped this would be one of those moments.

"At the press release yesterday, outside the station, did you see a guy wearing a raincoat and a trilby hat?" There. She'd said it. Possibly opening up a huge can of worms and disturbing the hornet's nest all in one go. She'd seen Jeremy in the sparse crowd that had assembled yesterday. She just didn't know if he'd seen what she did. Or *who*.

The silence on the other end of the line did nothing to dampen her nerves.

She bit her bottom lip as the seconds ticked by. Eventually, Jeremy spoke.

"As it happens, I did. Guy that looked like Philip Marlowe?"

Nicki's stomach flipped. "Do you know who he is?" She eyed the business card once more, and could almost hear Jeremy shaking his head in response to her question.

"No, sorry. Never seen him before. Is he local or an outsider?"

"That was something I was hoping you could tell me." Nicki sighed and slumped back in her chair. "You're sure you've never seen him before?"

"No, never," repeated Jeremy, taking what sounded like a slurp of tea or coffee in the background. Knowing Jeremy like she did, something stronger wasn't out of the question even at this time of the morning. "I'd remember someone like that. Want me to ask around?"

"Would you? There is one thing though."

"Oh?"

"He might not be a reporter."

"I see – and what makes you say that?"

Nicki hesitated, unsure how much she should divulge. She trusted Jeremy, no doubt about that. But she just wasn't sure she wanted to tell him everything just yet. "Just a hunch."

Jeremy paused again before replying. "OK, well I'll do some digging on your hunch. But it'll cost you."

Nicki raised an eyebrow. "How much?"

"You still owe me that dinner, remember? A table for two tonight is my price."

Nicki felt her smile returning. Jeremy was good company, so she could suffer an evening out if he was going to help her.

"All right, call me later." Nicki replaced the phone receiver and slid the business card back inside her pocket. With a sigh, she pushed herself back up from her chair and grabbed her coat.

* * *

*Thursday 1ˢᵗ November 2018*

11.20am

Duncan Jenkins tilted the computer monitor away from the harsh strip lighting overhead and frowned. He and Matt had trawled through what seemed like thousands of images from the CCTV cameras serving the Abbey Gardens and, apart from the initial sighting of Sophia and her family entering under the Abbey Gate, they had found precious little.

Until now.

"Here, Matt. Take a look at this." He nodded towards the screen and pulled his chair to the side, allowing room for his colleague to scoot his own chair over.

Matt Holland nudged his glasses up onto the bridge of his nose and peered at the monitor. Duncan had paused the screen on a still black and white image, taken close to the exit leading out onto Mustow Road. The quality wasn't great, the people captured in the frame appearing blurred and fuzzy around the edges, but there was no mistaking one of the figures in the very centre.

"That's the lad, right?" Duncan leant forwards and tapped the screen with his finger.

The image was of a young boy walking towards the exit, his back towards the camera. His head was turned at an angle, looking up at the figure by his side.

It was unmistakably Lucas Jackson – complete with his Batman cape and minus his red wellington boots.

"Can we enlarge it?" Matt looked on while Duncan worked on making the image fill the screen. Lucas was walking by the side of a man dressed in dark clothing. The man's back was also to the camera, showing no aspect of his face at all. He was merely a figure, dressed in black – with an arm stretched out towards Lucas at his side. Chillingly, as the image slowly enlarged, it was clear that little Lucas Jackson was holding the man's hand – a look of joy on his face, his mouth open mid-laugh.

Whoever had taken Lucas out of the Abbey Gardens, he'd done so willingly. The boy looked happy.

Duncan pulled up his emails. "I'll get this sent over to the boss."

* * *

*Thursday 1ˢᵗ November 2018*
11.30am

Nicki slipped her phone into her pocket and stood in the centre of the Abbey Gardens, giving it a 360-degree sweep. It looked so peaceful; the well-tended flower beds bursting with late Autumn colour, and squirrels foraging for food amongst the piles of fallen leaves. It seemed incomprehensible that something so tragic could have taken place just thirty-six hours ago.

The main entrance under the Abbey Gate was where Sophia Jackson and her family had been seen to enter the Gardens. And now, according to DC Duncan Jenkins, a young boy in a Batman costume was seen heading in the direction of the exit that led out onto Mustow Road at approximately 7.37pm, being led by the hand by an unknown man. Nicki shivered as she turned to face the direction of Lucas's last known steps. She'd asked Duncan to forward her the still CCTV image.

Had they left that way? Apparently, the camera hadn't picked them up actually leaving via that exit, but they were certainly heading that way. Nicki let her eyes sweep once again in a full circle. The exit via Abbey Gate was behind her – they could easily have turned around and left that way, slipping out unnoticed. In front of her was the exit via the footbridge over the River Lark – it may have been the closest exit to the inflatable slide, but Nicki dismissed it as an unlikely choice. The abductor would have to have had a vehicle parked somewhere close by, and this exit gave less opportunity for that.

Similarly, Nicki discounted the other exit that went via the rear of the neighbouring Cathedral. It would have involved walking a greater distance with the greater potential of being seen, and drawing attention to themselves.

Her gut told her Lucas was taken through the exit onto Mustow Road, or through the main entrance behind her. Both would have plenty of places where a vehicle could be parked close by. She'd left Holland and Jenkins the task of trawling back through CCTV of all roads surrounding both exits.

Turning back along the central path that would lead her back under the Abbey Gate, to where she'd parked her car outside the Angel Hotel, Nicki noticed how life in the Gardens was returning to some degree of normality. The inflatable slide was still in situ, still encircled by blue and white police tape, but the rest of the Gardens was being opened back up to the public.

However, it looked to Nicki as though the crowds were staying away; whether due to the freezing temperatures or maybe out of some form of quiet respect for the Jackson family. Whichever it was, today the Gardens were deserted.

Nicki buried her chin in her scarf and strode towards her car, feeling the phone in her pocket vibrate with an incoming message. Pulling it out, she saw it was from Duncan. With her heart in her mouth, she opened the email whilst unlocking the driver's door.

The image stilled her heart. The last known picture of little Lucas Jackson.

Nicki knew she now had to go and see Sophia – but it wasn't a visit she was looking forward to.

* * *

# Chapter Fifteen

*Thursday 1ˢᵗ November 2018*

  12.30pm

The house looked exactly the same as before. The curtains were still drawn, and as Nicki stepped inside the hallway, she noted the unopened post still on the doormat. Bending down to pick it up, she smiled at DC Tina Gallagher as the family liaison officer closed the front door behind her. Motioning for Nicki to follow, DC Gallagher led her into the front room.

Sophia was sitting in the same armchair, with the same empty look on her face.

"Mrs Jackson?" Nicki seated herself at one end of the two-seater sofa and reached across for Sophia's hand. It felt ice cold to the touch. Giving the hand a gentle squeeze, Nicki noticed only the briefest flicker of acknowledgement cross the woman's face.

About to ask how she was, Nicki bit back her words. Instead, she said, "is there anyone we can call to come and sit with you?"

Nicki had again noticed how Sophia Jackson was alone in her grief. No friends or family were visible; no one rallying around in her time of need. A brief shake of the head gave Nicki her answer.

DC Gallagher slipped into the other vacant armchair; there was no point offering to make a further round of tea – nobody would drink it.

"How is Amelia bearing up?" Nicki's question was as much directed to DC Gallagher as it was to Sophia Jackson.

"She's struggling, understandably," replied the family liaison officer. "Spends most of her time in her room." DC Gallagher gave a sad smile. "She still blames herself."

Nicki nodded. She knew just how the young girl would be feeling.

"Is there anything else you wish to tell me, Sophia? Or anything you wish to ask?" Nicki noted the folded up copy of the Daily Mail on the coffee table, with another headline about Lucas. There was no way of telling if Sophia had read it.

Sophia gave another shake of the head, continuing to stare towards curtains drawn across the bay window in front of them.

Nicki paused before bringing her phone out of her pocket. "I have a picture that I need to show you, but you may find it distressing. Are you sure I can't contact anyone to sit with you?"

Nicki detected a slight tensing of Sophia's jawline, but all she got in response was another brief shake of the head. Rising from the sofa, Nicki went to the grief-stricken woman's side and knelt down.

"We've found an image of Lucas on CCTV." Nicki turned the phone screen to face Sophia. "It was taken at 7.37pm and he can clearly be seen in the company of a man." Nicki watched as Sophia Jackson's head turned slightly towards the image. "The man can only be seen from the back, and the image isn't of great quality, but is it anyone that you recognise?"

Sophia's face remained stony. Her blotchy skin and glassy eyes told Nicki that the woman had cried herself dry. Several seconds ticked by before Sophia shook her head once again, and this time she spoke.

"He looks happy," she croaked, her voice sounding so brittle it might break. "Lucas. He's smiling."

Nicki's heart squeezed painfully inside her chest. "The man, Sophia. Do you recognise him?"

Sophia Jackson's shoulder heaved and her whole body shuddered. Another shake of the head. "No. I don't recognise him."

Nicki slipped the phone back in her pocket and glanced back towards DC Gallagher. She immediately saw a tell-tale look she recognised on her colleague's face. Straightening up, she touched Sophia on the shoulder.

"We're just going to go and make a fresh pot of tea. We won't be long."

Once in the sanctity of the kitchen and out of earshot, DC Gallagher turned towards Nicki, her own phone in her hand. "Sophia's been having some unwanted attention on social media. I've taken some screen shots."

Nicki took the phone from DC Gallagher and scrolled through the images. "How long has this been going on?"

"Those are the most recent ones. Online trolls mostly – blaming Sophia for Lucas's disappearance. Calling her an unfit mother, that kind of thing."

Nicki nodded. Unfortunately, social media made it all too easy for hurtful words to be splashed in front of millions; and those responsible safely hidden behind their anonymity. "I see. Has she said much about it?"

DC Gallagher shook her head. "No. It was Amelia who brought it to my attention. I think it's affecting her more. Sophia seems.... how can I put it?" The family liaison officer paused, her brow creasing. "Indifferent?"

"She really needs someone to be here with her. She's suffering all on her own."

DC Gallagher nodded. "And that's not all, I'm afraid. Those posts were just the tip of the iceberg." The family liaison officer again tapped her phone screen and handed it back to Nicki. "These go back further – before Lucas went missing." Nicki lowered her eyes to the screen.

The posts DC Gallagher had captured were full of hate; the words and imagery truly shocking. And each post had been shared hundreds, and in some cases thousands of times.

"Doesn't this kind of thing get blocked now?"

"If it does, a new account just springs up and it starts all over again." DC Gallagher peered over Nicki's shoulder. "You'll see in a lot of them, her employers have been added in."

Nicki handed the phone back and started towards the kitchen door. "Can you send me everything you've got? We'll have to dig into it."

Returning to the front room, Nicki saw that Sophia Jackson hadn't moved an inch. Nicki wasted no time and again knelt down by her side.

"Sophia? Why didn't you say you'd been attacked on social media? Some of those messages are vile. And the ones directed at your employers – they go back weeks." Nicki again gave Sophia's ice-cold hand a squeeze. "You should've said something - it could be important."

For the first time since her arrival, Sophia Jackson turned and looked at Nicki with empty eyes. She looked completely defeated and merely shrugged.

"Why? Those things were online way before Lucas..." The word 'disappeared' caught in her throat. A single tear squeezed its way out of her red-rimmed eyes and tracked down her cheek. "It's not connected."

"You don't know that, Sophia." Nicki got to her feet and flashed a look of thanks towards DC Gallagher. "We need to investigate the origins of these posts. And if they continue, you must tell Tina."

Nicki bid Sophia Jackson goodbye, noticing how the broken woman merely switched her gaze back to staring vacantly at the shrouded window.

* * *

*Thursday 1st November 2018*
   12.45pm


DS Graham Fox declined the offer of tea. "You think they gained access via the back door?" He nodded towards the door at the rear of the kitchen, currently being processed for fingerprints by a crime scene investigator.

David Marshall gave an affirmative nod. "Yes. I don't know why, but we'd left it unlocked last night. We never normally do that – we're quite fastidious with security but...we'd had some bad news yesterday and our heads were all over the place."

"I understand." DS Fox glanced around the rest of the kitchen. "And nothing of value was taken?"

A shake of the head, this time from David's wife, Anna "Not that I can see. Just a small amount of spare cash from my purse. It just makes me shudder that someone was in here - while we were sleeping."

DS Fox made another note in his notebook. The circumstances were alarmingly similar to the house he'd left just half an hour ago. The MO was identical. An unsecured back door. Small amount of cash taken. And nobody heard a thing.

"To be honest, I wasn't sure we'd been broken into to begin with. It all seemed so odd." Anna Marshall gave another shudder, her narrow shoulders heaving. "But then I saw the back door was ajar, so..." She broke off and covered her mouth with her hand. "And then we saw things had been moved in Jake's room."

"And is Jake your youngest?"

Both Mr and Mrs Marshall nodded.

"And just moved, nothing taken?" DS Fox flicked back a few pages in his notebook.

More nods. "Yes," replied Mrs Marshall. "Just moved. It was...creepy."

DS Fox snapped his notebook shut. "And what exactly was moved?"

It was David Marshall who spoke this time. "Our youngest is a big Thomas the Tank Engine fan. He always lines up his books on the bookshelf in a specific order before he goes to sleep. When he woke, they'd been moved."

DS Fox slipped his notebook into his back pocket. "And you think whoever came into your property last night moved them?"

Anna Marshall shrugged. "I...I can't explain it otherwise."

"Your son didn't just put them in a different order maybe? And forgot he did so?"

Mrs Marshall shook her head vehemently. "No. He's very particular like that. He wouldn't. He just wouldn't. He was very distressed this morning when he saw it."

DS Fox took several steps towards the door leading to the hallway. "May I take a look upstairs?"

Following David Marshall up the narrow staircase, DS Fox noticed how several of the stairs creaked loudly underfoot as they went. Jake's room was at the end of a short landing and the door was already open. The crime scene investigators had finished processing the small bedroom and it now lay empty.

"And where is your son now?"

"We sent them both next door to sit with our neighbour while..." Mrs Marshall had followed them up to Jake's bedroom. DS Fox turned to see fresh tears springing up in the corner of her eyes. She continued to wring a cotton handkerchief in her hands.

DS Fox nodded and gave what he hoped was a reassuring smile. "I understand. It's an upsetting thing to happen. You must be in shock."

Stepping into the small box-like bedroom, DS Fox noted a single bed pushed against the far wall and a slim single wardrobe by its side. There wasn't room for much else. At the end of the bed was a series of wooden bookshelves, brimming with toys and books.

"And which items had been moved?" DS Fox edged further into the confined space, allowing both Mr and Mrs Marshall to follow. As he did so, his eyes took in the matching Thomas the Tank Engine duvet set and curtains.

Anna Marshall pointed to the middle shelf at the bottom of the bed. "There. His Thomas books. He always lines them up in numerical order – he's obsessed with numbers. But this morning..." Her voice tailed off as DS Fox followed her gaze.

It was true. The books were now in a random order – not organised from one to twenty as they apparently should be. A fine covering of fingerprint dust remained on the shelving and DS Fox pulled out his notebook to make another entry. He would get the books bagged up and taken into evidence. It was a long shot, but...

DS Fox cast his gaze around the small bedroom. "Is your son a deep sleeper? He wouldn't have woken up if someone came into his room?"

Mrs Marshall shook her head. "He's out for the count. Nothing wakes him once he's asleep. I often have to shake him awake in the mornings."

DS Fox detected another shudder from the slightly-built woman's shoulders and immediately thought of his own children. The idea of someone being in your house, in your children's bedroom.... he quickly pushed the thoughts from his mind and edged back towards the door.

"He's nothing like me," Mrs Marshall added, following DS Fox and her husband out onto the narrow landing. "I'm such a light sleeper. I stir at every noise."

"And you didn't hear anything yourself?" enquired DS Fox.

"No, sorry."

As DS Fox headed along the landing back towards the stairs, he noted another door to the left and nudged it open with his foot.

"Sorry about the mess." David Marshall appeared at DS Fox's side. "We're having some work done – converting the loft space. Needed some decorating done." He nodded up at the small loft hatch in the ceiling.

DS Fox quickly scanned the room – noting how it was littered with workmen's tools. The room smelt of plaster, paint and sawdust.

Leaving the room behind, DS Fox popped his head in two more bedrooms – one belonging to the eldest son and one belonging to Mr and Mrs Marshall, as well as the family bathroom, but found nothing else of note. Arriving at the bottom of the stairs, DS Fox hesitated at the front door.

"The incident will be logged back at the station and we'll keep you informed as to any progress. You made initial statements this morning to the officers that attended?"

Both Mr and Mrs Marshall nodded.

"In that case, I'll leave you in peace. The crime scene investigators should be finishing up soon. I'll get them to bag up your son's books, the ones he thinks have been moved. So please don't touch them." He turned towards the door, his hand hovering over the handle. "But I do have to warn you..."

"I know, I know." David Marshall nodded and sighed, a rueful smile on his lips. "Domestic burglaries. You'll probably never catch them."

DS Fox gave an apologetic smile. "We'll see what comes of the forensics. But yes, you may not get the outcome you hope for."

DS Fox had a quick word with one of the crime scene investigators about bagging up Jake's books, before returning to his car. Sitting behind the wheel, he pulled out his notebook and pondered both the scene here with the Marshalls and the house he'd visited not half an hour before. The similarities were so striking it had to be the same perpetrator. After making another couple of notes at the bottom of the page, he thrust the key into the ignition and set off in the direction of the station.

\* \* \*

# Chapter Sixteen

*Thursday 1ˢᵗ November 2018*

  3.00pm

The idea of replacing the boy wouldn't leave him. Another one – or even two. He couldn't help the smile breaking out on his lips the more he thought about it. Even a second session in the padlocked room with Dad's old belt hadn't helped him to change his mind. Lucas Jackson needed to go.

He fleetingly wondered whether it was too soon. He'd had Lucas for only a matter of days and he was already getting bored with him. Was it too soon to go hunting again? Could he really replace him so quickly?

He'd taken Ivy and Oliver quite close together, almost two months apart, but this would only be a matter of days. Doubt fogged his mind, but all he could do was turn his thoughts back to his stepfather – which gave him all the reassurance he needed.

Hadn't Dad taken Sean quite soon after Jacob? It might not have been days in-between, but he was sure Sean had arrived at 5 Arlington Crescent not that long after Jacob had left.

The thought buoyed him. He remembered the day Sean Warren came to stay.

\* \* \*

5 Arlington Crescent

*Saturday 11<sup>th</sup> January 2003*

He'd watched as mum picked up her shopping basket and slipped her purse into her handbag. She looked nice. Her hair was styled into a neat bob, and she'd applied several strokes of blusher to her pale cheeks. She hid her eyes with a pair of dark glasses.

The freshly laundered and pressed pinafore dress hung from her tiny frame, a head scarf wrapped around her head. To him, his mother looked like a film star.

Dad had looked impressed too – he had that gleam in his eye again, and an odd-looking smile plastered on his unshaven face. He'd continued to watch as his father knelt down and unlocked the clasp around his mother's ankle, letting the chain fall to the floor with a clank.

Straightening up, Dad had pulled a stopwatch from his pocket and held it up in the air. "Off you go! Don't be late, I'm watching."

Mum had hesitated in the doorway, like a newborn bird hovering at the edge of the nest about to take that first leap to freedom. Except freedom would be short-lived for Mum that day. Thirty-seven minutes precisely. Dad had already timed exactly how long it took to walk to the corner shop and back again. Not a second more was allowed. She knew from bitter experience that timing was important.

Mum had soon scuttled away, pulling the door shut behind her.

He remembered looking up into his stepfather's expectant face, noting the gleam from earlier had intensified. Slipping the stopwatch back inside his pocket, Dad had gestured for him to follow.

"Come with me, son." His thick, gravelly voice echoed around the empty kitchen. "Your mother will be back soon. I have something to show you while she's gone."

As they climbed the rear staircase, he thought back to when Jacob had been with them. It had only been for a short time; he was sure. The boy had disappeared from the back bedroom almost as quickly as he'd appeared.

He didn't feel that he could ask his stepfather what had happened to Jacob. But he could read. He was a bright boy and had a reading age far beyond his years and he'd seen the newspaper headlines, immediately recognising the boy's picture beneath. According to the report, Jacob had been found naked and buried in a shallow grave on the edge of a forest. Subsequent newspaper articles mentioned injuries that his young brain found difficult to comprehend.

After Jacob had gone, his stepfather had seemed to relax and show him a long-overdue kindness that warmed his heart. What they'd shared together in the back bedroom had brought them closer; seeded a sense of trust between them, a secret that belonged to them and them alone.

As far as he was aware, his mother didn't know anything about Jacob - he'd been under strict instructions not to say anything. His stepfather had been very clear on that score. This was their secret, man and boy. *She wouldn't understand, son.*

So he'd kept quiet and enjoyed the new-found closeness with his stepfather. Even when he came home minus his school blazer and fresh cuts to his knees, his stepfather just smiled. The same smile that had lit up his face when he'd taken his belt off in front of the boy.

And here they were again, only weeks later, standing once more at the back bedroom door. The stopwatch was gently ticking away, the faint tick-tick could be heard through the heavy fabric of his stepfather's trousers.

He'd held his breath, feeling both excited and nervous at the same time – the heady mixture causing his heart to quicken. Clenching and unclenching his fists, he'd nervously jogged from foot to foot. His father caught his eye and gave a throaty chuckle.

*"That's my boy."*

The hinges on the door had recently been oiled, so they gave no sound when his father pushed it open. He watched as his father stepped forwards and disappeared from sight. Still hovering at the top step of the rear staircase, he'd felt his mouth twitch and his tongue turn dry. He wanted to see, but he also didn't want to see. It was an unnerving paradox for an eleven-year-old boy to be faced with.

Curiosity finally got the better of him and he pushed his quivering legs forwards to enter the back bedroom once again. The scene before him looked identical to the one before. The boy sat strapped to the same wooden chair in the centre of the room, stripped to his underwear, a gag wrapped tightly across his mouth that no doubt silenced his screams.

A pair of mournful, dark brown eyes peered out from pale and blotchy face – he could see the boy's tears had cascaded down his cheeks and already soaked the grubby rag that served as the gag. Once again, the boy's clothes were neatly folded up on the bed.

Dad had stood behind the chair, his hands placed lightly on the boy's shoulders. Curiously, the boy seemed to flinch under his stepfather's loving touch. Anger began to build within him from a place unseen and somewhat foreign to him. Anger at the boy's apparent fear and revulsion at his father's presence.

His father was the kindest, most loving person he'd ever known – and he felt enraged by the boy's reaction. He took a step closer.

"And here he is." Alan Woods tapped the shaking boy once more on the shoulders. "This is my son, Daniel. He'll be here, looking after you, just as I will. Say hello, Daniel."

Silently, he took another few steps forward until he was standing directly in front of the terrified boy. He crouched down so that his breath could be felt on the skin of the quaking boy's knees. For a moment or two, he merely stared up into the boy's frightened eyes, noting how similar he looked to Jacob - maybe a year or two older, no more - with the same pale skin, the same melancholy look, and the same rapid breathing.

He lowered his gaze and watched as the boy's narrow chest heaved in rapid succession, the sound of his breaths rasping through the fabric of the gag. Saliva was dribbling from either side of his mouth.

Without quite understanding what he was doing, or why, he reached out and touched the boy's knee. He felt the boy flinch and recoil under his touch, as if hit by a bolt of electricity.

He returned his gaze once again to the boy's dark brown eyes, noting an element of horror mixed in with their sadness. An exquisite trickle of excitement started to build within him. Touching the boy's knee once more, he again felt the boy recoil and try to tuck his legs out of reach beneath the wooden chair.

After a third touch, he straightened up and locked eyes with his father. A knowing look passed between them that required no explanation. He at last understood what it was that his father was doing here; that feeling of being in complete and utter control of another human being. He felt himself shiver. The feeling was like no other; an overpowering emotion that intoxicated the soul.

He hadn't touched Jacob. He'd only watched from the sanctity of a corner of the back bedroom. But now – a small smile crept onto his face, soon turning into a grin. The expression was matched by his father.

The tense silence of the back bedroom was broken by the chiming coming from the stopwatch in his father's pocket.

Mum would be at the shops now.

With a final squeeze of the boy's shoulders, his stepfather stepped around the wooden chair and gestured for his son to follow him out onto the landing. Once Mum was back home safe and sound, secured to the kitchen table, then they would return.

The boy merely whimpered as the door was pulled shut.

*His* nightmare was only just beginning.

* * *

*Thursday 1ˢᵗ November 2018*
3.45pm

Sean had stayed with them for longer; longer than Jacob had, he was sure. Maybe he'd been Dad's favourite – Dad did seem quite sad when it had been time for him to go. And there'd been far more visits to the back bedroom to see Sean than there ever were with Jacob. Sometimes, Dad even let him go up on his own.

He remembered the first time he'd entered the back bedroom alone, and Sean Warren had looked up at him. The look in the boy's eyes remained with him to this day, as did the thrill that followed.

In many ways, Sean and Oliver were very similar. They had the same chocolate brown eyes and the same initial fighting spirit. Spirit that was very quickly knocked out of them, courtesy of Dad's belt, but spirit all the same.

He'd enjoyed taking Oliver, but it had probably been his most risky attempt. The open air cinema had been far less crowded than he'd expected, and he'd worried that he'd be too conspicuous. But his worries had all melted away once he'd locked eyes with the little boy in the Spiderman t-shirt. Although he was sure he'd seen a little girl watching him, he knew his plan would work. And in the end, Oliver Chambers had come along quite happily.

* * *

*Wednesday 30<sup>th</sup> May 2018*

Oliver held onto his brother's hand as they picked their way through the scattered picnic blankets littering the field where the open-air cinema was in full swing. The evening was still warm and sultry, a promise of the summer yet to come, so he'd kept his shorts and favourite Spiderman t-shirt on. The Jungle Book had been good but he'd seen it countless times before. He didn't mind singing some of the songs and big Baloo was his favourite, but his legs were getting stiff from sitting in the same position on the picnic blanket for so long.

Mum had told them they could go and have a look around the stalls, maybe buy some sweets, so long as they weren't long. The next film started in twenty minutes but Oliver wasn't really sure if he wanted to see it – it was Snow White, and Snow White was for girls.

Heading out of the gate, towards the rows of stalls selling all manner of local produce, Oliver's nose wrinkled as they walked past a stall selling cheeses. Several more displayed local chutneys and cured meats. Oliver didn't know how anyone could eat anything that smelt so strange. He covered his nose and mouth with his hand and jogged along by the side of his big brother.

He knew where they would be headed. He'd seen the sweet stall on the way in – with tables piled high, full of all manner of multi-coloured confectionery. Everything he could possibly think of was there, and as they got closer the familiar sugar-scented aroma filled his nostrils.

Oliver clutched the coins in his pocket.

"You go and pick your sweets – I'm gonna try the shooting gallery over there!"

George was a lot older than him – fifteen. Oliver didn't quite know how long it would take him to reach fifteen, but he knew it was a long time. Mum always told him he needed to eat his vegetables to get as big as George, but George didn't like vegetables and always left them on his plate. But he was still big. Oliver didn't really understand adults sometimes.

The sweet stalls were busy with children, shrieking as they ran from table to table. Oliver felt uneasy being left on his own. Everyone was bigger than he was; and he'd never be able to push himself towards the front. His bottom lip began to tremble.

"Oh don't start whingeing now," huffed George. "Look. Here's an extra pound to spend. Just give me five minutes over there. You can't come over and watch, coz there's guns – you're too young."

George took Oliver by the arm and led him to the front of the first sweet stall, shouldering some other children out of the way. "See? There's your favourite cherry sweets on the top there. And the fizzy ones." George stepped back and started heading towards the shooting gallery. "Just stay there. Don't move. I'll be five minutes."

George was obsessed with guns. He wanted to join the Army when he left school; he couldn't wait. The teachers couldn't wait for him to leave, either – he could tell. Grinning, he handed over his money and picked up the rifle.

Oliver hovered by the first sweet stall as instructed, clenching his hand so tightly around his money that his hand began to hurt. He didn't like big crowds of people, but he didn't like the banging sounds from the shooting stall George was at either. He placed his free hand over one ear to try and block out the noise.

It was then that he saw a familiar face.

The man was staring down at him, and Oliver couldn't help but smile

"Hey, Spidey!" The man's voice sounded friendly. "How about we use your Spidey senses and choose some sweets?"

\* \* \*

*Thursday 1ˢᵗ November 2018*

   4.00pm

Yes, Oliver had been a good choice - and he'd been sad to let him go in the end. But he couldn't keep him forever – Dad had taught him that. At some point they all had to go. If he could find another one like Oliver, then he'd be happy.

He thought about whether he should take Dad's leather belt to the boy again. He'd spent much of the day with him, but the desire he was expecting to feel had already started to ebb away at the mere thought of the boy's name. He wasn't sure Lucas Jackson was worth the effort anymore.

Not now that he had another plan.

Now he'd made up his mind, the urge to go hunting again was almost overwhelming; it was all he could think about.

Lucas Jackson had knocked his confidence. But everyone was allowed one mistake, weren't they?

This time he needed to be sure he was hunting the right prey, but he already had a pretty good idea who was going to be next – he hadn't been able to stop thinking about them all day.

Yes, he knew exactly where to go. And the timing couldn't be more perfect.

\* \* \*

*Thursday 1ˢᵗ November 2018*

   4.45pm

Nicki leant over Duncan Jenkins' shoulder as he enlarged the CCTV image on his computer screen. It had been chilling enough to see on a phone screen, but now it was brought to life on the monitor it seemed even worse.

"Well, Sophia is adamant that she doesn't recognise him. But I guess we only have the back view..."

"It's the look on the lad's face I can't get out of my head." Duncan nodded towards the screen. "His poor little face. He's actually smiling. Looking up into that man's face and he's *smiling*."

The look on Lucas's face hadn't escaped Nicki's attention either. Just as it hadn't escaped Sophia's.

"Do you think he knows him?" asked Duncan, minimising the screen. Nobody wanted to look at the chilling scene any longer than they had to. "Is that why he's smiling?"

"Sophia's sure she doesn't recognise him, but..." Nicki shrugged. "Look, there's something else I need you to do. Still carry on with the CCTV, see if you can pick this guy up again anywhere else during the course of the evening, and also if any cameras pick them up after they left."

"I'll do that," jumped in Matt, seated at an adjacent desk. "I've already started."

"Good. So, Duncan, could you make a start on pulling Sophia Jackson's phone records and social media accounts? While I was there today, Tina showed me some pretty awful troll posts. Some are about Lucas – and how she's an unfit mother; similar to what's been cropping up in some of the newspapers today. But the ones I'm interested in pre-date Lucas's disappearance. She's had some very spiteful posts about her personally, some tagging in her employers. They're quite distasteful and disturbing. See what you can dig up."

"Sure, boss. You think that might be a lead?"

Nicki hesitated. "To be honest, I don't know. My gut tells me Lucas has been taken by the same person who murdered Ivy and Oliver. The MO is just too similar. But – if there's anyone else out there with a motive to cause Sophia and her family harm, then we need to follow it up." Standing up, she paused by Duncan's side. "Find out what you can about the employer, too. See if you can speak to them - see what their take is on it all."

Nicki headed for the door. As she did so she glanced at the wall clock

"And don't forget to go home, everyone. It's been a long day."

\* \* \*

# Chapter Seventeen

*Thursday 1<sup>st</sup> November 2018*

7.30pm

Mario's restaurant was busy for a weeknight but Jeremy had secured them a table at the back, nestled in a quiet alcove away from the hustle and bustle. Ever the gentleman, he pulled out Nicki's chair before she sat down. As she took her seat, she noticed the roses in a delicate china vase at the centre of the table, flanked by two candles. She shook her head and flashed a playful grin.

"This is strictly business, Jeremy, you know that."

The reporter gave a chuckle and took his seat opposite. "Well you can't blame a guy for trying." He gave a good-natured wink across the table, his chocolate brown eyes sparkling even in the muted light from the candles.

Jeremy Frost wasn't a bad catch. Thirty-seven and good-looking in a rough and rugged kind of way. His hair was cut short, with the habit of looking as though he'd just rolled out of bed – and he kept himself in shape playing five-a-side football for the local newspaper's team.

Jeremy himself made no attempt to disguise his soft-spot for the Detective Inspector sitting opposite him, making a beeline for her whenever their paths crossed – which, in a small town like Bury St Edmunds, could be more often than expected.

They ordered their drinks and began to peruse the menu in an amiable silence. Nicki wasn't one for eating out all that much, preferring to spend her spare time, such as it was, pounding the streets alone on her evening runs or sitting up on her rooftop garden with Luna for company. She felt safer like that. Somehow, being out and about in the big, wide world made her feel exposed.

Glancing around the rapidly filling restaurant, she surveyed the other diners as they took their seats or leant forwards across their tables in an intimate exchange of conversation. She always people watched wherever she went; it was a curse of the job. Letting her eyes roam the room, a familiar feeling started to grow. She couldn't get the thought of Lucas Jackson out of her head. It could be anyone, she mused, her eyes still searching the diners. Any one of them sitting right here, right now, enjoying a drink and a plate of pasta could be the one they were hunting.

Nicki shuddered and turned her attention back to the menu.

Jeremy eyed her across the table, his gaze narrowing. "You OK?"

Nicki caught his eye and gave a lop-sided smile. "Sorry. Mind on the job."

For the next hour they ate and drank and, if Nicki were truly honest with herself, she began to relax and enjoy herself for once. Slowly, all thoughts of the investigation began to slip from her mind. It wasn't until they ordered coffee to accompany the last bottle of red wine, that the real reason for the dinner was voiced.

Loosened by the alcohol, Nicki broached the question that had been on her lips all evening.

"Have you had a chance to find anything out about that guy at the press release?" She'd transferred the private investigator's business card to her purse, and could almost feel it glowing red-hot beside her inside her bag. Although she already knew the man's name – if indeed that *was* his name – she daren't tell Jeremy in case he asked her where she'd got her information from. Then she'd have to come clean about the words he'd spoken on the steps of the station – and then she'd have to tell him about Deano. Instead, she took a sip of the strong filter coffee, savouring the rich, velvety taste as it slid down her throat, and eyed her companion across the table.

Jeremy paused the methodical stirring of his coffee, a perplexed look crossing his face. He opened his mouth, then closed it again. Eventually, he resumed the stirring, adding another sachet of sugar. Locking eyes with Nicki, he shook his head.

"To be honest, he's a bit of a mystery."

Nicki's heart sank – those were not the words she wanted to hear.

"I ran it past Richard – he was at the press release, too – and he usually knows anyone who's anyone around here. But he hadn't seen the guy before, either." Jeremy paused and took a sip of his over-sweetened coffee. "Maybe he's a freelancer, or..." Jeremy cocked his head to one side and narrowed his gaze.

"Or what?"

"Or your hunch is correct – and he's not a reporter at all." Jeremy fixed Nicki with an intense look over the rim of his coffee cup, a smile teasing his lips. "Which suggests to me you already knew this and that maybe you're not giving me the whole picture?" He paused and intensified his gaze. "What exactly aren't you telling me, DI Hardcastle?"

Nicki brought her own cup up to her lips to hide behind, and averted her gaze. Jeremy was no fool.

Just as Nicki was searching for something to say, her thoughts were interrupted by a familiar voice.

"Hey, boss!" DC Darcie Butler appeared by Nicki's side, her eyes shining from presumably a mixture of happiness and alcohol. "Don't often see you out and about of an evening! Hiya, Jez!"

Nicki smiled and nodded to the vacant chair by her side. Jeremy raised a hand in greeting. "Good to see you, Darcie. Having a good night?"

Darcie sunk into the chair and started to giggle. She leant in towards Nicki and whispered excitedly. "I'm on a date!"

"Another one?" Nicki raised a good-humoured eyebrow and reached for the dregs of her wine. "Who's the lucky chap this time?"

"I'm not quite that bad! It's the same one who cancelled on me last time. We thought we'd give it another go tonight."

"And?" Nicki let a mischievous smile cross her lips. "What's the verdict? This one any good? Worth a second shot?"

Darcie began to giggle again, interrupted by several bouts of hiccups. Her pink cheeks shone in the hazy light from the candles. "He's quite nice, actually. Normal."

"Normal?" Nicki's attention was distracted by Jeremy tipping the rest of the contents of the wine bottle into Nicki's glass. She felt heat beginning to spread across her own cheeks. She would need to make this the last one.

Darcie nodded. "More than the last few anyway. Even got a normal job, too – a porter up at the hospital." She glanced over her shoulder in the direction of her table on the other side of the restaurant.

Nicki followed her gaze to a smart-looking, well-dressed man sitting on his own at a table for two. He did indeed, at first glance, look 'normal'. Whatever that was. Dark hair cropped short, and dark eyes from what she could make out at this distance. He looked freshly shaven and dressed to impress. Nicki gave an appreciative nod at her detective constable.

"I see what you mean – he looks promising."

"I hope you're not judging someone by their appearances alone, Inspector. How extremely shallow." Jeremy's eyes danced in the candlelight as he suppressed a grin.

Nicki returned the smile. "As if you men don't do exactly the same thing on a regular basis." She reached for the rest of her coffee. "What's good enough for you..." Her smile was joined by a raised eyebrow across the top of her coffee cup.

Darcie made to get up from the chair, her hiccups subsiding. "I'd better get back, we're onto dessert." She gave Nicki a wink and turned to thread her way back through the tables and chairs.

"Be careful, Darcie," warned Nicki, Darcie began to disappear. "You still don't know him that well. Get a taxi home."

Darcie raised a hand in acknowledgment and continued her journey towards her blind date.

"Youth of today, huh?" commented Jeremy, sinking the last of his wine. "What are they like? All this online dating. Wasn't like that in our day."

"I hope you're not insinuating I'm too old for that kind of thing?" Nicki gave her best headmistress-style glare across the table. "I'm mortally wounded!" She hid the emerging grin behind her cup.

Jeremy merely smiled and tapped the empty wine bottle. "Another?"

Nicki replaced her coffee cup on the table and shook her head. "Not for me I'm afraid. I'd better call it a night. Up early tomorrow, you know how it is."

Jeremy conceded and caught a passing waiter's eye, indicating they would like the bill. After a few moments of good-natured discussion, where Jeremy insisted it was his treat, they decided on a fifty-fifty split. Leaving the cash on the table, they started to retrieve their coats from the coat stand.

"I'll keep my ear to the ground about your mystery fella," said Jeremy, following Nicki towards the exit. "Someone, somewhere, must know who he is."

Nicki nodded her thanks and, after another reminder to Darcie to 'be careful' as they passed her table, they stepped out into the chilled evening air. Glancing at her watch, she hadn't realised how much time had passed – it was already quite late.

It was only a short walk back home, one advantage of living in the town centre, and Jeremy kept her company along the way. She felt relaxed and comfortable in his presence and even slipped her arm through his as they walked. There was no awkwardness on the doorstep, either – they knew each other far too well for that. Jeremy merely pecked her on the cheek and waved as he crossed the road to head back in the direction of his own flat. Not that he wouldn't have accepted an invitation in for coffee – he just knew that wasn't on the cards. Not yet. He was patient. And if he had learnt anything about Detective Inspector Nicki Hardcastle over the years, patience was what you needed in spades.

\* \* \*

*Friday 2nd November 2018*

12.55am

The house sat in darkness at the bottom of a slight dip in the road, the street lights already snuffed out, plunging the entire street into a claustrophobic shadow.

Which suited him just fine.

The gate at the side was unlocked, just as he knew it would be, and he slipped inside without making a sound.

The back garden was mostly laid to lawn, with a small patio by the back door. With no security lights he was able to move around unnoticed. With his gloved hands and thick woollen balaclava hiding his face, he was nothing more than a shadow creeping through the black stillness of the night.

He was able to quickly pick the lock on the back door. It opened easily and soundlessly, thanks to an earlier liberal application of WD40, and he walked into the darkened kitchen. The unique scent of the lubricant still lingered in the air.

The kitchen itself was compact and functional, leading out into a narrow hall that ran the length of the house. With a dining room and living room behind closed doors on the left, he made his way towards the foot of the stairs. Pausing only briefly at the bottom, he stretched his legs and hopped over steps number four, seven and ten, the ones he knew creaked beneath the slightest weight, and arrived at the top landing as silently as he had entered.

The air felt heavy with slumber; not a sound could be heard. Not even his own breathing. A trickle of excitement within him made him shiver. He had a good feeling about this one. He knew the room he needed was at the back of the house, so he silently padded across the carpeted floor. The door was ajar and, making no sound, he nudged it open.

Pausing at the threshold, he let his eyes adjust to the gloom. He made out the shape of a cabin-style bed on the far wall, a space for a desk and single wardrobe beneath. A set of bookshelves to his right appeared in his line of sight, together with a box of toys.

With nothing but the light from his own eyes, he cautiously stepped further into the room. He could see the mound of the sleeping child high up on the bed, but his own gaze soon turned back down to the floor. Seeing a selection of unidentified shapes, he bent down to inspect more closely – finding them to be scattered Lego bricks of all shapes and sizes.

With a gloved hand he picked up a piece and studied it. And then he smiled.

GUILT

* * *

# Chapter Eighteen

*Friday 2nd November 2018*
7.30am

Despite the late night, and a faint alcohol brain fog, Nicki managed to rise early and put in a circuit of the town's streets before sunrise. For some unknown reason she felt energised, even with only a few hours' sleep under her belt. Her evening out with Jeremy had been a good idea – and during the thirty or so minutes she spent pounding the pavements, she began to sort things out in her mind. With each stride, she began to put all the conflicting thoughts she'd had clogging her brain over the last twenty-four hours into some kind of order.

Caspar Ambrose could mean nothing. Maybe he was just fishing for a story on her childhood for some reason. She decided to leave it alone and see what happened. If she ignored his calls long enough he'd give up and, with any luck, she wouldn't hear from him again.

And the reports of Dean in the newspapers, linking him to Alan Woods, that was just speculation and nothing more. The man had been interviewed several times and denied any involvement. And that was good enough for Nicki. What possible motive did the man have to lie?

Arriving back at her house at a little after 6.30, she jumped into the shower and afterwards made herself a quick round of toast and coffee before setting off for the station. Being such a narrow lane, there was no resident's parking on her own street, so she often preferred to leave her car in the station car park.

She opened her office door just before 7.30am, the early morning weak sunshine now starting to break through and streak the sky with swathes of pink, orange and pale blue. It looked stunning – in sharp contrast to the overcast skies they'd ensured for the last few days - and Nicki arrived at her desk with a buoyant heart. They had a lot to get through on the Lucas Jackson case, but she felt energised and ready to tackle whatever the day threw at her.

That feeling lasted all of two seconds.

Slipping out of her coat, her eyes fell to the pile of messages in the centre of her desk – and the one on the top in particular.

'*Caspar Ambrose called – please call back (07700 900548)*'

Nicki's stomach clenched.

He definitely wasn't giving up.

\* \* \*

*Friday 2ⁿᵈ November 2018*

7.40am

The boy hadn't soiled himself overnight, which was an improvement, but he still needed to go. Last night had gone well; he'd seen exactly what he needed to see. The boys were perfect, and the next stage in his plan was already forming in his mind.

The Lego had been an extra touch, though. He smiled at the thought and hoped they appreciated the effort he'd gone to.

He was pleased that he didn't have to wait long to bring them home – the firework display was tomorrow. And he loved fireworks.

Reaching for the pot of moisturising cream, he proceeded to smother his face in the cooling lotion as he did every morning. He knew his scars were still there, deep down. They may have healed and the skin re-grown, becoming mostly invisible to the outside world, but he knew they were still there.

In a way, he missed them. They'd set him apart from everyone else; they'd made him different. But now? Now he was just like everybody else. Which was why he sometimes still liked to wear a mask, just inside the house, where nobody could see him. Just feeling the cloth against his skin made him feel safe and secure. Protected.

As he made his way up the stairs with a plate of sandwiches for the boy, he smiled. Whenever he wore a mask in front of Lucas, the boy physically shook. The paradox was intriguing. It used to be the sight of his scarred and acid-burnt face that caused people to recoil and turn away in revulsion.

He let a dry chuckle escape his lips, muffled behind the Mickey Mouse mask he'd chosen especially for the boy. He wondered what kind of reaction it would provoke. All children liked Mickey, didn't they?

* * *

*Friday 2nd November 2018*
   8.00am

"You all right, boss?" asked Darcie as she took a seat nearest to the whiteboards. "You look a bit peaky."

Nicki tried a smile. "I'm fine, Darcie. Just a headache."

Darcie raised her eyebrows. "Too much red wine last night?"

Nicki allowed her smile to widen. "Maybe, Darcie. Maybe. And what about yourself? Any lasting effects from last night?"

Darcie shook her head and beamed. "Nope. I was home before midnight. Cinderella would be proud."

Nicki turned her attention back to the room, which was now filling up. "Right – we've a lot to get through this morning, so if we could all take our seats?" Roy took the seat next to Darcie, DCs Holland and Jenkins filling in behind.

Nicki thrust her chilled hands into her pockets, instantly feeling the sharp edge of the private investigator's business card. She'd scrunched the telephone message up and thrown it in the bin along with the others. For now, she needed to put Caspar Ambrose out of her mind.

"It is now more than three days since Lucas Jackson disappeared. One significant development yesterday – we now have an image of the man we suspect of taking Lucas."

Duncan Jenkins activated the interactive whiteboard and a copy of the CCTV image filled the screen.

"He's of tall build, but we can only see him from the back. It doesn't give us a lot to go on, but it does show that Lucas appears to have gone with him willingly. I'm going to head out today to see both Ivy and Oliver's parents – bring them up to speed on the developments. I'll show them this image to see if they recognise him. Darcie, you're with me. While we're gone, Roy, can you delve into the Jackson family history a bit deeper – find out if there is anyone else we should be interested in. I especially want to know more about those two brothers of Liam's."

Roy nodded. "Yes, boss."

"Matt and Duncan. Carry on with trawling through Sophia Jackson's social media and phone records. Make sure we're not overlooking some other motive for targeting Lucas."

Both DCs gave affirmative noises and began pushing their chairs back towards the bank of computer screens at the rear of the incident room.

Nicki reached for her jacket. "And Graham?" She'd noticed DS Graham Fox skulking around in the far corner of the room, scowling at everyone as they entered. Sighing, not really having the energy for any of his attitude that day, she caught his eye. "How are you getting on with the burglaries?"

DS Fox continued to hover at the back of the room, pretending to fiddle with the hot water urn. He could feel Nicki's gaze burning into his back, right between his shoulder blades. "I'm processing them, what more can I say?" he replied, his voice gruff. He didn't turn around.

"How many have you got now? I heard there was another reported early this morning?"

DS Fox gave a noncommittal shrug. "Six so far. All going back to the beginning of last month. And yes, I heard about the one this morning. I'm adding it to the list – the very long list – and I'll head out there in a bit."

"I know it's not the most exciting caseload in the world, but you could put a bit more enthusiasm into it." Nicki slipped into her jacket and turned towards the door.

"It's volume crime, what can I say?" There's not a lot to get excited about." DS Fox slouched into a vacant chair and sat down.

Nicki opened her mouth to respond, but thought better of it. Sometimes things just weren't worth the breath. Exasperated, she motioned for Darcie to get her coat and follow. They needed to get over to see Ivy and Oliver's families.

DS Graham Fox and his tantrums could wait.

* * *

# Chapter Nineteen

*Friday 2<sup>nd</sup> November 2018*

*Friday 2nd November 2018*
   8.30am

The boy hadn't touched his sandwiches – instead he'd begun to cry again. He hadn't liked the Mickey Mouse mask after all. Irritation ripped through him as he jogged back down the stairs. He'd smacked the boy across the side of the head, knocking him from the chair, which had silenced his moans for a while. He'd added sufficient lashes from Dad's old leather belt just to make sure.

   With each stroke that hit the boy's pale skin, his determination to move on intensified. It was all he could think about. He couldn't wait to get rid of Lucas Jackson. Today was going to be the boy's last.

   For tomorrow heralded a fresh start.

   The phrase evoked a curious memory.

* * *

5 Arlington Crescent
   *Monday 25th October 2004*

Standing at the bottom of the rear staircase, he knew he still had time. His mother was busy checking the other bedrooms and wouldn't notice if he was gone for a few minutes. And a few minutes was all he would need – just to say goodbye.

Making the short journey up the stairs for the final time, he stood on the well-worn carpet of the landing outside the back bedroom. The door was shut but he knew it wasn't locked. Mum never locked it now, not like Dad did. Turning the handle, he gently pushed the door open.

One of the last things Dad had done was oil the hinges. He'd watched him do it - marvelling at how just a few drops could eliminate the squeak. It was something he knew he would always remember.

The room looked the same, but he knew it was very different. The bedframe was still there, stripped of its mattress, but the police had taken everything else. The mattress, the moth-eaten scratchy blanket, the chair. Even the bucket in the corner of the room. All gone.

The same could be said of Dad's personal things. His clothes. His shoes. His books and papers. His car. Everything seized and taken away. Mum didn't want any of it back; not one thing. It was as if she wanted to wipe all memory of him away, expunged from existence.

She'd ripped the boards down from the window, and weak sunlight now streamed in. It was strange, seeing the back bedroom like this. He was used to seeing it full of darkness and shadows. It looked odd in the daylight.

And it smelt different, too. Lemon scented cleaning fluids filled the air instead of metallic dried blood and acidic urine. Mum had spent hours on her hands and knees scrubbing the floorboards until her fingers bled. He knew because he'd watched her from the doorway, as slowly every memory of the man he looked up to was washed clean away.

Sighing, he turned his back on the bedroom and made his way down the rear staircase for the last time. The back bedroom may look and smell different now, but no amount of scrubbing could take away his memories of it. He would keep those locked away inside him where nobody else could reach them.

His mother had finished checking the upstairs rooms and now stood in the centre of the kitchen, two suitcases by her feet. They weren't taking much with them; just a few clothes and personal items. Everything else could stay. They were having a *'fresh start'*, apparently. It was a phrase he'd heard mentioned a lot over the last few months. He remembered feeling oddly confused when his mother had first told him they were moving. Moving? Leaving everything behind? Why would they do that?

His mother had tried to explain that after everything that had happened, they needed to leave; to have a *'fresh start'*. There was that phrase again. He felt quite happy with the 'old start' and didn't see why they needed to move.

His face was beginning to heal now – with much fewer trips to the hospital needed. The creams and ointments he had to use each day would lessen the scarring, so they had told him. He wouldn't miss school – not that he went there much anymore - but he would miss the house.

It was the only house he'd ever lived in. Or at least it was the only one he really remembered. He knew he'd lived somewhere else before, and had vague recollections of an apple tree at the bottom of a garden, but those memories had faded over time.

When he'd asked his mother what would happen if Dad came home and found them gone, her face took on a strange look. Her eyes glazed over and he thought he could see her thin shoulders judder; just for a second. Then she'd smiled one of her biggest smiles and told him that everything would be fine.

So, now, here they were on moving day. *'Fresh start'* day.

He'd heard the commotion outside long before he'd rolled out of bed that morning. The single pane of glass at his window did little to mask the noise. He'd carefully parted the curtains, trying to remain hidden from view. Dad always told him to beware of windows – too many people could see inside.

As he peeked around the side of the curtain, he saw several cars parked outside on the road - cars he hadn't seen before. And there were people. *Lots* of people. As his eyes adjusted to the early morning sunshine, he gazed across the heads of those that were gathered on the pavement. Several policemen were lined up at the front gate, their backs to the house, standing with their arms out wide. It looked like they were trying to stop the crowd surging forward and up the garden path.

A frown crossed his brow. Why were there so many people outside? And why did they seem to want to come up the path to the front door? Did they know it was 'fresh start' day?

He moved away from the window and started to get dressed, his mother having left his clothes out for him the night before, packing away everything else. Once dressed, he'd made his way down to the kitchen where the table was already laid for breakfast. The kitchen window was masked by a thin, net curtain and the back door was shut and locked.

His mother had smiled brightly from behind a box of cornflakes and started to pour him some orange juice. "Come on, then. Let's have some breakfast before we leave."

He'd taken his seat as instructed and reached for the freshly poured juice. Again, he'd wanted to ask why. Why they were leaving. But he knew that he shouldn't. He'd only get the same answer – something about a 'fresh start'. He didn't manage to eat much, just a few mouthfuls of soggy cornflakes before excusing himself. He wanted to visit the back bedroom, just one last time. If they really *were* leaving.

And now here they were - back in the kitchen for the final time. All their worldly goods packed away into two small suitcases. It wasn't much to show for a life.

Mum looked nervous and, from the faint smell of smoke in the air around her, he suspected she'd had a sneaky cigarette on the back porch before locking the door. She never used to smoke when Dad was here. He wouldn't let her.

Just as they stood there in the centre of the kitchen, a cry rose up from outside, followed by a cacophony of cheering. Fear flooded across his mother's face as her eyes flickered towards the shrouded kitchen window.

He moved too quickly for her this time, dashing to the sink and clambering up onto the draining board to peer out from behind the net curtain. He could see the crowds were much closer now, and it looked like even more people had arrived. Someone had jumped over the low picket fence and was being wrestled to the ground by two burly-looking police officers, the three of them writhing over the neatly cut lawn.

His mouth opened in wonder. What *were* they doing here? His attention was drawn to a man, who leapfrogged the fence and jumped over the wrestling bodies on the grass. He was making a lunge towards the front of the house.

In the man's hands was a tin of paint, the contents of which was then hurled through the air towards the front door. The sound of paint against the wooden door made a slapping sound and, before he knew what was happening, his mother had grabbed him off the draining board and pulled him in close to her. The smell of cigarette smoke was more intense as his face was pressed into the folds of her cardigan.

Leaving the breakfast things on the table, his mother nodded at him to pick up the smaller of the suitcases. Wordlessly, he did as he was told and followed her out into the hallway. With a battered suitcase in one hand, his mother painted a fierce and defiant look on her face and pulled open the front door.

The jeering and shouting, that had been muted whilst they were cocooned inside the house, now erupted and assaulted their eardrums. Two policemen were on the doorstep and herded them both along the garden path. As they were bundled towards the front gate, he glanced sideways towards the lawn and saw that all that remained of the earlier scuffle was some flattened grass and a lone policeman's helmet. His gaze came to rest on the house - the front door now coated with huge swathes of white, glossy paint, and further splatters decorating the brickwork on either side.

As they neared the front gate, the sound from the crowd intensified. His mother had her head down, staring at the path, her chin buried in the collar of her jacket – but he also saw silent tears streaking down her cheeks. Whilst his mother had her head down, he held his firmly up - openly taking in the angry and violent mob trying their best to surge towards them.

He tried to listen to what they were saying, but it was difficult to make out individual words. 'Murderer' was one he could detect. 'Paedophile' was another. Although he wasn't quite sure what that meant. 'You knew', 'rot in hell' and 'you witch' floated around as well.

The police herded them into the back of the waiting police car. He'd never been inside one before and the thought quite excited him. His mother quickly dived onto the back seat, dragging her suitcase behind her. Before he followed, he hesitated and looked back out towards the baying crowd. The picket fence now lay in pieces, and several of the crowd were now gathered on the front lawn.

He scoured the faces turned towards him. He saw angry faces; shouting faces; swearing faces. He knew he was meant to be scared of them, but he curiously found that he wasn't. Instead, they intrigued him. So much emotion, so much feeling, so much anger directed towards them.

All these people were here for *them*.

The realisation gave him a not unpleasant flicker of excitement in the pit of his stomach. They were famous. People knew who they were. The chanting and jeering didn't scare him – quite the opposite. He thought back to his father and wondered what he would make of all this. All this adoration being thrust towards them.

He stood there, drinking in the commotion around him for several more seconds before a police officer finally bundled him into the back of the car and slammed the door. As the car pulled away from the kerb and inched its way through the mob, he turned to look out of the side window and smiled. The empty beer cans thrown at the side of the car, and even the dog faeces smeared across the glass, didn't faze him.

Instead, he smiled.

\* \* \*

*Friday 2nd November 2018*
10.45am

Once again, DS Graham Fox found himself in the kitchen of a property, trying to reassure the homeowners that the person who'd broken into their house overnight was unlikely to return. For the most part, that was true. But the look on both Mr and Mrs Kennedy's faces spoke volumes.

They didn't believe him.

"And you're sure the door was locked?" DS Fox nodded towards the back door.

Neil Kennedy nodded. "I'm sure of it. I'm quite fastidious with security. I always check all doors and windows before we go to bed. I can't think that I wouldn't have done it last night." Confusion mixed with shock haunted his features.

"But you can't be a hundred percent sure?" DS Fox's pen hovered over a blank page of his notebook, noting the two empty bottles of red wine on the draining board by the sink.

"Well, I...I guess not, no." Mr Kennedy hung his head and rubbed a hand over his early-morning stubble. "But I'm so sure I locked it."

"And nobody heard anything?" DS Fox knew the answer before the question had even left his lips. He'd already skimmed through the initial statements both Mr and Mrs Kennedy had given to the attending officers earlier that morning.

Both Neil and Hazel Kennedy shook their heads as DS Fox snapped his notebook shut and glanced once more around the compact kitchen. It was a standard layout – sink underneath the window that looked out onto the back garden; cupboards on three walls above an expensive-looking granite worktop. A built-in oven and induction hob graced one wall, with a tall freestanding fridge-freezer opposite.

DS Fox stepped across to the fridge-freezer, noting the usual photographs and hastily written messages pinned to the front. A shopping list had been scrawled onto a ragged piece of paper, urging the next person to visit the shops to remember toilet rolls and potatoes. A calendar was pinned to the middle, set to yesterday's date, surrounded by pictures of smiling children.

"You have just the two children?" It was a statement rather than a question.

"Yes. Noah and Isaac," replied Mrs Kennedy.

"And you believe the intruder accessed your youngest son's bedroom?"

Mrs Kennedy nodded, her lips starting to quiver. "Isaac's room." Tears began to spring up in the corners of her already red-rimmed eyes. "I keep imagining what could have happened." She brought a hand up to her mouth to stifle a choked sob.

DS Fox tried his best at a reassuring smile. "From what we know about this particular intruder, he doesn't appear to intend anyone any harm."

"So what's he doing? He doesn't take anything of value." Mr Kennedy had an edge of irritation to his tone. "Why break in and not steal anything except a few quid from Hazel's purse?"

DS Fox could do nothing but shrug. "At this stage, we don't really know. But please be assured, he's most unlikely to return and we don't consider his motives are to harm." He knew his reassurances sounded hollow, but it was the best he could do. It was true – they didn't know what the intruder's motives were – whether he was searching for something in particular, or just wanting to cause fear. The latter he had certainly achieved.

DS Fox had already taken a look upstairs and seen the bedroom that the intruder was thought to have accessed. It looked like a normal five-year-old's bedroom, and nothing was thought to have been taken. Intriguingly, the intruder had stuck around long enough to make a fire engine out of the scattered Lego bricks that littered the carpet. Mr and Mrs Kennedy had been adamant the construction had not been there the previous evening, and their five-year-old son would not have been able to build it himself. The fire engine had been dutifully bagged up as evidence, although DS Fox doubted there would be any forensic evidence – and the pieces were too small for fingerprints.

After exchanging a few more well-meaning pleasantries, and answering their questions the best he could, DS Fox made his excuses and left Mr and Mrs Kennedy in peace, making his way back out to the car.

Before starting the engine, he sat behind the wheel and sighed. Was this really what his life now consisted of? Volume crime burglaries? Handing out false platitudes and home safety advice? He'd taken a swift look at the whiteboards in the incident room that morning, seeing how the Lucas Jackson investigation was progressing and what leads were being followed up. He'd listened to the briefing whilst pretending to busy himself at one of the computers, and then watched as one by one everyone left.

And while everyone else was out and about chasing down leads, he was chasing down Lego fire engines.

Biting back the bitterness that he knew he shouldn't feel, he gunned the engine of the Honda and headed back to the station.

* * *

2.30pm

The décor may have looked different, but the same feeling filled the air of the Chambers' family home as it had in the front room at Ivy McFadden's house not half an hour before.

Nicki waved away the offer of another cup of tea. Vanessa McFadden had insisted on making a fresh pot of tea, bringing it through with a cake stand filled with fresh cream horns and pastries. Both Nicki and Darcie had accepted a cup to be polite – which was too strong and too sweet – but declined the selection of high tea delicacies. Nicki felt as though the crumbs would lodge in her throat.

She'd seen the pain in Vanessa McFadden's eyes the moment they'd stepped over the threshold. She had tried to mask it, but grief always finds a way into even the most hardened of faces – no matter how hard you tried to stop it. It was pointless to even try – like trying to catch smoke.

The same look now graced the eyes of Helen Chambers. Her husband was busy in the shed, but she offered to go and get him if needed. Nicki shook her head – it wasn't necessary, just a courtesy call. Both families had already had contact from Norfolk Police, updating them on the developments in Suffolk surrounding Lucas Jackson, and Nicki didn't really have much by way of additional news for them. But she wanted to meet them – to put a face to the names she was reading about.

Vanessa McFadden had taken them upstairs to see Ivy's bedroom. They'd kept it exactly the same - as if the little girl had just skipped outside to play. Even the pile of clothes on the floor by the foot of the bed.

Nicki had seen it countless times before. Grieving families keeping the rooms of their loved ones exactly as they had been the last time they'd been inside those precious walls. As if it in some way preserved them – or their memory at least.

Nicki could remember Deano's room being kept in exactly the same way for years. She also remembered getting a severe ticking off from her mother when she'd gone into Deano's room and accidentally spilt a glass of Ribena on the carpet. Her mother had literally broken down in front of her, for just one glass of blackcurrant juice.

Nicki's father had taken her to one side to explain that it wasn't the Ribena; it wasn't the mess, or the scrubbing she'd had to do to get rid of the stain, that had upset her mother. It was the fact that now the carpet was clean – erasing that part of Deano's memory.

So Nicki understood.

She also understood the sad pair of eyes that watched her from the brown leather sofa. George Chambers sat glumly by his mother's side, clutching a stuffed toy on his lap.

Nicki had read enough of the file on Oliver Chambers' abduction and murder to know that George would be blaming himself. Of course he would. Nicki's heart almost split in two when she saw his bottom lip trembling.

But she was also relieved to see the comforting hug that came from Helen Chambers. It wasn't a stilted hug, or a forced hug, or a hug devoid of feeling. She knew an empty hug when she saw one – and this wasn't it. This hug was a real hug, warm and full of love.

Nicki was glad. She knew what it felt like to be starved of affection after your whole world had caved in; when you were feeling at your lowest, and the problems of the whole world were down to you and you alone. And all you wanted was the love from your mother.

Yes – Nicki knew exactly what that felt like.

George would be OK in time. He'd never be the same, not really, but he'd be OK.

After briefly outlining where they were with the investigation, Nicki brought out her phone and pulled up the CCTV image.

"Does the man on the right here look familiar to you at all, Mrs Chambers?" She passed the handset across to Helen Chambers. "Anything at all about him that you may have seen before?"

Nicki watched as Oliver's mother studied the image. She saw the grieving woman's hand hover over the screen, lightly touching it with a finger. Slowly, Helen Chambers shook her head.

"No," she whispered, her voice brittle. "No, I don't."

Nicki gave an understanding smile and took the handset back. Vanessa McFadden had given the same reaction. Neither woman had recognised the man leading Lucas Jackson out of the Abbey Gardens, albeit they could only see him from the back.

After declining another offer of tea, Nicki and Darcie made their excuses and left.

Back in the car, Nicki sighed and rested her hands on the steering wheel. It had been an emotional visit to both families – but it had to be done. She needed to look them in the eye and tell them how determined she was to find the man who had ripped their worlds apart.

George Chambers' parting words echoed around inside her head.

*"You will catch him, won't you? That man?"*

Nicki had nodded, promising that she would.

And, right now, it was a promise she intended to keep.

* * *

# Chapter Twenty

*Friday 2<sup>nd</sup> November 2018*
   7.35pm

It was late and everyone else had gone home. DS Fox sat hunched over his computer keyboard and enjoyed the silence. The incident room had been a hive of activity when he'd arrived back from visiting the Kennedys. Nicki and Darcie were still both out visiting the parents of Ivy McFadden and Oliver Chambers – he knew that because he'd taken a sly look at the whiteboards and had been listening at the early morning briefing. Holland and Jenkins were still trawling through the Jackson's social media accounts and Roy was huddled over his own computer monitor, deep in thought.

None of them gave much away, despite the prodding DS Fox gave them. Not long after, they'd all left for home.

It's like they don't want me to know. DS Fox took a bite out of the hot sausage roll he'd bought himself on the way back. They want to keep it all to themselves, hidden away like some big secret he wasn't a part of. And all he had was a file full of repetitive volume crime domestic burglaries to keep him occupied.

It felt like a demotion.

Taking another bite from his pastry, he again cast his eyes back to the statements taken from Neil and Hazel Kennedy. They were both uncannily similar to all the others on file, with only a few variations. But he felt he was at last getting somewhere. Usually the motive was the key – you unearth the motive, then it quite often led you to your suspect. But here, the motive was about as clear as mud.

So instead he'd asked himself why? Not why as in the motive, because he already knew that particular question was a dead-end, but why these people in particular? Why these particular houses? None of them seemed to know each other; they had no common workplaces, and the kids all went to different schools.

It had taken him hours, and just when he was about to give up and call it a night, he found it.

The penny finally dropped.

It'd been staring him in the face all this time, but he'd been too blind to see it.

Immediately, all misgivings and resentment at being shut out of the Lucas Jackson investigation disappeared into the ether. It no longer mattered. None of it.

Just to be sure, he cast his eyes over his notebook one more time and felt his stomach flutter.

This was it.

*  *  *

*Friday 2<sup>nd</sup> November 2018*
    8.00pm

Nicki had just tipped out Luna's dinner into her bowl when she heard the knock at the door. Standing rooted to the spot, empty cat food sachet in hand, she felt her heartbeat quicken beneath her dressing gown. A glance at the kitchen clock told her it was a little before eight o'clock.

Instantly, the vision of Caspar Ambrose filled her cluttered mind. She'd lost count of the number of phone messages that she'd now ignored; screwing them up and tossing them in the bin. He'd managed to track her down this far, so it wouldn't take much to find out where she lived. If he was a decent private investigator, he would find her - no matter how hard she tried to stay hidden.

The knock came again, louder this time. Nicki flashed a glance towards the rack of carving knives sitting by the side of the microwave and then instantly admonished herself at her overreaction. What was she expecting? The burglar? Some hooded assailant with a weapon? It was unlikely either would be so polite as to knock first.

Throwing the cat food sachet into the bin as she passed, Nicki headed out of the kitchen and towards the front door. With her blood pulsating wildly at her eardrums, she pulled her dressing gown tightly around her waist. It was at times like these that she wished she'd paid more attention during her self-defence classes – instead of giggling at the back and thinking about the glass of wine in the bar that followed.

Upon wrenching the door open, relief immediately flooded her face.

"Amy." Nicki felt her muscles slacken, releasing her tight grip on the door handle. "It's you."

Nicki's best friend frowned, peering out from beneath a heavy, dark fringe. "Of course it's me. Ta da!" Amy waved a bottle of wine in the air, a grin spreading across her face. "Wine night, remember?"

"Of course, of course. Come in." Nicki stepped back, breathing deeply to quieten her thudding heartbeat.

"You forgot." Amy stepped across the threshold, shedding her knee-length Burberry trench coat as she did so.

"No, of course I didn't," lied Nicki, forcing the door closed against the bitter chill from outside. She clicked the lock into place and smiled, sheepishly, at her best friend. "Who could forget wine?"

Amy headed for the sofa, folding her coat and placing it on the spare armchair. "Liar. You forgot I was coming." She flashed a grin at Nicki, clad in her pyjamas and dressing down, winking as she did so. "I'm heartbroken."

"Well, maybe I did a little." Nicki hurried to the coffee table and began scooping up the various loose Lucas Jackson investigation papers scattered across the top, shoving them into a folder out of sight. She hadn't been able to concentrate after arriving back from visiting both Ivy and Oliver's parents – so had rammed the paperwork into a folder and brought it home.

"I can go?" Amy raised her perfectly shaped eyebrows and inclined her head back towards the front door. "If you're busy? I know you're in the thick of things right now. We can do this another time?"

Nicki hurriedly shook her head. "No, no. It's fine. Welcome, in fact. I need to take a break from all this anyway." She slid the folder underneath the table and straightened up. "And wine is just what I need after today." No matter how hard she'd tried, she couldn't rid herself of the look on George Chambers' face that had haunted every minute of the journey home. Stepping around the sofa and heading towards the kitchen, she stopped to squeeze her friend's arm as she passed. "I'll get us some glasses."

With the wine poured, and the wood burner replenished, both Nicki and Amy settled down on the 'L' shaped sofa. Nicki found herself relaxing, finally releasing the pent-up tension she'd been harbouring since the knock at the door. She really had to start getting a grip.

"So, how's things with you?" Nicki took a large gulp of wine, savouring the chill as she swallowed. "Busy?"

Amy nodded as she pushed her heavy fringe out of her eyes. Her jet black hair was tied up into a high ponytail, yet still managed to reach to the small of her back. With a sharp bone structure and a perfectly proportioned heart-shaped face, her dark smoky eyes peered over the rim of her wine glass. "Very. The place was packed to bursting when I left. God knows what the wait time is – I daren't even ask. Certainly nowhere near the four-hour target." Amy worked as a senior A&E staff nurse at the West Suffolk Hospital, a small district hospital set in a beautiful location on Hardwick Heath.

"How come it's so busy?" Nicki topped up both their glasses with the rapidly decreasing wine.

"Everywhere's busy. Seems to be a lot of flu cases this year. And it's always busy around firework night. The Norfolk and Norwich have declared a major incident, so their A&E is closed." Amy paused to take a welcome glug of wine. "We're getting a lot of diverts. But we're already at high capacity anyway – we just can't discharge the patients on the wards into the community quickly enough to make way for the ones coming in through the front door. When I left, there were several ambulances queuing outside – something I've not seen in a long time. There's just no room at the inn."

"Must be tough." Nicki scooted back to the kitchen to grab some nibbles from the cupboard. "I don't know how you guys cope some days." She returned to the sofa, tipping out crisps and salted pretzels into china bowls before settling back down with her wine glass. "You must be shattered."

Amy gave a shrug and reached for a handful of crisps. "Pretty much - but you just keep going, don't you? You must know all about that – you look pretty tired yourself." Amy leant forwards and tipped the remains of the wine into their glasses.

Nicki punched her best friend playfully on the arm before grabbing some pretzels. "Thanks! I know I look a wreck."

"I didn't say wreck, I said tired." Amy grinned as she popped a crisp into her mouth. "Anyhow, a little bird told me you were out on the razzle last night with that reporter. Come on, spill."

Nicki spluttered into her glass, feeling her cheeks warming. "I was not out *on the razzle*! It was a quiet dinner. And before you ask, it was work."

Amy laughed. "If you say so. But that's not what my spy tells me."

"And who exactly is your spy, as if I can't already guess?" Nicki's own laughter joined that of her best friend – a friend who also happened to be the older sister of DC Darcie Butler. "Darcie needs to learn when to keep her mouth shut."

"We're just happy for you – getting yourself out and about. You spend far too much time locked away in here with just your cat for company."

Right on cue, Luna padded into the living room and hopped up onto Nicki's lap, looking for attention. Nicki obliged by giving a few head scratches, followed by a rub underneath the chin. "I don't lock myself away – I go out most evenings."

"Yes, on your own," replied Amy, draining her glass, her dark eyes sparkling. "All that running can't be good for you." She uncurled her legs and pushed herself up out of the sofa. "Any more wine?"

Nicki nodded. "In the fridge. Help yourself."

With a second bottle now open, Nicki settled back against the sofa cushions, stroking a sleeping Luna in her lap.

"How's Darcie getting on anyway?" Amy topped up both their glasses with the fresh bottle of Chardonnay. "She doesn't tell me much about work."

Despite her tiredness, Nicki couldn't help beaming. "Darcie's great. She's a really good police officer and she's settled into the role of DC a treat. She's a natural." Nicki knew how proud Amy was of her baby sister. "She'll go a long way, I'm sure. This is just the start for her."

"Well, she's got a great teacher," replied Amy, crunching on another handful of crisps. "She really looks up to you."

Nicki glanced down at her faded pyjama bottoms and well-worn slippers. "Well, I can see what a great role model I am – just look at me!" She took another large sip of wine and wondered if a few bowls of crisps would be enough to soak up the alcohol they were consuming at an alarming rate of knots. Maybe a takeaway later would be required to ward off a raging hangover the next morning.

Pushing the thought of the morning aside, Nicki turned to her friend. "Talking of Darcie, has she told you much about the new man?"

"Ryan?" Amy groaned. "She hasn't stopped going on about him for days. He seems nice enough, though, from what she's said. Not too sure where he's from - she's a bit vague on that. There's a hint of some rift with his family, but who has a perfect family, right? He seems OK anyway. I see him around the hospital."

"Ah, yes. I remember her saying. He works as a porter, is that right?"

Another nod from Amy accompanied another top up of wine. "Yes. Not been with us that long – only a few months I think. He comes down to A&E quite regularly. He's good with the youngsters - the kids. If we have to send them off for an x-ray or anything, he's really good at putting them at ease."

The evening progressed and soon the second bottle of wine was empty, as were the bowls of crisps and pretzels. They'd decided against ordering a takeaway. Instead, Nicki had knocked up a couple of toasted cheese sandwiches. She stifled a yawn behind her hand and stretched her legs to the end of the sofa.

"I think that's my cue to leave." Amy placed her empty glass onto the coffee table and stood up.

"No, you're fine. You don't need to run off." Nicki rubbed her eyes. "I'll make some coffee."

Amy shook her head. "No, I'll get going. I'm knackered myself anyway. And you need a decent night's sleep – no coffee before bed!"

Nicki smiled and pushed herself off the sofa. Glancing at her watch, she noticed it was just after eleven thirty. After helping Amy into her coat they both hovered by the front door.

"Are you sure you're OK?" Amy caught Nicki's eye. "You seem like you've got the weight of the world on your shoulders tonight."

Several times during the course of the evening, Nicki had almost blurted out everything to do with Caspar Ambrose. She'd transferred the business card to the pocket of her dressing gown and could feel its sharp edges whenever she moved. But if she told Amy about the card and the investigator, then she would have to tell her about Deano – and then she would have to tell her the truth.

And she wasn't quite ready for that. Not yet.

Nicki plastered another smile onto her face. "I'm fine, really. It's just work. This investigation. It's taking its toll on us all."

Amy nodded and stepped forwards to give Nicki a hug. The two friends embraced for several seconds before breaking apart. Nicki could feel tears pricking at the corners of her eyes. She hated lying to her friend, her *best* friend. But she couldn't tell her the truth – not yet.

"Well, you get yourself off to bed." Amy unlocked the door and stepped out into the cold. "And I hope you guys get a break on the case soon – and find that little boy. It's so heart-breaking."

Nicki nodded and watched her friend disappear into the night. Once she was out of sight, she closed the door and locked it. This time she slid the bolts home too, one at the top and one at the bottom – just in case. After gathering up the empty wine bottles, plates and bowls, she dumped them all in the kitchen sink. Washing up could wait until the morning.

For now, she needed sleep. For tomorrow, Lucas Jackson needed her to be at her sharpest.

* * *

Even at this time of night, DS Carl Bradshaw had been happy to take his call. They'd attended several courses together in the past, and sunk more than a few pints over the years, albeit not for a while. After exchanging the usual pleasantries, DS Fox quickly got to the point of his call.

DS Bradshaw had remembered the cases well and confirmed they were still open and unsolved. From his tone, DS Fox knew his old pal wasn't hopeful that status would be changing any time soon. Although DS Fox's next question sounded odd when spoken out loud, Carl Bradshaw didn't say so. And his response convinced DS Fox that his suspicions had been correct.

With the excitement still flickering in his stomach, he checked his watch and considered ringing Nicki. Deciding against it, he closed his notebook. He'd already spent hours going over the information until his head began to spin. The lead would still be there tomorrow. The boss was unlikely to welcome a call from him at this time of night.

Pushing himself up out of his chair, he stretched his arms above his head and heard his back creak in protest. He'd been sitting in the same position for hours, pouring over the paperwork, and clearly his vertebrae were angry. He felt hungry; the sausage roll from earlier now a long distant memory. Reaching for the jacket hanging on the back of his chair, he resolved to pick up a late-night takeaway on his way home.

As he powered down his computer monitor, his eyes lifted towards the whiteboards on the far wall. Operation Goldfish had now managed to cover three of them, with various leads highlighted as still under investigation. He knew the team was no further forward, not really. He could hear the discussions going on around him every day; it was hard to ignore.

But everyone was working flat out and covering all the angles that they should - they just didn't have that one lead, that one piece of evidence that broke everything else apart. Stepping across the room, he peered at the whiteboards more closely. The first board was dedicated to Lucas Jackson and his family. He noted the family tree diagram in the centre.

The second whiteboard detailed the other two cases now linked to Lucas's abduction. Ivy McFadden and Oliver Chambers. As his eyes scoured the boards he felt his heart rate quicken.

*Ivy and Oliver.*

Knowing Darcie had been trawling through the previous Norfolk investigations, he made a beeline towards her desk. Neat piles of folders and papers littered its surface, but it didn't take him long to find what he wanted.

With his heartbeat thudding loudly in his ears and his palms beginning to moisten, he took the files back to his own desk. Flicking his computer back on, he sat down. It couldn't be, could it? Opening his notebook once again, he skimmed his eyes over the entries he'd made from his late night telephone conversation with Carl Bradshaw.

And there it was.

DS Fox continued to stare at his notebook, then back at Darcie's files.

This was it. This was the break they'd been waiting for.

Dismissing the lateness of the hour, DS Fox reached for his phone.

* * *

# Chapter Twenty-One

1.35am

Nicki burst into the incident room, out of breath. She hadn't been asleep when the call came in – far from it. She'd gone to bed as soon as Amy had left, but sleep had evaded her. It had taken her less than a minute to pull on her jeans, and then she'd run the short distance to the station.

"What have you got, Graham?" Her voice was clipped. Frowning, she saw that the incident room was in total darkness and DS Fox clearly hadn't been home.

Graham Fox strode away from the window where he'd been pacing back and forth ever since placing the call. He pulled another chair across to his desk. "Here," he said, nodding at the seat. "I've got something you need to see."

In the intervening minutes, between summoning Nicki to the station and her hurried arrival, doubt had flooded in. What if he was wrong? What if it all came to nothing and he was left with egg on his face? *Again.*

Uncertainty clouded his clogged mind as he sat down and pulled his notebook towards him. Nicki followed, taking the seat next to him. He could smell a faint waft of something floral as she sat.

"What have you got, Graham?" she repeated, not attempting to hide the tiredness in her tone.

"I was working on these burglary reports when I found something."

Pushing aside the doubt, he opened the file on the domestic burglaries. As he did so, he felt the same flicker of excitement he'd felt earlier.

Nicki sighed and followed his gaze to the open file. She felt like quipping *'what kind of something drags me out of bed at half past one in the morning?'* but bit her tongue instead.

"I looked over the statements each of the homeowners gave, and then did a bit of digging of my own." He pulled out several sheets of paper from the file. "These are the burglaries I attended and I noted down a few things while I was there. Things that won't necessarily be mentioned in their statements. And something stood out, connecting them all."

Despite the hour, Nicki felt intrigued and leant forwards.

"All three houses I visited had been having some kind of building work done on their properties." He tapped one of the reports relating to David and Anna Marshall. "This one here – they're in the middle of a loft conversion. I saw the spare room with the building materials for myself."

Nicki nodded, her initial frown deepening. "I see. Go on."

"And here. Mr and Mrs Winters – they had some painting and decorating completed quite recently. I saw the empty paint pots and plasterboard out on the drive." DS Fox paused and tapped a third sheet. "And the last one I visited yesterday – Neil and Hazel Kennedy. They had some builder's sacks outside."

"And your point is?"

"I'm coming to that. Bear with me." DS Fox slotted the papers back into the file and pulled out several more. "These are the ones that Darcie visited. Darcie's own notes confirmed evidence of building materials at all three addresses.

"And you think...?"

"It always troubled me why nobody heard the intruder. Anna Marshall called herself a light sleeper. *'I stir at every noise'* were her exact words. No matter how careful this guy was, he would've made some noise at least. Unless..." DS Fox left the sentence hanging and caught Nicki's eye.

"Unless what?"

"Unless he'd already been inside the property before. The Marshall's house had really creaky stairs. It was one of the first things I noticed when we went up to see the kid's bedroom. There's no way anyone would have been able to climb those stairs without making a sound and alerting the one person who 'stirs at every noise', unless..."

"He already knew the stairs that were creaky," finished Nicki. "So, you think your burglar is a builder or handyman, and he's been inside the houses before?"

DS Fox nodded. "That's my bet. He could be using his day job to suss out the properties – and revisits them later, knowing which back doors are left unlocked, or maybe even stealing a key to let himself in. None of the properties report any damage to doors or windows."

Nicki nodded and shifted in her seat. The incident room was cold without any bodies to create heat, and she'd only managed to pull on a lightweight sweatshirt before rushing out of the house. What DS Fox had shown her certainly made sense, and it was good detective work. But there was one question at the forefront of her mind.

"This is all very good, Graham, but why the urgency?" She made a point of looking back at the wall clock and stifled a yawn. "Could this not have waited until morning?"

"I'm coming to that." DS Fox's eyes sparkled and Nicki detected a glimmer of a smile on his lips which he was fighting hard to suppress. "As part of my investigation into the burglaries, I put in a trawl for any unsolved cases with a similar MO. Unforced entry. Small amounts of cash stolen. That kind of thing. I got a few hits, some of which I discounted due to their localities. But a few stood out. There were five in total from neighbouring Norfolk, all in the last twelve months - but two caught my eye in particular."

DS Fox pulled his notebook closer towards them both and continued. "As I said there were five similar burglaries reported in the Norfolk area over the last year. I rang the detective in charge over in Norwich, who happens to be a mate of mine, and he confirmed that all five had evidence of current or recent building work having been undertaken."

DS Fox paused, noting that he now had Nicki's undivided attention, but there was still the faint edge of doubt clouding her eyes. She's still wondering why I've tipped her out of bed for this, he mused, as he flicked over the next page in his notebook. Time to put her out of her misery before she lost patience completely.

"It was then that I made the connection to your case – Operation Goldfish."

Nicki's eyes darted in DS Fox's direction, their cloudiness evaporating. "Operation Goldfish? In what sense?"

DS Fox tapped his notebook, unable to halt the grin spreading across his face. His stomach flipped in anticipation. "Look at the names of the families who reported similar burglaries in Norfolk."

Nicki's eyes followed DS Fox's finger, taking in the five listed surnames. Two stood out. She glanced at DS Fox, noting the grin still plastered across his face. With her heart racing, she took in the names once again. "Are you sure?"

DS Fox nodded. "Absolutely. Both Ivy McFadden and Oliver Chambers' parents reported similar break-ins. And look at the dates. Only days before their children were abducted. And Sophia Jackson's break-in was the day before Lucas disappeared. *And* all three had building work carried out recently."

DS Fox pulled the domestic burglary file back in front of them and flipped to a series of colour photographs. "Someone thought it worthwhile to take an outside shot of the back door at the Jackson's house."

Nicki's eyes fell onto the pictures of Sophia Jackson's kitchen door, noting the three builder's sacks lined up against the rear wall, awaiting collection. "How did we miss this?" she breathed.

"Nothing in the files for Ivy and Oliver mentioned the break-ins. It doesn't appear in any of their statements. And why would it? Compared with the disappearance of your child it would pale into insignificance. It wouldn't seem important. But it's a common thread with all three families."

Silence filled the incident room as DS Fox let his words sink in. His heart hammered as he fought to keep his breathing in check. He was onto something. It was just a question of whether Detective Inspector Nicki Hardcastle thought the same.

The seconds ticked by agonisingly slowly as Nicki flicked once again through the file, her eyes sweeping across the gathered information. Her mouth felt dry as her brain started to slot everything into place. Finally, she closed the file and looked up into DS Fox's expectant face.

"Call the rest of the team – I want them all here for a briefing at 5am." Nicki pushed herself up out of her chair. "Good work, Graham."

\* \* \*

# Chapter Twenty-Two

   *Saturday 3rd November 2018*
   5.15am

Everyone made it into the incident room by 5am, as asked, and the air was soon filled with an aroma of citrus and sandalwood, evidence of a number of hurried morning showers. Nicki encouraged everyone to grab a coffee before they sat down. They had a lot to get through and the day ahead was likely to be busy.

Standing by the main whiteboard, Nicki watched as Darcie and Roy settled at the front, Matt and Duncan behind them. Hovering by the hot water urn at the back of the room was DS Graham Fox. Nicki caught his eye and waved him forward, noting how he hesitated for a second or two before shuffling towards a seat at the back.

"Morning, everyone. Thanks for answering the call and coming in so quickly." Nicki took a sip of her coffee, still feeling the same spark of excitement that had seared through her when DS Fox had taken her through his findings in the early hours. Neither of them had gone home. A quick splash of water on her face in the women's toilets had refreshed her only momentarily. Her stomach growled with both hunger and anticipation. She was running on adrenaline right now and just hoped it would last the day.

Catching DS Fox's eye, she saw how tired he looked - his face blotchy, his suit crumpled. Nicki felt a genuine warmth towards the man who'd acted so prickly in her presence for so long – despite his exhaustion, his eyes still glimmered with hunger for the job.

Over the last few hours they'd worked together, side by side, going over the evidence for the burglaries and matching them to the Lucas Jackson investigation. It was just like old times. Two friends working alongside each other. She realised just how much she'd missed it.

Nicki cleared her throat, realising that every pair of eyes in the room were now trained on her. She put her mug of coffee down on the corner of a nearby desk and waved an arm towards DS Fox.

"Firstly, I want you all to welcome a new member to the team for Operation Goldfish. DS Graham Fox."

Darcie and Roy swivelled in their seats to flash confused looks in the direction of the somewhat dishevelled detective sitting at the back. "My my, Gray," remarked Darcie, her face sporting an impish grin. "You look like you've been up all night. Anyone we know?"

"Graham and myself have been together most of the night," continued Nicki. "But before you pass any more lurid comments, DC Butler, we've been here at the station." A smile twitched at her lips as she reached for her coffee mug again. "And, at last, I think that we might have that one breakthrough we've been waiting for." Nicki paused and stared directly across the room to DS Fox. "Graham?" She raised her eyebrows while taking a sip from her mug. "You want to come up here and explain to the rest of the team what you found?"

DS Fox felt his cheeks colour, turning his tired pallid skin a faint shade of pink. "I...well, I don't mind if you want to..."

"Nonsense." Nicki shook her head and stepped to the side. "This is your moment. You found this, so it's only right you get the chance to tell the team." She flashed him a reassuring smile. "Despite their reputation, they don't usually bite. Not this early in the morning, anyway."

DS Fox found a sheepish grin settling over his unshaven face as he pushed himself up from his chair and edged towards the front.

"Go on," whispered Nicki as he passed by. "You've got this."

Turning towards his audience, DS Fox felt a wave of pride start to build. He *had* been the one to discover this lead. He *had* stayed behind and put the work in. He *had* earned his place on this team. He glanced sideways once again to find Nicki's eyes and received another encouraging nod in return.

Some bosses would have reaped the rewards themselves, taken the praise for someone else's achievement, passed off a break in a case as one of their own. But not Nicki. She was fair and straight, and praise was given where praise was due. Even after the way he'd been treating her. He felt another jolt of colour head towards his cheeks – but this time it was from shame. Shame because of how he'd behaved towards his one-time friend; best friend even. He'd been a fool, letting jealousy and self-pity get the better of him and it wasn't something he felt proud of.

Swallowing, with his mouth feeling suddenly dry, he pushed aside the thoughts of his own conduct – that was for another day. Today was about a little boy called Lucas Jackson. He cleared his throat and began.

"So, as the boss has just said, we've been here all night working on a link between my burglary investigation, and your Operation Goldfish." He turned towards the fourth whiteboard and picked up a marker pen, catching Nicki's eye once again. She gave another nod of encouragement.

"A series of burglaries in the town, at least the ones that have been reported, started at the beginning of October." Uncapping a red marker pen, DS Fox wrote the first householder's name at the top of the board. "This was quickly followed by another." A second name was added to the list. "Both were quickly put down as simple domestic burglaries, although nothing appeared to have been taken from either property, other than a small amount of cash." Pausing, he glanced back to ensure everyone was listening – they were. He turned back towards the whiteboard. "Over the next four weeks, four more similar burglaries were reported at various addresses across the town." Four more surnames were added to the list. "Once again, the MOs between them all were strikingly similar. No forced entry, no damage to property, and only small amounts of cash taken. One of the houses was the home of Lucas Jackson." DS Fox took the pen and underlined the surname Jackson.

Clearing his throat once more, he turned to face the team. Another flicker of pride teased his insides as he saw everyone hanging onto his every word.

"As part of my investigation, I made a search of other unsolved crimes that had a similar MO – not just in this county, but elsewhere. I found five that fit the criteria over in Norfolk, and two stood out for me in particular."

DS Fox turned back to the whiteboard and wrote two more surnames in red marker pen. He hadn't finished writing the second name when he heard a gasp. Turning around, he saw Darcie's wide-eyed expression and open mouth.

"Ivy and Oliver!" she exclaimed.

DS Fox nodded, putting the cap back on the marker pen. "Both Ivy and Oliver's parents reported similar break-ins only days before their children were abducted. In Lucas Jackson's case, the break-in was the night before he went missing." He paused and turned towards Nicki. "As soon as I discovered this link, I brought the boss in."

"So they're connected," said Roy, shuffling forwards in his seat, his eyes still trained on the whiteboard. "You're saying your burglar is our killer?"

Nicki nodded at DS Fox to continue. "Once I saw the connection with the burglaries and the abducted children, I began to take a closer look." DS Fox turned and nodded towards the list of names he'd written in red marker pen. "It took some phone calls, but it became clear that each of these families had renovations, or some kind of building work, undertaken at their properties in the days before their break-ins."

Darcie gave another gasp. "The builder's sacks outside! I remember those!"

DS Fox nodded, and let a smile flicker onto his lips. "Yes. You helpfully made a note of those in your notebook, Darcie. It was a good spot. Which got me thinking."

"The builder is the burglar," commented Roy, slowly nodding as the cogs inside his head began to churn and slot into place. "And the burglar is our killer."

DS Fox gave another nod. "That's my take on it, yes. He knows how to get inside these houses without breaking in. Maybe he notices which ones don't lock their doors at night, or he even steals a key. But he's familiar with the layout of the houses, and how to move around at night making the minimum of noise."

As DS Fox placed the marker pen back in its slot on the whiteboard, a silence descended across the incident room.

"Oh my," breathed Darcie, the first to break the quiet.

"Thank you, Graham." Nicki stepped forwards and turned towards her stunned team. "So, this is the position we find ourselves in this morning. We find our builder; we find our burglar. And when we find our burglar..." She didn't need to finish the sentence. "Today is going to be a long day – there'll be plenty of actions to get cracking with."

"Do you think he's still alive, boss?" Darcie asked the question that everyone else in the room had been thinking. "Lucas?"

Nicki hesitated before replying. "We have to work on that assumption, Darcie. According to the post mortems, both Ivy and Oliver are thought to have been kept by their abductor for at least six days before being killed. If our killer is working to the same timetable, then we have a small window to find him alive."

"But you can't be sure?" pressed Darcie, her eyes glassy.

Nicki gave an apologetic smile and shook her head. "No, I can't be sure. But we have to think positively. We're under a tight time pressure here – every minute and every second we delay, the likelihood of finding him alive diminishes. But, for now, we must treat him as still being alive and go out there and find him."

"So, what's to do, boss?" Roy sat with his notebook open. "What's first?"

"Track down as many builders or handyman services as we can in the locality. And we need to go back to each family that reported a burglary - see what they can remember about builders working on their properties. Maybe they have contact details such as business cards or invoices. Or at least a name. Matt and Duncan, I want you both on that. Contact all the families apart from the Jacksons and also Ivy and Oliver's. Graham and I will deal with those."

Both detectives readily agreed, nodding and moving towards a set of computers at the rear of the incident room.

"Darcie and Roy. I want you to start with searching for the local builders. Both Darcie and Roy nodded. "Yes, boss," they replied in unison.

Just then, Nicki's mobile chirped. As she pulled it from her pocket she

187

noted it was a call from DC Tina Gallagher. Frowning at the time, Nicki answered the call.

"Tina? Is everything OK?"

"Yes, everything's fine. Sorry to call so early, but..." Tina broke off and Nicki heard muffled sounds as if the family liaison officer were moving, and then the sound of a door closing. "Sophia was up most of the night, and we had a chat."

"Go on."

"I got her talking about her family. About Liam. You know she told us that Liam's brothers, Marcus and Callum, lived abroad?"

"Uh-huh?"

"Well, they don't. Live abroad, that is. Marcus has his own place down on the South Coast, not far from their mother. And Callum apparently lives not far from Norwich."

"Norwich? Well that's only 40 minutes or so from here."

"Indeed. Thought you should know. Sorry about the hour."

"No, no, you did the right thing. Why would Sophia lie about where Liam's brothers were living?"

Nicki could almost hear Tina's shrug. "No idea. She was still reluctant to talk about them. But they're definitely not as far away as she led us to believe."

Nicki closed the call and turned back to face the team.

"Slight change of plan. Darcie and Roy. I want you to trace Marcus and Callum Jackson instead. Turns out Sophia has misled us on where they might be living. Find out all you can on both of them. And I mean *everything*. We need to rule them out."

Nicki then turned to DS Fox. "Graham, you and I are going to see both Ivy and Oliver's parents. They're not that far away. And you said you had a contact at Norfolk police?"

DS Fox nodded. "Yes, Carl Bradshaw. Detective Sergeant. He'll talk to us again if needed. He remembers both cases very well. Obviously."

"Good. It's a busy day, people. But it'll be a good day if we make progress. Get yourselves some breakfast and then crack on. We'll meet up again later for a briefing at two o'clock." Nicki picked up her cooled coffee and turned to head towards the door. She paused with her hand on the door handle. "And while you're out and about today, I need you all to be thinking about how this man manages to entice small children to go with him. How does he befriend them in such a short space of time?" The image of Lucas Jackson in the CCTV made her shiver. "Lucas Jackson was holding this man's hand. I want to know why. Sophia Jackson said she didn't recognise the man in the CCTV image – but could he be someone Lucas knew? Roy? Darcie? I want to know how well Marcus and Callum knew Sophia's family."

Darcie pulled her chair across to her desk. "Maybe if he's been in their houses before, as a workman, they feel like they know him?" she ventured.

"Mmmmm," replied Nicki, pulling open the door. "Possibly. But some random man they might've seen around the house? Would that really be enough?"

Darcie and Roy looked at each other and shrugged.

"It's a thought, guys." Nicki stepped out into the corridor, calling back over her shoulder. "But we need to keep thinking. Why do they go with him without making a sound? No shouting. No screaming. No nothing. There's got to be more to it."

As Nicki headed along the corridor in the direction of her office, she heard hurried footsteps behind her. Turning around she saw DS Fox heading in her direction, slipping a jacket over his crumpled shirt.

"Thanks for that, boss," he said. "It means a lot."

"No problem," replied Nicki, a smile creeping onto her face. "It was your lead, you deserved to break it to the team. And while I remember - before we head out - if our killer is targeting the children in houses he's worked in before, we need to alert the families that reported the recent break-ins. Discreetly, mind. We don't want to cause mass panic. You say there's been three since the Jackson's break-in?"

DS Fox nodded.

"Discreetly alert the families. Get a patrol car to drive past every so often. At the very least, stress they must not let their children out of their sight, not for a single second. Best thing they can do is stay home."

DS Fox nodded again. "I'll get onto it now. And thanks – again - for welcoming me back. To the team, I mean." Feeling a lump forming in his throat, he gave a cough and continued. "Thanks."

Nicki smiled and playfully punched him on the arm. "Come on, you. Make those phone calls, and then you can buy me breakfast before we head out."

\* \* \*

# Chapter Twenty-Three

*Saturday 3rd November 2018*

7.30am

Nicki had barely put the phone down from speaking to DS Carl Bradshaw about the break-ins at the McFadden and Chambers properties when her office door flew open.

"Boss!" Darcie burst in, a piece of paper clutched in her hand. She waved it in the air as DS Carter followed her across the threshold. "Good, you're still here. You need to see this." Nicki's eyes followed the piece of paper as Darcie thrust it down in front of her. "It's Callum Jackson – Liam's younger brother."

Nicki picked up the paper, letting her eyes scan the details. Then she saw what had got Darcie so excited. "We need to follow this up."

"Already done, boss." Roy stepped forward, another sheet of paper in his hand. "Arrested in 2015 for sex with a minor while he was living in Surrey. He was twenty-four at the time, the girl was fifteen. From the reports we were able to access, it was consensual and no force was alleged. It appears the girl told him she was seventeen."

"Hmmm." Nicki ran her eyes across the details one more time. "That's what they all say. What happened to him?"

"Pleaded guilty and sentenced to two years' imprisonment. Sounds like they possibly didn't believe him when he said he thought she was seventeen. Came out on licence after serving a year. Placed on the sex offenders register for ten years."

"And he's living near Norwich now?"

Roy glanced back down at the report in his hand. "Yep. About ten miles south. That's all we have on him so far."

Jumping up from her chair, Nicki reached for her coat. "OK. This Callum needs a visit. Give the local force a call and see if they have anything further to add before you rock up. Are you both happy to follow this up? I've got to head out with Graham to see Ivy and Oliver's parents again. See if they recall anything about their builder."

Both Roy and Darcie nodded.

"Good. I'll see you at the briefing at two."

\* \* \*

*Saturday 3<sup>rd</sup> November 2018*

7.45am

Sitting in his usual chair by the window, Callum Jackson gazed out from behind the thin, net curtains. It wasn't the greatest of views – looking out over the disused expanse of open ground where a car sales lot had once stood. Now it was nothing but a wasteland, left to rot; unloved and unkempt. Callum knew only too well what that felt like.

It was an ugly blot on an otherwise picturesque landscape, driving house prices and local rents in a never-ending downward spiral. Although that was something Callum, for one, wasn't too unhappy about.

He tossed the local newspaper to the floor. He'd searched the jobs section yet again and come up with nothing. Returning his gaze to the window, he felt the familiar feeling of despair. He had a lot in common with the old car lot. Both had been discarded without a second thought; kicked into touch and forgotten.

*Ruined.*

Reaching down for the can of cider by the side of his chair, he swallowed the small amount left in the bottom. Crumpling the can in one hand, he then launched it in the same direction as the newspaper. He'd been up and about early - replenishing his stocks of cheap beer and cider from what was left of this week's benefit payment. But now he was back home, the day stretched out in front of him like all the others. Days filled with nothing. Days filled with emptiness. Days where all he seemed to do was think.

He flicked the TV off with the remote – there was never anything worth watching at this time of the morning, just endless news programmes or other daytime nonsense.

Next to the TV was a battered bookcase he'd picked up at a local car boot sale. He wasn't a great reader – never had been – so instead of books the shelves were sparsely populated with DVDs, old motorbike magazines and a few photo albums. It was the photo albums that caught his eye on this Saturday morning; as they usually did when all he had to do with his time was think. Nothing to do but think about times gone by and a future so callously ripped from his grasp.

Anger boiled within him; another common occurrence these days. Pushing himself up out of his chair, he crossed the short distance and pulled out the largest of the photo albums from the bottom shelf, before returning to his position by the window. With the turning of each page, the anger lessened, and he felt a familiar tug on his heart. The images may be some years old but they never left him, not for one second. Since his release from prison, he'd studied these pages so many, many times – each one burned into his memory, never to be forgotten. Each and every face was a reminder of what he'd lost - how things used to be, and how things could've been.

Before it all went wrong.

Before his world came crashing down around him.

Before *her*.

The Princess of Wales's Royal Regiment had been his saviour. He hadn't been a model pupil at school; far from it. Always lagging behind his peers academically, preferring to spend his time out on the football field or, more often than not, slipping through the hole in the fence and disappearing into town with his mates. He'd been labelled as a lost cause quite early on in his school career and nobody, not even his parents, had expected much from him. So it had been to everyone's surprise, including his own, when he'd been accepted for army training as a new recruit with 'The Tigers'.

'*It'll do him good*,' had been his parents' response. '*Teach him some discipline.*' '*It'll be the making of him, just you wait and see.*'

Hot tears pinched at the corners of his eyes. The anger was now returning in spades. He'd been happy then. The army had offered him the support and camaraderie that no one else could. He'd felt, for the first time in his life, that he belonged. That he *fitted*.

Following in Liam's footsteps had been a challenge. Liam was the eldest and the golden child of the family. He could do no wrong in the eyes of their parents. An exemplary student, gaining straight 'A's across the board, he'd sailed through his army training and very quickly been singled out for promotion. Everyone knew he was on course to reach high office – Captain or Major material. Maybe even higher.

Nobody expected much from Callum.

Snapping the photo album shut, he sank back in his chair and closed his eyes, pushing away the tears that threatened to spill. He hated anyone seeing him cry, and Marcus was only upstairs. Clenching his eyes tightly shut, he fought against the anger welling up inside. It was all that bitch's fault. *She* did this to him; ruining the only career that had ever felt right for him. Taking away his one dream, his one chance of making something of himself.

*It was all her fault.*

\* \* \*

*Saturday 3ʳᵈ November 2018*
    8.15am

The two wooden chairs sat side by side in the centre of the small bedroom.

Excitement flickered within him. Tonight was the night.

He glanced over at the roll of carpet positioned against the wall next to the metal-framed bed. It had taken quite an effort to drag the roll upstairs from the back of the van. He couldn't ask his brother for help; not now. It'd taken all of his strength to reach the top.

Padding over to the carpet, he kicked the side with his foot. Lucas Jackson's head poked out of one end, just enough to see his tangled mop of sandy hair with a pale and lifeless arm stretched out next to it. He ought to unravel the whole roll, wrap him back up more tightly this time – and poke that arm back inside. But he didn't have the time. Or the inclination.

His mind was on other things. He glanced back towards the two chairs and smiled at the thrill of anticipation it gave him.

Lucas had been a mistake from the very beginning, he knew that now, and the sooner he got rid of him the better. He'd thought about dragging the carpet downstairs and shoving it into the rear of the van – but he knew he didn't have time. He hadn't chosen a dump site yet, and he didn't want to rush that part this time. It needed careful thought.

And what if the carpet unravelled part way down the stairs? He'd have to start all over again. No. The boy wasn't going anywhere. Not now. Once he had the other two safely back in the room, he'd deal with Lucas Jackson.

* * *

# Chapter Twenty-Four

*Saturday 3rd November 2018*

12.35pm

Nicki slotted the keys into the ignition of her Toyota, but before switching on the engine she turned towards the passenger seat. "It never gets any easier, does it?"

DS Graham Fox shook his head and ran a hand through his matted hair. He knew he looked like he'd slept in his clothes and hadn't shaved for a week – but he also knew that neither Ivy nor Oliver's parents would have noticed. "Those poor people," he sighed. "I can't even begin to imagine what they must be feeling."

Nicki let her hands fall into her lap as she cast a glance back out towards the home of Oliver Chapman. Her visit yesterday had been bad enough, but the return journey today had seemed even more so, if that were possible. The intervening months since the children's disappearance had barely made a dent in the sorrow each family still faced. It was likely that no amount of time ever would. Grief would linger for them like an unwelcome guest, one way or another.

And then Nicki had rubbed even more salt in their wounds by asking about the odd-job man both families had engaged just before their children's disappearance. Rapid connections followed, everything steadily slotting into place - and then the gut-wrenching realisation hit them like a freight train.

They'd invited him into their house.

It was something Nicki knew they would never forgive themselves for, no matter how much time passed. Another stake hammered home; another nail in the coffin that harboured their guilt.

Guilt.

There was that word again. That small word that merely festered and grew; leaching out like some uncontrollable virus, consuming everything in its path.

Neither family had been able to shed any more light on the identity of the killer they'd unwittingly welcomed into their lives. Ivy's father said he thought the man's name was Tom or Thomas. Mr Chapman had thought it was Max. Neither had any form of contact details and neither had been presented with an invoice – just a cash-in-hand job, cheaper with no VAT or books to go through. It had suited everyone. Both families said he'd merely turned up on the doorstep, saying he was working in the area, and did they have any odd jobs needing doing? No job too big or too small.

Switching on the engine, Nicki pulled the car away from the kerb and headed for home. The trip had been disappointing, with no further leads to help them track down who their elusive builder might be. She only hoped Matt and Duncan were having better luck.

Nicki wasn't a pessimist by nature, but she doubted very much would come of it. The initial euphoria of Graham's discovery was now going stale.

As she swung the car around a roundabout, her mobile rang. Using the car's hands-free unit, Nicki answered the call from Tina Gallagher. "Tina? What's up?"

"Just a bit more information on Liam's brothers that I managed to tease out of Sophia. Marcus was the only one of the family that didn't join the forces – he apparently has a small handyman business based on the South Coast. Sophia says she hasn't seen or heard from him in years. And Callum? Did you know about his sexual offences conviction?"

Nicki nodded and pulled out to overtake a lorry. "Yes, we got news of that this morning. Darcie and Roy are heading out to see him."

"I'll keep trying to get Sophia to open up, but it's hard work."

"You're doing great, Tina. Thanks." Nicki ended the call and turned towards DS Fox. "You thinking what I'm thinking?" Nicki immediately placed a call to Roy's mobile. "Roy? Where are you right now?"

"Just about to leave to go and see Callum Jackson," replied Roy, sounding like he was outside. "Darcie's driving."

"Well apparently, Marcus Jackson has a building company or handyman service. After you've called in on Callum, I want you tracking him down. We're on our way back to the station right now."

"Will do, boss. I've a mate who works down in Sussex. I'll give him a ring."

Nicki cut the call and swung the Toyota back out into the fast lane, taking another glance at the passenger seat. "You OK there, Graham?"

DS Fox nodded, but continued to stare out of the window. "It's at times like these that you think about your own family. About how things can change in a matter of seconds – suddenly your whole world is turned upside down."

Nicki murmured her agreement. "It sure does. Life can be cruel."

DS Fox pulled his gaze away from the countryside flashing past the window. "I want to say sorry – again. For how I've been lately."

Nicki let a frown graze her forehead as she flashed a look of concern at her colleague. "What do you mean?"

DS Fox gave Nicki a rueful smile and bit back the chuckle on his lips. "Don't pretend you don't know what I mean. We both know I've been a right dick lately. More than just lately."

"Well..." Nicki slid another sideways glance towards the passenger seat. "Now you put it like that..."

DS Fox let the laugh escape this time. "You're too kind. I've been an arse and you know it. And I'm sorry. Really sorry. I'm getting my shit together, I promise. And it won't happen again."

Nicki gave a shrug and turned her attention back to the road in front. "We all have our demons, Graham." She tried to push the image of Deano out of her head. "It's what makes us human."

DS Fox cleared his throat. "My wife left me – last year. Took the kids and moved in with her new bloke." The statement hung in the stuffy air of the Toyota, the only sound being the rumble strips on the tarmac below.

# CHAPTER TWENTY-FOUR

"Jesus, Graham. I had no idea. I'm really sorry."

It was DS Fox's turn to shrug. "It's been on the cards for a while – apparently. I was so blinkered with the job, I never noticed how unhappy she was. How unhappy I was making her. It's my own fault."

Nicki shook her head and slowed the car down for a tight bend. "I'm sure it was more than just you and the job. It takes two to make a relationship work...and two to make it fail." Nicki paused. Hark at her giving relationship advice. She swallowed back a bitter laugh. "So where are you living now?"

"I had to sell the house, so I'm living in a really shitty little room above a kebab shop at the moment."

"I'm really sorry, Graham. I mean it."

"Not as sorry as I am." DS Fox returned his gaze to the window. "Not about Debbie and me – that ship has long since sailed. I know that now. But about you – and the team. I've let you all down badly by being such a prick."

"Well, you've more than made up for it with your shout about our killer being linked to your burglaries. You're forgiven. You're a good man, Graham Fox. And an outstanding detective." She paused and gave him a playful poke on the arm. "Although the team will be expecting doughnuts as recompense."

\* \* \*

*Saturday 3rd November 2018*
    12.45pm

Marcus Jackson made sure the door was firmly locked before he made his way downstairs. He hadn't told Callum what he was doing, or why he was spending so much time upstairs. Callum wouldn't understand – not fully.

His younger brother hadn't questioned him when he'd turned up on his doorstep two months ago. He'd told their mother he was moving in with Callum to keep an eye on him – and to help him with job applications. And that was a joke in itself. No prospective employer would go anywhere near Callum; not now. Not when they took a look at his record. A brief look at his

CV and his application would go to the bottom of the pile. If not the shredder.

But that wasn't the real reason Marcus had landed on his younger brother's doorstep. Marcus had other plans, over and above getting Callum some minimum-wage job with a zero-hours contract.

Marcus neared the bottom of the stairs as an image of Sophia Jackson filled his head.

Sophia Jackson.

That woman had succeeded in ruining the Jackson family. She'd ragged their name through the mud and killed their brother. Not a day went by when Marcus didn't think of Liam – and the part his so-called loving wife had played in his death.

Standing by the side of Liam's coffin on that overcast April day, he'd made his promise – touching the side of the rosewood box as he did so. One day he would make her pay.

And it was a promise he intended to keep.

Callum was sitting, just as he always was, in the chair by the window – an empty can of cider crumpled on the floor. At least it was just the one.

His brother's once muscular physique had wasted away – much like the scene opposite the house. He didn't look after himself properly, surviving on a diet of cigarettes and alcohol mostly. Seeing the physical deterioration of his brother before his very own eyes stoked the anger that was so often bubbling just beneath the surface.

Sophia Jackson.

If there was one thing Marcus Jackson intended to do, it was to ruin her life – just the way she'd ruined theirs.

\* \* \*

*Saturday 3<sup>rd</sup> November 2018*
   1.05pm

"So, what's the score with this one?" Roy turned and looked through the passenger window at No 6 Beech Grove. They'd parked opposite, by the side of an expanse of wasteland that stretched as far as the eye could see. The remains of a burnt-out car sat not far from the roadside – they assumed it was a car, although its true identity had been torched beyond recognition.

Darcie flipped open her notebook. "Place is rented in the name Callum Jackson. Been here for the last eighteen months. He was released from prison in 2016 after serving half of a two-year sentence. No employment records since being dishonourably discharged from the Army. Youngest of the three brothers."

Roy went to open the door when his mobile chirped. Pulling it out, his eyebrows hitched. "Well, this is somewhat timely. My mate at Sussex Police has got back to me already. Apparently, Marcus Jackson no longer lives in his house down there – according to a neighbour, he's just gone to stay with his brother..."

Both Roy and Darcie's gaze returned to the front of No 6 Beech Grove.

"And currently he has two vehicles registered in his name. One of which is a white van, registration number..."

"DE16 XEW," finished Darcie, her eyes now trained on the white van parked on the driveway.

Roy nodded. "Well, it looks like he's at home."

Darcie led the way towards the house. The front garden was devoid of anything but some patchy grass, with an equally patchy gravel path leading to the front door. The double garage at the side was shut fast. As they approached, both noted the heavy curtains still shrouding all the upstairs windows despite it being past midday.

"Are you sure we shouldn't call this in?" Darcie's hand hovered over the door.

"We're just here for a friendly chat. If we suspect there's anything untoward about either of them, I'll be the first to radio for back-up."

The first series of raps on the weathered front door elicited no response. After a pause, Darcie rapped again, louder this time. It took a third round of knocking before any movement was seen through the frosted glass at the side of the door.

"Callum and Marcus Jackson?" Darcie peered through the side window.

"Police. Open up."

Darcie was about to knock again when they heard the lock turn. With warrant cards at the ready, they both stood back and waited for the door to open.

The first figure they saw was tall. Still dressed in a pair of crumpled pyjama bottoms and an equally crumpled t-shirt, Marcus Jackson's imposing frame filled every inch of the door frame.

"What d'you want?" His expression gave both Darcie and Roy no doubt that their unannounced presence was decidedly unwelcome.

"Sorry to disturb, Mr Jackson – is it Marcus or Callum?" Roy stepped forward, warrant card held high. "I'm DS Royston Carter from Suffolk Police and this is my colleague DC Butler. We just have a few questions to ask if that's all right? May we come in?"

Marcus Jackson hesitated, his eyes flicking from Roy to Darcie and back again. He folded his arms across his chest and maintained his stance. "What's it about?" He focused his gaze on Roy, his jaw tightening with every word.

Roy held his gaze without flinching. "It won't take long. But I think you might prefer it to be discussed inside, Mr Jackson." Roy made a point of glancing over his shoulder at the street beyond. "You know what neighbours can be like."

A flash of irritation crossed Marcus Jackson's brow, but he gave a curt nod and stepped back. "Well, make it quick. I'm busy."

Roy led Darcie into the narrow hallway. It smelt musty, as if the doors and windows hadn't been opened in a while. The stale aroma of last night's cooking hung in the air. Marcus Jackson stood in the centre of the hall, the same rock-hard stance as he'd had in the doorway. Legs planted apart, arms folded across his muscular chest, he prevented Roy or Darcie from advancing more than a few feet.

"May we step inside?" Darcie nodded at a closed door that she presumed led to a living room.

Marcus Jackson held his position. "What you have to say you can say right here."

Before either Roy or Darcie had the chance to reply, the door to the living room opened and Callum Jackson stepped out into the hall.

"Who is it, Marc? What's up?"

Callum Jackson, ex-infantryman with the Princess of Wales's Royal Regiment, portrayed a very different image than that of his older brother as they stood side by side in the hallway. Callum was lightly-framed, with not an ounce of meat on his bones. His face was drawn and pale, his limbs scrawny. In contrast, Marcus Jackson posed a daunting figure. Taller and broader, his muscles rippled beneath his tatty t-shirt.

"You must be Callum." Roy exchanged a look with Darcie as he stepped forward. "DS Royston Carter, Suffolk Police. This here is DC Butler. Glad to find you both at home. We'd like to ask you some questions."

Callum Jackson cast a worried glance towards his brother. "What...what's this about, Marc? What do they want?"

Marcus Jackson flashed a look that told his brother to be quiet. Callum obeyed and shrank backwards. The taut muscles on Marcus Jackson's neck flexed. "Let me handle this." Rocking back on his heels, he switched his contemptuous gaze back to the detectives blocking his hallway. "Say what you've come to say, then you can leave."

Roy slipped his warrant card back inside his pocket. "Just a moment or two of your time, that's all. How well do you know Sophia Jackson?"

\* \* \*

# Chapter Twenty-Five

*Saturday 3$^{rd}$ November 2018*

2.00pm

Upon returning to the station, DS Fox had set about trawling back through the phone book, Yellow Pages and local websites to continue the search for the builder. It was a painstaking and thankless task. Matt and Duncan had returned from visiting the other families, but all were very vague as to who exactly they'd invited into their homes. Somewhere in there was a stark lesson to be learned – but now wasn't the time.

They'd made a brief stop on their way back to call on Sophia Jackson. She, too, had been unable to say exactly who had carried out the decorating at her home and Nicki had once again shown her the CCTV image of Lucas hand in hand with his abductor. Once again, Sophia denied recognising the figure.

Tina's revelation about Marcus Jackson was starting to unnerve Nicki. But surely if the man with Lucas had been Marcus, Sophia would have recognised him? Her own brother-in-law?

DS Fox followed her into the incident room armed with two coffees. "Still nothing credible on the online search, but I've just had an update on the three families we've alerted about the break-ins. The first two are happy staying at home and have no plans to go anywhere."

Nicki nodded. "Good. What about the third family?"

"Apparently, the Kennedy's haven't been at home today. And the number given on the case file is just ringing out."

Nicki frowned. "OK. When we're done here, can you swing by their house again and check if they've returned? Then update me."

"Sure."

Matt and Duncan entered the incident room and Nicki looked at her watch again. "Has anyone seen or heard from Roy or Darcie?"

Blank looks all round confirmed what Nicki had already suspected. Pulling her phone from her pocket, she quickly scrolled to Roy's number and gave it another call. It went to voicemail. With no time to lose, Nicki started the briefing.

"OK. Let's begin. We're at day four of Operation Goldfish. Matt? Duncan? Would you like to kick off and tell us what you've managed to find out from the other families?"

Matt Holland nodded and flipped open his notebook. "We managed to speak to all the families concerned. Most recalled a plain white van, no markings or wording on the outside. No mention of a registration number. The guy apparently gave a variety of names, none of which I think we can safely assume was his real one." Matt flicked to another page. "He was always paid in cash, so no bank details. At a couple of properties, he left behind a business card – again, none of the names checked out. And no physical address was ever given."

Nicki nodded. It was exactly what both Ivy and Oliver's parents had said.

"But we do have a fairly decent description," added Duncan. "Tall, with a fairly muscular build. Dark hair, closely cut. Clean shaven. And all mentioned seeing a facial scar around the jaw area."

Nicki's eyebrows raised. "A scar?" Neither Ivy nor Oliver's parents had mentioned a scar. But then again, she hadn't asked. Silently admonishing herself for not probing more deeply about the builder's description, Nicki gave both Matt and Duncan an appreciative nod. "That's interesting. Good work. Anything else?"

"Most described him as quiet, kept himself to himself while working and always wore gloves."

Nicki sighed. "Well, that puts the dampener on my next suggestion that we reprocess the houses for further fingerprints."

Nicki glanced at the wall clock above the whiteboards. It was now almost two-fifteen and there was still no word from either Roy or Darcie. It was unusual for at least one of them not to have checked in if they were running late. Nicki pulled out her phone again to give Roy another call but, as she did so, the handset started to chirp.

"Darcie," greeted Nicki, breaking into a smile. "I was just thinking about you." She paused and listened to the voice on the other end of the line, the smile quickly dropping from her face. "Where are you now?" After a brief response, Nicki nodded curtly. "OK, I'm on my way."

Snapping the phone shut, she turned towards her team, her face white. "Darcie and Roy are at the hospital. Roy's been attacked."

* * *

# Chapter Twenty-Six

*Saturday 3rd November 2018*
2.45pm

A&E was busy but at least everyone in Waiting Room B appeared to have a seat and there were no waiting ambulances queuing outside the doors. Nicki first spotted Darcie and Roy sat in the far corner, the latter with a pad of gauze held up to his nose. She then spied Amy behind the main reception desk and headed her way.

"Hey, Nicki," greeted Amy. "It's all go here today." She nodded in Roy's direction. "Your man over there is just waiting for an x-ray slot."

"Any lasting damage?" Nicki glanced over her shoulder, noting the blood decorating Roy's shirt.

"Looks worse than it is, I suspect. The x-ray will confirm if anything's broken." Amy reached across the desk. "Take him some fresh gauze, he looks like he might need it. And I'll chase up the x-ray slot."

Nicki threaded her way through the quiet chaos and sat down next to Roy. "You look a bit battered, Roy. You OK?"

Roy gave a smile behind the bloodied gauze. "Just a scrape, boss. I'm fine."

"The guy was a complete maniac," blasted Darcie, shaking her head. "We were only asking a few general questions about his relationship with his brother's family, Sophia in particular, and he just flipped. I'm not even sure what it was we said that tipped him over the edge. It all happened so fast."

"Don't concern yourselves about it right now." Nicki handed Roy the fresh pad of gauze and took the bloodied one in exchange. "It'll all come out in the wash. I take it he's been arrested?"

Darcie nodded, defiantly. "I did it myself at the scene, then called for backup to take him away. I'm guessing he's in a cell right now."

"Well, we can let him stew for a while. You're more important than he is right now." Nicki eyed the rest of Roy's injuries. As well as the bloodied nose, which may or may not be broken, there was an impressive swelling developing across his right cheekbone and around his right eye. A cut above the right eyebrow was oozing a slow trickle of blood.

While she was appraising Roy's injuries, Nicki saw Darcie's face light up. Following her DC's gaze towards the reception desk, she saw a vaguely familiar figure talking to Amy. Darcie gave a small wave, followed by a huge smile.

The boyfriend. Nicki had already forgotten the man's name.

Her gaze followed Darcie's new man as he wheeled a young boy towards a set of chairs, and presumably his parents, and then made his way back along the corridor towards the main hospital. Nicki felt the familiar cogs starting to whirr inside her brain, making connections it hadn't done before. Springing out of her seat, she headed towards Amy, who noted the pensive look on Nicki's face as she approached.

"What's up?"

With the gnawing feeling in her stomach growing by the second, Nicki's gaze drifted towards the exit where the porter had disappeared only seconds before. "He was wearing a mask." She turned back towards Amy, her frown deepening. "That guy – Darcie's new beau. He was wearing a mask."

\* \* \*

*Saturday 3ʳᵈ November 2018*
  2.50pm

Ryan Hodges made his way to the children's ward on the second floor, his mask safely stowed away in his pocket. The corridors were a little quieter upstairs, contrasting with the hustle and bustle of the A&E department below. But he really preferred the hospital at night; at night it was peaceful, on the whole. And quiet. Sometimes the only thing you could hear was the squeaking of your shoes on the highly polished floor beneath you.

Using his ID badge, Ryan buzzed himself into the children's ward and headed towards the desk. He smiled as he recognised the nurse standing at the computer monitor. "Evening, Charlene," he greeted, flashing a smile that made the dimples on either side of his cheeks deepen. "You have a job for us?"

He nodded at his colleague who had already arrived and was leaning up against the nurse's station.

"I do." The nurse tapped the computer keyboard as she spoke. "Timothy Green. Young lad just over there. Needs to go to theatre for an emergency appendicectomy."

"Ready to go now?" Ryan cast his eyes over towards the bed nearest to the nurse's station.

Charlene nodded. "Yes, good to go. He's been prepped but is understandably quite anxious. We hoped he might have got away with conservative treatment, but his abdominal pain has worsened throughout the morning – so the surgeons want him in theatre straight away." She looked up from the computer screen and smiled at Ryan. "You might need to work your magic."

Ryan returned the smile. "No problem, I've come prepared!"

The two porters turned towards their waiting patient. As expected, the young boy looked pale and frightened. Ryan assumed that the two people sporting equally anxious expressions by the boy's side were his parents. He also recognised Dr Francis, Consultant Anaesthetist, hovering by the end of the bed and nodded in acknowledgment.

Ryan immediately went to the boy's bedside and crouched down. "Hey, Tim. How're you doing? I hear you've got a painful tummy?"

The boy's red-rimmed eyes widened with renewed fear.

Ryan gave one of his best smiles and continued. "Well, the doctors here are going to make you feel better. So, when you wake up, you don't have that horrible tummy pain anymore. That's good, right?"

Ten-year-old Timothy Green stared at Ryan for a few seconds, before slowly nodding his head.

"He's worried about the anaesthetic," whispered the woman Ryan presumed was the mother. "He won't let anyone touch him."

Dr Francis stepped forwards. "IV access is proving too difficult, so we're going for a gas induction."

Ryan nodded. He'd noticed the boy's pale arms lying outside the hospital blanket, with the evidence of numerous attempts to get an IV line into him. Attempts that had clearly failed. "And does that worry you, Tim? Having a mask on your face to help you go to sleep?"

The boy nodded, his eyes welling up with a fresh bout of tears. He pulled the blanket up towards his chin.

Ryan smiled again and reached into his pocket. "Well, you don't need to be scared of masks. Look." Bringing out a handful of cloth masks, he spread them over the bedcovers. "Who's your favourite? You like Spiderman? The Marvel characters?" The boy's eyes flickered hesitantly towards the masks. "I've got Captain Marvel here, and The Hulk. But my favourite one is this. Look."

Ryan pulled out a cloth mask with a picture of Shrek on the front and brought it up to his face, popping the elasticated bands around his ears. The boy's eyes widened again, but this time the fear etched onto his face seemed to subside a little. A small smile flickered at the corners of his mouth.

"See, masks are fun! They don't need to be scary. Do you want to try one on?" Ryan patted the bedcovers next to the remaining masks. "Go on, choose one."

The boy looked down at the pile of cloth masks. After a few moments, his fingers stretched towards a mask of Bart Simpson.

"Ah, good choice!" Ryan helped the boy bring the mask to his face and fasten the straps around his ears. "See, nothing to it. The mask they give you just before your operation might look a bit different, and it might feel a bit different, but it's just a mask. Just like this one."

The boy's eyes started to gleam, but this time with something other than tears. Ryan was convinced that, beneath the cloth mask, the boy was smiling.

A look of relief flooded the faces of both parents.

"Do you want to keep it on?" asked Ryan, straightening up by the boy's bedside. "While we wheel you down to theatre?"

The boy nodded.

Ryan glanced sideways towards Dr Francis. "Looks like we're good to go."

* * *

*Saturday 3rd November 2018*

3.30pm

Darcie led Roy back towards the reception desk where Nicki was nursing a strong black coffee that she didn't really want.

"How did it go?" Nicki noted the bloodstains on Roy's shirt had now dried and his nose had, at last, stopped bleeding. "Good news?"

Roy began to nod, then wished he hadn't as pain seared through his skull. "Nose isn't broken, but the cheekbone has a small fracture. And there's a few cracked ribs, too. I've got some painkillers and apparently we can go." The relief in his voice was palpable.

"And concussion," added Darcie, clutching a packet of medication in her hand.

"Take him home, Darcie. I've got a few things to do, then I'll see you back at the station." Nicki watched as Darcie hooked her arm through Roy's and started to guide him towards the front entrance. Before they'd got far, Nicki called out. "When you saw Marcus, did you see any kind of scar on his face? Around the jaw?"

Darcie turned and shook her head. "Not that I can recall...Roy?"

Roy matched Darcie's shake of the head, wincing as he did so. "No, nothing. And I got a pretty good look at him before he decked me." With another pained smile, he let Darcie lead him outside.

Nicki pursed her lips. Several of the families had reported seeing a scar. Did that now put Marcus Jackson out of the frame? Confusion fogged her mind and she took another sip of the bitter, black coffee. As she did so, the image of the departing porter filled her head once more.

"Do you think he might talk to me?"

Amy looked up from the computer monitor and frowned. "Who?"

"The porter. Darcie's new man."

"Ryan? Why would you want to talk to him?"

Nicki hesitated. It was the mask that had caught her attention. The *mask*. *He puts children at ease by wearing a mask.*

Could it really be that simple?

Nicki's frown deepened, as did her grip on the coffee cup. "Does he have a scar on his face?"

* * *

# Chapter Twenty-Seven

*Saturday 3$^{rd}$ November 2018*

3.45pm

"Coffee?" Nicki pressed the button on the self-serve coffee machine in the hospital canteen.

Ryan shook his head. "No, thanks. I'm not really on a break."

Nicki paid for her coffee and then led the porter across to the visitor's tables on the far side of the canteen, away from any prying eyes and waggling ears. Taking a seat, and indicating he should do the same, Nicki took a moment to blow across the top of her coffee mug and gather her thoughts

"Tell me," she began, her voice calm and even. "How long have you worked here?"

A look of surprise crossed the porter's face. "At the hospital? Um, about three months. Why?"

Nicki ignored the question. "And where did you work before that? You're new to Bury, right?"

Ryan hesitated, a steely expression replacing the earlier look of surprise. "This and that. I moved around. Where's this going?"

Again, Nicki ignored the question and took another sip of the cooling coffee while she composed herself. Everything screamed at her to stop this line of questioning; to stop questioning him at all. DCI Turner's voice hammered inside her head. Stop, Nicki. *Stop.*

She was on shaky ground procedure-wise, she knew that. It was as if she'd taken PACE and just ripped it up and thrown it out the window. If she truly suspected him, she should end it now; caution him and take him to the station.

But she didn't. Instead, she placed her coffee cup down and gazed across the table. She noted the hardened look on the porter's face was now joined by a similar look in his eyes. As she watched the muscles in his jaw tighten, her gaze was drawn to a pale white scar along one side of his jaw.

"How did you get that scar?"

The steely look in the man's pale green eyes now turned into something more hostile. He broke Nicki's gaze and glanced down at his watch. "Look, I'm not sure what this is all about, but I've got a job to do." He made to get up. "In fact, my shift ended fifteen minutes ago, so I don't even need to be here."

"Well, I beg to differ." Nicki stood up at the same time and brought out her warrant card, holding it just a matter of inches from Ryan Hodges' face. With the DCI's voice screaming at her from every crevice of her mind, she succumbed.

"If you're not needed here then you won't mind accompanying me to the station where we can continue our little chat more formally."

\* \* \*

*Saturday 3rd November 2018*
4.45pm

With Roy now safely tucked up on his sofa beneath a blanket, with a pot of tea by his side, Darcie pushed open the door to the incident room.

"You still here, Gray?"

DS Graham Fox nodded towards his computer screen. "Thought I'd keep trying to locate local builders. But everything's a dead end. But hey, how's Roy? I heard he got whacked?"

Darcie grimaced. "Don't get me started. That Marcus Jackson's a maniac and wants locking up. Roy's OK. Battered and bruised. A fractured cheekbone.

Some cracked ribs. Probably concussion, too."

"Is he being interviewed – Marcus?"

Darcie shook her head. "Not yet. The boss says he can stew for a while. She called me when I was over at Roy's. She wants me to go back through the files on Ivy and Oliver – looking for any mention of masks."

"Masks?"

"It's a theory she has on how the children seem willing to go with him. How he puts them at ease somehow. Maybe he has a funny mask or something. The boss thinks she remembers reading something, somewhere – that somebody mentions a mask, or a costume. I think I do, too, but I just can't remember where."

"Spiderman." DS Fox pushed himself out of his chair and headed over to Darcie's desk, starting to pull the files on Ivy and Oliver out of the towering pile. "It was Oliver."

Darcie frowned as DS Fox took Oliver's file and began leafing through the papers. "Here. Statement of Matilda Davenport, aged thirteen. It's hidden away but she mentions seeing a man with a Spiderman mask on. Wasn't Oliver wearing a Spiderman t-shirt when he was abducted?"

Darcie's eyes gleamed as she took the statement from DS Fox's hands. "Oh my God, you're right – I *knew* I'd seen it somewhere. And yes. Oliver had a Spiderman t-shirt on when he went missing. But is that plausible? That he just wears a mask to win their trust?"

DS Fox shrugged. "It could work, I guess. Who knows? My kids love any kind of dressing up …" DS Fox stopped abruptly, mid-sentence, and strode across to the whiteboard, grabbing a red marker pen on his way.

"Gray?" Darcie watched as DS Fox hovered in front of the whiteboards.

"We now think our killer is the burglar, correct?"

Darcie nodded.

"He accesses the houses of his victims in the middle of the night, not taking much of value. We've never really understood why that is. So, what if that's just a cover? A distraction? The real reason for breaking in is not to steal, but to access the children's bedrooms."

Darcie paused and then gave a slow nod. "OK, go on."

"The real reason he breaks in, in the dead of night, is to take a look in the kid's rooms - and what do the bedrooms all have in common?"

Darcie began to shrug.

"TV characters. Every one of them has some kind of TV or movie character theme. So, what if he goes into their rooms to see what TV characters they like? So..." DS Fox paused, holding Darcie's gaze. "So, if he needs to wear a mask...."

Darcie's eyebrows shot up a notch. "He knows which one to pick."

"Lucas was obsessed with Batman, yes?"

Darcie nodded. "His room was full of it."

Using the red marker pen, DS Fox wrote 'Batman' next to Lucas Jackson's name.

"And Oliver's room had Spiderman everywhere, yes?"

Darcie nodded again while watching DS Fox write Spiderman next to Oliver's name. Out of the file in his hands, he pinned up a photograph of the six-year-old's bedroom, showing a duvet set and curtains covered in images of Spiderman.

"What about Ivy?" DS Fox returned to Darcie's desk and pulled out Ivy's file. After flicking through several pages, he pulled out a scene of crime photograph from the little girl's bedroom and pinned it next to her name. "Peppa Pig."

"Ivy was wearing a Peppa Pig coat when she was abducted," breathed Darcie, her eyes shining.

Both Darcie and DS Fox stared in silence at the whiteboard.

After what seemed like an eternity, Darcie reached for the phone. "I'm calling the boss."

* * *

# Chapter Twenty-Eight

*Saturday 3<sup>rd</sup> November 2018*

5.15pm

The change in venue had done nothing to soften the expression on Ryan Hodges' face. After being arrested and cautioned in the canteen, Nicki had considered calling for back-up to transport them back to the Police Investigation Centre, but he'd come surprisingly willingly. There was also a part of her that didn't want to alert Darcie to what was happening – if indeed anything *was* happening. By taking him herself, direct, she could avoid that confrontation.

On arrival, he was booked in by the custody sergeant and then taken straight to one of the holding cells. Nicki's phone had rung almost the minute the door was locked. It was Darcie, firstly informing her about the statement of Matilda Davenport and the Spiderman mask and then going on to explain DS Fox's theory on the burglaries.

By the time the conversation had ended, Nicki was more convinced than ever that the man they were looking for wore a mask.

Not quite revealing where she was, or who she was about to interview, Nicki told Darcie to continue searching through all the witness evidence for any more references to masks. And to tell DS Fox to take a break – to go home for a change of clothes and a freshen up. He'd been on the go for forty-eight hours solid, and if Nicki was verging on exhaustion then he would be too.

Now seated opposite her, in the smallest interview room she could find,

Ryan had succumbed to the offer of a coffee and now sat nursing the polystyrene cup of murky brown liquid in his hands. Nicki cleared her throat and turned on the tape. "The time is five-fifteen on Saturday 3rd November 2018 and present in interview room number one is myself, Detective Inspector Nicki Hardcastle, and..." She looked pointedly at Ryan Hodges from across the small table. "Please state your name for the tape."

The porter's jaw clenched before he replied. "Ryan Hodges".

"As you may know, Mr Hodges, we are investigating the disappearance of six-year-old Lucas Jackson, who disappeared from the Winter Fayre in the town on the evening of Tuesday 30th October."

Ryan's expression remained stony, his eyes lowered to the table.

"Let's start with the basics. How long have you worked at the West Suffolk Hospital, Ryan?"

The porter's eyes remained trained to the battered wooden table.

"It's not a trick question, Mr Hodges." Nicki leant back in her chair, her gaze fixed on her suspect. His body language was telling her he was hiding something – his entire body was tensed, his muscles taut, and he refused to make eye contact. "How long have you worked at the hospital, Ryan? You said to me before that it was about three months. Is that right?"

Ryan Hodges still kept his eyes lowered and his mouth shut.

"OK, let's try another. How long have you lived in Bury St Edmunds?"

The same stony silence filled the air of the interview room.

"OK. How about before Bury? Where were you born?"

Ryan Hodges began picking at the polystyrene coffee cup, refusing to meet Nicki's gaze.

Irritation started to seep into Nicki's tone. "Mr Hodges. Did you understand the caution that was read to you when you were arrested and which was repeated on your arrival here?"

Slowly, the porter began to nod.

"For the purpose of the tape, Mr Hodges has nodded." Nicki paused and glanced at her watch. Time was ticking by and they were still no nearer to finding Lucas Jackson. The small window of opportunity to find him alive was narrowing by the second. "And you understand you have the right to legal advice and have a solicitor with you in interview? Both of which you have, at present, declined?"

Again, the porter gave a slow nod.

Nicki pursed her lips. "Again, for the purpose of the tape, Mr Hodges has nodded." Shifting in her chair, Nicki edged closer to the table, reducing the amount of distance between them. She eyed him steadily. "Do you know the Jackson family, Mr Hodges?"

Ryan Hodges eventually raised his gaze from the polystyrene cup. "I don't know anyone called Jackson."

"And what about Ivy McFadden and Oliver Chambers?"

A frown creased Ryan's brow as he lowered his eyes once more. "I've never heard of them."

Nicki raised her eyebrows. "Really? That surprises me. Do you read the newspapers, Mr Hodges? Or watch the TV? Do you own a smartphone or use the internet?" Nicki paused. "If you do any of these things, Mr Hodges then you cannot fail to have come across these names over the last few days."

More silence stretched out from across the table. Nicki saw the muscles at the side of the porter's jaw clench. He was hiding something; she could tell.

"So, I'll ask you again. Do you know Lucas Jackson, Ivy McFadden or Oliver Chambers?"

Ryan Hodges sighed. "OK. I recognise the names, but I don't *know* them. I've never met them. I have nothing to do with them."

Nicki cocked her head to the side and considered her next question. "Where were you last Tuesday evening? The day Lucas Jackson disappeared."

"Whoa, hold on." Ryan Hodges sat bolt upright in his chair and held his hands up in front of his face. "You can't seriously think I had anything to do with that lad going missing?"

"Well that's why we're here, Mr Hodges. You tell me."

The deafening silence from earlier returned and the porter flashed a hot look across the table. "I had nothing to do with it."

"Then you won't mind telling me where you were on the night of Tuesday 30th October." Nicki tried to keep the edge of irritation from her voice.

"I can't remember. I was probably at work."

"Ah, yes. Work. Let's go back to my first question. How long have you worked at the West Suffolk Hospital, Mr Hodges?"

The porter shrugged. "About three months."

"And before that?"

Ryan Hodges again dropped his gaze back to the coffee cup and resumed his picking.

Nicki sighed, not attempting to hide her annoyance from her tone this time. "Mr Hodges, it won't help your situation by choosing to answer some of my questions and not others. Do I need to remind you of your caution?"

The wall of silence continued.

"What about the masks and that scar on your face?"

\* \* \*

*Saturday 3rd November 2018*

5.15pm

Despite still wearing the same suit he'd worn all day, and indeed yesterday, DS Fox decided he had time to make the call to the Kennedy's house on his way home. One more stop wouldn't make any difference, or make him look any less crumpled.

Darcie had called Nicki about the Matilda Davenport statement and Roy's own theories about the killer – but he needed a break. He hadn't been home since Thursday night, and lord knows how long it'd been since he'd last slept. So, Darcie had told him to go home, to get some rest and freshen up.

He'd promised he would, but he just needed to do this first.

The Kennedy's hadn't been home all day – the last patrol car had passed by an hour or so ago, but the house still looked deserted. Similarly, calls to the one mobile number they had on file for the family continued to ring out before going to voicemail.

The house looked just as DS Fox remembered it from his last visit. The driveway was empty and there were no lights visible inside, despite the encroaching darkness. It certainly did look as though the family were not at home.

He parked the car on the road outside and quickly jogged up the garden path. He rang the doorbell and then gave the door a few hefty knocks for good measure. After thirty seconds or so, he repeated the process.

Standing on the doorstep, thrusting his hands into his pockets against the developing chill, he waited. The night was going to be another sub-zero one if the plunging temperatures around him were anything to go by, and the welcome thought of a hot shower and an equally hot curry filled his thoughts. He was slowly getting used to being a bachelor again, although it'd taken a lot of getting used to coming home to a cold and empty flat. He was getting there, but he was finding it tough.

With still no response from inside, DS Fox stepped across to the well-tended front garden and peered in through the bay window at the side. It was difficult to see anything in the dark, so he pressed his nose up against the chilled glass and cupped his hands around his eyes. The window misted over with his warm breath.

Definitely no lights on inside and nothing was moving.

Just then, a voice startled him, and he jumped back to see an elderly lady standing by the garden gate belonging to the house next door. The tiny-framed woman was engulfed in a thick, woollen shawl. "They're not in, my dear."

"I'm sorry?" DS Fox stepped off the grass and made his way back down the garden path.

"Hazel and Neil. They're not in. I'm assuming that's who you're looking for?" The old woman's piercing blue eyes peered at him through the dark. "They went out earlier this morning."

DS Fox glanced back towards the empty house. "You have any idea when they might be back?"

The old lady shrugged beneath her shawl. "I'm really not sure, sonny. Quite late I would imagine. They've gone to that fireworks display in Thetford."

A frown creased DS Fox's forehead. A fireworks display. Why did that ring a bell with him? As he returned to the pavement, heading towards his car, it suddenly struck him.

*The flyer on the outside of the fridge.*

He'd seen it in amongst the shopping list for toilet paper and potatoes, the calendar stuck on yesterday's date, and the various photographs of grinning children. He remembered it now, with a clarity as sure and sharp as the frost developing around him; the flyer tacked to the fridge door advertising the display at Thetford, together with four tickets.

"The children were very excited," added the old woman, starting to shuffle up the garden path towards her front door. "Haven't stopped talking about it all week. I help out with baby-sitting occasionally," she explained. "But I think they were looking forward to the fairground rides more than the fireworks, if the truth be told." The old lady started to chuckle, which soon turned into a chesty cough.

"Rides?" DS Fox stopped in his tracks, his hand hovering above the driver's door handle.

"Yes. A little fairground as well as the firework display. It'll cost Hazel and Neil a fortune, the amount of rides those two will want to go on!" More laughter and coughing followed. "I must get myself back inside now, my dear. My chest, you see. This cold and damp weather plays havoc with my asthma."

DS Fox nodded and watched the old woman continue to shuffle towards her front door.

Thetford firework display. And fairground.

Suddenly, all thoughts of a hot shower and curry evaporated as he wrenched open the door of the Honda.

He needed to get back.

* * *

*Saturday 3rd November 2018*
5.35pm

Tina Gallagher nudged open the door to Amelia Jackson's room, and popped her head around the side. She saw the twelve-year-old sitting on the edge of her bed, phone in hand, her cheeks streaked with fresh tears. With a heavy heart, she placed the plate of sandwiches and glass of milk she'd brought with her onto Amelia's dressing table, and sat down at the young girl's side.

"What's the matter, Amelia?" DC Gallagher placed a comforting hand on the shaking girl's shoulder.

Amelia's shoulders heaved and another round of sobs escaped her mouth. She wiped her eyes with the back of an already sodden hand and angled her phone screen towards the family liaison officer.

"I was just looking at photos of Lucas."

DC Gallagher took the phone and scrolled through countless pictures of the six-year-old. Some were taken out in the garden, or in the park, others were at home indoors – but in all of them his unmistakable cheeky grin stood out. She could feel her own heart aching and squeezed Amelia's hand in comfort.

"You should eat something. Or have a drink at least."

Amelia shook her head. "I can't. I feel so sick all the time. I just can't believe I won't see him again." The words caught in the back of her throat as she broke out into another sob.

"Sssshhhh," hushed DC Gallagher, letting Amelia's head rest on her shoulder. "Lucas wouldn't want to see you like this." As she stroked the young girl's hair, she glanced back down at the phone screen. There were literally hundreds of pictures, taken from when Lucas was a baby right up until the day he went missing.

*The day he went missing.*

DC Gallagher scrolled to the most recent set of photographs and felt her heart stop.

\* \* \*

*Saturday 3rd November 2018*
  5.45pm

Nicki switched on the tape recorder again and sat down. A request for a comfort break to speak to the duty solicitor had seen an immediate change in Ryan Hodge's demeanour.

"OK," he began, staring down into a fresh cup of weak coffee. "I moved here four months ago from Norwich. For two years prior to that, I resided at Her Majesty's pleasure in Norwich prison. I was released in July. The hospital job is my first since coming out of prison and I didn't want to blow it. I haven't told anyone at work about my past. Just, obviously HR, who needed to know. I haven't told Darcie. I didn't want her to break things off before she got to know me. I wanted her to give me a chance."

Nicki quickly made the mental calculations. If what Ryan was now saying was the truth, then he was in prison at the time both Oliver and Ivy were taken. Biting her lip, she nodded at him to continue.

"You asked about my parents. They live in Shropshire and I don't have much to do with them. That's about it."

"Can I ask what you were inside for?" Although Nicki knew she could easily find out, she wanted to hear him say it.

"It's no secret. It'll be on your system somewhere. It was an assault where a guy ended up in intensive care. I wasn't the one that threw the punch, but we all got sent down. I swear I'm not involved in anything like that anymore – one reason I moved away. A clean slate. Leave the past behind. Or so I thought."

Nicki's own hardened expression softened as she listened. He could be spinning her a pack of lies, but there was no reason right now to disbelieve him. It could all too easily be fact-checked; he'd be a fool to have made it up, especially now that he'd had legal advice. Not that it had stopped anyone in the past.

Ryan looked up and locked eyes with Nicki, noticing her gaze drifting to his chin. He gave a half-smile and pointed to his chin. "I got this after an altercation inside, just after I was locked up. Some guy took umbrage at something I said and knifed me across the face. I got solitary confinement, he got transferred to the psychiatric wing."

A mixture of emotions swamped Nicki's brain. Relief that Darcie wasn't involved with a child killer, but disappointment that they appeared to be back to square one and no closer to finding Lucas Jackson.

And time could very well be running out.

Nicki's phone buzzed in her pocket, the screen telling her it was a message from DC Gallagher. Switching off the tape recorder, Nicki made her excuses and left the interview room.

\* \* \*

*Saturday 3rd November 2018*
   6.10pm

Seeing the advert for the fireworks on the fridge door had been a sign – a gift from above. It had to be. He'd only stepped into the Kennedy's kitchen to apply some WD40 to the door hinges - the wife had mentioned that they squeaked - and that was when he'd seen it. In amongst the shopping lists, till receipts and photographs of two blonde-haired smiling children, the advert and tickets to the firework display.

No one had seen him snap a quick copy with his own phone.

Yes, it was definitely a sign.

The room was ready back at the house; the chairs in place and Lucas Jackson dealt with. It had given him a strange thrill to see the two chairs there, side by side. He didn't know why he hadn't thought of it before.

He still needed to get rid of the rolled up carpet, though - but he'd been too caught up in his new plans to drag it downstairs into the van. It would have to wait now. He didn't have time. And Lucas Jackson wasn't his problem anymore.

Pulling the van out onto the A134 he let a smile graze his lips. Tonight was going to be a very special night. Maybe the best one yet. He knew there would be an additional police presence at the display, that was inevitable, but that made the plan he'd made this time even more exquisite.

He'd be untouchable tonight.

Switching on the radio, he found a 1980s pop station and whistled along to 'Sweet Child O' Mine' - making his grin widen by the second.

GUILT

* * *

# Chapter Twenty-Nine

*Saturday 3$^{rd}$ November 2018*

6.30pm

DS Fox drove while Nicki made some calls. It wouldn't take them long to get to Thetford – especially with the assistance of the blue lights - but it was still time that they didn't have. After alerting Norfolk Constabulary to the situation, Nicki asked them to secure the site as much as they could and begin the search for the Kennedy family. She snapped her phone shut. What more could she do?

Ryan Hodges had been remarkably good natured when Nicki had released him from caution and told him he was free to go. She was ready for a tirade of abuse, but instead he seemed to want to help and apologised for his earlier uncooperative behaviour. Memories of his previous incarceration had clouded his judgment. Before leaving, he did make the comment that the cells here at the Police Investigation Centre were a million times better than those he'd experienced before. Expecting the cold damp cells to be filled with deep-seated competing aromas of stale urine, vomit and body odour, he'd been pleasantly surprised at the almost clinical feel of the PIC's cells.

Ryan had also given her some useful insights into his own use of masks to pacify the children at the hospital – and the more he spoke, the more Nicki became convinced.

Their killer wore a mask.

And now they had a picture of him.

GUILT

DC Gallagher's earlier message was accompanied by a picture of Lucas Jackson at the top of the inflatable slide in the Abbey Gardens. The image had stilled her heart the moment she saw it. Amelia had forgotten she'd taken photos of her brother literally minutes before he vanished. And in the last one, he could be seen smiling and waving towards a figure waiting at the bottom of the ball pit. A figure that until now had meant nothing to anybody.

The man was side-on this time, and could be seen with his hands raised in the air, clapping as Lucas prepared to head down the slide. He looked like a proud father, a proud parent cheering on his boy.

But he wasn't.

He was a killer waiting to snare his prey.

Waiting for Batman.

Nicki had had a brief word with the custody sergeant at the Police Investigation Centre about Marcus Jackson. She was now increasingly sure he had nothing to do with Lucas's disappearance and she was happy to hand him over to be interviewed about the assault on Roy.

She had bigger fish to fry than Marcus Jackson.

They only had a vague description of the family to go on. DS Fox had spent only half an hour in their company, but it was better than nothing. It had crossed Nicki's mind to order a cancellation of the event altogether, but that had the potential to cause mass panic amongst the crowds already there. The thought of a human stampede was equally as dangerous as the killer they were hunting. There'd been enough bad press lately not to voluntarily invite another disparaging headline.

But probably Nicki's chief overriding factor in letting the display go ahead, if she was honest, was that the killer would be spooked if it was cancelled. He could then immediately disappear underground – and if that happened, their chances of ever finding Lucas Jackson alive were reduced to zero.

Nicki's eyes were glued to the clock on the dashboard, which seemed to have stopped still, or maybe even going in reverse. Darcie sat in the back of the car, her face taut. She poked her head in-between the two front seats.

"You really think he might be wearing a mask?"

Nicki waved her phone in the air. "Yes I do. You only have to look at the photo taken in the Abbey Gardens." The image on Amelia's phone had clearly shown the man standing side on – a mask of The Joker on his face. "Or at least some form of disguise or costume to make this poor kid go with him. What do we know about the children, Graham?"

DS Fox accelerated past an articulated lorry and sped down the opposite lane of the A134, sirens blaring. Thankfully, at this time of night the road was quiet and the Honda was behaving itself for once. He really needed to take it to the garage to get the starter motor looked at, but there were never enough hours in the day. He rubbed the tiredness from his sleep deprived eyes. "There's two children. Both boys. Noah is the eldest, aged eleven. Isaac is the youngest. Five years old. It was his bedroom that we believe the intruder accessed. That's pretty much all I know."

"What do you remember about the youngest boy's bedroom?" Nicki braced herself against the dashboard as DS Fox swung the car back onto the correct side of the road to avoid an oncoming motorbike. "If we think our guy targets the children's favourite TV characters or suchlike – what do you recall from the bedroom of this Isaac?"

DS Fox frowned as he negotiated a set of traffic lights, speeding through on red. "I recall lots of Fireman Sam memorabilia. He had the curtains, duvet set, that kind of thing. And lots of Fireman Sam books on the bookcase. And then there was the Lego model."

"Lego model?" Nicki matched DS Fox's frown.

"There was a Lego model left on the side. Both Mr and Mrs Kennedy swear blind it wasn't there the night before, and Isaac wouldn't have been able to make it himself." DS Fox cast a sideways glance at Nicki. "It was a fire engine."

Nicki raised her eyebrows at the same time that Darcie's phone pinged with an incoming message. Her head appeared between the two front seats once again.

"Roy's tracked down a photo of the family. I'll forward it to your phones."

* * *

*Saturday 3rd November 2018*

6.50pm

Hazel and Neil Kennedy handed their tickets over at the gate and led both Noah and Isaac into the field. There were two police constables at the entrance, and a quick glance around the gathering crowds told them that there were plenty more on view.

"Why are the police here, Mummy?" asked Isaac, grabbing hold of his mother's hand and jumping up and down excitedly at her side.

"They're just here to watch the fireworks, honey," replied Mrs Kennedy, flashing a look towards her husband. "Just like we are." They'd discussed whether they should make the trip or not, in the light of what had happened to that poor boy in the Abbey Gardens, but decided it would be safe enough. Surely the event wouldn't go ahead if it was thought to be dangerous? They agreed they wouldn't let the children out of their sight, and the increased police presence seen on arrival reassured them further.

"No they're not," chirped Noah, grinning. "They're here because those kids got killed and another one's gone missing."

Mrs Kennedy shot a dark look at her eldest son. "That's enough, Noah," she scolded. "Don't go scaring your brother." It was hard to shield him from the news these days; he was old enough to read it for himself now. And, of course, it was everywhere you looked - twenty-four hours a day.

"Who's gone missing, Mummy?" Isaac looked up at his mother with wide, staring eyes.

"No-one, sweet pea. Your brother was just messing about." She pulled her youngest son in close and gave him a hug. "Hey, look over there, why don't we start with the tea cups?"

\* \* \*

*Saturday 3rd November 2018*

6.55pm

The air was thick with the aroma of frying sausages and roasted chestnuts, but he wasn't hungry. Wandering through the crowds, he delighted in how no one seemed to give him a second look.

He knew he would recognise them when he saw them. It was the mother he remembered the most. She'd always been in the house when he was working, decorating the downstairs bathroom. The father he didn't see so much; just occasionally first thing in the morning before he went to work. But he still had the man's image burned in his memory. The children he'd only had a passing glimpse of as they set off for school. But what he'd seen had been enough.

They were the ones.

He'd never taken two at once before and the idea made him nervous as well as excited. What would his father say? Would he slap him on the back for making such a bold choice? Or would he tell him he was taking too many risks and it was foolhardy?

He dismissed his father's voice from his mind. Tonight was *his* night. If he could take two, which he knew he could, then he would. They were no nearer catching him than they were at the beginning; he could tell. The newspapers were starting to turn on the police, as they inevitably did, accusing them of incompetence and failing in their duty of protecting the public. Which they weren't; not really. How could they be expected to catch him when he was impossible to find?

Stifling a chuckle, he felt another smile tickle his lips.

As he sauntered through the crowd, his eyes swept the many faces wrapped up in hats and scarves, searching for his targets. He'd taken the decision not to use a mask tonight – tonight he would face the world and show them who he really was; the man *behind* the mask.

And so what if they saw his scars? He wasn't ashamed of them anymore.

After one complete circuit of the field, he started again. It was still early and plenty of people were still piling in through the entrance. Glancing at his watch, he saw it was approaching seven o'clock. The fireworks weren't scheduled to begin for another hour – he still had plenty of time to find them.

And he knew he would.

He always did.

* * *

*Saturday 3<sup>rd</sup> November 2018*

7.05pm

"We'll have to split up." They'd arrived at Thetford in less than twenty minutes, thanks to DS Fox's advanced driving skills and a relatively clear road. Nicki's eyes surveyed the scene, seeing the enormous field stretching out in front of them already filling up fast. It would be like looking for a tiny needle in a very large haystack. "I'll take the left side," she added. "Darcie – you take the right. Graham, head up the middle section."

Both nodded in agreement.

"And stay in touch. Phones on at all times. Report *anything* that looks out of place."

"And there really is no tannoy system?" Darcie glanced around. "No public announcements?"

"Apparently it's not working," replied Nicki, irritation edging her tone. "I'm just hoping they get it up and running soon though. A public announcement would be the easiest way to get the Kennedy's attention."

Darcie and Graham began to head towards their allocated sections of the field, but before they were out of earshot, Nicki called out. "And remember to look for masks."

After watching Darcie and Graham disappear, Nicki began to make her way over to the left side of the field. She'd immediately noticed the amount of uniformed officers in attendance once they'd stepped through the entrance. It reassured her to some extent, but it also reminded her how precarious the current situation was. There could be a child killer in this very field - right here, right now – and the thought chilled her to the bone.

Nicki found herself looking at each and every face that passed; both searching for the Kennedy family, but also their suspect. It still worried her that the public announcement system wasn't yet in operation. There was a tannoy system erected but it wasn't working - something to do with the weather had been the conclusion.

A light drizzle was settling in, combining with the chilled air to give the odd flurry of tiny snowflakes. It wasn't much, and the hope was the freshening breeze would clear the skies before the firework display started. A huge bonfire had been lit at the far end of the field and Nicki could see many of the crowd already drifting towards it.

Heading in the general direction of the bonfire, Nicki passed several local produce stalls; one selling the famous Newmarket sausages they had at the station canteen, another selling local cheese and wine.

Moving on, she passed several small fairground stalls, watching as excited children attempted to 'hook a duck' and win a prize. She studied each and every smiling face as she passed by, but couldn't spot the Kennedy family anywhere.

Two fire engines sat at the edge of the field, with their doors open and swarms of children attempting to climb inside. Good natured fire-fighters let them hold a real hosepipe and sound the horn. Nicki moved closer, scrutinising each and every face. None of them looked like the blurry photo they had on Amelia's phone or the CCTV picture from the Abbey Gardens, and none of them looked like the Kennedys. Nicki couldn't get the image of Isaac's bedroom full of Fireman Sam memorabilia out of her mind. She made a mental note to return to the fire engines on her next circuit. Moving around the coils of hosepipe, she headed towards the bonfire.

Trepidation had initially flooded her thoughts when they'd set off from the station. Another fairground. Another reminder of Deano. But the urgency of the investigation had taken over and all thoughts of her younger brother were pushed into the background as soon as they'd piled into Graham's car and began their journey.

But now she was alone with her thoughts, images of Dean tumbled uncontrollably through her mind, one after the other. It was the smell that usually triggered it – the aroma was everywhere you turned.

Candyfloss.

She'd expected it to happen at some point that night, how could it not?

But when it did, it hit her hard. She brought a hand up to cover her nose and mouth - but it was too late and the sweet, sickly aroma wrapped itself around her nostrils.

As her head began to throb, the sound from the crowds began to fade into the distance and just one distinctive voice called out.

Deano.

All she could hear was Deano's shrieks of delight coming from the green caterpillar ride; laughing and waving his hands as he completed another circuit. Nicki clasped her hands to her ears, but it still didn't deaden the sound. Second by second the sound intensified until she could hear nothing else pulsating inside her ears. Stumbling across the tufted grass, she headed unsteadily towards the bonfire, leaving the stalls behind and, with them, the sickening candyfloss scent.

* * *

*Saturday 3rd November 2018*
   7.15pm

Isaac leapt off the tea cup ride, his eyes shining and a broad grin plastered to his face. He began jumping up and down on the spot. "Again, Mummy! Again!"

Hazel Kennedy scooped him up into her arms and pressed her face against his cold cheek. She could still smell the citrus shampoo in his freshly washed hair, over and above the burgers and hot dogs from a nearby stall.

"All right, one more go. But then it's toffee apples!" Mrs Kennedy lowered Isaac to the ground and watched him scamper off back towards the ride, climbing aboard the nearest tea cup decorated with bright yellow dots and daisies. She turned to her eldest son. "Go and sit with your brother. Just for one more go." Pressing a five-pound note into his hand, she gently nudged him towards the ride.

Noah sighed and pursed his lips, but headed back towards the tea cup. He wasn't too bothered about anyone seeing him from school. As far as he knew, no one was coming tonight – so he was pretty sure he wouldn't get teased at school for being on such a sissy ride.

While the tea cups began to swirl once again, Hazel Kennedy slipped her arm through her husband's and rested her head against his shoulder.

"I'm glad we decided to come," she murmured, snuggling further into Neil's padded jacket. "The boys are having so much fun."

Neil Kennedy nodded and leant in to kiss the top of his wife's bobble hat. They'd agonised for hours over whether to make the trip. Everything in the papers and on the news made for heart-breaking reading.

Initially they'd decided to cancel, and to get refunds on their tickets. The thought of a child killer on the loose was frightening. But the look on the boys' faces had swayed them to change their minds. They'd been looking forward to it for weeks. It was something they always did as a family - had done for the last three years - spending the day in nearby Great Yarmouth, walking along the deserted seafront, playing in the arcades, and eating fish and chips out of paper with wooden forks. And then, in the evening, they would head back to Thetford for the fairground and fireworks.

They'd scoured the event's website and found no information that it was to be cancelled, although there was a section informing them there would be an increased police presence and security checks where necessary. They felt reassured - so long as they were sensible, everything would be fine.

And the numbers of uniformed police they'd seen patrolling the field convinced them they'd made the right decision. Last night they'd told the boys they had to stick together at all times; to never lose sight of one another, not even for a second. If anyone came up to them that they didn't know, they should shout and scream their very loudest.

Both Noah and Isaac had found this particularly funny, spending the rest of the evening practicing their loudest screams. At one point, Hazel went next door to dear old Mrs Cooke to let her know that the children were not injured or being attacked, and it was just a game.

The break-in had unnerved them, but with only a few pounds stolen they tried to put it behind them. The Lego fire engine had been more disturbing – and the thought of someone prowling around the house while they slept, and entering Isaac's bedroom…it didn't bear thinking about.

Neil Kennedy shivered and then felt his wife squeeze his hand. She'd pulled her head away from where it had been resting on his shoulder. The tea cup ride was slowing down and coming to a stop.

Isaac jumped down from the ride. "Can we have toffee apples now? And burgers?! And can I go and see the fire engine?!"

Hazel Kennedy smiled as her youngest son catapulted into her side, and ruffled the top of his head. "Put your hat back on and yes, we'll go and get a toffee apple. And yes you can go and see the fire engine. But we'll leave the burgers until later, when the fireworks are about to start. Let's just wait for your brother."

＊ ＊ ＊

*Saturday 3rd November 2018*
  *7.25pm*

It felt liberating without the mask. He was glad he'd chosen to leave it behind this time. And the more he mingled with the crowd, the more he knew it'd been the right choice. There were no face painting stalls that he could see, so wearing a mask this time would have made him too conspicuous. He silently congratulated himself for his foresight. Dad would've been proud.

The smell of fried onions and sweet toffee apples grazed his nostrils, but despite his stomach being empty he didn't give them a second look. Hovering by the cheese stall, which was offering small samples of cheese with bread and olive oil dips, his eyes scoured the queues waiting for the free tasters. None were the Kennedy family; he was sure of it.

Turning his back on the cheese stall, he strolled away. He needed to maintain his edge. The hunger he felt in his stomach wasn't for food.

Passing another hot roasted chestnut stall, he headed in the direction of the bonfire. That was where he needed to be. The younger boy was obsessed with that Fireman Sam character; that much had been evident from his bedroom. So where else would he be, but by the biggest bonfire his young eyes had ever seen?

He'd checked out the two fire engines that were on one side of the field. None of the families shrouded in hats and scarves were the Kennedys. But he'd check again later, just to be sure.

As he neared the fire, the crackling from the flames intensified and he felt a pleasant warmth on his cheeks. And that wasn't all. In front of him, almost within touching distance, was a family of four. With a quickening heart, he lengthened his stride a little, closing the ground between them. A familiar flurry of excitement began to build in the pit of his stomach.

It was them. He was sure of it, even with their backs turned towards him. The way the mother held her head just to one side as she walked; the way the father's shoulders sloped underneath his jacket. The mother's hair was buried beneath a bobble hat, but when she turned her head to the side, exchanging words with her husband, he saw the familiar upturned nose and the outline of her perfect heart-shaped lips.

It was definitely them.

Breathing hard, he changed direction to skirt around the side. He saw a solitary stall - selling a variety of fluorescent headbands, wands and other useless plastic nonsense that hard-pressed parents would feel obliged to buy their offspring as they waited, impatiently, for the fireworks to begin. He headed in its direction.

Two uniformed police officers strolled towards him. He smothered the smile that was itching to burst onto his lips as he received a brief nod of acknowledgement from one of them as they passed.

He returned the nod and smiled to himself.

If only they knew how close they had come.

* * *

# Chapter Thirty

*Saturday 3rd November 2018*
   7.35pm

Isaac curled his hand around the toffee apple stick and grinned. The smell of the sticky caramel was making his mouth water. He wasn't all that fond of apples – Mum would try and make him eat one every day, something about 'keeping the doctor away'. But he didn't like the skin or the pips inside, and sometimes they tasted too sharp. There would always be one in his lunchbox for school – but he often swapped it for a packet of crisps with Alfie Burrows. And he hadn't seen a doctor for a *very* long time – not since he'd fallen off the climbing frame in the park and banged his head. And he was sure that, even if he *had* eaten an apple that day, he would still have fallen off.

But *toffee* apples were different. They weren't *real* apples.

He sunk his teeth into the sticky coating, biting into the crisp apple beneath. A mixture of sweetness from the toffee and tartness from the apple filled his mouth as he chewed, and he happily bounced along beside his parents as they made their way towards the bonfire at the top of the field.

Noah had won him a huge bag of sweets on the Hoopla stall, and he thrust his other hand in his pocket to keep them safe. As they walked towards the bonfire, the shouts and shrieks from the fairground rides behind them faded further and further into the distance. Ahead of them, sparks crackled and spat from the fire, the flames stretching higher and higher into the crisp night air. Isaac could soon feel the warmth of the flames caressing his frozen cheeks. The drizzle that had started when they'd arrived had now disappeared, replaced by a bitingly cold wind. The clouds had parted to reveal a clear night sky with a full moon and winking stars. A perfect night for fireworks.

A metal safety barrier circled the bonfire, preventing anyone from getting too close. Mr and Mrs Kennedy stopped at the railings and gathered both boys around them.

"Wow!" breathed Isaac, his mouth full of toffee apple. "That's the biggest fire I've ever seen!" He'd wanted to wear his Fireman Sam costume, but Mum had said it wouldn't be warm enough. But she'd relented and let him put on his special anorak that he'd got for Christmas with its Fireman Sam logo on the front.

Both Mr and Mrs Kennedy laughed and let both boys lean up against the railings to watch the flames. The fireworks were meant to be starting at eight, in just under half an hour's time – they'd have the perfect grandstand view if they stayed here.

With both boys contently munching on their apples and watching the developing fire, Neil Kennedy turned towards his wife and whispered in her ear. "I spied a stall selling mulled wine not too far back. Shall we treat ourselves?" He gave her gloved hand a squeeze.

Hazel Kennedy glanced over her shoulder. There was, indeed, a stall selling hot drinks, including mulled wine, not too far away - she remembered inhaling the enticing aroma as they'd passed by. Her stomach rumbled and the thought of some warming German red wine made her shiver with pleasure.

"I don't see why not." Her eyes sparkled and she returned the squeeze. The feeling of someone having been in the house in the dead of night still made her shiver. Her overactive imagination had started to wonder where else he'd gone while they slept and what else he'd seen. The thought made her shudder. A glass of wine was just what she needed. "Shall I wait here with the boys, or shall we all go?"

Crowds had started to fill the gaps alongside the railings, with the time for the fireworks getting closer. Hazel noted several uniformed police officers strolling in amongst them.

Neil Kennedy followed his wife's gaze and saw the same police officers milling amongst the crowds. "They'll be fine here for a few minutes, won't they? They can save our spot, otherwise we'll be right at the back when the fireworks start. There's plenty of people around, and the police are only over there." He nodded towards two officers leaning up against the railings only three or four metres away, chatting to three children who were waving sparklers in the air.

After instructing Noah and Isaac to stay exactly where they were, and not to talk to anyone, Mr and Mrs Kennedy strode off towards the mulled wine stall. Hazel took a glance back over her shoulder to see both boys standing exactly where instructed, eating their toffee apples, both mesmerised by the rising flames.

The smell of warming red wine filled her nostrils as she linked her arm back through her husband's. Yes, a glass of wine was just what she needed.

\* \* \*

*Saturday 3rd November 2018*
  7.35pm

Stopping adjacent to the stall with its fluorescent paraphernalia, he turned and trained his eyes on the Kennedy family. They'd made their way, as expected, towards the metal railings that surrounded the roaring fire. He could see both boys' faces were shining in the glow of the flames. Such young and innocent faces.

His stomach fluttered in anticipation.

All he needed to do was wait, he was sure of it. His instincts had never let him down before; he just needed to be patient. The two uniformed officers he'd seen only moments before were now leaning up against the metal railings only a few metres away from the boys. They appeared to be chatting to some children who were playing with sparklers, no doubt reminding them of fire safety.

It's not the sparklers you need to be wary of, he chuckled to himself. It's me.

After another minute or so, he saw both Mr and Mrs Kennedy turn and walk away from the boys. They appeared to be heading towards a stall selling mulled wine. He couldn't think of anything worse – warm wine. The mere thought made his nose wrinkle.

The boys, however, remained standing by the metal railings.

Knowing he only had a small window of opportunity, he started walking towards the bonfire. He strode confidently past the two officers, still ensconced in telling the children about firework safety, and felt a chuckle rise up within him.

This was going to be even easier than before.

* * *

*Saturday 3rd November 2018*
7.45pm

No matter how much distance she tried to put between herself and the candyfloss stall, the sickly aroma trailed after her. The smell flooded her nostrils and coated her tongue, refusing to release her from its clutches. Time spun backwards and she was ten-years-old again.

And it was then that she saw him.

Deano.

He was there, standing right in front of her; his round, smiling face glowing from the frosty air. His wide mouth grinned, revealing that empty space where the tooth-fairy had taken away her latest prize.

Deano.

Nicki's heart melted and swelled at the same time, a surge of love bursting through the man-made barriers she'd erected so painstakingly over the last twenty-two years. The caterpillar ride had come to a stop and Deano was looking at her, imploringly, desperate for another go.

"Go on," she murmured, feeling herself sway on the spot. "Go on, Deano."

She watched as Deano clambered aboard the bright green carriage, already shrieking with excitement.

She knew it wasn't real. It *couldn't* be real. But yet it was as real as the ground she stood on. Deano was no more than six feet away. If she stepped forwards she could even touch him.

Love poured into every crevice of her being. Unable to drag her gaze away from his tiny frame, swamped inside his winter coat, and the bobble hat tugged down over his head, everything else around her faded into the background. It was as if the sound dial had been turned down and life was on mute.

Feeling herself swaying again, she put an arm out to steady herself and immediately felt someone grab her wrist and then her elbow. Not taking her eyes from Deano for one second, she felt her legs buckle and a pair of arms lowered her to the ground. Cold, frosted grass came up to meet her.

"Boss?"

A voice she faintly recognised floated through the air. It was a soft voice, sounding distant and muffled.

"Boss?" The voice was louder this time, and stronger. With her vision beginning to clear, her eyes came back into sharp focus. The sound of laughter and shrieking from all around flooded her ears once more, life's sound dial finally turned back up to high.

The caterpillar ride had disappeared.

And so had Deano.

"Boss? Are you all right?" The voice now registered with her, and she turned her face towards DS Fox, who was crouching down by her side, a look of concern etched onto his face. "You nearly went over there."

Nicki looked down at the legs curled beneath her. They felt strange – tingling and numb, but not because of the cold. She could feel her own heartbeat thudding and her blood pulsating at her temples. She began to nod. "I'm fine."

Her own voice sounded detached, as if it were a million miles away from her body. She started to scramble to her feet, acutely aware that she was sitting on the muddied, frozen grass and people around were starting to notice.

"Whoa, easy does it." DS Fox's grip on her elbow tightened, helping her to her feet. "Slowly, now – lean on me."

"I'm fine, Graham. Really." Nicki's cheeks began to flush as realisation dawned. There was no Deano. No caterpillar ride. It had all been in her mind. "I just felt a bit faint."

"I've sent Darcie to find some water." DS Fox guided Nicki towards the edge of the field. "Then maybe you should go and sit back in the car."

"No." Nicki's voice was sharp. "We don't have time." Clarity returned in spades, the chill wind hitting her squarely in the face, bringing her abruptly to her senses. "We need to find the Kennedys." She extricated herself from DS Fox's concerned grip and began brushing herself down. There was a damp, muddy patch on the back of her jeans and her hands were wet. "We need to keep searching."

"At least have some water, boss." Darcie had arrived with a bottle of Highland Spring, thrusting it towards Nicki. Her face mirrored the same concern as DS Fox's.

Gratefully, Nicki ripped the lid off the bottle and drank a quarter without stopping for breath. The ice-cold liquid burned her throat but cleared her mind. "We need to keep searching," she repeated, screwing the lid back on the bottle and handing it back. "They've got to be here somewhere."

"I tried the mobile again, boss, but it's not picking up. Maybe they left it behind?" Darcie turned to look towards the entrance, where yet more people were streaming in through the gate. "Is that tannoy up and running yet? There's so many people still arriving."

"I'll go and check." Nicki straightened her shoulders and started walking towards the entrance. "Darcie – stay around here and keep watch on those still arriving. Graham – you head back up to the top, by the bonfire. All little boys love a bonfire. And the fireworks are due to start in ten minutes."

DS Fox nodded and strode away in the direction of the flames.

"You really think they're here, boss?" Darcie followed Nicki towards the entrance. "And the killer, too?"

Nicki gave a faint shrug. "I've no idea, Darcie, but we have to assume so."

She stopped as a stream of people passed them by, all wrapped up in winter hats and scarves. "You stay here and keep a look out. I'm going to see what's happened to that bloody tannoy."

* * *

# Chapter Thirty-One

*Saturday 3rd November 2018*
    7.50pm

A quick glance around told him that Mr and Mrs Kennedy were nowhere to be seen. Tut-tut. A smile twitched at his lips. Some people would never learn. The papers had been full of it for the last four days, and still they let their guard down. They really were making it far too easy for him.

As the flames crackled and spat in front of them, neither boy seemed to notice him as he edged closer.

"Hey, you two."

Both sets of eyes, complete with their reflections of the bonfire, turned in his direction. He remembered them more now – from their photographs on the fridge door. With sandy-blonde hair and bright blue eyes, they looked a mirror-image of each other, even down to the small, upturned snub-nose and dusting of freckles on each cheek.

Now he had their attention, he knew he only had the one shot at this. At any moment, they could scream and raise the alarm – and he could find himself ensnared. *Caught.* And then everything would be over.

The thought gave a renewed edge to his building excitement.

"How d'you both like the bonfire?" He crouched down by their side. Eye level was important; his father had told him that.

The older boy was hesitant at first, but his younger brother showed no such qualms.

"It's great! I love fire! I want to be a fireman when I grow up!"

He resisted the urge to laugh out loud and smothered the developing smile on his lips. *I know. I've seen your bedroom*, he wanted to say. *I know everything about you.* Instead he said, "is that right? Well that's a very good job to have."

He then turned his attention to the older one. If there was going to be a problem, he would be it. "And what about you, young man? What do you want to be when you grow up?"

He again masked his developing grin.

*I already know.*

Noah looked at the man crouching down by his side and bit his bottom lip. He wasn't supposed to talk to strangers, he knew that. Especially after what he'd read in the papers. He didn't always understand everything he read, but he knew enough. And it'd been on the news every night on the TV. What had Mum and Dad told them to do if a stranger approached them? Shout and scream as loud as they could? But this was different. This wasn't a stranger – this was a man they could trust.

"I want to be like you when I grow up," he replied, his eyes shining and a smile breaking out on his face. His top lip glistened with apple juice and toffee.

I know.

"Is that so?" He smiled and nodded towards his two new friends. It was at that moment that he knew he'd succeeded. They would come with him; that much was guaranteed. And silently, too. "Well, I'm sure you'll make a mighty fine policeman one day, son."

He stood up and brushed a hand down the imitation policeman's uniform he had so skilfully acquired before setting out on tonight's mission. It had been a brilliant idea, possibly his best yet. When he'd finished looking into the younger boy's bedroom and seen all the Fireman Sam memorabilia, an idea had formed in his head. But then, on a whim, he'd also popped his head into the older boy's room next door and his plans had changed in an instant.

"What happened to your face?" It was the smaller boy that spoke this time. He was looking up and pointing with a sticky, toffee-apple finger.

Instinctively, he brought a hand up to his jaw and stroked the scar he knew was there. Visible at this distance, he knew the boys had seen it as soon as he'd crouched down and spoken. But neither seemed wary of him - or his scar.

He knelt back down so he was again on the same eye level as both of them.

"Well, I was caught up in a fire – a bit like this one here." He nodded towards the raging bonfire which was increasing in heat and intensity as the seconds went by. "I was rescuing two little boys just like yourselves." The lie tripped so easily off his tongue.

Both boys' eyes widened, awe etched onto their glowing faces.

"But everything's all right now." He smiled again, knowing that it was now or never. The longer he stayed, the more people would be alerted to his presence. And the more chance they would be able to give a description of him when they were inevitably asked later. He needed to get this part of the plan over with. "Anyway, you're Noah and Isaac, right?"

Both boys barely hesitated before nodding.

"Well, I've a message from your Mum and Dad. They asked me to come and tell you to meet them by the burger stall. They'd come over and get you themselves but there's a very long queue and they don't want to give up their place."

He watched as the little boy, Isaac, began to jump up and down at the thought of a burger, but his brother was a little more hesitant. He noted the faint flicker of doubt entering the older boy's eyes and knew he needed to act fast.

"You won't remember me, but I know your Mum and Dad. You live in Henley Road, right?"

Both boys nodded. The doubt in the older boy's eyes began to fade.

"And your Dad works for British Sugar, at the factory?"

More nodding followed and the rest of the doubt left Noah Kennedy's eyes.

"Well, you're right to be wary of strangers. But I'm a friend of your Mum and Dad's. *And* I'm a policeman, so you can trust me." Plastering his best smile onto his face, he straightened up. "So, shall we go and get that burger? We'll need to hurry if you want to get back for the fireworks."

Both boys obediently left the safety of the railings and began to follow.

247

He flashed them a wide smile. "Come with me. I'll show you my police van on the way."

* * *

*Saturday 3rd November 2018*
7.55pm

DS Fox pushed his way through the burgeoning crowd. People were surging towards the bonfire, desperate to get a good position for the fireworks that were due to start at any moment. He studied each and every face that came into view, but no one matched that of the Kennedy family. They were running out of time, he could feel it. With his heart racing, he reached the metal railings circling the bonfire and scoured the faces turned towards the flames.

None of them were the Kennedys.

Pushing back through the crowds, he headed towards a St John Ambulance which was parked in front of a high hedge. Pulling out his warrant card, he approached the two volunteers standing by the vehicle's open rear door.

"DS Graham Fox, Suffolk Police. I don't suppose you've seen a family that looks like this?" He held up his mobile phone with the picture of the Kennedys. "I know it's a long shot, but..."

One of the volunteers, a tall man with a shock of black curly hair and an equally impressive moustache, stepped closer and peered at DS Fox's phone. All the while, the detective's own eyes continued to scour the crowds milling behind him. As he turned his attention back to the St John Ambulance volunteer, a huge boom erupted and the sky was filled with a flurry of sparks and crackles.

A collected roar escaped the mouths of the crowd surrounding the bonfire. The firework display had started, and with every eruption the ground shook beneath their feet. Rockets shot high into the sky, exploding in a series of multi-coloured rainbows – reds, yellows, oranges and purples – the once jet-black sky now a haven of colour.

The St John Ambulance volunteer handed DS Fox back his phone, accompanied with a slight nod of the head.

"I think I might've seen the two wee kiddies – but not the parents."

DS Fox blocked out the deafening sounds around him and stepped closer, his heart thumping. "You did? Where? How long ago?"

"Yes, I'm sure of it now." The curls on the St John Ambulance volunteer's head bobbed as he nodded his head once again. "There were two boys – looking very similar to that picture. They went through that side exit there just a few minutes ago." He pointed towards a break in the hedge. "Dropped their toffee apples on the ground as they went."

DS Fox's eyes followed the man's arm, spotting the exit. "A few minutes ago, you say?" DS Fox took a couple of steps across the grass towards the break in the bushes and peered out into the road beyond. He noted the row of cars parked along one side and instantly recognised it as the road where he'd parked his own car, a little way down on the left towards the main entrance. Returning to the field, he stepped over the discarded, half-eaten toffee apples lying on the grass.

"But, hey. I'm sure they're fine," called out the bushy-haired St John Ambulance volunteer. "They weren't on their own. They were with one of your lot."

\* \* \*

*Saturday 3rd November 2018*

7.57pm

The slap came from nowhere and landed on Isaac's cheek, knocking him sideways.

"Shut up!" he growled, spit frothing at the corners of his mouth. "Didn't I tell you to be quiet?!"

"Don't hit my brother!" yelled Noah, trying to scramble to his feet. He'd been thrown into the back of the nondescript white van, landing in a heap next to several sacks of builder's sand. A slap that felt more like a punch hit him square in the jaw and split his lip. He landed back on the floor, blood dripping down his chin.

This wasn't how it was meant to be. He grabbed a coil of twine from the racking at the side of the van. They were meant to come quietly, like the others did. They'd been fine until he'd opened the doors of the van. He'd seen the look of disquiet enter the older boy's eyes when he'd nudged them both forwards and asked them to get in the back of a 'real police van'.

Both boys suddenly erupted into ear piercing screams, so loud they almost rocked the van's sides. Such loud screams from such very small mouths. They needed to be silenced, and quick.

Two swift punches to the smaller boy's head soon quietened him down, and another kick to the older boy's stomach left him doubled over in pain, unable to make a sound. But he knew it wouldn't last long. Abandoning the twine, he reached for two oily rags and stuffed one in each boys' mouth, watching them gag and try to spit them out. Taking advantage of the quiet, he picked up the coil of twine once again and began to wrap it tightly around the older boy's wrists.

The boy kicked out with both feet, wrenching his body from side to side, but he was no match for his captor's powerful grasp. Slowly, the boy succumbed and his wrists were securely trussed together. Within seconds his ankles were also secured.

The younger boy was cowering in a corner on the opposite side of the van, his body shaking and his face wet with tears. He felt a small smile trickle onto his lips. This one wouldn't be quite so much trouble. It took less than a minute to tie both his ankles and wrists, and throw him into the same corner as his brother.

He didn't know how much time had passed – probably not as much as he thought – but he knew he needed to get a move on. The boys would be missed before long and he needed them to be as far away as possible when the alarm was raised. He could hear the firework display was now in full swing, the whizzes and bangs of the fireworks overhead thudding into the night sky. It would buy him a little time – but not much.

\* \* \*

# CHAPTER THIRTY-ONE

*Saturday 3rd November 2018*
7.57pm

"One of our lot?"

The St John Ambulance volunteer nodded. "Yes. Police."

The frown on DS Fox's forehead deepened. A police officer? Had the boys been found by one of the local force and taken to safety? The thought rushed through his head but before he could make any sense of it a series of rockets screeched into the night sky above them, exploding one after the other. The sound was deafening. Screams and yells from the watching crowd followed.

DS Fox could barely hear himself think and turned away from the noise. As he did so, he detected a different sound in amongst the whooshing, thumping, and crackling from overhead.

It had been faint and distant, but he was sure he'd heard something.

His gaze dropped to the ground where the discarded toffee apples still lay.

And there it was again. Different in tone to the screams from the crowds flooding the air; different to the screech of exploding fireworks overhead. But it was a sound that was unmistakable.

A child's scream.

And this scream was full of fear.

\* \* \*

# Chapter Thirty-Two

*Saturday 3rd November 2018*
  8.00pm

Nicki held the phone to her ear as rockets screeched overhead.

"Yes, Sir. We've done an initial sweep. As yet, we've been unable to locate the family." As she listened to the DCI's response, Nicki continued to scan the faces of the latecomers still piling through the entrance. "Yes. The tannoy system's been down, but it's fixed now and we're about to get an announcement put out any minute." Nicki paused and nodded. "Of course. I'll update you as soon as I hear anything." She ended the call.

"Right, let's get this announcement up and running. Darcie – stay and keep an eye on the entrance. Call me if you see anything."

Darcie nodded and watched as Nicki hurried over to the tent that housed the public address system. She just hoped they weren't too late.

\* \* \*

*Saturday 3rd November 2018*
  8.00pm

The road was deserted as far as he could see – just a line of cars parked one behind the other along one side. DS Fox knew his own car was parked towards the left hand end, down by the main entrance. He'd managed to squeeze it

252

into the last available space, moving a couple of 'do not park' traffic cones out of the way.

A police officer.

He couldn't get the idea out of his head. Any thought that the boys had been taken to safety by one of their Norfolk colleagues dissipated almost as soon as it had formed in his mind, and he'd run back out through the side exit into the road. But a quick glance from side to side saw no movement. Nothing at all. Nobody.

Nicki's phone was engaged when he'd tried only moments before. As he broke into a run, heading up the deserted road to the right, he pulled his own phone out again and stabbed the screen once more. There was still no one and nothing all around him. No sounds, except the thumping and screeching of fireworks overhead.

He'd heard a scream; he was sure of it. Two screams even, maybe more. And they weren't just shrieks from the crowd. There was no joy in the sounds that had reached his ears. The line of parked cars stretched out into the distance beyond and nothing in the road looked out of place

Nothing except the van.

DS Fox slowed down and jogged towards a battered looking white van, facing away from him and parked several metres ahead. Glancing once again in both directions, he noted it was the only van in a sea of cars. For that reason, and that reason alone, it stood out.

With his mouth painfully dry and his chest heaving, he quickened his step. With his phone to his ear, he heard the familiar engaged tone. Swearing under his breath he ended the call. As he neared the van, the rear doors flew open and a figure jumped down onto the road.

DS Fox froze to the spot. The man was dressed in a familiar-looking black uniform, and as he turned to head towards the driver's door, the detective caught a glimpse of the printed word on the back of the man's jacket.

POLICE

\* \* \*

*Saturday 3ʳᵈ November 2018*

  8.00pm

"Where are they?" Hazel Kennedy's voice shook as she spoke. The fireworks had just begun and were exploding above their heads. Roars of delight erupted from the crowd around them, but even the intense heat from the flames of the bonfire just metres away did nothing to warm her chilled heart. "They should be right here."

Both Mr and Mrs Kennedy snapped their heads from side to side, searching along the entire length of the metal railings where they'd left the boys only minutes before. They saw plenty of smiling, laughing faces, mostly children, but they weren't Noah or Isaac. Even the two police officers were still there, chatting to the children waving sparklers.

Nausea welled up inside her and she fought hard to keep it down.

"Where are they, Neil?" she repeated, straining to make herself heard. A huge rocket exploded right above their heads and shook the ground beneath their feet.

Neil Kennedy pushed his way back through the crowd and started shouting. "Noah? Isaac!" His voice did little to carry above the screeching fireworks overhead. "Noah!" he yelled, louder and more frantic this time, his face contorted in fear and panic. "Isaac!"

Hazel Kennedy dropped her plastic beaker of warm mulled wine and clung to his arm, her fingers painfully digging into his flesh despite the thickness of his padded jacket. "Where are they, Neil?" she wailed, tears gushing down her cheeks. "Where are they?"

But nobody seemed to notice their plight. Everybody's eyes were trained skywards, absorbed in the light show being played out in the skies above.

* * *

*Saturday 3ʳᵈ November 2018*

  8.01pm

DS Fox stabbed at Nicki's name once again whilst tearing down the pavement towards his car. There was no time to lose; he couldn't let the van get away. Throwing the handset onto the front passenger seat, he dived behind the wheel. He heard the van's engine roaring into life and knew he needed the Honda to start first time.

Looking through the windscreen, he saw the van had pulled out and was already heading away from him. Thrusting his key into the ignition, he turned it – but received only a spluttering noise in response. Shit, not now, he cursed, slapping the steering wheel and twisting the key once again.

More spluttering filled the air.

Think, think, think. DS Fox commanded his brain to function, sweat now pouring down the back of his neck and pooling in the centre of his back. With his heart hammering painfully inside his chest, he shoved the phone into the hands free set and stabbed at Nicki's name again.

Giving the key a final twist, the Honda roared into life at the very same second Nicki answered his call.

\* \* \*

*Saturday 3rd November 2018*
8.02pm

The oily rag was making him gag, and the twine around his wrists cut painfully into his skin. As the van lurched violently from side to side, he found himself thrown back and forth across the floor. Managing to roll himself to the side, he pushed himself into a sitting position, leaning up against some old rolls of carpet. His lip stung where the man had punched him, and he could still feel a trickle of blood along his lower jaw and chin. A few spots dripped down onto his anorak.

Noah looked across to the other side of the van and saw his younger brother crying. No sound escaped Isaac's mouth, the oily rag absorbing any sobs, but he knew he was crying all the same. He watched his brother's shoulders heaving up and down as his tiny body quivered in the dimness of the van.

All around them were piles of materials; builders' sacks stacked on top of each other, and various buckets and pieces of wood. The van had a musty smell, tinged with oil or paint, and various rusty-looking tools hung from hooks on the side walls. Each time the van swung around a corner, they clattered against the metal side and Noah feared they would fly off and embed themselves into their flesh.

He shivered and began to cry. It had all been his fault, he knew that. Mum and Dad had told him repeatedly not to talk to strangers – but that's exactly what he'd done.

But the man was a police officer – they could trust a police officer, couldn't they? They taught you that in school – if you need help, ask a police officer. And this one was a hero – he'd been burned rescuing children from a fire. Surely that made him a good person and someone they would be safe with?

Confusion wracked his body and swirled inside his brain. He didn't understand. The man had told them this was a police van; that he'd show them the inside before they went to meet Mum and Dad for burgers. He'd told them they'd see where real-life criminals were locked up before being taken to the police station in handcuffs.

Noah had felt excited by the thought. Just wait until he told the others at school that he'd been inside a real police van! And seen a real set of handcuffs!

But there were no handcuffs. And this was no police van.

The van made another screeching turn and Noah was flung once again to the floor, landing face down. With his head turned to the side, all he could see was his brother's shaking body and tear stained cheeks. He wanted to call out for his Mum, but the rag smothered his cries.

\* \* \*

*Saturday 3<sup>rd</sup> November 2018*
    8.02pm

"Would Mr and Mrs Kennedy, from Bury St Edmunds, please make their way to the front entrance. That's Mr and Mrs Kennedy - please proceed to the front entrance urgently."

Nicki brought the phone to her ear, covering the opposite one with a gloved hand to cut out the noise. With the fireworks now in full swing, it was virtually impossible to hear anything clearly. Even the announcement over the tannoy had been lost amongst the roars from the crowd and the explosions in the sky. She only hoped the Kennedys could hear it.

"Graham?" she replied. "What's up?" She noticed that she had missed several calls from him in the last minute or so while she'd been on a call with DCI Turner. "Where are you?"

"What is it, boss?" Darcie stepped closer, a concerned look flooding her face as she saw Nicki's cheeks turn white.

Nicki held up a hand, her face continuing to drain of colour as she listened to DS Fox's frantic cries. "OK. I'll radio it in – white van leaving the scene. Which direction?" Nicki began to run towards the main entrance, waving at Darcie to follow. "Stay with them."

\* \* \*

*Saturday 3ʳᵈ November 2018*
*8.03pm*

DS Fox cursed again as he saw the van's brake lights disappear out of sight. He wrenched the steering wheel hard left to pull out from behind the line of parked cars, but instead of racing off in pursuit, he hit the brakes and brought the Honda to a sharp halt. He knew this area pretty well – he'd done an advanced driving course around these very same roads not so long ago.

The direction the van had sped off in led to a junction – a no-through road on the right meant the van would be forced to turn left. It would then be forced to make an identical left turn not long after, as the only other option was a private farm track. The van would end up driving in a complete circle, finishing up on the road behind him.

As his mind raced, an idea flickered into his mind.

It might just work.

In that split second, he made the decision. Slamming the car into reverse, he drove at speed back along the access road, in the direction of the main entrance. If he could just get there in time, he might be able to head them off.

Flooring the accelerator, DS Fox reversed at maximum speed – the car's engine protesting, violently. With an arm across the back of the front passenger seat, his gaze was fixed out of the rear window and the approaching intersection with the main road.

He didn't know how much time he had, or even if the van had already sped past. Or maybe it'd attempted that farm track after all. But all he could do was hope and pray that he was right and will the Honda to go faster.

Reaching the junction with the main road, DS Fox swerved violently around the last parked car and screeched across the carriageway without slowing down.

He hadn't seen the van; not until it was too late.

Focusing his gaze out of the rear window, the first he knew of the impact was the passenger side door crumpling inwards and the sensation of flying glass peppering his face.

After that, there was nothing.

* * *

# Chapter Thirty-Three

"The doctor hasn't cleared him fit to be interviewed yet. We're waiting on another CT scan and a bed on the ward." The senior staff nurse had a kind face and was just doing her job – and Nicki regretted the tone of voice she knew was about to decorate her next words.

"I don't care. He's talking to me – fit or otherwise."

"But..."

Nicki strode away from the nurse's station and headed towards resus number 1. The curtains around the cubicle were drawn tightly shut, shrouding its latest occupant from prying eyes. A uniformed constable stood outside.

Nicki ripped the curtains aside, oblivious to the commotion she was causing. The cubicle was full of bodies but Nicki only had eyes for one.

"Where is he?" Nicki stood by the man's side, her tone sharp and hostile. He wasn't asleep, she could tell. His eyes were closed but the man was awake. There was a bandage around his forehead, with signs of fresh blood seeping through into the fabric - presumably from where his head had hit the steering wheel in the impact. Both eyes were starting to blacken around the edges, and his nose was swollen with blood encrusted around each nostril. The neck collar had been removed after an x-ray cleared him of any spinal injury. Nicki already knew that, beneath the thin hospital blanket, he sported a fractured collarbone, a fractured pelvis and several cracked ribs.

An IV drip stand next to the bed was pumping him full of fluids and painkillers. She felt like ripping the line out from his hand and making him suffer. Anger rose uncontrollably within her. Why should he be pain free when Sophia Jackson was wracked with agony every single minute of every single day? As she looked on, her loathing for the man on the resus trolley intensified.

He had no name – a fact declared on the computer system when he'd been triaged on arrival. He'd refused to speak on being extricated from the remains of his crashed van and had no identifying documents on him. One thing for sure, though, was that he wasn't a policeman. The uniform that had been cut from his body now sat in plastic bags awaiting removal for forensic examination.

"Where is he?" Nicki repeated, stepping closer to the trolley and leaning towards the figure swathed in hospital blankets. An ED Consultant tutted and flashed Nicki a dark look, but she ignored him. Two ED nurses and the surgical doctor on-call stepped out of her way. Anger surged uncontrollably through her veins and she had to fight the renewed urge to grab him by the throat and beat the information out of him one way or another. "Lucas Jackson. What have you done with him?"

As she inched closer, she detected a flicker at the corner of the man's bloodied mouth. With her fists balling at her sides, anger flooded her system and fuelled the overwhelming desire she felt to inflict pain on another human being. Unable to stop herself, she raised a hand - just as the curtains behind her swished open.

"Inspector?"

\* \* \*

*Saturday 3rd November 2018*
9.45pm

The door to the semi-detached house was easily breached with the help of a sturdy shoulder and a Norfolk Constabulary boot. It splintered on impact and, after PC Donovan removed the jagged wood around the edges, Darcie stepped inside.

The house smelt musty; abandoned and unlived-in. And it felt cold. So very, very cold. The floor in the hall was littered with unopened post. PC Donovan flicked the light switch on the side-wall with a gloved hand, but nothing happened. The door to the neighbouring front room was already wide open – again PC Donovan tried the light switch inside. Still nothing. The electricity looked as if it had been disconnected.

A quick search of the rooms downstairs revealed nothing - the house giving the impression that it was nothing more than a shell. No furniture to speak of – just a tatty, battered looking sofa in the front room, with a multitude of cigarette burns on the arms. Darcie used her torch to illuminate the rest of the space. There were no pictures on the walls; no bookcases; no TV; no nothing. A worn carpet was underfoot with the faint edges of where a rug used to live.

At the rear of the house, the kitchen was in darkness. All the cupboards were empty, the fridge and freezer long since disconnected. Satisfied there was no sign of Lucas Jackson downstairs, they moved upstairs, careful not to touch anything as they went. For all they knew, the house could turn out to be a crime scene and need processing later – the very thought churned Darcie's stomach as they climbed. Swallowing past the dryness constricting her throat, she followed PC Donovan to the top.

Upstairs housed three bedrooms, and PC Donovan quickly confirmed the first two were empty of furniture and devoid of any signs of life. In the third, he stopped on the threshold, turning to beckon Darcie closer. Even in the darkness of the upstairs landing, his face looked ashen.

With her heart in her mouth, Darcie stepped through the doorway.

A single wooden chair sat in the centre of an otherwise almost empty room, a single coil of rope curled up beneath. The single window on the far wall was boarded up, with just a small, metal-framed bed beneath. Using her torch, Darcie illuminated the walls – noting the patches of creeping mould and thick nests of cobwebs in every corner. She felt herself shiver.

As she continued to sweep the torchlight around the room, the metal-framed bed once again caught her eye. Even from this distance she could make out the tell-tale blotches of blood on the stained mattress – but hanging over one of the bedposts was the sight that chilled her heart.

The red long-sleeved t-shirt was unmistakable. Darcie recognised it from the photograph in Oliver Chambers' murder file as being the clothes he was wearing when he was abducted.

Swallowing back the acrid taste of the bile that threatened to make an appearance, Darcie stumbled backwards. Reaching the landing, she pulled out her phone. She needed to speak to Nicki - she'd only managed to leave a garbled voicemail message before she'd jumped into PC Donovan's patrol car.

Thoughts of DS Fox filled her mind as she scrolled through to Nicki's contact details, her hand shaking. The vision of his bloodied, lifeless body being carefully cut free from the remains of his car would stay with her forever.

Shuddering once again, she beckoned PC Donovan to follow her back downstairs. The discovery of what could only be Oliver Chambers' Spiderman t-shirt in the upstairs room, meant the whole house was now a crime scene. And just because Lucas wasn't here now didn't mean he hadn't been at some point. The chair and the coil of rope upstairs had frozen the blood in her veins. Maybe both Oliver and Ivy had been here before...Darcie swallowed more bile. Those poor children.

Holding the phone to her ear, she heard the line ring out before switching to voicemail. She left another brief message for Nicki to call her. The initial euphoria of finding the address where they might find Lucas had very quickly evaporated, leaving a hollow, sick feeling inside. If Lucas had been here, he clearly wasn't now.

Biting back the tears that threatened to spill, she herded PC Donovan outside to start setting up a cordon.

* * *

*Saturday 3rd November 2018*

10.05pm

Hazel Kennedy pulled both her children close, tears cascading down her cheeks and dripping onto the tops of their heads. She felt Isaac flinch under her touch.

"Sorry," she whispered, releasing her grip.

Both boys had been found relatively unscathed in the back of the van, something which had astounded the paramedics attending the scene.

When Hazel and Neil had arrived at the entrance after hearing their names announced over the tannoy system, they were just in time to witness the crash between DS Fox's Honda and the battered white van. Even with the thumping fireworks overhead, the sound of crunching metal and shattering glass had pierced the air.

It had been Noah, banging on the inside of the van, and both boys screaming, that had alerted those on scene that there was someone in the back. The two fire engines that had only minutes before been a child's playground, were swiftly brought into action; their first job being to extract an unconscious DS Fox from the remains of his vehicle.

Although badly shaken, the impact had merely flung both boys against several rolls of carpet and they suffered only minor injuries. As a precaution, they were brought to the Norfolk and Norwich Hospital, where Isaac was to have his wrist x-rayed in case there was a fracture. But the signs for the pair of them were good. An overnight stay on the Children's Ward was being arranged, just to be on the safe side.

"I can't believe we were so stupid," breathed Hazel, watching Noah lead his younger brother towards a pile of comics on a table in the corner. "I just can't believe we did that."

The family had been allowed to sit in one of the relative's rooms while awaiting an x-ray slot for Isaac. Neither Hazel nor Neil relished being the focus of attention out in the waiting room. News had already started to trickle through about what had happened – and being on the receiving end of any number of judgmental stares was not what was needed right now.

They already blamed themselves – they didn't need anyone else to point out their guilt over what had happened or how foolish they'd been.

Neil came to sit beside his wife, his own hands shaking. "I know. I know. But it's over now. They're safe."

Fresh tears squeezed from Hazel's eyes as she leant against her husband's shoulder. "But it could so easily have turned out differently," she whispered. "I'll never forgive myself as long as I live."

Neil kissed the top of Hazel's head and merely stroked the back of her hand. There was nothing he could say or do to make her feel any better – or himself, for that matter. And there was a part of him that didn't want to feel any better. He *should* feel sick. He *should* feel responsible. He *should* feel his whole world was on the verge of crashing down around him.

And he should feel guilty.

Because he was.

He'd been the one to suggest leaving the boys on their own. Not Hazel – *him.*

And it was the one decision that would haunt him for the rest of his life.

They'd been told by a very sympathetic police officer at the scene that the boys would be spoken to by specially trained officers in due course – but for now they just needed to make sure both boys were well. The investigation as to how they came to be in the back of the van could wait.

"At least they had the foresight to scream," muttered Hazel, as she watched her two sons flicking through a selection of Marvel comics. "Other-wise..." She broke off and buried her face in her hands.

The evening spent teaching the boys how to scream at the tops of their lungs had paid off – something that had literally saved their lives.

Just then, the door to the relative's room opened and the young paediatric nurse who'd been looking after them since their arrival gave a warm smile. "We've an x-ray slot for this young man now," she said, nodding towards Isaac who was absorbed in a Spiderman comic.

He looked up, a red wheal developing on his forehead from where he'd collided with the roll of carpet. "Can I bring this with me?" He waved the comic in his good hand.

Hazel smiled and got to her feet, brushing away her remaining tears. "Of course you can, tiger. Come on. Let's go and get some photos of your arm."

\* \* \*

*Saturday 3rd November 2018*
10.15pm

Nicki watched from the main waiting room as the trolley was wheeled away towards the CT scanner. With his eyes still closed, to all intents and purposes the man looked unresponsive – but Nicki knew better. As, no doubt, did the experienced trauma team surrounding him. As the trolley disappeared from sight, she pulled her phone from her pocket and noticed the voicemail icon flashing with two missed calls from Darcie.

After being asked in no uncertain terms to vacate resus cubicle 1, Nicki had stepped next door to where DS Fox was being treated. She dutifully stayed out of the way this time, but was relieved to hear that her friend and colleague was alert and conscious. He was hooked up to various lines and monitors, but he still had a smile – albeit pained – on his face. Nicki stayed long enough to hear that he was stable, before heading out of resus cubicle 2 and heading for the corridor.

Raising the handset to her ear, she headed towards a vending machine. Her near-fainting episode at the fireworks display seemed a lifetime ago, but her body was telling her that she needed liquid. Punching in the code for a black coffee, Nicki listened to Darcie's first voice message. She sounded breathless, verging on frantic, and in the background was the sound of slamming car doors and sirens.

"Boss, it's me. A vehicle check on the van has thrown up an address in a village a few miles away. We're heading there now, it's not far. The local force is providing backup. I'll fill you in on what we find when we get there."

Nicki watched the machine spit out a stream of hot water and waited for Darcie's second message to play.

"Boss – he's not here. Lucas. The place is deserted but, I don't know, he might have been here at some point. There's…" Darcie's voice hitched and

Nicki thought she could hear the sound of the detective fighting back a sob. "Oliver's t-shirt – it's here. There's a chair. Rope. And blood. It's sickening. We've secured the place for the crime scene guys. The van was registered to a Mr Alan Woods. I'll get his name put in the system. Call me back."

Nicki stood and stared at the freshly poured cup of coffee standing in the drip tray, her feet rooted to the spot.

Alan Woods.

That couldn't be right, surely? A trickle of fear spread along Nicki's spine and all thoughts of sitting with a coffee while waiting for her suspect to return from the scanner evaporated in an instant. Instead, she turned on her heels and began to stride towards the exit.

"Miss? Your coffee?" A young man who'd been waiting patiently behind Nicki at the vending machine called out after her, pointing towards the abandoned cup.

Nicki didn't lessen her stride. Raising a hand in the air, she called back over her shoulder. "You have it." Disappearing through a set of double doors she soon reached the outside; the rush of cold night air on her skin sharpening her senses.

Alan Woods.

It made no sense. A myriad of jumbled thoughts coursed through her cluttered mind, as she strode past the entrance to A&E and rested against a concrete bollard. How could that be possible? With her phone still clutched in her hand, she stabbed a finger at one of the contacts and willed it to be answered.

After three rings it was.

\* \* \*

# Chapter Thirty-Four

Nicki found herself a concrete bench just around the corner from the A&E entrance.

"What do you need to know?" Jeremy Frost's tone sounded alert, despite the late hour.

"Everything," she replied. "Everything you can find out about Alan Woods."

"I'll ring Adam. He's been writing articles in the Guardian recently, and did a piece on the Woods case the other day. I think he's working on a biography of the guy – so he'll know everything there is to know." Jeremy paused before continuing. "Can I ask why? Why the sudden interest in Alan Woods at this time of night? Where are you?"

Nicki hesitated and bit her lip. Jeremy was a good friend and an even better source of information at times. But she needed to tread carefully. He was still a journalist at heart. "I need to go. I'll fill you in later. OK?"

She ended the call and stood up from the bench. The cold concrete had numbed her legs.

Alan Woods.

He quite clearly wasn't the man currently languishing in a hospital trolley under the CT scanner right now. Because Alan Woods was at this point in time imprisoned and serving a life sentence for murder.

Tapping her phone impatiently with her finger, Nicki decided to return Darcie's call. Irritatingly, the call went straight to voicemail so Nicki left her own message before returning in through the A&E front entrance.

"Darcie. That name – Alan Woods. It can't be him. Keep digging. And let me know what you find."

\* \* \*

*Saturday 3rd November 2018*
   10.25pm

Darcie stood just inside the remains of the broken front door, one foot still on the threadbare doormat. PC Donovan had gone back to the car to radio his own unit and update them. They'd managed to secure an outer cordon as best they could; a crime scene investigation team were on their way. All they could do now was secure the scene and wait.

Although there'd been no sign of Lucas, Darcie's stomach had clenched at the vision of the Spiderman t-shirt hanging over the end of the bed upstairs. The post mortem photographs of little Oliver's body had then flooded her brain. How the poor little mite must have suffered. Pushing the images from her mind, Darcie turned her attention to the pile of unopened post that littered the carpet at her feet. Bending down, she noticed most were flyers from local takeaways or other junk mail. There were a few 'to the occupier' circulars in brown envelopes and a hoard of plastic charity bags asking for donations.

She wanted to get back to the station. Roy had insisted on coming back in, and she needed to check he was all right. And then there was Graham. There'd been no word from the hospital other than a hurried message that he'd arrived in A&E.

As she continued to sift through the post, a single letter caught her eye.

\* \* \*

*Saturday 3rd November 2018*

10.30pm

Amy informed Nicki that her suspect had been found a bed on one of the wards upstairs and was being transported there straight from the CT scanner. Thanking her best friend, Nicki noted the pensive look on Amy's face.

"What is it?"

Amy beckoned her closer to the desk and placed a hand on Nicki's arm. "It's your colleague. The one you came in with?"

Nicki felt her blood chill. "Graham? DS Fox?" She glanced towards the second resus cubicle where she'd left him.

Amy nodded. "He's been rushed to theatre. Literally just now. There's a note here to call you and let you know."

"Why? What's wrong with him? He was fine when I last saw him." Nicki remembered leaving DS Fox on the resus trolley, the dogged detective giving her the thumbs up despite being in obvious pain. According to the ED Consultant his vital signs were good and they were waiting for a bed on a ward.

Amy could do nothing but shrug. "I don't know, I'm afraid. Theatres are upstairs – your best bet is to head up there. They'll be able to tell you more."

How she managed to keep herself upright, Nicki hadn't a clue, but she arrived outside the Main Theatres reception window with her heart hammering. All thoughts of Alan Woods and the man being wheeled up to Ward F6 were cast aside. Right now, Graham Fox was her only concern.

Steeling herself against the wall, Nicki rang the bell. It was an anxious few seconds before the call was answered. She then listened as a gentle voice confirmed that DS Fox had indeed been rushed into emergency surgery only minutes before.

After being cut from the wreckage of his car, pale and lifeless, he'd regained consciousness in the back of the ambulance. The primary survey and trauma CT on arrival at A&E had confirmed no significant intracranial injury, just a deep laceration to the scalp and multiple cuts to the face from shattered glass. A dislocated shoulder, fractured sternum and several cracked ribs would all heal in time. But as Nicki had disappeared outside to speak to Jeremy, his condition had deteriorated, his vital signs plummeting. They now suspected that the force of the gearstick into his abdomen had caused massive internal bleeding.

Right now that was all that they could tell her. She was welcome to wait, but he was likely to be in surgery for some time.

Nicki stumbled away from Main Theatres. Her anger now resurfaced and she headed along the corridor in the direction of Ward F6. If anything happened to Graham, then she wasn't sure she would be able to control herself. She no longer cared what rules or protocols there might be for visiting the ward at this time of night – the man was going to talk. And then he was going to pay.

Arriving at the entrance to Ward F6, she pressed the buzzer until the door was released. Warrant card at the ready, she thundered through towards one of the bed spaces at the far end, outside of which she was relieved to see the uniformed constable still on constants. Wrenching back the curtains, Nicki stepped in and approached the bed.

The whiteboard on the wall confirmed that the man still had no name, but that didn't deter Nicki from towering over the figure swathed in hospital blankets

"Tell me where he is," she fumed, leaning onto the bed with both hands. She could feel the sweat beginning to prickle underneath her hair line. "I know you can hear me, tell me where Lucas is!"

The man remained motionless, but Nicki again saw the faint flicker of a smile at the corners of his mouth. Without thinking, she lunged forwards, ready to rip the lines from his body and drag him from the bed.

"Tell me where he is, you no-good piece of shit!"

Just then the curtains were pulled back and the on-call Registrar for Ward F6 appeared by her side.

"This man needs to rest." The Registrar's expression made it quite clear that Nicki's presence wasn't welcome. "He's in no position to be questioned overnight, and you being here is disturbing the other patients."

Not wanting to cause more of a scene than she already had, Nicki allowed herself to be shepherded off the ward and back out into the corridor. It had taken all her strength and resolve not to cause him even more damage than he'd suffered in the crash. She wasn't one to lose her temper, but he was testing her patience to its very limits. The smile that played on his lips when the doctor wasn't looking almost tipped her over the edge.

And the scar.

The scar had been noticeable as soon as Nicki had stormed into the A&E resus cubicle.

They had their man. Even if he had no name.

Before leaving the ward, she told the uniformed officer on watch outside the bed space to contact her as soon as the man showed any signs of lucidity. Nicki was pretty sure he was faking, but as soon as he was awake she wanted him placed under arrest.

And it was something she wanted to do personally.

Sitting down on one of the visitor chairs outside the ward, she felt her phone buzz in her pocket. It was a call from an unknown number.

"Is that Nicki Hardcastle?" the voice on the other end enquired. "Detective Inspector Hardcastle?"

Nicki found herself nodding. "Yes, speaking."

"Hi, it's Adam Sullivan. Jeremy asked me to give you a call. You wanted some information on an Alan Woods?"

Nicki felt her heartbeat quicken. "Yes, yes I do. Thanks for getting back to me so quickly."

"No problem. Jeremy might have told you, I'm doing a biography of sorts on Woods. Well, child killers in general, really. And it's the 20th anniversary of his first victim this year. The Guardian is going to do an article nearer the time and print an extract from my book, if I ever get it finished."

Nicki pressed the handset closer to her ear as two porters wheeled a patient on a bed along the corridor in front of her. "Go on."

"As you probably know, Alan Woods was arrested in 2003 for the abduction and murder of two boys – Jacob Ayers and Sean Warren. He went on trial in early 2004 and was convicted of both offences. Currently serving a life sentence, he's unlikely to ever be released." Adam paused. "At the time of his conviction it was thought he could be responsible for other unsolved child murders – it was felt unlikely that Jacob and Sean would be his only victims. He eventually admitted to three further murders - two in 1998, and one in 1999. It was put to him that there might be more, but he denied involvement in any other child abductions."

Nicki blinked back the vision of her brother as it swam in front of her eyes. "Go on," she croaked.

"At the time of his arrest he was living with his wife and stepson.

"And where are they now?"

"After his conviction, the police moved the family to a safe house for their own protection. There was a lot of bad feeling in the local community, as you might imagine, and the house was regularly targeted by vandals. Several attempts to firebomb the property led to them being offered alternative accommodation."

"Witness protection?"

"No evidence of that, no. If it was offered, then it was turned down. I managed to trace the wife to just east of Cambridge – she now goes under her maiden name of Sutherland and by all accounts is leading a relatively normal life."

"And the stepson?"

"He's a bit more problematic. There's plenty of information about Daniel Woods during his school days, but not much thereafter. It's as though he's just dropped off the face of the earth. He's either dead, abroad or he's changed his name. But there is one other thing of note. My initial enquiries unearthed an incident that happened at school, not long after his stepfather's conviction. Acid was thrown into his face by a fellow pupil, causing facial burns and scarring. I might have some more on that. I'll try and dig it out."

The ice in Nicki's veins chilled even further. "A scar, you say?" Although her mind was already cluttered, images flooded back of their suspect. And the scar visible on his lower jaw. "How old would he be right now?" Nicki tried to do the arithmetic in her head.

"Well, he was thirteen when his stepfather was convicted – so that would make him around twenty-seven now."

# CHAPTER THIRTY-FOUR

Nicki found herself nodding. The age fit nicely.

"Are there any photographs of him?" Within a split second of her posing the question, she could almost hear the reporter shaking his head.

"Not that I've been able to find, no. As he was a child at the time, he was kept out of the media for obvious reasons. I tried the school before, but they weren't all that helpful. I could try again?"

"If you could, that would be great."

Nicki thanked Adam and closed the call. Was the man currently up on F6 Daniel Woods? Alan Woods' stepson?

Just as she was trying to process everything the reporter had divulged, her phone buzzed again in her hand. This time it was Darcie.

"Darcie," answered Nicki, her voice somewhat breathless. "I was just about to ring you. I think our man is Daniel Woods."

"That's exactly what I was going to say!" replied Darcie. "I found some post at the property with his name on. Daniel Woods. There's not much, but..."

"Well, I'm betting he won't be using that name anymore, but run it through the system anyway. See what you come up with. Any kind of alternate address for him – somewhere where we might find Lucas. Anything at all."

"Will do, boss. Roy's checked the van's details. No transfer of ownership since it was registered back in 1996."

They had their man, Nicki was sure of that – and they now had his name. But she still had to make him talk. "How is Roy, anyway? He should be home nursing his injuries."

"He was. But he got wind of what was going on and insisted on coming back in to help. He's at the station now, doing all the ringing around and leg work. I'll get him to run the name through the system. I'm making my way back to the station now that the scene of crime guys have turned up here." Darcie paused, her voice catching in her throat. "I told him about Gray. How is he?"

Nicki swallowed before replying, her stomach clenching tight. "He's in theatre, Darcie. It doesn't sound good."

Nicki closed the call. Pushing herself up out of the visitor's chair, she decided to leave Daniel Woods for the time being – he wasn't going anywhere - and made her way along the corridor back towards main theatres. She had no energy left in her to keep walking. She'd just wait outside until there was news, no matter how long it took.

As she arrived outside theatre reception, she pulled out her phone again and made the call she'd been avoiding for the last three days.

* * *

# Chapter Thirty-Five

*Sunday 4<sup>th</sup> November 2018*

6.15am

The words swam in front of her eyes in a teasing, taunting dance - once seen, they could never be unseen. She'd bought several different newspapers over the last few days, her stomach clenching tighter and tighter with each one that dropped into her shopping basket. The shop owner had raised an eyebrow as he scanned the barcodes, but not a word was said.

She didn't need to read them really – she already knew what they would say. Unless you lived under a rock, it was impossible not to have heard. The media had taken the story by the scruff of the neck and were not letting go.

Lucas Jackson was the little boy's name. She'd seen his photograph in the newspapers earlier that week, and the image of his cheeky smile had stayed with her long after the effects of the alcohol she'd consumed to dull her senses had worn off. She'd tipped the rest of the bottle down the sink. Alcohol couldn't help her now. And it couldn't help Lucas Jackson either.

Only she could do that.

Folding up her copy of the Daily Express, she placed it on top of all the others on the occasional table that sat by the side of her armchair. The headlines may be different in each, but the message they all conveyed was identical.

*We need to find the boy. We need to save the boy.*

Accusations of police incompetence were flung around wildly in amongst the appeals for help from the public. But she knew it wasn't the fault of the police. There could be only one person to blame.

Reaching across the stack of newspapers, she picked up her most prized possession. The photograph had aged over the years, now protected inside the cheap plastic photo frame she'd bought in the local pound shop. Her eyes became glassy, as they often did when she thought about her boys. She ran a quivering finger across the surface, touching each of their faces in turn.

My boys.

Her heart heaved when she asked herself the inevitable question, '*what did I do wrong?*'

It was a question she'd never managed to answer.

The eldest two stood beneath the apple tree at the bottom of the garden, smirks plastered across their faces. A smile teased at her own lips as she thought back to the day the camera had captured this snapshot of their life; the day before everything had changed. Five minutes before the picture was taken, they'd been given a stiff talking to by their father, and a swift smack to their backsides, for climbing the apple tree and throwing apples at their younger brother.

Lowering her gaze to the bottom of the photograph, she saw the tell-tale fruit lying at their feet. They'd meant no harm – just boys being boys. It'd been a hot summer's day and the tree was just asking to be climbed.

But their father hadn't seen it that way. He'd been furious, striding out across the garden from where he'd been watching them from the sanctity of his study, dragging them from the branches by their legs. All the while, their younger brother had watched, open-mouthed, as the drama unfolded in front of him.

She let her finger hover over the youngest boy. He was crouching down on the grass at his brothers' feet, the smile on his face stretching from ear to ear. His bare knees were caked in dirt from where he'd been playing on the ground with his trucks.

Daniel.

It was the only photograph she had of the three of them together. A shiny polaroid capturing the last day of happiness before it all went wrong. That very night, their father – her husband of ten years – walked to the pub at the end of the road and never came back. The next morning, she discovered that he'd packed a small suitcase and taken the housekeeping money from where she always kept it in a biscuit tin by the kettle. And he'd taken the polaroid camera with him, too.

The only time she heard from him again was when the padded envelope landed on the doormat with the divorce papers inside.

The boys had been confused at first, especially Daniel, but as the days stretched into weeks, and the weeks into months, the eldest two rejoiced in the knowledge that he wasn't coming back. They were able to climb the apple tree to their heart's content, and nobody would be there to drag them back down again or whoop their behinds.

No, the eldest boys thrived in the absence of their overbearing father. But it'd been the little one that had worried her the most. He'd idolised his father, following him around the house and demanding stories at bedtime. His absence created a huge chasm that she struggled to fill on her own. She would often find him curled up on his bed, sobbing his heart out, wondering why his Daddy had abandoned him.

She brushed a silent tear from her cheek and placed the photograph back down on the table. She could have saved him. She could have turned his life around and made him into a decent human being. But she didn't. Instead, she set him on a path that would ultimately end up destroying his life – and those that had the misfortune to come into contact with him.

It's my fault, she breathed.

*It's all my fault.*

\* \* \*

*Sunday 4<sup>th</sup> November 2018*
6.40am

As Nicki leant up against the wall outside main theatres, exhaustion threatened to overwhelm her. Her body sagged, and if it wasn't for the bricks and mortar behind her, she would've slipped quite happily to the floor. The adrenaline of last night had now completely drained away, replaced with intense fatigue. Now entering forty-eight hours with no sleep, Nicki's body was flagging. She'd refused to go home, wanting to be here the minute Graham woke up.

She sipped on a black coffee loaded with sugar, and forced her eyes to focus.

After six hours in theatre overnight, with a repair to a lacerated kidney and partial removal of his spleen, Graham had been returned to recovery. The surgeon had told her he was doing 'as well as could be expected' and was currently 'comfortable'.

Nicki wasn't sure that was an accurate description of how Graham would be feeling right now, but she was thankful he appeared to no longer be in danger. She'd managed a few words with him as he came round from the anaesthetic, but was quickly ushered away to let him rest. He'd given her his customary 'thumbs up' gesture as she'd departed.

Nicki took another sip of her coffee and winced at the bitter taste. She was glad she'd pulled him onto the team for Operation Goldfish. Without him, they were unlikely to have got to where they were today. Daniel Woods was under guard in a hospital bed and unable to harm anyone else.

But they were still no closer to finding Lucas.

They may have saved Noah and Isaac Kennedy from a horrific ordeal, but they still hadn't found Lucas.

Nicki's stomach churned at the thought

Just as exhaustion was winning the day, Nicki's mobile chirped.

* * *

Sunday 4<sup>th</sup> November 2018
  6.40am


"Where are the Kennedy family now?" Roy closed the last of DS Fox's burglary files. Darcie had persuaded him to go back home for a rest and a shower, but he'd returned not long after and insisted he keep working. It was heading towards seven o'clock and the skies were only just starting to lighten.

Darcie looked up from her computer screen. "They were advised at the scene to take the boys to hospital to get checked over, but they just seemed to want to take them home. I'm not sure what happened after that." She rubbed her eyes, the effects of the strong black coffee she'd made herself drink were wearing off. "If they'd come to the hospital here, then I'm sure the boss would've said. They could've gone to the Norfolk and Norwich I suppose? It's a bit further but..." Darcie shrugged and turned back to her computer screen. "We'll need to speak to the boys at some point – they're valuable witnesses."

Roy nodded. "Put in a call to the local force and see where they went, would you?" Pushing himself up out of his chair, he reached for the jacket he'd hung over the back, wincing as he did so.

"Where are you off to?" Darcie frowned. "You know you really ought to be at home, resting. Nicki will have a fit if she finds you back here again."

"I'm fine. It's just a few cuts and bruises."

"And a fractured cheekbone, and suspected cracked ribs. *And* possible concussion."

Roy gave a pained smile. "As I said – cuts and bruises." He slipped his jacket on, successfully hiding the wince from Darcie this time. "I'm heading over to the Kennedy house. They're the only ones who haven't been asked about any contact details for their builder."

"We've already established he's too clever to have left his real address behind."

"I know." Roy headed towards the door, pulling out his car keys. "But it needs checking out anyway. And I need the fresh air. I'll be there and back in no time. They might not be at home, anyway. Then I'll go home, I promise."

Darcie watched as Roy disappeared out into the corridor and turned her attention back to her search for Daniel Woods. Everything she'd tried had drawn a blank. Nicki was most probably right – he wasn't using this name anymore, and the chances of finding him were diminishing rapidly. She contemplated making another strong coffee, in need of the caffeine hit, but the thought churned her stomach.

She'd heard nothing more from the hospital. The last she'd heard was that Graham was in emergency surgery, but that had been hours ago. The thought of what might be happening, or had already happened, squeezed her insides. Blinking back tears that threatened to spill, she angrily punched the name Daniel Woods into yet another system and prayed.

\* \* \*

*Sunday 4<sup>th</sup> November 2018*
6.40am

"Detective Inspector Hardcastle. I got your voicemail."

Nicki hovered at the top of a deserted stairwell, close to the entrance to main theatres. The hospital was still sleeping and no one was in earshot.

"Don't get too excited. I need a favour." Her voice was taut, matched by the look on her face. It wasn't a call she'd planned on making, but as she'd stood outside main theatres late last night, waiting for news on Graham, it was the only call she thought might help. Adam Sullivan might find out what was on public record, but she felt this required something somewhat deeper.

"A favour?" Intrigue swept Caspar Ambrose's tone. "You ignore my calls for several days and now you want me to do you a favour?"

Nicki paced from side to side in the confined stairwell. "Yes. Yes, I do. How much do you know, or can find out, about Alan Woods' family?"

The line remained silent and Nicki began to wonder if Ambrose was still there. "The Woods family," she repeated, an edge of frustration to her tone. "You're familiar with the name? How much do you know?"

"Of course I'm familiar with the name," came the eventual reply. "And I know enough. What is it exactly that you're after?"

"The stepson of the family – Daniel Woods. I need to know what he changed his name to, because we're pretty sure he has. And I need to know his current address."

"That could be like looking for a white cat in a snowstorm."

"But you can do it? You have contacts?"

There was another heavy pause before Ambrose continued. "I can, and I do."

"Then do it. A little boy's life could be at stake here."

Nicki heard the rustling of paperwork in the background. "Is this the best number to reach you on?"

"Yes, anytime."

"Then I'll do what I can, Detective Inspector. But on one condition."

Nicki felt the blood beginning to ignite in her veins. "Condition?"

"Yes." There was further rustling in the background before Caspar Ambrose spoke again. "Meet with me."

"Meet with you?"

"Yes, meet with me. If you want information on this Daniel Woods, then my price is a portion of your time. You won't regret it."

\* \* \*

# Chapter Thirty-Six

*Sunday 4ᵗʰ November 2018*

   6.55am

She'd let the cup of tea go cold by her side. Glancing down, the photo of her three boys by the apple tree was still clutched in her hands. With the room now lightening with the hint of the breaking dawn, she placed it back on the table with a shaky hand and started to rise. As she moved, she felt her bones creak. The years were catching up with her now; her joints protesting in earnest as she pushed herself up from her chair. Pain shot up the backs of her legs as she crossed the carpet to take the tea cup back to the kitchen at the rear of the modest bungalow.

   Her ankles were often the worst; stiff and sore most of the time. She'd tried to put the past behind her, block out the memories, but the discomfort she felt on a daily basis was a constant reminder of the past that refused to be buried.

   The chain he'd used to fasten around her ankles, locking her to the kitchen table for hours at a time, may have long since been removed, but its memory still lingered. The thought made her feel sick. Every day she could feel the cold, hard metal against her skin, chafing her as she shuffled across the linoleum floor. She glanced down at her slipper-clad feet, knowing they were now free and unchained – but her mind often played tricks on her and told her otherwise.

   The photograph of the boys under the apple tree returned to her mind as she tipped the cold tea down the sink. The eldest two had escaped, and she was thankful for that. When she'd moved in and married Alan, after a whirlwind three-month romance that she now bitterly regretted, he'd put his foot down at her three children accompanying her. The house was too small, had been his excuse. An excuse she'd swallowed and accepted at the time. Packing the eldest boys off to stay with her sister had been a wrench, the hardest thing she'd ever had to do – but looking back on it now, it was an act that had saved them. They'd been brought up in the care of a warm and friendly family, saved from the vile existence they would have endured at Arlington Crescent.

But her sister hadn't room for all three – so her baby boy, the apple of her eye, had stayed with her.

She'd let Daniel down; she knew that now. She should've insisted that he go with his brothers – insisted that her sister make room for him. Anything to take him away from that fearful place.

But she hadn't. She'd held him close and told him that everything was going to be all right.

Alan had been kind at first – they'd been welcomed into his home and life looked to be good. But she had no idea what lay around the corner; what nightmare was about to be unleashed. It happened so gradually, the control and coercion, that she couldn't quite remember when it started. But before she knew it, she was trapped.

Shaking the unwanted memories from her head, she shuffled back to the front room. She felt her eyes drawn, once again, to the stack of newspapers by the side of the armchair. The headlines burned her eyes. She'd not read the articles in full; she didn't need to. Her conscience told her everything she needed to know.

It was him; there was no doubt in her mind.

Daniel.

Mixed feelings threatened to drown her. He was an exact copy of his father – not his real father, of course, but the only father he'd ever really known. The only father who'd taken an interest in him. A father that had moulded him, nurtured him, *created him*.

The very thought sickened her to the core.

She'd let him down once before, she couldn't let him down again. She had to do what was right this time.

With a heavy heart, she slipped herself back down into the armchair and reached for the phone.

* * *

*Sunday 4<sup>th</sup> November 2018*

   6.55am

The Kennedy's house sat in semi-darkness, the sun only just starting to make its early morning appearance. With no car on the drive, it was clear to DS Carter, as he pulled up outside, that the family weren't at home. He guessed they'd succumbed to the suggestion to take the boys to hospital for a check-up, and were probably still there, what with waiting times such as they were. He dialled the mobile number they had on file, just in case, but the call went to voicemail. He declined to leave a message.

Stepping out of the car, Roy pulled his jacket around him to ward off the biting chill that had descended overnight. His whole face throbbed. The painkillers issued by the hospital were barely making a dent.

Ignoring his discomfort, he made his way up the short garden path, immediately noting that the front door was made of strong UPVC and would likely withstand any feeble attempt he might make to gain entry. He didn't fancy shouldering it, given his fragile state. And in any event, he didn't really have the right to break the door down. Not now.

As he turned to walk towards a side gate that presumably led around to the back, a movement flickered to catch his attention.

"Hello, sonny. Are you looking for Hazel and Neil?"

An old woman peered across the top of a well-manicured hedge that separated her house from the Kennedy's. Even in the dimness of the morning light, Roy could see she had a wild expanse of wiry, white hair and the clearest set of piercing blue eyes he'd ever seen. She was small, tiny even – with a bulky knitted shawl draped across her narrow shoulders.

"I'm sorry?" Roy took a step nearer to the old woman, the faint waft of lavender meeting his nostrils.

"Hazel and Neil Kennedy. Are you looking for them? Only they didn't come back last night. It was the firework display, you see. They go every year. That's what I told that other nice gentleman. He was looking for them, too."

A faint frown hovered over Roy's brow. "The other gentleman?"

The old woman nodded. "Yes. The policeman. And a very nice young man he was, too. Said he was looking for the Kennedys. I told him they'd taken the boys to that firework display."

"Ah, that would've been my colleague, DS Fox." Roy brought out his warrant card. "I'm DS Roy Carter. I don't suppose the Kennedys gave you a spare key to their house?"

The old woman shook her head. "No, dear. There was usually always one of them at home – for the children, you see."

Roy nodded and began to back away. Short of smashing a window, he didn't quite see how he was going to be able to get inside. And he was pretty sure he'd have some questions to answer when he got back to the station if he did. Darcie was right – the guy wouldn't have slipped up and suddenly left his home address behind.

"OK, thanks anyway. Never mind." Roy gave the old woman a smile, pain shooting across his cheekbone as he did so. It didn't go unnoticed.

"You poor boy – what's happened to your face?"

Roy gave a nervous laugh, another stab of pain hitting him squarely between his bruised eyes. "I'm fine. A little accident, that's all."

"Arnica, my dear."

"I'm sorry?" Roy had half-turned away from the woman, intending to head back towards his car.

"Arnica. It does wonders for bruising. If you wait there, I'll fetch you some."

Before Roy had a chance to politely decline, the old woman had shuffled off back inside her front door, emerging less than a minute later with a tube of ointment in her hand.

"Dab that on your bruises three times a day." She held the tube out over the top of the hedge. "You mark my words - you'll be better in no time."

Roy accepted the ointment and nodded his thanks. "You're most kind. Thank you."

"Natural remedies are the best," she added, pulling her woollen shawl more closely around her shoulders. "None of this fancy factory-created chemical nonsense. Plants and herbs will do you far more good. And take some green tea – that'll heal you from within."

Roy began side-stepping back along the garden path, waving the tube of ointment in the air. "I'll remember that. Green tea. Thanks again."

The old woman beamed, her bright blue eyes blazing even in the dull haze of the breaking dawn. "You're most welcome, sonny. You're far more appreciative of my advice than that other man. Quite rude he was, if I'm honest. And all I was doing was trying to help."

Roy hesitated, almost at the pavement. "What man was that? My colleague? DS Fox?"

The old woman shook her head. "No, no, my dear. The builder Hazel and Neil had in to do their decorating. All I said was that he could use some aloe vera on his face, where he has his scars, and he fair near bit my head off."

\* \* \*

*Sunday 4<sup>th</sup> November 2018*
7.00am

Darcie ripped open the bar of Dairy Milk and sunk her teeth into the rich chocolate. She closed her eyes and let the velvety sweet texture flood her mouth. It wasn't until she'd stood up, to go and get something from the printer, that she'd felt the first wobble. With her head swimming and her eyes beginning to blur, she'd had to grab hold of a desk chair to stop herself from falling.

Now armed with a black coffee and a bar of chocolate, she sat herself back

CHAPTER THIRTY-SIX

down at the computer screen and forced her eyes to focus. Looking down at her watch, she frowned. Roy shouldn't be working, not after taking such a hefty whack from Marcus Jackson. He'd hit the deck pretty hard. She picked up her phone, deciding to give him a quick ring, but the call wasn't answered. She left a brief message, telling him to go home or at least come back to the station. Just as she ended the call, the desk phone behind her started to trill.

"DC Butler," greeted Darcie, stifling a yawn as she leant back in her chair to pick up the receiver.

"I've someone on the line insisting they speak with DI Hardcastle."

"She's not here – still up at the hospital." Darcie took another bite from her chocolate bar. "Can you take the details and she'll call back when she can?"

"I tried that." The voice on the other end of the line paused. "She's insistent on speaking to DI Hardcastle right now. I can't seem to placate her or convince her that taking a message is the best I can do."

Darcie sighed, taking a mouthful of the hot, black coffee to wash away the chocolate covering her tongue. "Put her through. I'll do what I can."

"Thanks, Darcie."

There was a brief pause while the call was connected. Darcie pulled a notepad towards her and bit the top off her biro. When the voice eventually came through it was barely audible.

"Hello? DC Butler, here. You sound very faint." Darcie frowned. "Can you repeat that, please?"

There was another brief delay before the voice spoke again, accompanied by the sound of a muffled sob.

"My name is Linda. And I know the person who's taken that young boy."

\* \* \*

*Sunday 4<sup>th</sup> November 2018*
7.05am

Roy ushered the old woman into the darkened hallway of her house, the

287

reluctant dawn not yet reaching inside.

"He wasn't very pleasant to me, I can tell you that."

Elsie Cooke, as Roy now discovered, had lived in Henley Road for the last ten years and knew the Kennedy family well.

She shuffled further back inside the house, waving for Roy to follow. There was a small lamp on a telephone table just inside the hallway, giving out a faint glow to illuminate their way.

"Can I get you a cup of tea, dear?" Elsie disappeared into the kitchen. "You look like you've seen a ghost."

Roy followed, his mind continuing to whirr. "No, I'm fine, really. Do you think you could tell me more about this man – this builder that was working next door? Do you remember what he looked like?"

The old woman turned towards Roy and nodded. "I might be old but my eyesight is 20/20. I even recognised him when I went to get Clarence his favourite tuna in jelly from the corner shop."

As if on cue, at the very mention of his favourite food, a large ginger tabby cat appeared and began to wind himself around the old woman's ankles.

"Oh, Clarence!" she chuckled, trying to extricate herself from the mewing cat. "It's not breakfast time yet, Go on, shoo!"

The cat took no notice and continued to perform its figure-of-eight dance in between Mrs Cooke's legs, until she bent down to scoop him up into her arms, her face shining. "Fifteen and still going strong, aren't you, my boy?" She gave Clarence a head rub and received a rhythmical purr in response.

Roy was still standing in the doorway between the hall and the kitchen trying to untangle the old woman's words. "The corner shop. Where would that be? And when were you there?"

The old woman gave a faint frown before replying. "It would have been last Wednesday. I always treat myself to a slice of Battenberg on a Wednesday. There's a little parade of shops – a hairdresser, a bakery, and a little shop on the corner. It's a good ten-minute walk from here, but the exercise does me good! Keeps me young, so the doctors keep telling me." She chuckled to herself, turning away and depositing the cat onto the kitchen worktop "Are you sure I can't make you a nice cup of tea? I've got Earl Grey?"

Roy took a step forward, shaking his head. "No, thank you. I really am fine. Is there anything else you can tell me about him? The builder? When you saw him in the shop, what was he buying? Did you see what car he had?"

Roy knew he was bombarding the poor woman with far too many questions all at once, one after the other, but his mind was careering out of control and he was unable to stop himself. Mrs Cooke seemed unaware and continued to busy herself filling the kettle and then switching it on – despite Roy declining a cup of Earl Grey, it looked like she was making one anyway.

"He didn't buy much, as I recall. A loaf of bread and a newspaper, I think. Maybe something else – I couldn't quite see everything." The old woman turned towards the worktop and brought down two bone china cups and saucers from the cupboard above. "I tried to stay out of his way, you see. I didn't want him to see me. Not after he was so rude to me about the aloe vera. And I was only trying to help."

Roy nodded. "Did you see where he went after? What kind of car he had? Was he alone?"

Too many questions again, all tumbling out of his mouth at the same time. His detective training in the questioning of witnesses had gone sailing out of the window. Elsie didn't seem to mind and proceeded to place a tea bag into each cup, the kettle having reached the boil and switched off.

"There was no car, my dear. He walked home. He doesn't live that far away."

Roy felt his mouth drop open. "You *saw* where he went?"

The old woman nodded, pouring hot water onto the tea bags. "I'd already finished my shopping – two tins of Clarence's favourite and my Battenberg – so I followed him out of the shop. He turned right, and walked up the road heading towards the community centre. I decided to walk that way too – I can get back home that way, it just takes a few minutes longer, and it was a nice enough morning for once. He walked quite fast, as I recall - all the way along there for a good five minutes. I had a job to keep up, what with my legs. Then he went inside one of those big houses set back from the road – the ones that back onto the school. His was the one at the very end – with a double garage and a high hedge all the way around."

Roy pulled his notebook and mobile phone from his pocket. "Can you tell me the name of the road again?"

The old woman placed the freshly brewed cup of Earl Grey on the worktop in front of Roy and sighed. "I'm afraid my memory rather lets me down these days. Eyesight is as sharp as a pin, but simple things…" She shook her head. "Simple things just disappear."

"But it's the road next to the shops? Do you happen to know the name of the road the shops are on?" Roy could tell by the look on Elsie Cooke's face that she didn't.

"It's just a few streets away from here – it's not far. As if you were heading towards that nice pub with the garden?"

It was now that Roy felt the acute disadvantage of being the new boy in town. He hadn't a clue where the old woman was talking about. He hadn't been out in this part of the town before – or if he had, he didn't recognise any of it. He had no idea where the parade of shops was, let alone the pub. He silently cursed himself for his lack of local knowledge.

After politely taking a mouthful of the freshly poured Earl Grey tea, Roy bolted out of number 23 and dashed for his car.

\* \* \*

# Chapter Thirty-Seven

*Sunday 4<sup>th</sup> November 2018*

7.50am

"And where is she now?" Nicki hurried across the station car park, her phone clamped to her ear. The moment the call from Darcie came through, she'd abandoned her vigil outside main theatres and raced out of the hospital to flag down a taxi.

"She's here. I got a local patrol car to bring her straight in – she wasn't that far away. I've just put her in your office for now as I wasn't sure what else to do with her." Darcie's voice was strained. "Should I move her to an interview room?"

Nicki shook her head as she barged through the front entrance. "No need. I'm here now. Be with you in two shakes."

Racing up the stairs, taking them two at a time, Nicki burst into the incident room. It was deserted except for Darcie hovering by one of the whiteboards. The young detective swirled round at Nicki's approach.

"What can you tell me about her? Who is she?" Nicki wrenched off the scarf that was wound too tightly around her neck. Her throat felt dry and constricted. "Is she for real?"

"Says her name is Linda. She won't say anything else. Just says she knows who our man is. She knows who has Lucas."

Nicki's eyes widened. "Anything else?"

Darcie shook her head. "She won't say anything else to me. Clammed right

291

up. Says it has to be you."

Nicki turned on her heels and headed towards her office, waving at Darcie to follow. "Come with me, Darcie. I might need you to take notes."

Darcie hurried after her, grabbing her notebook as she did so. "How's Gray?"

Nicki paused at the entrance to her office and gave Darcie a tired smile. "Better. Out of theatre and fingers crossed he should be OK."

Relief flooded Darcie's face as she followed Nicki over the threshold into the office.

Inside, a small-framed woman was perched on the edge of one of the visitors' chairs. She looked like a bird, so tiny and delicate, as if she might snap in two at any given moment. Her face was thin and pointed, her greying hair scraped away into a high and hastily arranged bun. Red-rimmed, raw eyes looked up to meet Nicki.

"Linda?" Nicki moved closer, noting how the woman seemed to visibly tremble at her approach. She looked terrified, clutching a ragged handkerchief in her quivering hands. "My colleague here tells me you have some information that might help us?" She slipped into one of the vacant visitors' chairs beside the shaking woman. "Would you like a cup of tea?"

The woman shook her head but remained mute.

Nicki nodded, discreetly, at Darcie to get the notepad ready. "You rang to say you knew who had taken Lucas Jackson?"

The woman began to nod, slowly at first but then more fervently. She brought a trembling hand up to her face to brush away the fresh tears spilling from her eyes and smoothed away several stray strands of hair from her damp cheeks. "Yes." Her voice was barely above a whisper. "Yes I do."

"In your own time, Linda." Nicki reached forwards and placed a hand on the woman's arm, feeling the angle of her bones through the thin fabric of her jumper.

The woman's voice, when it returned, was a little stronger. "The man in the newspapers," she began, her chest heaving as she took another deep breath. "The one you're looking for – for abducting that young boy."

"Lucas? Lucas Jackson?" Nicki gave the woman's arm another gentle squeeze. "What is it you would like to tell us, Linda?"

The woman looked up, a fresh stream of silent tears streaking her cheeks. She gave Nicki a wan smile. "The man you're looking for - he's my son."

Nicki looked up, sharply. "Your son?"

The woman nodded, wiping her cheeks with a shaky hand. "Yes. My son, Daniel."

"Is your surname Sutherland, Linda? Linda Sutherland?" Nicki's mind raced back to her conversation with Adam Sullivan late last night. "Your husband was Alan Woods?"

Linda Sutherland shuddered, together with another nod. "It's my maiden name. I don't want to be a Woods anymore."

Nicki understood perfectly. No explanation was needed. "Linda, is Daniel using a different name? Is he using your maiden name? We can't seem to locate anyone called Daniel Woods." At first Nicki thought Linda hadn't heard her. The poor woman's head hung in despair, tears dripping from her chin. "Linda?"

Linda Sutherland's shoulders heaved, and she raised her gaze to meet Nicki's. "Craig. Craig Sutherland. All my boys went to using my maiden name after – well, after what happened. No one wanted to be connected to a Woods."

Nicki bit her lip, wondering if she should tell the fragile woman seated next to her that the man they suspected of abducting Lucas Jackson, and possibly murdering others – the man that was her son - was currently in the town's hospital.

Nicki decided that piece of information could wait for now.

"Linda – this is really important. Do you happen to know where your son – Craig – has been living?"

\* \* \*

*Sunday 4<sup>th</sup> November 2018*
  8.00am

Darcie brought in two cups of fresh coffee then left Nicki and Linda Sutherland alone. Hurrying back to the incident room, she pulled out her phone and placed another call to Roy. He hadn't returned her call from earlier and it was starting to worry her. What if he'd collapsed somewhere? He'd ignored everyone's advice to rest at home, despite the potential concussion diagnosis. The call went, predictably, to voicemail once again and Darcie left another brief message for Roy to get his backside back to the station.

*They had a name.*

She first tried searching the database, but that soon turned up a negative result, as expected. Any hopes for a quick resolution as to where Craig Sutherland might be living now were instantly dashed. Linda had told them that she hadn't been in touch with her son for many years and didn't have a current address for him.

Of course he wouldn't be in the system, she mused, reaching for the chocolate she'd abandoned earlier. He's clever. He wouldn't be on any police radar that was for certain. That's how he'd evaded detection for so long. And who knows...maybe Ivy and Oliver weren't his first? Maybe there were more victims that just hadn't been discovered yet.

The very thought churned her stomach and she pushed the bar of chocolate out of reach.

For the next ten minutes she searched database after database but everything came up with a blank. The guy just didn't seem to exist – anywhere. The initial euphoria at discovering his name was deflating by the second. Darcie even punched his name into Google but the only results were for a 1960s Scottish footballer, and an Australian soap actor, both of which she immediately discounted.

Darcie checked her phone again - there was still nothing from Roy. Just as she looked back up at the wall clock, the man himself came crashing into the incident room, out of breath from sprinting all the way in from the car park.

"Shit, Roy, where've you been?" exclaimed Darcie, as he almost collided with a desk. "Be careful, you'll hurt yourself again! I've been calling you."

Roy waved a hand, dismissively, in the air. "No time, Darce. I got a flat tyre on the way back, and my phone's dead. But, I think I know where our man lives!"

Darcie's eyes widened. "You do? How in God's name...?"

Roy threw himself into the vacant chair next to Darcie. "We need to get hold of Nicki. Is she still at the hospital?"

"No, she's back here. I've left you messages, where the hell have you been?"

"No time to explain – get Google Maps up. Find the street where the Kennedys live. Henley Road. I've been running around town for ages trying to get my bearings, but it's no use."

Darcie did as instructed and pulled up a Google Maps view of the town.

"The Kennedys live on Henley Road – at number 21." She hovered the cursor over the street address. "That's it right there."

Roy nodded, his chest still heaving from running up the stairs. "Yep, and I've just met a Mrs Elsie Cooke who lives on the right. Number 23."

"Who's Elsie Cooke?"

For the next minute, Roy told Darcie what he'd managed to glean from the old woman at number 23 about the Kennedy's builder. "Find me a parade of shops, no more than a ten-minute walk from the Kennedy's house. I had a quick look around, but I couldn't find the damned thing,"

Darcie immediately enlarged the map and highlighted two potential rows of shops. "There's one, here, on Scammel Road. That's about a ten-minute walk from the house. Then you've got another parade of shops over here." Darcie pointed the cursor at a road several streets in the opposite direction. "Again, about a ten-minute walk – maybe slightly longer."

Roy's eyes darted across the screen. "What about a pub? And a school? She mentioned the shops were on the way to the pub, and our man's house backs onto the playing fields of some school."

Darcie typed 'school' into the search bar and they both watched as little red dots populated the map.

"There!" Roy tapped at one of the school locations on the screen. "It's close to that first row of shops. Where's the nearest pub?"

Darcie pointed at the screen. "There a big Harvester pub right there on the corner."

Roy's eyes sparkled with renewed vigour. "That's got to be the one, look."
He trailed a finger from the parade of shops, turning right as Elsie Cooke said
they did. The road swept up for a short distance before Roy tapped the screen
on a row of properties that backed onto the playing fields of a secondary
school. "That's it – it has to be. No 6 Hawthorne Avenue."

\* \* \*

# Chapter Thirty-Eight

*Sunday 4<sup>th</sup> November 2018*
8.15am

Both coffees sat untouched on Nicki's desk. She'd managed to get a brief but surprisingly detailed history from Linda Sutherland – albeit in fits and starts. But as the woman began to talk, her voice became stronger and the words began to flow more freely. And it made for shocking listening.

Moving from one failed marriage straight into another, her eventual entanglement with Alan Woods had no doubt set in motion the events leading up to the position they all found themselves in today. And Linda clearly blamed herself, that much was evident from the way she spoke. Years of guilt were etched deeply into her careworn skin.

Guilt.

Something Nicki was already well versed in. She pushed her own thoughts about Deano to one side and regarded the woman sat only feet across the desk from her. The more she spoke, the more guilt she unburdened, and the more visibly she shook. Nicki felt enormous pity for the woman – none of this was her fault, although she knew she wouldn't see it that way.

As the woman spoke, it became more and more apparent that she had no idea her son had been in the area, and more importantly, was now at the town's hospital. Nicki knew she needed to break the news, gently.

"Linda. There was an incident last night – an attempted abduction of two young boys. We currently have a man at the hospital who we believe could be

your son, Daniel. Would you be willing to come to the hospital to confirm?"
Nicki eyed Linda across the desk, watching her shudder. "You don't have
to."

Linda eventually gave a nod. "I've not seen Daniel since he was seventeen.
Not really. One day he was there – the next…" Linda's voice tailed off.

Nicki tried a brief smile. Her heart ached for the poor woman. "When did
he change his name to Craig Sutherland – was that before or after he left
home?"

"Just before. He hadn't finished school, dropped out before his exams.
Things were difficult for us, after Alan went to prison. And then there was….
the incident."

The incident.

Nicki cast her mind back to Adam Sullivan telling her about the acid attack
on Daniel Woods. "That must have been a very traumatic experience for you
both. Did he receive any counselling afterwards?"

Linda shook her head, her shoulders heaving. "The school wanted it
brushed under the carpet. I…I didn't have anyone to turn to. We just tried
to deal with it as best we could. On our own." Fresh tears began to course
down the woman's cheeks.

"Any contact over the years at all? You say you didn't see him, but did he
keep in touch by phone, or letter?"

Linda paused and rubbed her damp eyes with the already sodden handkerchief. She tentatively reached for the cup of cooling coffee, then changed
her mind and returned her trembling hand to her lap. "I'd hear from him
from time to time. When he needed money. He got himself odd jobs as a
handyman, I think, but it was quite sporadic. Cash jobs only. I don't think
he even had a bank account."

Nicki nodded and bit her lip. Her thoughts turned to Lucas Jackson. He'd
been missing for almost five days now, and by her reckoning had been alone,
wherever he was being held, for the last twelve hours at least.

If he was still alive.

"Are you sure you don't know where he's been living? Any address at all?
Somewhere local?" As Darcie hadn't come thundering through with any

search results for Craig Sutherland, she had to assume no news was bad news on that front.

Linda began to shake her head, and then stopped, a look of faint horror in her watery eyes as she looked up and caught Nicki's gaze. "Surely he wouldn't go there?" she whispered, more to herself than anyone else.

"Go where, Linda?"

Linda's face lost even more colour. "His brother, James. He rents a house here. But they haven't spoken in over twenty years, at least. James won't have anything to do with him. Won't entertain him for a second." An image of the sunny afternoon in the back garden underneath the apple tree swam in front of her eyes. "Surely he could never have gone there?"

"Linda? Do you have an address for me?"

* * *

Sunday 4$^{th}$ November 2018
8.15am

Darcie hit 'print' and raced over to the printer to retrieve the paper as soon as it was spat out.

"6 Hawthorne Avenue," she repeated, looking at the map. "We need to tell Nicki."

Roy led the way, sprinting along the corridor towards Nicki's office. Ordinarily, they would've knocked first and waited to be invited in – but these weren't ordinary times.

Roy flung the door open and stood, breathless, in the doorway, his eyes shining.

"Hawthorne Avenue," he announced, at the exact time the very same words escaped the mouth of Linda Sutherland.

Darcie dodged around Roy and handed Nicki the printed map. "It's the house on the corner." She picked up a red biro from Nicki's pen pot and placed a circle around the address.

Nicki glanced down at the map and then up at Linda. No words needed to be exchanged; no questions required an answer. No verification at all. A simple nod was enough.

Nicki sprang from her seat. "Right, I need patrol cars out to that property immediately. And an ambulance. Darcie, get on the radio and see who's available. You can drive me." She reached into her pocket and flung a set of car keys at Darcie. "I'll meet you outside."

Nicki grabbed her jacket and locked eyes with Roy. "Good work, Roy. But I need you to stay here and look after Linda." She saw a brief flicker of disappointment cross his face and gave him a reassuring smile. "You've done brilliantly, Roy. But you've a head injury and I need you to take a break. You shouldn't even be here. Sit down with Linda until I call in."

Roy stepped back into the corridor as Nicki and Darcie rushed out. He felt the pulsating adrenaline surge through his veins, his heart pumping wildly. And although part of him was desperate to follow his colleagues out of the station, his head was banging.

Squinting up at the ceiling, he felt the overhead strip lights sear his eyes and the throbbing at his temples increased. As he lowered his gaze towards Linda Sutherland, he blinked away a succession of pin-prick stars that flashed in and out of his vision.

Clutching at the door frame, he felt his legs start to wobble.

"Are you all right?" Linda pushed herself up out of her chair and cautiously approached, a look of concern across her face. "You look awfully pale."

Roy attempted a smile but felt his face turning strangely numb and his vision instantly turned to blackness.

* * *

# Chapter Thirty-Nine

*Sunday 4<sup>th</sup> November 2018*

8.40am

The journey didn't take long but to Nicki it felt like hours. Hawthorne Avenue was only a few streets away on the other side of Moreton Hall, but the roads were deserted at this time on a Sunday morning, so Darcie put her foot down. Two other patrols in the area were also heading there, and an ambulance had been requested. It was anyone's guess who would get there first.

Nicki braced herself against the dashboard as Darcie threw the Toyota over a series of mini-roundabouts. The road they were after was just up ahead. Passing the row of shops Roy had spoken briefly about to Darcie, and where Elsie Cooke had started to follow Daniel Woods home, Nicki let her eyes search through the fronts of the houses as they sped past. Everyone appeared to be asleep – houses lying dormant, shrouded behind thick curtains, shielded from the grey Sunday morning unfolding before them.

Darcie brought the car to a stop outside number six. They were the first to arrive, but only by a matter of seconds. As soon as Nicki had opened the passenger door and placed one foot on the pavement outside, two patrol cars complete with blue flashing lights approached from around the bend.

Nicki wasted no time and sprinted up the garden path, immediately disappearing from view behind the high hedges that masked the house from the road. Whoever lived in this house wanted to hide from the world.

Darcie and four uniformed officers followed in Nicki's shadow. After hammering on the sturdy UPVC front door and getting no response, Nicki decided to head around to the rear, beckoning the others to follow. If the brother was here, he wasn't answering. In the back garden, the rear kitchen door looked kickable and Nicki gave the nod. It took several attempts but the door soon gave way to a welcoming sound of splintering wood.

Inside, the house stood in a muted gloom. Darcie snapped on the light, but the low wattage bulb swinging from the centre of the ceiling only gave a dim glow. The kitchen itself was neat and clean, a solitary mug and side plate on the draining board was the only indication of human habitation.

Moving swiftly out into the hall, the four uniformed officers spread out, checking all of the downstairs rooms first for any signs of life. It quickly became apparent that there was none. The front room was again neat and tidy, a two-seater sofa with two armchairs faced the window, a TV set in the corner next to a standard lamp. A coffee table sat on a deep-pile rug, a paperback book and folded up newspaper decorated its surface.

But everywhere was deathly quiet and still.

The search moved upstairs, Nicki reaching the top of the landing first. Immediately she detected the cloying smell of bleach assaulting her nostrils and pinching her eyes. As she stepped forwards, the smell of bleach was joined by something else. Something beyond the acrid aroma of cleaning fluid; something she'd smelt too many times before.

It was the unmistakable scent of death.

Taking a deep breath, she headed along the landing towards the one door at the end that was closed – closed and padlocked. As she walked, the smell intensified, forcing her to place a hand over her nose and mouth. The smell of decay was everywhere. With her heart thumping, sickened to the core, Nicki closed the gap between herself and the padlocked door.

On her left, she passed the entrance to an upstairs bathroom. A quick glance inside told her all she needed to know about the origins of the smell.

The body had swollen grotesquely; the torso and limbs bloated almost beyond recognition, the skin discoloured. Putrefaction was well underway, judging by the noxious odour that hung in the air. Lying face up in the bath, the man's eyes stared lifelessly towards the ceiling. Stepping away from the door, Nicki fought to keep down the bile threatening to erupt from her stomach, waving Darcie and the other officers past. The contents of the bathroom could wait; there was nothing anyone could do for the poor unfortunate soul now.

Keeping a hand clamped to her mouth, Nicki headed towards the padlocked door. As she neared, a set of blue flashing lights flickered through the window on the landing behind them – a window that looked out over the front of the house and the road beyond. The ambulance had arrived. Nicki's stomach heaved as she turned back towards the locked door.

"We need a set of bolt cutters."

No sooner had the words escaped her mouth than a pair of bolt cutters appeared, brandished by a uniformed officer.

"Always in the back of the car, just in case." The officer stepped forward and made short work of the padlock.

As the door was pushed open, the smell of bleach intensified, pinching at the corners of their eyes once again. Nicki's gaze flicked back towards the bathroom and the remains of the unfortunate James Sutherland – for she was sure that was who was lying in the bath. The aroma of his putrefying flesh followed them, clinging to their skin and clothes.

Bile threatened to make another return to her throat as her thoughts turned to Lucas Jackson. Stepping into the room, Nicki noticed the window on the opposite wall was boarded up, plunging the room into darkness. Darcie tried the lightswitch, but nothing happened. Nicki pulled a pen torch from her pocket and swept the beam around the room. The walls had evidence of mould creeping up from the floor, thick cobwebs clung to the corners. Nicki wasn't the only one who shivered.

A bed frame sat in a far corner with just a cheap, thin mattress on top and a sleeping bag. The only other furniture of any description in the room were two identical wooden chairs sitting in the centre. Next to each was a coil of rope. Nicki's already fast-beating heart quickened. Two chairs; two sets of rope. All ready for Noah and Isaac.

Shuddering at the thought, Nicki took another tentative step inside, her palms thick with sweat and her breath coming in short, sharp rasps. Dropping her gaze, she noted the floorboards beneath her feet looked recently swept and cleaned, the chairs in front of them spotless. More bleach teased her nostrils.

Nicki swept her torch to the left side of the room and froze. Her horrified eyes widened as she took in the roll of carpet pushed up against the wall. Focusing the torchlight, she quickly swept it up and down the carpet's length, coming to rest on the mop of sandy hair clearly visible at one end, together with an outstretched arm.

Neither the head nor the arm moved.

Nicki ran to the rolled up carpet, throwing the torch to the floor. Her eyes had already started to burn with hot tears.

She began to grapple with the heavy carpet, trying desperately to unravel it. Darcie rushed to her side to help. It took two uniformed officers, one at each end, to manoeuvre the carpet out from where it had been wedged up against the wall, swinging it out onto the bleached floorboards.

By this time two paramedics had made their way upstairs, escorted by two more uniformed officers, and entered the cramped room with their kit bags and stretcher. As they placed the stretcher down, the carpet unfurled before them.

The first sight of Lucas Jackson's lifeless body caused Nicki's knees to buckle.

* * *

# Chapter Forty

*Sunday 4$^{th}$ November 2018*

10.45am

Sophia Jackson's face matched the colour on the walls of the relative's room. If there was a colour that was paler than white, then that was the shade that decorated her skin. She waved away the offer of a fresh cup of coffee; as she had the previous four.

She hadn't spoken much since the knock at the door that morning. Nicki didn't blame her. There were no words that could possibly express how she was feeling right now.

The only sound in the room was the faint ticking from the wall clock, marking the passing of time that had no real meaning to anybody. Nicki watched Sophia from across the low rise table that separated them, noting how she'd aged over the last five days. Her previously bright complexion was pallid and stale. Her eyes, once shiny and sparkling, were cloudy and dull. Her skin sagged and deep, dark, bruise-like circles hugged her eyes. She looked as though she had neither eaten nor slept since Lucas's disappearance.

Nicki also noticed Sophia's fingernails - once beautifully shaped and painted, each was now bitten to the core, the skin around them ragged and bleeding. Anger welled up inside her once more, an emotion she'd gotten to know far too well of late. Unbeknown to Sophia Jackson, the man responsible for Lucas's abduction was lying in this very same hospital, only a minute or so walk away from where they sat right now. Nobody had imparted that fact to her yet, and when she found out, Nicki wasn't quite sure what to expect. Sophia Jackson didn't strike her as the violent type. But you could never tell, not truly.

As the minutes ticked by agonisingly slowly, the door creaked open to interrupt the silence. A nurse popped her head around the doorframe, a tired and well-practised smile on her face, glancing warily at Nicki before she spoke.

"Mrs Jackson? Would you like to come and see Lucas now?"

Sophia hesitated, as if the mere suggestion of movement was outside of her control. She raised her heavy-lidded eyes just as Nicki stepped forward and offered a hand to help her up. Following the nurse out of the relative's room, Nicki guided Sophia along the corridor, aware that if she were to let go at any moment then the poor woman would most likely sink to the ground.

Nicki had accompanied many a relative to view the body of a loved one before, and the overwhelming surge of grief and heartache that followed was no different to that being experienced by Sophia Jackson right at this very moment. For days she'd been living in torment, imagining and expecting the worst, being confronted by vile accusations in the press of not looking after her son properly. For letting him out of her sight; for allowing him to be taken. She was to blame.

It's all your fault.

Nicki squeezed Sophia's chilled hand as they arrived at the door to the Critical Care Unit. Guilt was something she could relate to. And right now, Sophia Jackson was wracked with a mixture of guilt, pain, sorrow, and anger – all mixed together in a heady cocktail. She was a ticking time bomb, ready to explode.

But Sophia Jackson was also able to express another emotion in amongst the anger, sorrow, and guilt – an emotion that only an hour or so ago had seemed impossible to comprehend.

Relief.

The nurse led them to a bed space where Lucas Jackson's pale face peered out from the equally pale pillows around his head. Despite being severely dehydrated, tipping his tiny body into acute renal failure, his physical condition was surprisingly good.

Tears cascaded down Sophia Jackson's cheeks as she gripped Nicki's hand. Nicki felt the woman sway as they stood by the side of the bed and guided her towards a chair by her son's bedside. She stepped back and watched as Sophia leant forwards, holding Lucas's face in her hands, her tears dripping onto his bedsheets.

"Andrea, here, will be able to answer any of your questions." The nurse nodded towards the critical care nurse adjusting Lucas's IV drip. "And the doctor will be along to talk to you shortly. I'll leave you to it." The nurse gave another tired smile and left.

Nicki hovered by the end of the bed, feeling both conspicuous and intrusive. What Sophia Jackson was experiencing right now should be private.

Lucas Jackson's eyes remained hooded and sleepy, but apparently his vital signs were good. Seemingly lifeless upon their discovery of the coiled carpet, the paramedics at the scene had detected both a faint heartbeat and shallow breaths coming from his tiny body.

Severely hypoglycaemic and dehydrated, Lucas's body had begun to shut down. Before being loaded into the ambulance and blue-lighted to the nearby hospital, the paramedics inserted several lines, struggling to get access to begin with, to administer life-saving saline and glucose infusions.

Lucas had remained unconscious throughout the journey to hospital, but upon being unloaded at the other end, his eyes had begun to flicker.

As they'd unfurled the carpet back at the house, Nicki had stared in horror at the bloodied wounds on Lucas's limp body. Deep gouges and welts all across his back and thighs; weeping abrasions to each ankle and wrist. Even his face hadn't escaped the terrible onslaught, swollen and bruised with dried blood matted throughout his hair.

But he was alive.

The physical injuries would heal in time, but Nicki knew the real damage was unlikely to be visible to the naked eye. She didn't need to read his hospital notes to know that.

Escaping with his life was only the first hurdle in his recovery. At six years old, the hope was that whatever he'd experienced at the hands of

Daniel Woods, he would forget – in time. But there was every chance that he wouldn't. Not entirely. He was likely to need a great deal of psychological support over the coming months, and even years, to enable him to live his life again.

But at least he was alive.

Nicki watched the critical care nurse update Lucas's medical notes while Sophia Jackson remained clamped to her son's side, never taking her eyes off his pale and limp body for even a second.

The relief in Sophia's eyes was something that would stay with Nicki for as long as she lived; eyes that had just about given up all hope of ever seeing her son alive again. She felt a lump form in her throat and bit back the tears that again threatened to erupt. Nicki's thoughts turned to Amelia. She hadn't accompanied her mother to the hospital; sitting with a neighbour was what the reports had said. Nicki could almost visualise her young face when she'd been told the news that her brother had been found alive. No longer would she have to carry the burden of blame – no longer have to face the enormity of being *responsible*.

For the Jacksons, the guilt they'd buried so deeply could start to diminish.

It was a feeling that Nicki could only dream of.

Pushing away her own tangled thoughts, Nicki turned them instead towards the man responsible for the family's anguish.

"Mrs Jackson? Sophia?" Nicki stepped forward to the end of Lucas's bed. "Will you be all right if I step out for a while? There's somewhere I need to be."

Nicki took her leave and headed out of the critical care unit, pulling out her phone as she did so.

"Darcie? Where are you?" Listening to Darcie confirming she was at the front entrance, Nicki pushed her way through a set of double doors and headed for the stairs. "OK, wait there. I'm coming down."

Nicki flew downstairs and rushed outside, spying Darcie waiting next to one of the ambulance bays. As she began to cross the road, a set of headlights swept around the corner and a taxi came to a halt by their side.

Daniel Woods' mother exited from the rear of the taxi and stood in the centre of the road as it departed. Her face was the same colour as the heavy grey skies overhead.

"Linda." Nicki stepped out and herded the woman towards the front entrance. "Thank you for coming." She glanced back over her shoulder at the departing taxi and frowned. "But where's DS Carter?"

Linda accepted the guidance into the foyer of the hospital. "He felt unwell just as you left. Fainted right at my feet, he did. Someone from downstairs came to take him home. I told them I was happy to get a taxi here on my own."

Nicki smiled, gratefully, and led the woman past the cafeteria that was just opening up. The smell of bacon and eggs turned their stomachs as they headed towards the stairs.

It was a moot point really, getting Linda to identify her son. They all but knew him now to be Daniel Woods. And they had Lucas. The risk the man posed, as far as they knew, was now over. Linda had yet to be informed of her other son, James's, death – his body still in situ in the bathroom back at the house on Hawthorne Avenue, awaiting the attendance of the pathologist and crime scene investigators. The house would be a crime scene, two crime scenes in reality, and that kind of information could wait...for now.

Nicki knew her way to ward F6 and pressed the buzzer by the door. It took a minute or so for the call to be answered, and on production of her warrant card she and Linda were quietly ushered inside.

The ward was relatively quiet, the breakfast rounds having long since been cleared away. Daniel Woods' bed was at the far end of the ward and Nicki led Linda towards it, relieved to see the uniformed officer still stationed outside the closed curtains.

Nicki nodded at the officer and then turned to face Linda once again. "You don't have to do this."

"I know." Linda gave a weak smile. "But I want to."

Nicki stepped back. "Don't stay long. You don't have to say anything – in fact, I'd advise that you don't."

Linda nodded, her face taut. Her tears from earlier had now dried, leaving behind red, puffy eyes and blotchy skin. Nicki guessed that she'd cried so much that there were no tears left. Emotionally, the woman was drained.

Nicki drew back the curtains and stepped out of the way, feeling her stomach churn. It had to be remembered that this woman hadn't seen her son for twenty years, and now faced the prospect of never seeing him again for a good while longer, except on a prison visit. And she had yet to be told about the death of her other son. She strained her ears to hear above the general murmurings and hubbub of ward around her. She thought she could possibly hear a sharp intake of breath, maybe even a gasp. But then it was over and Linda stepped back out from behind the curtain.

A simple nod was all that followed.

Nicki squeezed Linda's arm and gave her a reassuring smile. But she now knew what she had to do, stepping back inside the curtains, Nicki regarded the figure they now knew to be Daniel Woods. He was awake, eyes open, staring expressionlessly up towards the ceiling.

"Daniel Woods." Nicki stepped closer, cutting the distance between herself and the bed. "I'm arresting you on suspicion of the abduction of Lucas Jackson. I am also arresting you on suspicion of the attempted abductions of Isaac Kennedy and Noah Kennedy." She paused. She wouldn't add the murder of James Sutherland to the list just yet. That was something his mother, just on the other side of the curtain, didn't need to hear quite yet. "You do not have to say anything. But it may harm your defence if you do not mention, when questioned, something that you later rely on in court. Anything you do say may be given in evidence."

\* \* \*

# Chapter Forty-One

*Tuesday 6<sup>th</sup> November 2018*

5.00pm

"Here we are again, Roy." Nicki flashed a grin and placed a pint of Greene King IPA in front of DS Carter, seating herself at the solitary table in The Nutshell.

"Thanks, boss." Roy returned the grin and reached for the glass.

"It's not boss in here, remember?" Nicki picked up her wine and raised it in thanks towards the barman. They'd replenished the stocks of her favourite Chenin Blanc. "How're you feeling, anyway?"

"Good," lied Roy, taking his first sip and trying his hardest to mask the flash of pain that crossed his cheekbone as he swallowed.

The wince hadn't gone unnoticed across the table. "Take a few days off, Roy. I mean it. You took some battering, and the hospital warned you about concussion. You passing out like that was a sign."

Roy managed a small shrug while he took another mouthful. He did feel quite sore and bruised. Collapsing like that had come out of the blue and scared him a little. Not that he would admit to it.

"I'll be fine. Desk duty only. I promise."

"Hmmmm." Nicki shook her head and smiled. Roy would be a good addition to her team, she could feel it. "It was a bit of a baptism of fire, your first few days with us. Things aren't always quite like that around here."

Roy grinned behind his pint glass. "I enjoyed it. Getting my teeth stuck in right from the beginning."

"You're lucky you still have your teeth," laughed Nicki, returning the grin. "We've charged Marcus Jackson with GBH, by the way – the noises from the CPS are that he'll plead guilty. So you can put the whole sorry episode behind you." Nicki paused, placing her wine glass back down on the beer mat in front of her. "But then there's the whole harassment charge to deal with."

Roy frowned as much as his battered head would allow. "What was that all about?"

"When Marcus was arrested, there was still the possibility he could be involved in Lucas's disappearance. The house was searched, but instead of Lucas we found a multitude of laptops and other mobile devices.

"They're still being analysed but it appears Marcus was conducting some kind of vendetta against Sophia Jackson – online mostly. Stirring up trouble with her employers, the HMRC over her child tax credits, and was even opening accounts online in her name and running up huge debts. The guy wanted to ruin her."

Roy's painful frown deepened. "But why?"

"Apparently, he was pretty tight-lipped in his first interview – advised by his solicitor not to say anything until they knew the full extent of the evidence against him. He's been bailed but I'm guessing that when he's interviewed again he'll change his mind. But I have my hunches."

"And they would be?" Roy had heard about Nicki's famous 'hunches'.

"Well, there's clearly animosity between the Jackson family and Sophia. Once Liam died she was virtually cut off from them – excommunicated, if you will. In particular, the brothers - Marcus and Callum – expressed an intense level of hatred towards her. You should see some of the emails and texts sent to her – they're appalling."

"What did she do that was so bad?"

"You know Callum's conviction for underage sex all but ended his Army career?"

Roy nodded and took another mouthful of his beer.

"Well, investigations suggest that it was a tip-off from none other than

Sophia Jackson that led to his downfall. Callum's life has pretty much gone down the toilet since then. Dishonourably discharged from the army, a two-year prison sentence and ten years on the sex offenders register. He's largely unemployable. I wouldn't be surprised if he held a distinct level of hatred and blame towards Sophia for that."

"And that's enough? For Marcus to wreak a war of revenge on her, on behalf of Callum? Seems quite excessive."

Nicki shook her head and took another sip of wine. "That's just the tip of the iceberg. I poked around into the circumstances of Liam's death – Sophia was always quite vague around what happened when she was asked by Tina Gallagher. Clammed up as soon as his name was mentioned. But his photograph is everywhere in the house. She clearly loved him."

Nicki paused as another customer entered the snug confines of The Nutshell, bringing the tight space almost to capacity. She edged closer to the table and lowered her voice. "Liam was killed after an all-night drinking binge. His car left the road and hit a tree. He was five times over the legal drink-drive limit and there were traces of cocaine in his system."

Roy's eyes widened. "And they're blaming Sophia for that?"

"You didn't hear me say this. But rumour has it that there were tensions in the marriage over Sophia's insistence that Liam leave the army. She didn't want to be an army wife anymore, not with a young baby. Lucas was eighteen months old when Liam died. She wanted her husband back at home, safe and sound. By all accounts it caused a huge family rift. The military is in the Jackson's blood. Generation after generation have either been in the Army, RAF or the Navy. It seems that Sophia was putting pressure on Liam to quit. Who knows what she did - threatened to leave him, I don't know – but he eventually agreed and handed in his papers. That was the week before he died."

"And so the whole family blames her."

Nicki nodded. "It would appear so. If she hadn't forced him to make that decision, he wouldn't have gone on a drug and alcohol binge and wouldn't have ended up wrapped around a horse chestnut tree."

"That's rough."

"Indeed it is."

They sipped their drinks in amiable silence for a while, as the skies darkened outside. Nicki drained the last of her wine and turned towards her newest detective. "So, Roy, has the role of DS lived up to your expectations so far? The last time we were here you mentioned you wanted to make a difference."

Roy let his pint glass hover in front of his lips. "I think so. We got the bad guy in the end and saved three kids' lives. So that's good for me."

"Pity we weren't quick enough to help James Sutherland. The evidence suggests he died pretty much as soon as Woods moved in."

"Has Daniel Woods been charged?"

Nicki nodded. "Three counts of murder – Ivy, Oliver and James. Plus, the abduction of Lucas and attempted abduction of Isaac and Noah."

Roy let out a breath. "He'll not be seeing the light of day again."

"No, I think that's pretty much guaranteed. A bit like his stepfather."

"Do you believe people like him are born that way? Destined for that path the minute they take their first breath?"

Nicki toyed with her wine glass. "Well, that's a discussion that needs another drink!" She turned round and caught the barman's attention, indicating that they were ready for round two. Once the drinks were in place, she eyed Roy across the small table. "Are killers born or created? Nature or nurture?"

Roy reached for the second pint. "It's an interesting concept. What's your take on it?"

Nicki cocked her head to one side and thought for a second. It was an age-old question that most police officers asked themselves at some point in their careers. "Well," she started. "Take our Daniel Woods, for example. His real father, his biological father, left him when he was young. As far as I know he wasn't a criminal. Therefore, you could say that he didn't inherit any criminal genes. And, as far as I know, his mother wasn't a criminal mastermind either."

"So, not genetic then? Not nature making him turn out the way he did?"

Nicki paused long enough for another mouthful of wine. "I don't think for one second it's that simple, Roy. There is some support for there being a 'criminal gene'. Something in someone's genetic makeup that predisposes them to a career of crime, to make bad choices. And maybe there is something in that. But in Daniel's case? I think his stepfather – the one who brought him up and had the most influence in his life – had a bigger part to play. Unfortunately, I think his fate was sealed the very moment he set foot inside that house as a young boy."

"So, nurture then?"

Nicki shrugged. "In his case, I think his upbringing would have shaped him as an adolescent and as a young man. There's no question his stepfather was a perverted child killer – and who knows what really went on inside those four walls when Daniel was growing up. We can only imagine. Couple that with the abandonment issues he might have had following his real father walking out on the family when he was little, and then the bullying at school. It all makes for a very toxic mixture."

"I know plenty of people whose parents split up when they were small, and plenty who were bullied at school – I was – and I didn't grow up to be a serial killer." Roy reached for his half-drunk second pint. "There's still an element of choice."

"That's very true, Roy. That's very true. So, I guess the answer is - I don't know."

Nicki's second glass of wine was almost empty, and she was contemplating whether she should make it a third, when her mobile phone vibrated in her pocket. Pulling it out, she recognised the number straight away.

She'd resisted Caspar Ambrose's insistence on a meeting – she hadn't needed his help with Daniel Woods in the end. The pieces had fallen into place of their own accord.

But the private investigator had refused to give up.

"Angel Hotel Bar. 10 minutes."

Irritation prickled Nicki's skin. Just who did he think he was? She'd called him in a moment of madness, a moment of weakness when she hadn't known who else to turn to.

And now he wasn't letting go.

"Another?" Roy held his empty glass in the air.

As tempted as she was, Nicki shook her head. "Not for me, Roy. I'd best be off." She started to gather up her bag and jacket. "And I mean it about taking a few days off. You've been in the wars – and you can't be too careful with head injuries."

"Boss," saluted Roy, giving one of his impish grins that told Nicki he would be at his desk first thing in the morning.

Nicki knew better than to argue and merely waved as she turned towards the door. "See you, Roy."

The air outside was cold and crisp. A perfect night for a run. As she turned for home, she hesitated and let her eyes wander along Abbeygate Street in the direction of the Angel Hotel. She could be there in a minute, two max. Find out once and for all what it was that he wanted with her – what he wanted with Nicola Webster.

She hovered, undecided, on the pavement. Then she took one step, then another towards the Hotel, her feet seeming to make the decision for her. Trepidation filled her soul. So much so that she thrust her hands into her pockets and forced her feet in the other direction. In the direction of safety. In the direction of home.

Once inside, she threw several logs into the wood burner and then collapsed back onto the sofa. Peeling off her jacket, she kicked off her boots and sank back against the cushions. Sighing, she closed her eyes.

The last week had taken it out of everyone. But even as she'd wiped the whiteboards clean of everything to do with Operation Goldfish, Nicki knew it was only a matter of time before the next complex major investigation popped up to take its place. And she still had a mountain of other cases vying for her attention on her desk.

Luna, detecting that this might well be a good time for some pampering, leapt up onto Nicki's lap and began her ritualistic kneading. Without needing to open an eye, Nicki gave the Russian Blue cat a series of gentle strokes along her back, with a soft rub behind the ears.

The warmth from Luna's body and the heat from the wood burner lulled Nicki into a delightful sense of contentment.

She couldn't quite tell how long she'd been asleep, but it was long enough for the wood burner to have reduced itself to a pile of glowing embers and for Luna to have slunk off to find somewhere cosy to spend the night.

Nicki blinked rapidly, trying to will herself into full consciousness. She hadn't meant to drop off like that – she'd been thinking of going for a run. As she blinked away the blurriness from her eyes, she saw that the mantelpiece clock showed it was 11.30pm. A run was out of the question, if it had even been one in the first place.

As she stirred, Nicki felt a cold chill at the base of her neck – in contrast to the warmth still seeping out from the slumbering wood burner. She glanced over at the kitchen door, but found it was closed. As was the front door. But she could still feel a chilling draught from somewhere.

Frowning, Nicki pushed herself up from the sofa and stumbled over to the open-plan stairs. Hovering at the base, she craned her neck up towards the first floor landing. Had she left a window open upstairs?

Sighing, Nicki began to pull herself up the wooden stairs. Her legs felt weary and she really needed her bed. She rarely opened the windows upstairs, concerned that Luna might be adventurous and get out, so she couldn't quite understand in her head where the cold draught was coming from.

Popping her head into the bathroom, she was relieved to see the single window was firmly shut. The same could be said for her bedroom, with Luna curled up fast asleep in the centre of the duvet on the double bed.

The air outside on the landing was, however, still chilled and Nicki's eyes gravitated towards the hatch in the ceiling that led to the rooftop garden.

Surely not?

She never left the hatch open. Never in a million years. But as she raised her gaze to the ceiling she saw that the opening was ajar.

Pulling the access ladder down, she quickly ascended the steps. The hatch was indeed open – a two-inch gap all around. It was as if she hadn't slotted it into place correctly the last time she'd been up there. And when had that been, exactly? Try as she might, she couldn't quite remember. Two nights ago? Three?

Surely it hadn't been open all that time? She would have felt the cold draught by now.

With a fluttering sensation in the pit of her stomach bordering on panic, Nicki pulled herself up through the hatch and onto the rooftop itself.

The sky above was inky black – no cloud cover to snuff out the winking stars. It was a perfect evening for relaxing back on her rooftop lounger and losing herself in the wide expanse of the universe.

But not tonight.

Tonight it felt different.

Now up on the roof, Nicki searched through the darkness. She snapped on the solar powered night lights to illuminate the space. Everything looked like it should, nothing unusual or out of place.

And yet there was.

Something was very different.

Turning a full circle, Nicki checked that she was alone. It was a compact rooftop garden space and there was nowhere to hide. For that, Nicki was thankful.

Crossing over to the rooftop furniture – just a lounger and a small table – Nicki noted everything was in order. Everything was exactly where it was meant to be. Nothing was out of place.

And yet everything was.

What pulled her attention down onto the rattan lounger, Nicki would never know. Some unseen force from within, pulling her, guiding her, urging her forwards.

It was a 5" x 7" photograph – her eyes making sense of it before her brain caught up. A photograph that she knew should not be there. Not up here. Not on the roof.

Nicki instinctively turned around once more, checking she was alone on the rooftop. She was. Nothing had changed, except everything had.

Inching closer, Nicki leant down and picked the photograph up, her hand shaking. But she no longer felt the cold. Instead, her whole body was awash with heat. She could feel the pounding of her heart, the throbbing of the blood in her veins. Her hot breath billowed out into the chill night air.

The picture was of a man

Initially, Nicki's brow creased with confusion. What was some random photograph of some equally random man doing on her rooftop garden?

And then she looked at the photograph again.

It was the eyes that did it. And the smile. Definitely the smile.

It may have been twenty-two years since she'd looked into those chocolate-brown eyes, but it felt as though it were yesterday.

Deano.

With her heart thudding painfully inside her chest, Nicki felt her head swim. Uncontrollable thoughts vied for attention. How could this be? It couldn't be Deano. It just couldn't. It made no sense.

But it looked just like him.

Nicki felt her legs shudder and begin to give way, collapsing down onto the rooftop lounger. As she did so, her phone vibrated in her back pocket.

Pulling it out, the message on the screen almost stilled her heart.

"I know where he is."

**THE END**

\* \* \*

*Message from the Author*

Although Cambridge-born, Bury St Edmunds in Suffolk has been my home since 2008. It's a lovely place to live and if you ever get the chance to visit then it's well worth it! A small market town, dating from about 1080, it even boasts its own cathedral. Bury St Edmunds is the base for the Greene King brewery, and is also where you will find the British Sugar factory which produces Silver Spoon sugar. I have made use of some local landmarks in the writing of Guilt, although I have exerted some artistic license for some road names.

The Nutshell does exist and is, indeed, the smallest pub in Britain. Sitting close to the town centre, it is worth a visit even if just to ask the barman the origins of the mummified cat above the bar!

The Abbey Gardens also exist and are one of the focal points of the town.

On the site of a former Benedictine Monastery, the Gardens are one of the most tranquil and beautiful places to sit and watch the world go by.

# Acknowledgements

There are a large number of people I need to thank for helping me get this far with the publication of Guilt. Firstly, I must thank PS Rebecca McCarthy of Suffolk Police who has been on the end of my sometimes odd-sounding questions and queries on police procedure! If there are any remaining inaccuracies, then I can assure you that they are mine and mine alone! I must also thank Tracey Proctor for being my 'go-to' person for anything to do with forensics.

Huge thanks also to Amy Ranner and Rebecca Bone from West Suffolk Hospital, who both helped with all sorts of queries regarding the hospital scenes.

Then I have a whole host of people who have helped Guilt become the book it is today. My heartfelt thanks go to Sarah Bezant, Sue Scott and Jane Badrock who all read Guilt in its early stages and helped me to polish and shape it into the final product. There are then also my friends and colleagues at Question Mark Press. Jim, Matt, Jane, Emma, Duncan, Donna, Zoe, LB, Kate, Marisa, Michael...the list goes on! And of course my ever faithful group of Advance Readers - Agnieszka Andrzejak, Peter Woods and Ian White. I also need to thank Amanda Wills for the loan of the name of her gorgeous cat Luna!

And finally it is you - the readers! Without you, none of these books would ever see the light of day. I thank each and every one of you.

The next DI Nicki Hardcastle book is due for release in 2022. Can't wait that long? Catch up on the DI Jack MacIntosh novels - the fifth book in the series - 'Hangman's End' - is due for publication in January 2022.

To keep up to date, there are various ways to keep in touch:

www.michellekiddauthor.com - join my author newsletter for information on future releases and special offers.
   www.facebook.com/michellekiddauthor
   Twitter @AuthorKidd
   Instagram @michellekiddauthor
   www.questionmarkpress.com

**Books available from Question Mark Press**

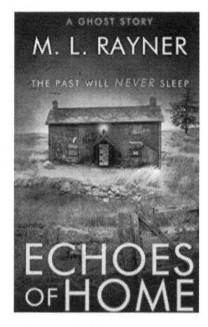

**?**

**Question Mark Press**

Printed in Great Britain
by Amazon